WHITE LIES

"Great stuff."

—*The New York Times*

"[Stone is] prickly, intelligent, wary, and amazingly resilient. . . . Suspenseful, dark and disturbing, *White Lies* features a fascinating heroine and a gripping story about sex offenders and their victims."

—*Wisconsin State Journal*

FAULT LINES

"An excellent novel. . . . A breathless, action-packed finale. . . . Anna Salter provides another compelling look at the criminal mind."

—*Chattanooga Times* (TN)

"Offer[s] a more realistic side to forensic psychology than many recent thrillers."

—*Publishers Weekly*

"A fast-paced novel with lots of little twists and turns and surprises. A quick, fun, hard-to-put-down read."

—*The Pilot* (Southern Pines, NC)

"Steadily gripping in its psychology. . . . There are shocks here, and each plot twist turns on a kink in an insanely brilliant mind."

—*Kirkus Reviews*

SHINY WATER

"The best first novel I have ever read. Anna Salter takes us into the disturbing world of forensic psychologist Michael Stone with just the right amount of wit and humanity. Don't miss this memorable debut."

—Anne Perry, author of *The Whitechapel Conspiracy*

"Forget about your demolition experts and your air traffic controllers; Michael Stone, the stressed-out heroine of Anna Salter's jolting debut mystery, *Shiny Water*, has the real job from hell. A forensic psychologist at a Vermont hospital, Michael carries a caseload that would make the angels weep. . . . [An] interestingly abrasive protagonist, whose own testy personality gives her a sharp perspective on her difficult patients and a dangerous edge when she testifies on her behalf in court . . . [where] a misapplication of justice . . . turns Michael into a tiger for the truth. . . . [Salter] handles this touchy material with integrity, tugging on our hearts even as she ties our nerves in knots."

—*The New York Times Book Review*

"Fascinating reading. . . . Salter introduces a heroine whose wit and courage shine through."

—Tess Gerritsen, *New York Times* bestselling author of *Gravity*

"A terrific tale with plenty of twists and turns and an almost lethal twist of the tail."

—*The Toronto Star*

Books by Anna Salter

Shiny Water
Fault Lines
White Lies
Prison Blues

Published by POCKET BOOKS

PRISON BLUES

Anna Salter

POCKET BOOKS

NEW YORK   LONDON   TORONTO   SYDNEY   SINGAPORE

For information regarding special discounts for bulk purchases, please contact Simon & Schuster Special Sales at 1-800-456-6798 or business@simonandschuster.com

This book is a work of fiction. Names, characters, places and incidents are products of the author's imagination or are used fictitiously. Any resemblance to actual events or locales or persons, living or dead, is entirely coincidental.

An *Original* Publication of POCKET BOOKS

POCKET BOOKS, a division of Simon & Schuster, Inc.
1230 Avenue of the Americas, New York, NY 10020

ISBN: 0-671-02353-5

First Pocket Books printing January 2002

10 9 8 7 6 5 4 3 2 1

POCKET and colophon are registered trademarks of Simon & Schuster, Inc.

Front cover illustration by Lisa Litwack
Photo: Photonica

Printed in the U.S.A.

For
Jazzy wazzy wo
And Blako, too

Acknowledgments

As always, I am grateful for my agent, Helen Rees. If Helen were brokering the Arab/Israeli conflict, we'd have peace by now. Also, I would like to thank Sandi Gelles-Cole, who works with me on editing these books before they are submitted for publication. Her input is substantial and much appreciated.

My friend and mentor at Harvard, Sunny Yando, really taught me how to write. As her Teaching Fellow at Harvard, I sat with Sunny until two A.M. on the fourteenth floor of William James Hall, reading psychology papers from students. We could have finished earlier if Sunny hadn't been editing on the basis of literary merit as well as scientific accuracy. She just couldn't help it: she would edit out redundant words and phrases and change graceless language—all the time unknowingly teaching a young graduate assistant looking over her shoulder how to write.

I like to write accurately, as do most authors, and experts have been generous in assisting me on technical material. I would like to thank Ardis Olson, M.D., and Steve Kairys, M.D., long-term friends and former colleagues at Dartmouth-Hitchcock Medical Center for going over the medical sections of this book. Lynn Copen, victim witness advocate and former police officer, edited the material for accuracy about guns.

I very much appreciate Cindy O'Donnell, Deputy Secretary of Corrections for the State of Wisconsin, Gary McCaughtry, Warden of Waupan Corrections Institution, and Jodeine Deppish, Deputy Warden of Waupan, for their helpful input about prisons.

The warden in this book makes a few cynical comments about his Department of Corrections higher-ups. My day job as a psychologist in the field of sexual abuse has brought me into extensive contact with correctional systems and I want to make it clear that the character's views in this book about "headquarters" actually do not correspond to my experience. I was in New England for over twenty years and now work in Wisconsin. Vermont Corrections has been a pioneer in the development of effective treatment programs for sex offenders for well over a decade. Wisconsin Corrections has a well-deserved national reputation for overall high quality programming in the correctional field.

The sadists, psychopaths and pedophiles in my books are not drawn from specific individuals, but the overall portrait is accurate. I started writing partly because I was so annoyed with the inaccurate portrayals of sex offenders and psychopaths in fiction and media, in general. The motivations, the patterns of thought and behavior that I saw in fiction rarely corresponded to what I saw in real life.

"JUST ANOTHER DAY AT THE OFFICE," I SAID TO ADAM OVER dinner. "My new client lost track of his penis. Same old. Same old."

Adam stopped eating. "Excuse me."

I shrugged and shifted my mammoth belly in the chair. Nothing felt comfortable anymore. I couldn't find a way to sit that worked. Sleeping wasn't an option and moving was a joke. I had to be getting close to delivery. Officially there was a couple of months to go, but my body was so distorted I couldn't have picked any of my body parts out of a lineup. I figured that had to be a clue.

"Nothing new about this one," I said. "I hear that kind of thing all the time." I wasn't kidding. As a forensic psychologist who deals with sex offenders daily, I have an entire collection of excuses for criminal behavior—one of the finer collections, in my opinion. "He didn't exactly commit a sex crime," I added. "He just lost track of his penis. Not nearly as creative as the guy last week."

Adam rolled his eyes.

"Yeah, heck of a thing," I continued. "I hate to be sexist here, but I never get that from women. What happens? You guys just turn around and it's gone or something? I've never yet encountered a woman who lost track of her vagina. You wake up in the morning, it's just where you left it the night before. You go to work. There it is. Who loses one?

"The one last week was better. He claimed a vagina just flew across the room and landed on his thumb. This must be some sort of male thing, losing track of penises, ducking flying vaginas."

My favorite police chief bristled slightly and picked up his dinner plate to take it to the sink. I kept forgetting that Adam, like most men, didn't appreciate being lumped in with sex offenders, not even jokingly. "It's not a 'we guys' kind of thing," he said over his shoulder. "I tend to know where mine is and I can't remember the last time I ducked a flying vagina."

I came up behind him at the sink and put my arms around him. Unfortunately, my belly was so big they only went halfway. I leaned forward and put my head on his shoulder and started gently kissing his neck. "So where is yours now?" I asked between kisses.

"Where would you like it to be?" he said, and I could feel the smile starting through the muscles of his neck.

"Hell's bells, Gary. It's been ages. How are you and how is life out there at Nelson's Point? Any good riots lately?" The last time I'd been at Nelson's Point Correctional Institution my conversation with Gary Raines, the warden, had been interrupted by a correctional officer rushing in to tell him there were rumors from several snitches that C block was going to riot in the cafeteria that evening.

But that had been years ago. I had interned at Nelson's Point way back when Gary was a regular correctional officer. It had taken him only a decade to climb the ladder to warden but he had been the boss for at least five years now. I had seen him only occasionally since I'd left—mostly when I came out to assess a sex offender for the court, which didn't happen all that often.

I shifted the phone on my shoulder and tried to catch my breath as I eased slowly into my desk chair. Could chairs shrink? This one seemed to be getting smaller daily. I was an early bird and usually in my office in the Department of Psychiatry at Jefferson University Hospital before anybody else. Corrections, however, ran on an even earlier schedule than I did, and the phone had been ringing when I walked in.

"No riots," he said, "although life's been interesting. You sound out of breath. Have you been running?"

"No," I said, "just walking across the room. Never mind, I'll tell you about it when I see you." Of course when I saw him I wouldn't need to tell him anything. "So what's been interesting?" I was between clients and didn't have much time to chat.

"Well, I just walked out a psychologist who was caught having sex with an inmate, somebody you know."

"The psychologist or the inmate?"

"The psychologist."

"Who?"

"Eileen Steelwater."

"No," I said, astonished. "You fired Eileen? For having sex with an inmate? It can't be. You can't be serious?" Eileen and I had been interns together at Nelson's Point years and years ago. Eileen had mousy brown hair.

No, I thought, hair was never mousy, people were. Eileen was a mousy, brown-haired woman who always played by the rules. She'd driven me crazy with her acceptance of the kinds of silly regulations that correctional institutions feel obligated to promulgate.

Eileen had always parked in the far parking lot where she was supposed to. She never tried to bring an aluminum can into the institution. She never kept a pocketknife in her bag to slice an apple at lunch. She never lost her ID. Her car keys were always locked in the lockers where they should be. If she ever broke a rule, I never knew it. I thought Eileen probably had nightmares about forgetting to sign out.

I had moved on, the anarchy gene in my soul uncomfortable living with the conformity prisons required. I left a little regretfully, though; there has always been something about extreme environments that attracted me. Eileen had settled in, happy with the job security—crime is a growth industry—and comfortable with the orderly world all those rules made.

"I know," Gary said. "Crazy, isn't it? I don't think there's a person here who would have believed it if she hadn't gotten caught with her pants down, literally. She can't deny it. And she's not one bit sorry. She's up on charges, Michael, there being a little thing like the law against staff having sex with inmates. I don't know if she'll beat that or not but her license is gone, for sure."

"Jesus," I said. "What the hell happened to Eileen? Did she have a psychotic break?"

"Not that you could tell," Gary said. "Although with most psychologists it's hard to know."

I didn't argue with him. I thought as a group we

were crazier than most, although not as crazy as psychiatrists—but that was little consolation.

"Anyway, I'm hoping you can bail us out," Gary said. He was my kind of no-nonsense guy and he wasted less time in small talk than I did. He had worked his way up from correctional officer to warden and he had the straight talk I had always liked in cops.

"She was running a sex offender treatment group when this happened. The whole thing's a mess now. I don't want the group to end like this. Makes us look bad. Somebody bangs the shrink, the group falls apart. How's the whole thing going to look when one of these guys applies for parole? 'I was working hard in treatment, sooooo hard, when the therapist started screwing one of the inmates and they just canceled the group. . . .'"

"Not to mention what they learned from this," I said dryly. "They must have seen him grooming her."

"Trust me," Gary said. "This guy didn't groom anybody. You'll see what I mean. Can you do it? Take over the group until we can hire a permanent replacement? Just one group, twice a week, no big deal."

"Gary, I'm pregnant. I'm delivering within a couple of months."

"Pregnant?" Gary said surprised. "Gee, well, that's great. Just great. Um, a couple of months," he repeatedly thoughtfully. "All right, I'll take it. I'll just have to find somebody else by then."

"But—" I started. I hadn't exactly agreed to this.

"Group starts tomorrow at two. Meet you at noon. I'll take you to lunch. Fill you in."

"Gary, let me think about this." I should really think about this and call him back. Some day my propensity for snap decisions would get me into trou-

ble—as if it hadn't already. But then again, life would
be a little dry without them.

"Oh, heck, all right," I said. "Why not?" I'd had to
cancel the kid part of my therapy clients because I
couldn't get up and down from the floor anymore. I
had room on my schedule and somehow I was more
than curious to know what had turned a rule-bound
but decent woman named Eileen Steelwater into someone who would flout her ethical code as a psychologist, throw her job, her career and her license right out
the window and not be one bit sorry.

I stood staring up at the walls of Nelson's Point
Correctional Center. It was the oldest prison in
Vermont and it was built before prisons got into aes-
thetics: no attempt had been made to soften the con-
tours or hide the inevitable razor wire. The walls went
straight up like a fortress, with towers sprinkled at inter-
vals and razor wire stretched between them. The morning was raw—winter never let go of New England without a fight—and the razor wire glistened with ice. I
have long ago lost all sense of the terror of razor wire. It
glistens in the summer sun like sprung coils of mirror
slivers and dazzles so much in the winter ice that it hurt
your eyes. Could be I'd been working in the field too
long if I was considering razor wire an aesthetic touch.

Prisons drew me in some strange way and they
always had. It was something about how clear life gets
when all the frills are stripped away. What was in front
of me wasn't all that different from the Antarctic or
Everest, from life on a wagon train or a life raft. It's just
that the deprivation and the dangers here were
human-made, that's all.

But it wasn't all deprivation; with the bad came a

strange intensifying of the good. All my life I would remember a cup of tea someone handed me once on a 14,000-foot mountain summit after I had been sick all night from some bad water. The sun had broken through, raising the temperature to the tolerable and I had sat up for the first time. Someone reached in my open tent and handed me a steaming cup of tea. The sunlight had shafted across his hand and the steaming cup, and it had brought tears to my eyes. I had peered in many cups of tea since then looking for a trace of the solace that one cup brought.

I stopped staring at the walls and went inside to the main desk. There was a memo at the desk allowing me in. The officer pushed the sign-up book over and picked up the phone. "Warden Raines will be coming out to get you," he said, raising his eyebrows. In a few minutes, I heard the sound of more sliding steel and Gary walked out.

He had put on a few pounds over the years and it had softened some of the harder edges in his face. But his shoes were still black and shiny and his shirt still white and tucked in so tightly it looked like he'd practiced on hospital beds. Gary was ex-military and he might as well have had a sign on his forehead.

"Michael," he said, stopping dead in his tracks. He started laughing. "My God, you're enormous. What are you having, a baby or a tractor trailer?"

"I appreciate your sensitivity, Gary. It's always good to laugh at a pregnant woman. Make some more comments about my totally deformed and misshapen body." I said it solemnly but Gary wasn't fooled. I was proud as hell of my huge belly and the healthy baby inside and it showed.

"But you were such a skinny little thing," he said.

The officer was staring at Gary, making me wonder if he'd ever before seen the jovial side of him, but Gary and I went way back to when I was an intern and he was a correctional officer. We'd been part of a group that had had a few beers after work now and then—a group that had included Eileen Steelwater—and both of us had dropped fifteen years at the sight of each other. From the reaction of the officer, maybe Gary was acting like a real grown-up these days.

Lunch was in the Make-Shift Café just down the street from the prison. The day was warming up and Gary and I walked. The sign out front advertised the country's most "Un-American Apple Pie, Nothing Like Your Grandmother's." Vermont was full of former hippies from the sixties who had just never moved on. They had settled in for the long haul, keeping both their dope and their sense of humor. Walking into one of their strongholds was like walking into a time machine. Waiters with ponytails wore tie-dyed tee shirts among signs that advertised the Make-Shift was a "communal restaurant," with lengthy explanations on the wall of what that meant. Cooks and cleaners were paid the same. Tasks rotated. Decisions were made communally.

Amazingly the system had worked for twenty years now and was still going strong. Glancing around at the cast of characters, though, it looked like the players had changed since last I'd been there. The current crop of waiters looked too young to be real hippies, more like hippie wannabees who collected Pink Floyd and had to ask their mothers to tell them what the sixties were really like. Whatever.

"You come here much?" I asked Gary. "I haven't been here in ages."

"Only on special occasions," he said. "Hasn't changed much."

"Brings you back," I said.

"Surely does." We were seated now and staring at menus that offered a variety of tofu and grain dishes, surprisingly good, if the food was like it used to be, although the descriptions managed not to give a clue.

"You still like being a warden?" I put the menu aside and looked at Gary.

"Most days," he said. "I hate to admit it but I like running the show—whatever small piece I get to run. The problem is I spend half my time at Headquarters trying to deal with higher-ups on the food chain. Not to mention the endless media-sucking politicians making one crazy law after the other. 'Tough on crime' has become a goddamn mantra. They don't give a shit whether any new piece of legislation will work or not, just whether it looks good. I swear to God we've had laws passed in twenty minutes without a moment's thought about their impact. But we've been luckier than some states. Some states have passed laws abolishing parole and then they're amazed that they have to build about eight new prisons. Hello. Anybody home?

"The prison's not nearly as bad as the politicians—although we do have our moments. Last week we found out some guys made a thirty-two-foot ladder in shop. Pretty good ladder, tall enough to clear the wall. Metal, no less, well-built—only held about three hundred pounds per step. Seems they got something out of shop. Snitch turned them in the night before nine of them were going out. It would have made some interesting headlines."

"Thirty-two-foot ladder?" I asked. "When did you start making ladders in shop?"

"Give me a break, Michael. We don't make ladders in shop. We make planters, things like that."

"How do you make a thirty-two-foot ladder in shop and have no one notice?"

"Now, that's the question, isn't it?" he said. "Likely somebody who was supposed to be supervising was playing cards or standing around chewing the fat."

"Where'd they hide it?"

"They didn't hide it. It was sitting right out among the tools and the lumber."

"Wow, you sure do run a tight ship here."

"Heck," he said. "That's nothing. We had a guy last year who wove a rope out of dental floss. Pretty good rope, too."

I paused, trying to imagine a rope made out of dental floss. "Doesn't that take a lot of dental floss?" I asked, finally.

"A whole lotta dental floss," he said. "Now we have to make sure they only get dental floss in small pieces. One more thing." I looked over to see the couple at the next table staring at us curiously.

Gary followed my gaze. He shrugged and said more quietly, "Good thing we weren't talking about my new guest."

"Who's your new guest?"

"He isn't here yet but he will be. Clarence."

I sat back and just looked at him. "Well, aren't you lucky?"

"He's gotta go somewhere."

"Why don't I think folks were lining up?"

Gary shrugged. "Nobody knows he's coming. I don't think even the inmate grapevine has it."

"That's a first. How'd you manage that?"

"I didn't tell the staff. Nobody knows but me and the Commissioner."

"They're not going to like it."

"Who's they?" he said. "Nobody's going to like it. The staff won't want him. The inmates will go after him. The media will hound us unmercifully every time he hiccups."

"You seem pretty calm."

"Same ol', same ol'."

"I'm sorry," I replied, "but Clarence isn't same ol'."

"I don't know," he said. "Seems like there's been a lot of them by now. Bundy, Dahmer, Gacey."

"None of them attacked kids," I said. We were both whispering conspiratorially. "Nobody else cut their penises off and kept them in jars on his nightstand. Nobody, not even the worst of the worst, is going to be happy about this." It was true. The prison had its hierarchy of what was acceptable and what was not. Child molesters weren't generally liked, but there were so many of them now that they weren't harassed like they used to be. But mutilating children was just too freaky for inmates to accept. And the fact that they were *male* children just made it worse. The inmates would all be wondering what Clarence would do now that he didn't have access to children anymore.

"Everybody needs a hobby."

"Gary, you're sick. Even I can't laugh at Clarence."

"I gotta do something. Might as well laugh. I'm stuck with him. But at least I've got a good shrink around. I'll drag you into it if it gets too bad." He looked up as if testing the waters.

"Drag me into what?" I said. "You're the one who'll need the shrink, not Clarence. Dealing with people like Clarence will make you crazy. Besides, we don't know what to do with someone like that any more than you do. Does the phrase 'meaner than a snake' mean anything up here? Well, forget what the court whores say. Terminal meanness is not a mental illness. Man needs an exorcist, not a psychologist."

"Man needs a state with capital punishment, if you ask me."

"You could argue that," I replied. "Even those of us who are queasy about the state killing people start thinking about it when someone like Clarence shows up. Not that the inmates won't take care of that for you."

"Not on my watch," he said, grimly. "I'd ship him to a state that would fry him in a second, but nobody's getting him while it's my job to protect him." He was looking down at the menu, trying to sound casual, but there was nothing casual in his voice.

I looked at him, surprised. Call me callous, but if protecting Clarence from the consequences of his evil nature had been *my* job, I'd have taken it seriously enough but I doubt I would have sounded as *passionate* about it as Gary did. "Better your job than mine," I said mildly. I started to say more but just then the smell of approaching food wiped all capacity for thought from my pregnant brain. Nothing, but nothing, interfered with eating these days.

I arrived at the group room and called up the operator to get the guys moving to group. Given it was maximum security, guys didn't just get to wander around the corridors. They couldn't leave their units to go anywhere until it was announced over the loudspeakers. Once the announcement came they'd be given a

pass with the time left on it and allowed to go to
group by themselves. I'd collect the passes and give
them back after group with a new time when they
headed back to the unit.

All of that was for security reasons, of course, but I
had a different reason for wanting to be there before
anyone else arrived. Especially in the first group session, I liked to see how each of the men handled
themselves when they were brought in. Transitions
give you a chance to see who sits where, who looks at
whom, who greets whom, all those little things that
give you information about who's who in the invisible
hierarchy that dominates a prison. I could find out
sooner or later by listening in group, but I was coming
in late and I needed to jump start my learning curve.

The first man came in and broke into a grin when
he saw me. Undoubtedly there was a bet going as to
who could seduce this group leader, given what happened with the last one. Pregnant or not, seducing the
group leader would always be a major coup. He looked
around and grinned even broader when he realized he
had a few minutes alone with me. "Well, hello," he
said slowly, "you're Michael?"

I stood up and extended my hand. "I'm Dr. Stone,"
I said with a good deal of distance in my voice. "And
you're . . ."

"Leroy," he replied.

"Ah, Leroy Warner," I said. I had read as much as I
could of the charts after lunch and I knew who was
supposed to be showing up. "Mr. Warner, have a seat.
The others will be with us shortly." He nodded and sat
down. We looked each other over silently for a
moment. Leroy was a small African-American man
with short curly hair and a wiry frame, and he looked

street smart. He grinned again and broke the silence, "You sure you gonna make it through the group? You don't look like it."

I didn't say anything at all.

Leroy glanced at the door. He didn't have much time and the first gambit hadn't worked. "I'd be happy to fill you in on who's coming," he said. "I know all these guys. Tell you who's who."

"That won't be necessary," I said. "I'd rather make up my own mind." If there was one rule about inmates, it was never take anything from them. It set up a private alliance. It meant you owed them—both to them and to you. And it was hard to figure out which had worse consequences in the long run—their thinking you owed them or your thinking it.

He started figuring again, but before he had time to make another run at me the door opened and a small, nervous white guy walked in. Child molester, I thought immediately as he glanced at me and looked away. The old-fashioned kind, the kind that are scared of women and just sort of generally pathetic.

I had barely greeted him and told him to find a seat, however, when the door opened again and a man the New England Patriots would have drafted in a heart-beat walked in. His shoulders filled the narrow door-way and angled down to a youthful waist. He even had that football neck on him, the one that's wider than the head.

He paused when he saw me, then picked up the youthful strut, that shoulder-rolling walk that is half walk, half dance. A weight lifter for sure; his biceps stretched the tight tee shirt as he crossed the room, something I was sure he knew. His head was shaved and his bald ebony skin seemed to shine. Both seated

inmates seemed to freeze for a second when he came
in and then both looked quickly away. Impressive the
way he had managed to intimidate them without saying a word. Whoa, here was somebody high up in the
hierarchy for sure.

I said nothing and he stayed silent too as he slowly
ambulated over to a seat at the far end of the semicir-
cular chairs and sat down. He had gotten as far away
from me as he possibly could. He stretched his feet out
and crossed them, put his hands behind his head and
leaned back. I looked down at my sheet. Only one
armed robber in the bunch. Had to be him. "Mr.
Avery," I said.

He said nothing and just stared at me intently.
Outside of prison, looking someone in the eye was a
sign of truthfulness; inside, it was a sign of defiance.
"I'm Dr. Stone," I went on, as though his behavior was
perfectly normal, which—in context—it was. "Glad to
have you. We'll get going in a few minutes as soon as
everyone arrives." I was acting as though I hadn't even
noticed his hostility, which was the safest way to deal
with it. It took some of the oomph out of an act to
have the audience miss it.

Four others arrived in rapid succession, all of them
looking at me and then immediately greeting or nod-
ding or otherwise acknowledging Avery, none of them
pulling the cool routine as he had done. I noticed
none of them sat next to him, either. Maybe they
didn't want to impose. Last guy would have to sit next
to him, like it or not.

The last to arrive surprised me. He was a white guy,
tall and distinguished-looking, and he had the kind of
white, even teeth that suggested expensive orthodon-
tics. Bad teeth are a mark of poverty in this country

and most inmates had teeth that would make a dentist cry. Even Teeth didn't look like he came from the criminal subculture and he didn't have the manner either. He smiled warmly at me and said, "Jim. Jim Walker," holding out his hand. We could have been at a rotary meeting.

"Dr. Stone, Mr. Walker," I replied. As I shook his hand I noticed the smile hadn't moved up to his eyes. The skin around them stayed smooth and the only wrinkles were the usual age wrinkles a man in his thirties would have, no smiling crinkles at all. That told me something. I knew the research that shows when people genuinely smile, the whole face lifts and the eyes crinkle upward. But in phony smiles only the mouth moves and nothing happens around the eyes.

The nonsmiling eyes were watchful and very bright. "You can't teach quick," John Wooden, the great UCLA basketball coach had once said, and he might as well have been talking about the mind as the body. I didn't need an IQ test to tell me this guy was smart—you couldn't look at his eyes and think otherwise. But being bright might or might not get him points in the prison. Smart was harder to place in the hierarchy than Avery's physical prowess and cold intimidation. He'd rank if he was a jailhouse lawyer and used his smartness to aid the other inmates. It would be dangerous for him if he used it to put people down.

I pegged him for fraud and a date rapist. Well, he had to have some kind of sexual conviction or he wouldn't be in the group. But unfortunately, date rapists rarely drew time so there must have been something else. I didn't know yet because I hadn't had time to read all of the files before group.

To my surprise, Avery started the group. "How's the ho?" he said. The group got very still and everybody looked at me.

Anger shot through me in a nanosecond and I pushed it down just as fast. This wasn't about calling Eileen Steelwater a whore. This was about dominance in the group. Blow it now, ignore what Avery said, show fear, lose control of Avery and the group was over. No point in coming back. Likely everybody in the room knew this was coming but me. Avery had probably bragged about what he was going to do to the new group leader.

I stared at Avery without speaking for a few seconds and just let the tension build. It made a statement I wasn't going to ignore it and that I wasn't going to be intimidated. It also gave me time to figure out how to handle it. Really, I didn't have a lot of choices. Give him orders and he'd risk seg to defy me. There would be too much face loss if he took orders. Ignore it and he'd take over. Give him choices, however, and he'd likely make a reasonable one. He wasn't trying to get thrown out of the group. He was just making a run at the group leader.

I spoke very carefully. "Mr. Avery, it's your choice whether to be in this group or not. I'm not making you or anybody else come. If you choose to be here, you'll follow the rules just like everybody else. They won't be any different for you than for anybody, including me. So let's go over them."

I turned to the group. "No disrespecting anybody in this group. Not anybody in it. Not anybody outside it. No violence, of course. No intimidation. No threats. No name-calling. No putting anybody down. No staring people down. Anybody got a problem with that, now's the time to speak up. Be a shame to waste your time and mine."

Avery snorted but he didn't speak. The snort was face-saving and I ignored it. I took a deep breath and looked around. Two runs at the group leader and we were about one minute into the first session. I'd say we were par for the course.

"All right," I said. "Now here's the deal. I am taking over the group for Dr. Steelwater, who everybody knows is no longer working here." There were several snickers and a few sly smiles. "I'm not going to discuss what Dr. Steelwater did or didn't do that resulted in her leaving the prison. I don't actually know very much about it. I suspect everybody here knows more about it than I do or thinks they do, anyway. What's important here, however, is not what Dr. Steelwater is doing with her life, it's what you are going to do with yours. What treatment is about—as I hope you know by now—is giving you choices.

"Anybody here crazy about spending the rest of their life in prison?" I paused and looked around. "If you are, you don't need this group. If you'd actually like to get out, stay out and have a life, then maybe it's got something to offer you." Nobody spoke although everybody except Avery appeared to be listening. He was, too; he just didn't want to get caught doing it.

"Okay, I want to go around again and this time I want to hear what each of you has been working on in group." All eyes had been on me until I said that. Suddenly, there was a massive shift of gazes to the floor, the door, the walls. More than one inmate glanced over at Even Teeth, Mr. Walker. Only Avery didn't change. He stared straight ahead just as he had since he first sat down.

I sat back, wary and a little alarmed. Didn't these guys know what they'd been working on? Why the sudden avoidance? I swung to Walker. Everybody else seemed to think he had the answer and I was curious why. "Mr. Walker? What about you?"

His smile wavered for just a second and then he got it set in place. "Me?" he said slowly. "Well, let's see. I've been working mostly on my depression. I've been quite depressed about my situation." He was watching me closely, looking to see if he should go on. "Eileen . . . I mean Dr. Steelwater, was very helpful to me in managing it. I was even suicidal for a while."

I just stared at him. "In group?" I said slowly. "In a sex offender group, you were working on depression?"

He glanced around for support. "Well, it was pretty bad," he said. "I couldn't do the regular sex offender work that depressed."

But Walker showed no clinical signs of depression. He wasn't slowed down in speech or movement. It didn't look like he'd lost any weight and he didn't even look particularly sad. He was interpersonally responsive—I'd say he was even kind of perky. But even if he had been depressed, standard practice was to refer a client with mental health issues to psychological services, not to try to treat them in a sex offender group that was supposed to be working on, well, sexual offending.

I was stymied. I didn't want to get into criticizing Eileen on the first day of group—or the last one, for that matter. But this didn't sound good at all. I looked around the room. "Okay," I said, "who's next?" But nobody spoke.

2

I STARED AT THE MAN'S SHIRT HANGING CASUALLY OVER THE back of a chair in my living room. In *my* living room. I sat down on the couch opposite the chair and just looked at it. "I'm not sure you belong here," I said slowly to the shirt. "No offense, but I'm just used to living alone and I'm not used to finding men's shirts in my living room. I mean, you're a perfectly nice shirt but I'm not sure you really should be here, hanging around like that. I mean maybe visiting on the weekend or something, but you just look like you think you *live* here hanging over the back of that chair."

I waited for a moment but the shirt didn't comment and I sighed and got up. I walked to the sliding glass door and stared out at the deck and the small stream beyond. It wasn't that Adam was hard to live with, exactly. In fact, I had enough reality testing to know which of us a jury would describe as "difficult." But right or wrong I had this thing. For me, the idea of two people sharing the same house was like two people sharing the same skin.

The sound of a key turning in the lock interrupted

my obsessing. I winced just hearing it. Jesus Christ, I'd
almost forgotten I'd given him a key. Did I really give
him a key? Why not just hand over the title to the
house? What was I thinking?

Adam walked in and smiled, which only made me
feel worse. I glanced around; there was no place to go.
Everything was so small. If you were here and somebody else was here you were going to be together,
that's all. I tried to contort my features into a smile
and then realized it wasn't going to work. I couldn't do
this tonight. A woman has to know her limitations. I
walked casually over to my jacket and picked it up.
"Going somewhere?" he asked.

"Yep, I'm going to have dinner with Carlotta."

He frowned. "Funny, I ran into her today. She didn't
mention it."

"That's because she doesn't know about it yet," I
said. I kissed him lightly and left.

Looking at my grim face, Carlotta hadn't objected
to dinner at all. Not that she would have, anyway. She
was my oldest friend, going all the way back to college.
It had taken years and years but I had mostly forgiven
her for wasting her six foot frame on modeling when
there was basketball to be played. For her part she had
mostly given up worrying about my propensity for
going under the boards with guys who had me by a
hundred pounds and six inches. She had almost given
up saying it was a sign of dementia.

We both took the view that men would come and
go but that women friends were permanent. So I had
every reason to expect sympathy for my present
dilemma. It didn't involve basketball or danger or anything Carlotta found completely obnoxious about me.

It involved men and *there* we were usually talking the same language. So over dinner at Sweet Tomatoes I raised it. "Carlotta, he's living there. I mean, he was just staying over now and then but now he's *living* there."

"So."

"So . . . I don't know."

"He's a hassle?"

"No."

"Throws his dirty clothes all over the house?"

"No, he's pretty neat."

"You don't like him anymore?"

"I like him just fine."

"No fun in bed?"

"That'll be the day."

"Snores?"

"I don't know. I'm too tired to listen."

"He's got some bad habit too embarrassing to tell me about?"

"Nothing's too embarrassing to tell you about."

"You're fighting?"

"Not really."

"He's upset about the pregnancy?"

"He's thrilled about the pregnancy."

"So?"

"So . . . I don't know."

Carlotta took several bites of her salad before speaking. "Michael, Adam's not the problem. You're the problem."

"I never said I wasn't," I said defensively, but somehow this wasn't going as I had expected. You're supposed to get a biased view from your friends. They are supposed to make you feel better when you act like a jerk, not worse.

"You need a good shrink."

"I am a good shrink."

"Doesn't count."

"But who could I see? I know everybody up here. That's the problem with a small town." It was true. Jefferson University was one of the few major hospitals in the country located in a small rural area. That's because everything was small in a rural state like Vermont. We only had 500,000 people in the whole state. If we got together there wouldn't be enough of us to make up a large suburb of a major U.S. city.

"Go see Marion."

"Marion?" I knew instantly who she meant. She was a small-boned woman in her sixties who wore her silver hair cut short and curly. Rumor was she had retired from her very full practice in Boston and moved to the area. Supposedly she was keeping her hand in, seeing a few people part time. She had started coming into Psychiatry to hear Grand Rounds and attend some seminars. I had only met her briefly. That hadn't stopped me from having instant opinions about her. The first time I saw her I had pegged her as a hot-tea drinker, the kind whose house is never messy, whose clothes are always hung up and who are never rushed or scattered. Of course, that was total fantasy on my part. I didn't know her at all.

"Supposedly she's psychoanalytic. Seriously psychoanalytic. She was a member of the Psychoanalytic Institute in Boston, for Christ's sake. You know how I feel about that."

"Jesus, Michael," Carlotta said disgustedly. "One excuse after the other."

"One session," I said.

"Hey, you're not bargaining with me. He's not living in *my* house."

I camped out in Carlotta's guest bedroom for the night. It wasn't a problem; I always kept a travel bag in the car for impulses like that. Actually, I'd been known on occasion to go directly from a meeting to the airport and head for my beloved North Carolina coast on impulse. I was a little too pregnant right now to pull a stunt like that—as in, airlines wouldn't let me fly—but Carlotta's house felt just fine.

Carlotta and I had even been housemates for a while and it always amazed me I could share a house with a friend but not a lover. Maybe it was because Carlotta's house was an old Victorian with enough room for a small village. Or maybe it was because you weren't connected to friends in the same kind of way. It might be deeper but it was different; there wasn't so much "we-ness" in that friend thing. Whatever.

Carlotta didn't object to my staying over, except for one minor comment about my cowardice. Actually, Carlotta didn't like me that far out in the country anyway given how pregnant I was, so she wouldn't have minded if I'd moved in full time for a while.

I didn't call Adam, but ten to one Carlotta did, no doubt to tell him not to worry. I didn't think Adam had any right worrying about me and I couldn't stand the sense of being tied down that checking in every five minutes brought. I knew Carlotta thought I was unreasonable about this but she didn't argue about stuff like that anymore; she just did whatever she pleased, which I couldn't argue with because that was my whole point.

* * *

I woke up cheerful, having exercised some small adolescent rebellion at my new-found status as a "couple" and found myself thinking about Eileen Steelwater instead. I needed to ask her about the group, get her input on the different offenders, but I just couldn't make the call. What I really wanted to ask her wasn't any of my business.

Psychiatry was buzzing when I got to the hospital and I made my way past a full waiting room through the double doors to my secretary's desk. My secretary, Melissa, was holding the phone a few inches from her ear with one hand and propping up her forehead with the other. I could hear the yelling before I even got close.

We had a range of customers in Psychiatry from the walking wounded to the truly crazy to the totally obnoxious. The walking wounded were just regular folks like the rest of us who got depressed or had marital problems and/or had kids who didn't do their homework. The truly crazy were a world away; they saw things we didn't see and heard things nobody should hear, and suffered endlessly. But they weren't the problem; they were mostly why we were there. They were just plain ill and they were more preyed upon than preying.

It was the folks euphemistically called "personality disorders," whom laypeople called "jerks," who did the yelling. They yelled at us and their families and their friends and anyone else who crossed their paths. Their lovers considered suicide and their therapists routinely considered selling hot dogs for a living. Somebody had tied into Melissa and I didn't interrupt. It seemed impolite to bother someone while they were being beaten up.

I was halfway down the hall going through my pink slips before I saw the message from Eileen. If there's no such thing as telepathy, why is it half the time when you're thinking of someone, they call you? I went straight to my office and called her back but the conversation was short and awkward. She didn't want to talk on the phone, which was fine with me. I wasn't sure this would be an easy conversation and I needed to see people to exercise the minuscule amount of tact I owned. I didn't even think about suggesting the Make-Shift Café. Eileen had been wearing round collar blouses in the sixties and singing her sorority song. Tie-dyed tee shirts made her nervous. At least the old Eileen wouldn't have been comfortable there. I wasn't sure what to expect from the new one.

I don't like to put things off so I suggested lunch right away, today. Eileen was out of work and didn't seem busy so it was fine with her. On the way I decided that I might as well drop the pretense I was just there for info about the group and tell her the truth. Maybe it was morbid curiosity, maybe it was for old times' sake, but she had been a colleague once and something of a friend, and I just didn't get it.

She was already seated but stood up and waved when she saw me. My mouth dropped and I found myself scrambling to keep her from seeing it as I walked over. She must have put on forty pounds and her ankles looked as swollen as mine. She didn't look well, not well at all physically, and it seemed a lot more than depression.

She looked just as surprised to see me. "Michael," she said simply, staring in amazement at my huge belly. The moment she said my name fifteen years dropped in a heartbeat. People change the way they look but not the way they sound. It's not the same over the phone, but in person, close your eyes and listen to someone you haven't seen for years and it's as good as an old song to take you back.

We both sat down. "I didn't know you got remarried," Eileen said.

"I didn't."

"But . . . ?"

"I'm living with the baby's dad—well, sort of—but we're not married."

"Same old Michael," she said, sounding almost bitter. Over what, I wondered.

"Well, that's true," I said, taking the bull by the horns. "I probably am the same-old-Michael whatever that was, but you aren't, Eileen. I don't understand what happened and that's the gospel truth. When I knew you, you'd get upset if someone forgot to fill in a time sheet. I just don't get it. What happened?"

"It's not important," she said. "That's not what I wanted to talk to you about."

"It isn't?" I said, puzzled. "So what is?"

"It's the group. It's about someone in your group."

I relaxed a little. This was surely a better way to start than my blunt frontal attack. Let Eileen talk a little about an area where she could help me. "Who?"

Eileen paused, "It's difficult to know where to start." I waited.

"It's about Jim," she said.

"Ah, Jim," I replied. "What about Jim?" I had pegged Jim for a psychopath and was waiting for Eileen to confirm it. Maybe she was going to warn me about him.

"He's innocent."

"Excuse me?"

"I know you're going to find this hard to believe, but he's innocent."

"Innocent?" I couldn't believe she'd said it. After group I had sat around reading the files. Jim was a lawyer who'd been screwing his down-and-out desperate divorce clients who were fearful of losing their children. He seemed to know just who was frightened enough and poor enough—as in couldn't afford a different lawyer—to go along with it. When one resisted, he threatened her. When she told him she'd take him to the ethics board, he beat the living hell out of her. So much for the smooth smile and the polite manner. "Innocent of what?" I replied. "He beat a woman unconscious. What are you talking about?"

"That's what I'm trying to tell you, Michael, if you'll just listen. He was framed. He didn't beat anybody. His ex-wife had that woman beat up. He didn't have anything to do with it. And he certainly didn't coerce anybody into having sex with him. Why would a man like Jim need to do that? Those women wanted to have sex with him. They seduced him. Oh, I know he shouldn't have done it. But he is a man and you know how men are about that sort of thing."

I sat blinking and trying to figure out what to say. Eileen hadn't just lost her boundaries. She'd lost her mind.

"Eileen," I said softly, and realized I sounded like I was talking to a child. "Have you read Jim's records? They're pretty compelling. What gave you the idea he's innocent?"

"The records are lies, complete lies. Well, it can happen, Michael. You know the legal system isn't perfect. It does make mistakes."

"So how did you figure out he was innocent? Where did you get this information?"

"I know what you're driving at, Michael. Yes, I got it from Jim, but I've talked to his family, too. The trouble he got in growing up, his mother said it was just scapegoating. He only fought because he had to. He was just the kind of kid other kids like to torture. Jealous, probably, because he was smart. I don't know. You're the one who treats children. But I'm telling you he's not a criminal. He didn't do any of this stuff. I'll have proof soon. I've hired a private detective."

"You've hired a private detective? No offense, Eileen, but what about you? Unless you've won the lottery, you're going to have enough trouble paying your own legal bills. You're going to be up on charges for whatever went on at the prison: in this state it's illegal to have sex with an inmate. I can't be telling you anything you don't know. Why are you spending money on a two-bit psychopath instead of taking care of yourself?"

I knew it was a mistake the moment I said it. Eileen's eyes instantly hardened. She straightened her back and replied frostily. "He's not a two-bit psychopath, Michael. He's a fine, decent man who has been wrongfully imprisoned. Doesn't that mean anything to you?" She raised her chin. "And I'm doing all right financially. I sold my house, so I do have the capital to hire a private detective if I want to. Not that it's any of your business."

The waiter interrupted to ask what we wanted to eat. I started to snap at him but thought better of it. It was hardly his fault Eileen Steelwater had gone bonkers. We both stared gloomily at the menu. Eileen seemed to be fighting tears. I ordered two cheeseburgers, French fries, and a milkshake. Nothing Eileen could possibly say could interfere with my appetite. I didn't know who I was hosting in that bubble in front of me but if this kept up, it was going to come out looking like a Sumo wrestler.

Eileen ordered a cup of tea and some toast. I noticed her hand shook slightly as she picked up her water and slowly sipped it.

"How did you get to know Jim?" I said. There was no point in arguing with her.

"In the group," she said.

"But you didn't get all this out of the group? So how did you get to know him outside of group?"

"Actually, it did start in group," she said. "That man Avery," she looked up at me. "You must have met Avery."

"Go on."

"Well, he was giving me a hard time and Jim confronted him. It was very brave of Jim. Avery could have killed him. Avery did threaten him over it but he wouldn't back down. I don't know what would have happened if Jim hadn't gotten between Avery and me. I might not be here today," she said melodramatically.

That's true, I thought. She might be still working at the prison, still have her license, her house and her reputation.

"Eileen, I don't want to upset you but I can't lie to you. Didn't you ever consider that Jim might have set that up with Avery? It's the oldest con trip in the book—protect a staff member from another inmate and they're indebted to you forever." I said it almost plaintively. It seemed so obvious what had happened. She'd worked in prisons for years. How could she not have figured it out?

"I don't want to upset you, Michael, but everybody knows you're cynical about inmates. If Jesus Christ were imprisoned you wouldn't believe He was innocent."

"Get real, Eileen. We're not dealing with Jesus Christ here. Besides, we're running treatment groups, not trials. You can't second-guess the court system; you've only got one side of the story. You're not even hearing from the victim. Half the time when you get the victim reports, the offender just happened to leave out most of the evidence."

"But what if someone *were* innocent?"

"He should get a good lawyer. Someone who could help him with the legal system, which we can't." The baby shifted again and I winced. Silence fell while I fidgeted trying to get comfortable.

"Are you all right?"

"Oh yeah, it's just normal aches and pains." I sighed. "I don't want to argue with you, Eileen. Tell me more. . . . How did you get to know him?"

"I started individual counseling sessions with him. Really, he needed more than just the group."

I winced again but this time it had nothing to do with the baby. "Why was he having all this therapy if he was innocent?"

"He was depressed. Who wouldn't be if they were falsely imprisoned?"

"So why was he in the sex offender group?"

"Well . . . it wasn't clear that his conviction would get overturned—don't look at me like that, Michael. You've said yourself that justice doesn't always work the way it should. If his conviction didn't get overturned, he needed treatment on his record to apply for parole."

"So he really wasn't working in treatment at all; he was just there to make it look good on his records."

"Actually he was very helpful to the other inmates. He's very insightful."

I started to open my mouth but realized my voice was not going to sound the way I wanted it to. It seemed to have a life of its own sometimes and now it was trying hard to yell at Eileen. I wrestled it to the mat before I spoke. "How insightful?"

"Pardon?"

"Did he ever get personal with you?"

Eileen picked up her toast, then put it down. She took a sip of tea instead. Buying time. "Not really," she said finally, without looking up.

Suddenly I felt a rush of the old warmth for Eileen. You gotta like someone who can't lie any better than that. There was something so sad and innocent about someone who didn't know the first, most elementary thing about lying—that you should look someone straight in the eye.

We waffled through the rest of the lunch, both of us disappointed in the other. Eileen seemed to be fighting tears because I wouldn't believe her and try to help the man she believed in. I was just baffled by her obsession with him and her obliviousness to her own peril.

It wasn't until later that afternoon that I realized I had gotten completely detoured. I hadn't asked the most important question of all. Eileen had had sex with a *different* inmate, not Jim, an inmate she didn't even mention. Which didn't make any sense at all.

3

I WAS AS NERVOUS FOR MY FIRST THERAPY SESSION AS ANY other new client. Maybe more nervous; knowing more didn't always help. Marion had agreed to see me at the end of the week, which was really pretty quick, and I wasn't sure why. True, she was new in the area so she might not have picked up many cases yet. Or maybe I sounded urgent. I hoped I didn't sound *that* urgent. Jesus, I hated being on the needy side of things.

For once I was right; she was a hot-tea drinker and she immediately offered me some as well. She was wearing a long black wool skirt with a black turtleneck and her short silver hair shone in contrast. She looked somehow more informal than I had expected from a psychoanalytic type.

Her office was a surprise, too. It was located in her home—not uncommon for therapists in Vermont—but it surprised me by how informal it was. There was an old, heavily stuffed couch set on a thick, full rug and fresh flowers on a table next to it. Her seat was an easy chair that looked old and comfortable and there was an identical one next to it. Clients could choose to sit on the couch or the chair.

There were a series of photos of the same tree on the wall, taken in different seasons and under different light conditions. I was pretty sure that she had taken them. The photos were too patient and there was too much love for that tree for them to come from a pro.

I stood looking at the photos, teacup in my hand. They were as close, I knew, as I would ever get to learning anything about her. "I knew someone once who was in art school," I said. "I asked him what he was painting. He said he was doing some still-lifes of three eggs and a bottle. Six months later I ran into him and asked him again. He said, 'Three eggs and a bottle.'

"I said, 'But that's what you were painting last time.'

"Oh, it's all right,' he replied. 'It doesn't have to change, because I do.'"

I turned and saw her smile. "Sit down," she said quietly, "and let's begin."

"So," she said, when I was seated. "Why are you here?"

"My boyfriend has moved in."

"And?"

"I don't know."

"You don't like him living there?"

"It's not about him."

"What's it about?"

"What I lose."

"Which is?"

"Living alone."

"Tell me about living alone."

"Whoa," I said. "Don't you want to know my history? My earliest memory? The whole early-childhood bit?"

"Actually," she said, taking a sip of tea, "I want to know about the problem."

I sighed. This was psychoanalytic? I concentrated on trying to put it together. "I don't know how to say it. The house . . . It's being in a house when no one else is there. I like empty buildings, always have. They have a sense about them. You can't feel the spirit of a house when somebody else is in it. People take up so much *space*. They do. They hide any sense of a place. Walk into an empty house—I don't even turn the lights on most of the time at night when I come home—the moonlight slants through the glass front of the A-frame in these patterns. It makes these sharp patterns across the couch . . ."

I paused but she said nothing, so I went on.

"I sit out on the deck at night, facing the woods. With no light, after a while you can see things in the woods. The woods become this live thing and you don't even notice yourself any more. Wallace Stevens wrote about it. He talked about the night becoming the book and you becoming the night, something like that . . ."

She still didn't speak and I couldn't tell if she was getting it. I didn't even know what I was saying, really. I tried again. "In the morning there is this silence until I open the skylight above my bed and then all I hear are birds. I sit in bed and drink my morning coffee and listen to the birds. I don't have to worry about anybody else. Not what they want. Not what they think. I don't feel at peace around people in the same way. Do you know what I'm saying?"

"Michael," she said softly. "There have always been women who loved solitude. It is not a crime if you are one of them. However . . ."

"However what?"

"You're pregnant."

I looked down at my belly. "Oops," I said.

"I think, my dear, you are in very deep denial. Whether this man of yours stays or not, your solitude is gone. You have just made a twenty-year commitment to living with another person. There will be someone there, Michael, when you wake in the morning and when you go to bed at night. Babies are not jobs that give you weekends off. Not even the nights will belong to you. Life with this man is likely to seem like complete solitude by contrast."

"Yikes," I managed to squeak before panic closed my throat entirely.

"Adam," I said, climbing into bed without even taking my clothes off. "I'm thinking about getting an abortion."

Adam turned over and looked at me. "Michael, you're in the eighth month."

"What? You're saying this is impractical?"

"It's called birth."

"Um . . ."

"Getting nervous?"

"Well, I just realized I'm not going to be pregnant forever."

"And . . ."

"Someone else is going to be living here."

"Besides me?"

"Well, we haven't really settled that, have we? I mean, I don't know whether to count your stuff in my

250 things or not." I never owned more than 250 things at a time. It was just this 'rule' I had.

"Yes, we've settled it and no, you don't have to count my stuff in your 250 things."

"What about the baby? Do we count the baby's stuff in my 250 things?"

"The baby's a person. She gets her own 250 things."

"You don't know it's a girl."

"What would have happened if I'd said, 'he'?"

"Good point."

"Go to sleep, Michael. Things will look better in the morning."

"What a stupid thing to say," I yelled. "They will not look better in the morning. That's the kind of dumb-ass thing people say when they don't take you seriously."

Wearily, Adam turned to face me. "You're right," he said sitting up. "Things won't look better in the morning. They're not going to look better for a while. But I know you. The problem is you haven't seen her face. That's all."

I swallowed hard and looked at him.

"Go to sleep, Michael," he said. He lay back down but reached back and put his hand across my belly, across the face I hadn't yet seen.

I looked at his hand and my belly, then I lay down. Suddenly I wasn't worrying about my precious solitude anymore. I was seeing faces: all different, all small. Strange that I'd never thought about it before. I put together noses and chins and cheekbones; hazel eyes and blue eyes and brown eyes, one after the other until a great fog eased into my mind.

I woke up to the sound of a ringing phone. Adam was gone even though it was a Saturday—cops didn't

keep the kind of hours the rest of the world did. It was
full daylight and for a moment I was disoriented trying to figure out how late it was. I reached for the
clock to turn it toward me and knocked it over instead.
When I finally got it off the floor, I shook my head in
disbelief. Jesus Christ, it was eight o'clock. Why didn't
I just sleep for the next two months? The answering
machine was just starting to pick up when I finally got
to the phone.

"Michael, this is Brenda." I closed my eyes. This was
no way to start the day. My cousin Brenda almost
never called me unless it had to do with Mama.

"Brenda? All right. Don't tell me. What's she up to
now?"

"Michael, glad to talk to you, too. And I'm fine,
thank you for asking. How's your pregnancy going?"

"Sorry, you know how crazy Mama makes me. I'm
fine, I guess, if you discount the fact people back up
and go around when they see me coming down a
shopping aisle. I've only gained seventy pounds and I
have two months to go."

"You couldn't have. Bless you, girl. You were such a
little thing."

"Not anymore. I look like I'm standing in front of
one of those fat mirrors at the fair. How are you doing,
really?"

"I'm doing fine but you're right about your mama.
I'm worried about her. She's gone to Las Vegas again."

"Again? What do you mean 'again'? When did she
go the first time?"

"Land sakes, Michael, I took her after Christmas. I
thought you knew."

"How would I know? Mama doesn't tell me anything. You took her to Vegas?"

"Well, yes," Brenda replied. "Now you know my daughter-in-law Betty Lou works for a travel agent. She got us a real good deal on a trip. Got us a room at the Bellagio. I tell you I have never seen anything in my life like it. I think all of Wilson's Pond could have fit in the lobby and left room over. They said it cost over a billion dollars to build."

"And Mama?"

"Well, she just had the best time. She perked right up. She'd been looking a little down at the mouth, you know, since that long flu bug she had this fall, and I thought the trip would do her good. But Michael, I swear to God if I'd known what was going to happen I would never have taken her."

"I'm not following you, Brenda. What happened?"

"Well, we were no sooner back than she was gone again. I tell you she's been to Vegas three times since Christmas and it's only the beginning of March. Then Clem Johnson called me this morning and I thought I'd better call you."

"Clem who?"

"You know Clem. He was only a couple of years behind you in school. He's Billy Johnson's son worked over at Stevens Marina. Don't you remember? Clem married Jonathan Rilley's daughter down on Harker's Island after that worthless, no good Thompson boy ran off and left her high and dry with two boys to raise. That's been ten years now. Clem's been working at the bank, gosh, I don't know how long, seems like forever. He took Mr. Everson's job as vice president when he retired four or five years ago. He's done real well for himself—"

"Brenda—"

"I'm getting to it. It seems like you are always in

such a hurry, Michael. It can't be good for you to always be that much in a hurry. Anyway, I know he wasn't supposed to tell me but he was worried. He's known your mama forever and he was wondering if everything was all right."

"Why?"

"Why what?"

"Why was he wondering?"

"Well, I'm trying to tell you if you'll let me. She took a hundred and ten thousand out of her retirement fund, that's why, and wouldn't tell him a thing about it. Told him it was none of his business; well, you know your mama. I told him she was in Las Vegas and my guess is she took the whole kit and caboodle with her. I don't know what she's thinking of. I have never known your mother to act that way."

"What? My mother has taken a hundred and ten thousand in cash to Vegas? You must be joking."

"Well, I don't know it's cash. I didn't ask him that."

I was stunned. Mama was not the most predictable person in the world, but she had never gambled that I knew of. Unfortunately, I could see Mama and Vegas. At seventy-six, she still favored bright lights and wore sequins more than her L. L. Bean daughter ever had, but she had always restricted her wanderings to the Grand Ole Opry. I always thought it was the size of the Grand Ole Opry Hotel that drew Mama more than the music. The Pentagon would fit in the Grand Ole Opry Hotel and leave room for a small city. Mama didn't actually like country music but did like grand. Mama had always liked grand.

And that's where Vegas would definitely draw Mama. But three times in two months? A hundred and ten thousand in cash? Maybe she'd decided at seventy-six she didn't have anything to lose and she'd go out with a bang. But if that's what she was thinking she was surely wrong, because my mama would live forever. She had never had anything wrong with her but one hemorrhoid operation thirty years ago she was still mad about. Besides, even God wouldn't want to take on my mother.

"Do you know where she's staying? The Bellagio?"

"No, I don't know, but I don't think it's the Bellagio. She likes to try different ones. Last time it was New York, New York. Said it couldn't hold a candle to the Bellagio. Said the glass works on the ceiling at the Bellagio was the prettiest thing she had ever—"

"Brenda . . ."

"Betty Lou'll know. She makes all her travel arrangements."

"Why didn't Betty Lou warn you she was doing this?"

"Betty Lou didn't have to warn me. Your mama told me. She told me she was going."

"Did you ask her why?"

"I didn't have to ask her. She told me. Said she had a good time."

"Jesus, Brenda, you should have gone with her."

"Well, that's easier said that done, Michael. I can't just take off from the pharmacy every whipstitch. But I did offer. She said she didn't need anybody to go with her. Said she had a man who went with her. Said he was going to be her business partner."

"Oh my God. Who?"

"How would I know?"

"You mean it isn't anybody from Wilson's Pond?"

"Oh, I'm pretty sure it isn't anybody from Wilson's

Pond. I would have heard if anybody from Wilson's Pond was traipsing out to Las Vegas with your mother. That would've been all over town by now. No, I think it's somebody she met out there."

There was silence while I tried to take this in. "Brenda, can you find out where my mother is staying and call me?"

"Well, I can surely do that. I'll call Betty Lou right now. I'm just as sorry as I can be, Michael. I feel like this is all my fault."

"It's not your fault, Brenda. You ought to know that. Nothing's anybody's fault when it comes to Mama."

I hung up and tried to take it in. Vegas. Drive-through chapels and billion-dollar hotels. Restaurants with ten genuine Picassos on the wall next door to chapels with Elvis impersonators who will marry you drunk or sober—although I sincerely hoped most people were drunk who let Elvis marry them.

If money was the American religion then those billion-dollar hotels were the closest this country would ever get to cathedrals. And just like the European cathedrals, they were built on the backs of the poor and the middle class and they, too, sold salvation. Only salvation in this country meant getting rich. The only difference was that American cathedrals were more efficient. No more simply walking down the aisles with plates asking for donations. They had installed cash extraction machines, milking stations by the thousands on the ground floor that people—amazingly—voluntarily hooked themselves up to.

It was a brilliant business. The cash extraction machines ran like IV drips twenty-four hours a day, slowly, insidiously pulling cash from the thousands who sat patiently pulling the levers and pushing the buttons—credit cards accepted.

But what was my mother doing in Vegas? Had she morphed into one of those little old ladies with a cigarette dangling from her mouth, feeding quarters and pulling the levers at seven-thirty in the morning? Mama reinvented herself regularly but this was a hard image to buy. A hundred and ten thousand dollars was a lot of quarters. No, if Mama was in Vegas, she'd be looking for action and she'd have higher stakes in mind than quarters.

4

I HARDLY NOTICED THE DRIVE TO NELSON'S POINT FOR GROUP on Monday I was so busy obsessing. Clearly, there was going to be B.B. and A.B.: life Before Baby and life After Baby. Marion had a point: if I couldn't cope with a guy in the house, how would I cope with a baby? Adam was at least reasonably sensitive to that space thing I had, but you couldn't exactly expect a baby to make allowances for my poor mental health.

And then there was Mama. Mama was on the back roads of my memory, as the song went. No, not the back roads. If it was Mama, it was more like the river in *Deliverance* running in the back of my mind. Brenda hadn't called back all weekend, which worried me a little. I couldn't say Mama and I were close—more like mutually suspicious countries with a common border—but I did hate to see her ripped off.

I had plenty of time to obsess since there was a tractor in front of me with a deaf farmer on it who showed no intention of letting me by. Tractors doing twenty miles an hour were a fact of life in Vermont and the narrow winding roads meant you just lived with it.

It was a gorgeous day for mud season—which usually had more personality than good looks—and if I weren't afraid of being late to group I wouldn't have minded a slow drive through the countryside. Old farmhouses and red barns were dotted here and there on the open hillsides and the breeze had a crisp, sweet smell to it. The promise of a Vermont summer was definitely in the air, like the undercurrent running through children right before Christmas. Heaven, after all, was a movable feast and every summer it set up a brief camp in Vermont.

The farmer made me late and I was still obsessing, so when I arrived at the prison I was distracted and slow to notice that something was different. The phones at Nelson's Point were ringing off the hook, and the officer on the desk seemed to be simply ignoring them.

"What's going on?" I said when the phones finally got through my personal fog. I was past the metal detector and holding my freshly stamped hand under the fluorescent light for the officer behind the bulletproof glass to see. It always took a while to get into a maximum security prison and there was no such thing as a door you could open yourself. I figured if you worked here long enough you'd go home one day and stand outside your front door waiting for it to spring open.

"Oh, they shipped Clarence in a couple of days ago," the officer at the desk behind me replied. "The phone hasn't stopped ringing since. Media's on a feeding frenzy." What was harder than dealing with the media when they were on a rampage? Some things, I thought. Maybe bullfighting in a red dress or swimming nude with piranhas. But then again, maybe not.

The steel door finally opened and I hurried off to the next one. I finally made it through all the doors and was just heading down the hall toward the group room when I saw Gary come out of an office and head up the same corridor. I started to call out to him to wait up when I saw Avery coming the other way. The words died in my throat. Avery was staring intently at Gary as he walked, something I knew Avery's subculture did not think respectful. But that wasn't so rare. What stopped me cold was not just that he was looking right at him, it was *how* he was looking at him.

It brought back a memory. I once had a friend with a seriously vicious dog she loved very much and I had come over to spend the day to try and make friends with it. I was sitting in a chair and I very slowly leaned down to pet the dog. The dog's eyes changed for one second, and then she went for my throat. It had all happened too fast for me to move. But it was not the teeth catching my shirt as I jerked away that I remembered. It was the eyes. They had turned hard and reptilian in a way I couldn't begin to describe. One thing I knew: in that split second I saw what the zebra saw right before the kill.

Avery turned to go into the library and I realized I had been holding my breath. I literally wasn't sure he wouldn't attack Gary right on the spot in front of me. I called out to Gary and he turned and smiled in a distracted kind of way. He waited while I caught up.

"What is the deal with you and Avery?" I asked.

"What?" he said.

"That look?" I said. "The one like he'd like to take your throat out with a spoon. That one."

"Oh, that," Gary shrugged and picked up his beeper, which had just vibrated. He looked at it and

sighed. "It's a long story," he said. "I'll tell you sometime. We've got a new guest," he added. "Clarence has
arrived. Kind of taking up a lot of my time right now.
You here for the group?"

"Yep."

"Let me know how it's going," he said. "Catch you
later," and he was already moving away.

I watched his receding back for a minute, still feeling uneasy. For a moment I had the impulse to call out
to Gary, say something more about it, but I didn't
know what. An inmate gave the warden a dirty look.
Big deal. But then again, I had seen dirty looks before
and this one was different—I'd bet on it.

I unlocked the group room and called the operator
to get the guys moving to group. Technically there
wasn't a problem if I was late. The door would stay
locked and the guys would stay on the unit or wherever they were. But it annoyed the hell out of staff
when people didn't call for them on time because
some of the inmates would be just standing around
waiting for the call, which meant staff also ended up
standing around and waiting.

It only took a few minutes and one by one they fil-
tered in, some scurrying, some dawdling, some with
furtive glances here and there. Only Avery owned the
strut. Really, you could tell most of what you needed
to know about people in a prison by the way they
moved. Fear showed up in a walk faster than in a
Rorschach. Bravado and cockiness could be displayed
in every step.

In the larger culture, your house, your neighborhood said who you were. In the ghetto, it was cars,
since nobody owned a house. In a prison, things got
down to more basic elements. All you had was you:

everybody lived in a cell and everybody got around by walking. But people were people and status was eternal. How you moved told people who you were. Slinking and swaggering replaced buying and owning and muscle under the skin was an adequate substitute for power under the hood.

The last to enter was Leroy Warner, street smart and canny, he moved like a ferret to his seat. The moment he sat down, I started "layout," the standard beginning of group. We should have done it last time but I was too busy dealing with the transition from Eileen to me. So this was really the first session where we could focus on their offenses.

Layout meant each man stated his name, admitted he was a sex offender, recited all the molestations and rapes he had ever done—which often took quite a while—described how he would have escalated if he hadn't gotten caught, revealed any deviant thoughts and fantasies he'd had during the previous week (yeah, right) and how he had handled them, said what he'd done for homework, and put something on the agenda about sexual deviancy to discuss this week. It wasn't for the faint of heart.

I deliberately started on the opposite end of the group from Avery. I wanted the group to get into a rhythm before I had to deal with him. Completely aside from his issues with Gary, I was remembering the problems he caused me last time and was anticipating more.

I picked a pathetic-looking child molester to begin. His name was Adrian Speare. He took a deep breath and said, "My name is Adrian. I am a sex offender. I molested my two children, a boy and a girl. I fondled my little boy and inserted my finger in my little girl's vagina. I started molesting when I was a teenager. I molested the girl next door when I was fourteen and she was six." All this time he hadn't looked up.

"I molested all the time until I got caught. I'm guessing I have maybe eighty to a hundred victims. If I hadn't gotten caught I would have just kept going. I don't think I would have escalated. I was already anally raping little boys and raping little girls with my finger and that's what my fantasies were about." He paused. "I saw a child on TV this week who looked a lot like one of my victims and I got a hard-on." He glanced up briefly to see how the group was taking this, then went on. "I punished the impulse by snapping the rubber band on my wrist. But it didn't work too well. I still had some fantasies. He looked depressed. "Okay, what else. For homework I've been working on all the factors that led up to my assault and I want to discuss my risk factors."

He looked around the room. I didn't blink an eye. Adrian's story wasn't new to me. Unfortunately, child molesters like him were a dime a dozen in prison. Avery, on the other hand, looked openly disgusted but didn't say anything. He was the sort that thought child molesters were "perverted," while he—since he only beat women up, brutally raped them and occasionally pimped a few—was a "real man."

On the other hand, the child molesters saw the rapists as sick because they were *violent* whereas—in the child molesters' minds—they were only guilty of loving children too much. No matter what folks did, they always had an excuse.

I wrote Adrian's agenda item on the blackboard and moved on. We'd do layout with everybody before we went to the agenda.

"Mr. Terrance," I said. Terrance was the youngest

offender in the group at eighteen. He came from the usual background of juvenile justice, i.e., trouble in school to early crime to failures at diversion and finally off to juvi jail. He wasn't just a sex offender. He was one of those kids who didn't know anything but crime of one sort or another. This was his first time in treatment and he was new to the group. I didn't really know if he was going to cooperate or not. He'd hardly said anything the first session. He was the only one in the group who hadn't been there for the debacle with Eileen.

"I don't know about this. I'm just going by what I heard, you know. I, um, did something to my brother and two of his friends. I didn't hurt um none. I just traded um some cigarettes." He paused.

"Any other victims?" I prompted.

"Nope," he said. "Well, I did touch a little girl once but I don't know if that counts."

"Why not?"

"Her mother told me I could, if I'd get her some crack. She already had her in some child porn and stuff." My stomach turned.

"Do you know her name or where to find her?" I asked.

He shook his head. "No, I met her in a crack house. I wasn't doing none. I was just looking for my brother Daryl. I didn't give her no crack." As if somehow that made it better.

I resisted the impulse to shake my head in disbelief. It was the world he lived in and he knew already the rest of us didn't understand it. "It counts," I said softly. "Just because she had a lousy mother doesn't make it okay to molest her."

I let him go after that. He didn't understand the rest

of layout yet and he'd done pretty well in admitting anything. I'd be surprised if that was really all the victims he had but it was a lot better start than most people made in treatment.

We moved around the group pretty smoothly after that until it was Avery's turn. I barely looked at him, deliberately making things as casual as possible and as much like the others as I could. "All right, Mr. Avery, your turn," I said.

He looked back at me, no doubt trying to figure out how to play it. I suspected he would have liked to say "fuck you" but, for whatever reasons, he wanted to be in the group and not cooperating at all would have gotten him thrown out. So there was pressure to come up with something.

"My name is Avery," he said, finally. "And don't none of you chumps forget it." As if anyone was in any danger of forgetting Avery. "I don't belong here with you perverts. All I did was catch a little ass. That weren't nothin'—"

"Mr. Avery," I said, interrupting. "Just the facts. How many victims did you have?"

"I've caught a little ass now and then. Mostly they thank me for it after."

"Mr. Avery, we've got work to do. I suggest we put on the agenda that you need to figure out how to do a decent layout. Let's move on."

The whole group looked at Avery to see how he'd react. He glared at me like I was lunch but I just said calmly, "Next." The truth was we didn't have time for Avery's grandstanding and if he started it, I wasn't going to oblige him by giving him air time. Jim looked uncertainly at Avery—he was the only one left—but when Avery just sat there, he started in.

"My name is Jim Walker," he said. "Everybody knows I'm an attorney. I was fooling around with some clients—I admit it—when one of them caught me with someone else and got jealous. She manufactured a beating charge—"

"Whoa, guys," I said. "It looks like half the group has forgotten how to do a decent layout. Okay, let me remind everybody. We are not here to retry these cases. If you think you're innocent, take it to the courts but—an innocent man can't be treated for a problem he doesn't have. So if you're completely denying the offense, you belong in court or in a denier's group, but not here. Everybody straight with that? To be in this group you have to have a problem. Otherwise, it's a waste of everybody's time. Mr. Walker, you got a problem or not?"

Working with sex offenders, psychopaths and sadists was a world away from working with victims. Treating victims required a soft and supportive touch. Try that with offenders and you were toast. Your treatment group would end up functioning like a gang and running credit card scams over the prison phones. Or you'd end up in bed with one of them, like Eileen.

"Well, I *was* fooling around with clients. And some people thought that was unethical because I was their attorney."

"And what kind of clients were these?"

"I was a divorce attorney."

"How many were women in custody fights and afraid they'd lose their children?"

"I don't remember."

"Maybe for your assignment today you could check that out," I said, "and report back." I turned to the group. "I'm getting a little confused, guys. Didn't you go over this stuff before? Before I joined the group when Dr. Steelwater was running it? How come almost nobody can do a decent layout?"

A couple of people snickered and no one answered. I hesitated. Sooner or later we'd have to talk about Eileen but I wasn't sure if now was the time. For one thing, I didn't know enough about what really happened in group to challenge anybody if they started lying through their teeth. Jesus. How would I get the info? Eileen wouldn't tell me anything except how wonderful Jim was. If I asked the group, Avery would start in on Eileen as the "ho."

But something had happened because this group was off track, badly off track. Half the group was lying or denying their offenses and they shouldn't have been—not at this point in treatment. This group had been meeting for well over six months, for Christ's sake. Anybody who was still denying should have been thrown out long ago. What the hell had Eileen been doing?

And what was even more frustrating was she had left almost no notes behind. Where there should have been progress notes on each and every session, there were only lists of who attended. I was used to sloppy record-keeping in some prisons, but this went way beyond the norm. And it was light years away from what I would have expected from Eileen. I couldn't find anything in the records at all to say what anybody was working on.

Actually, there were some things. Which made it even weirder. The first couple of months the records were decent. Individual notes on each group member after each session. But then it had just stopped. Maybe

Gary's theory that Eileen had had a psychotic break wasn't so farfetched after all.

"All right guys, never mind. Let's just cut to the agenda. We just can't spend all day on layouts. Most of you need to work on your layouts but we'll come back to them another time. Mr. Walker, is there anything you want to put on the agenda?"

"Sure," he said. "Clarence."

There was a dead silence in the group.

"All right," I said. "What about Clarence?"

"Man's gonna die," Jim said cheerfully.

"What? You mean if he comes out in general pop?"

"Don't matter. It won't matter where he is."

I looked around the room at the silent faces. Everybody except Avery was looking at the floor, the door, the walls, anything but me or Jim. Avery was just staring straight ahead. It seemed odd to me it was Jim saying this and not Avery. Avery blustered and fumed. Jim smooth-talked but he didn't look like the type to threaten. Was he trying to warn me? Was there a plan afoot already?

"Is that a rumor, Mr. Walker, or a promise? I mean, what are you saying? If somebody kills Clarence, they'll spend eons in seg—no electronics, no visitors, just sitting in a cell and staring at the wall—plus get a life sentence for murder. Anybody care about Clarence that much? That they're ready to spend the rest of their life in prison for him?"

Again, no one but Jim spoke. "If they're caught," Jim said softly.

"I think you can count on their getting caught," I said sharply. "I've spoken with the warden on this one and he'd make it worth somebody's while to tell. He'd chase Clarence's killer as if he'd killed the Pope.

Nobody gets a free shot at Clarence just because of who he is. Everybody understand that?" Again there was silence.

There are all kinds of silence. There's a blank silence with a soft feel to it and an embarrassed silence that's all angles and edges. But this silence was chock full, just bursting with the unsaid, the half-spoken, the unacknowledged. It was more pregnant than I was and I had the feeling I was the only one who didn't know what it was about. Something was going on and everybody in this group knew what it was but me.

When group was over I walked back to my office, uneasy. I never knew how much to trust my gut. Occasionally it was right; sometimes it wasn't. But, for what it was worth, my gut hadn't liked the *way* Jim had said that Clarence would die. There was something in the voice I couldn't place; I just didn't know him well enough. It was almost a kind of glee and it sounded absolutely and completely certain. I was just sitting there brooding about it when the phone rang. "Ah, Michael," Julie said. "Gary would like to see you—yesterday."

"About?"

"She'll be right over," she said smoothly to someone on the other end.

"I'll be right over," I echoed and hung up. Puzzled, I headed for the administrative wing. Before group, Gary hadn't had time to say two words. Suddenly he just had to see me?

"Go on in," Julie said, when I finally arrived at the office, six steel doors later. "They're expecting you."

The "they" didn't really register, so I was brought up short when I walked into Gary's office to see two people sitting in the room with him. Gary stood up

behind his desk and waved me in, looking relieved.
"Come on in, Dr. Stone," he said. I blinked at the "Dr."
but did as I was told. The older couple sitting in the
chairs turned hopefully to look at me.

"This is Dr. Stone," he said to the couple. "Dr.
Stone, Mr. and Mrs. Clarence. Dr. Stone is currently
running the sex offender group in the prison and if
your son needs any kind of assessment, she'll be the
one to do it." I would have shot Gary a look at being
blind-sided like that—it was the first I'd heard of it—
but given the older couple was still looking at me
hopefully, I didn't. The truth was, I suspected Gary
had me there for moral support as much as anything.

I held out my hand and introduced myself, looking
them over carefully. You can't assume anything when
you're dealing with the parents of monsters. Clarence
may have tortured and mutilated children but that
didn't actually tell me anything about his parents.

Sometimes the parents of killers were the worst of
parents. They had beaten the kid, sexually abused
him, emotionally degraded him and given him an
upbringing Stephen King wouldn't write about. You
could see why he had become a killer. Sometimes, on
the other hand—especially when dealing with psychopaths, which seemed to be some kind of innate
thing—the parents were nice enough folks who were
just as bewildered as the rest of us. These latter were
by far the worst to deal with. They were just in so
much pain.

Clarence's parents looked as though they were in
their sixties but it was always hard to say. Traumatized
people looked a lot older than they were, and finding
out your son was a serial killer was about as bad a
trauma as a parent could face. Mr. Clarence was thin

and wiry and looked, really, like a small greyhound. His hand was bony and papery dry.

Mrs. Clarence was thin, too, although slightly taller than her husband but with much less vitality. Her hand was absolutely limp. Both faces looked mild but his mother's looked faded, like all life had been sucked out of it. From her limp handshake I did not think she had ever been the power in the family, if there was one. But who knew? It was like looking at a house after an earthquake hit and trying to figure out what it had been like before.

I eased into the chair and said softly, "I'm so sorry. It must have been quite a shock."

Mr. Clarence glanced over at his wife, but she showed no signs of speaking so he cleared his throat and said, "Well, it was. We had no idea. . . . He won't talk to us."

"Your son won't talk to you?"

He shook his head.

"Since when?"

He glanced at his wife again. "Not since he was arrested. . . . We don't know anything."

"What do you mean?"

"We don't know how he's doing. We still love him," he said defiantly, his voice picking up strength when he said it. "I know you find that hard to believe." He looked at Gary and at me. His head was up and he was leading with his chin but he was blinking rapidly. I didn't know what the blinking meant. Maybe it was a tic or maybe he was fighting tears. "He's still our son," he said and his wife put out her hand and covered his for a moment. At the contact he seemed to crumble. He slumped in the seat and his shoulders rounded as though his chest had just caved in. He lowered his head and cried.

She patted his hand quietly and then reached into her pocketbook. I thought she was reaching for a Kleenex but she pulled out an old photograph of a child. He looked about five years old and he had an infectious grin and a mop of brown hair with a prominent cowlick in front. He sure hadn't looked like a killer then.

"Look at him," she said so softly I had to lean forward to hear her. I took the photograph she offered. "Look at him," she said again. "What happened?"

I stared at the photo and then looked up. Gary looked pained. Give him the toughest inmate in the world and he was unfazed but he hated dealing with victims and their suffering. I wondered how they had even gotten into his office. Wardens didn't usually deal with families but, say what you will, celebrity cases were different. For my part I had no earthly idea how to help these people.

"Mr. and Mrs. Clarence," I said. "I don't know what happened. I agree with you. He looks like a perfectly normal boy. These things are mysteries sometimes that nobody understands. You do the best you can and you think everything's fine and something is terribly wrong that nobody even knows about.

"You're going to need some help with this. Just with surviving this and getting through it." But even as I said it I knew parts of them wouldn't survive, hadn't already. Grief was like that. It killed whole parts of you and some of them grew back and some didn't.

"You need to see a counselor. Please don't just dismiss the idea. You need someone to talk to about your son and about what happened. I can give you some names but I can't see you myself, because I may be involved with him at the prison."

At this Mr. Clarence straightened up, pulled a Kleenex out of his pocket and blew his nose. Then he said, "We didn't come about us, Doctor. We want to be sure our son's okay. That he's safe and well. Since he won't talk to us, you're the only people we can ask. His attorney won't talk to us. He says our son won't give him permission."

Gary and I exchanged glances. We both knew his attorney. Boyle was a grandstanding type who always had his eye on the headlines. Clarence would have been his ticket to network news, not his parents. He could likely have helped these people out more than he had. "I haven't spoken with your son," I said.

Gary interrupted. "I'm sure Dr. Stone will be glad to interview your son and inquire about how he's doing. You have to understand, he does have rights to confidentiality and if he tells us not to repeat to you anything he says, we can't. However, I'm sure she will be able to tell you how he looks and if he seems well."

I really did want to kill Gary at that point. He was dumping the whole thing on me just to get the parents off his back. Instead, I just nodded. Despite my irritation, he did have the right to assign it to me if he wanted to and somebody had to try to do something for these folks.

"And you can be assured of one thing," Gary said, "We will treat your son like any other prisoner. I feel we do a good job here in the prisons in Vermont. The staff is very professional and your son will get good care." I winced inwardly. What Gary was saying was true for other inmates—but I wasn't as sure that Clarence would be quite as okay here as Gary sounded. The problem was *who* he was. Nobody really knew how the other inmates would deal with it. But what could Gary say? Somebody might try to kill your son?

"Will you tell him something, for me?" his mother said, turning to me. "Will you tell him we love him and we'll always love him no matter what he's done."

"I'll tell him," I said. "You might want to give him some time. Sometimes people come around later on. He may want to have more contact later, after he settles in." Hope, even the tiniest bit, was something to hold on to and they didn't have a whole lot else. Unfortunately, what I was really thinking was that Clarence might get bored enough to talk to them. Or if he was really psychopathic he'd figure out a way to use them somehow, which would mean he'd be happy to talk to them. But they wouldn't see anything like that. All they would see was the little boy in the picture.

When they left Gary put his head in his hands. "Shit," he said. "I hate that. I don't know how you do it. Give me every Clarence who ever lived but keep those sad, lonely, old people away from me. You deal with them, Michael. I just don't have the heart for it." He sat up. "Are they for real?"

I sighed. "They could be," I replied. "You never know with these guys. Some of them just seem to be on some kind of trajectory from the start that nobody can deflect. If Clarence has cigarette burns though, I'd change my mind.

"By the way, what are you going to do?" I asked. Gary knew what I meant. There was always a question about whether someone like Clarence could be protected in general population or needed to be in segregation. "Somebody in group today said he'd die, in or out of seg. I don't know if it was just big talk."

"They always talk big," Gary said. "I'm letting him out. He doesn't want to be in solitary. He knows the risks and he says he'd rather die than live like that. His attorney is supporting him. Says we don't have the right to isolate him against his will. He's wrong about that; I could keep him in seg against his will—hell, he's here against his will—but bottom line is I agree. It's cruel and unusual to keep him in. Anybody would go crazy by themselves in a six by eight rectangle twenty-four hours a day. Don't forget he's going to be here for the next fifty years or so."

"Your call," I said, but I didn't feel easy about it. I didn't know Jim from a can of paint, but he didn't strike me as a braggart. Too slick for that, plus he struck me as the type who'd get whatever advantage he could by snitching. Maybe I'd better check to see if he had something to sell.

"You want me to go see him?" I said. "See if he'll talk to his parents? Not that it will do the slightest bit of good."

"Couldn't hurt," Gary said.

He was wrong but I didn't say it. I wasn't any threat to Clarence—that much was true—but viciousness hurts anybody who goes near it. Clarence would find a way to take a bite out of my soul; people like that always did.

I walked out in the hall and started to head for my office, but stopped. Why put it off? I'm the sort who speeds up through intersections, anyway, and talking with Clarence was likely to be a miserable experience, so why not get it over with? I headed for the yard and the path to segregation.

Seg was in a separate building—it might as well be a separate planet for all the similarity it had with normal life, even in a prison. I took a deep breath before I pressed the buzzer that requested entry. The door swung open promptly and the noise hit me like a force field.

Seg was always noisy. The place always seemed to have standing waves of anger bouncing off the walls. Most of the inmates weren't there because they were new; they were there because they had done something egregious to other inmates or to staff. Some were angry about being there; others were angry just because that's who they were. Anger wasn't always a fleeting state of mind. For some folks it was part of the fabric of their souls.

I hated seg. The place was heavily staffed with officers standing around everywhere and despite that, or maybe because of it, the atmosphere always felt ominous. When inmates were out of their cells there were always two staff on each side walking them wherever they had to go and they always had their hands on the inmate. That alone would have driven me crazy.

On the other hand, staff were dealing with people who put pencils through other people's eyes and it wasn't a good idea to give one of them a running start. There was just nothing pretty about violence and no "pretty" way to handle it. In seg, the prison got down to its worst elements: unpredictable violence and the overwhelming force it took to contain it.

I waited for Clarence to be brought to an interviewing room. He didn't know me and didn't even glance my way as they walked him by. The officers holding him looked hyperalert: everybody in the world knew who Clarence was and what he'd done. He was shorter than both of the officers by a head, but they were handling him with the same wariness they might have had with Mike Tyson in tow.

He looked smaller than I expected. You don't get much sense of scale from newspaper photos and somehow I always have some kind of naive belief that evil should look evil. What was I expecting: big, bulging muscles and a leering grin? Too many Saturday morning cartoons as a kid. Instead, the guy walking by, staring impassively at the floor, was small and nondescript. From my angle, I couldn't read much of anything on his face. He was thin and he didn't look strong but he was moving quite precisely. Where had I seen that precision of movement before? I remembered a couple of memorable scrapes with people moving like that and they had both turned out to be a lot stronger than they looked.

I stood outside the glass door to the interview room for a moment, looking in. For some reason I was in no hurry for this interview to start. Clarence sat looking down at the floor, and I could see the bald spot on the top of his head. His skin was pasty, the kind of sickly white that looks like it has never seen daylight. He was shackled to the seat and the shackles looked ridiculous on his frail body. He looked far more pathetic than evil. I sighed. I didn't have any sympathy for this man. He had mutilated preschoolers, for Christ's sake. But it was an awful waste of a human soul.

I started to open the door and stopped, suddenly realizing that I was actually nervous. It was this pregnancy thing. I was pretty sure I could move very fast if I needed to *normally* but right now . . . face it, the walk light was gone by the time I got halfway across a street. Hell, just walking across a room took me half the room to pick up speed and the other half to slow down. Say what you will about seg and officers everywhere and shackles to the bench, you were just better off not trusting people who made a habit of killing other people and who had nothing left to lose.

I shook my head, annoyed at my sudden feeling of vulnerability and started to reach for the door. At that moment Clarence looked up and saw me. For a moment the hair stood up on the back of my neck. I almost stepped back I was so surprised. I had certainly interviewed some weird and very mean folk before and the hair had never stood up. What on earth had caused it?

He continued to look at me and I realized his face was totally empty. He was looking at me the same way he'd look at a chair or a table. People's faces are never completely expressionless when they look at someone else. Just seeing someone else looking back produced something, made something happen in the face. But this man's face held nothing at all. Is this what evil is? I thought. Not bulging muscles and a leering grin. Just this vast emptiness at the heart of things. "That's why misery is; nothing to have at heart," Wallace Stevens wrote. But this man had held something at heart and it had been dreadful. I opened the door and walked in.

"Mr. Clarence," I said. "I'm Dr. Stone. I'm a psychologist at the prison and your parents have asked me to see you."

"They've got nothing to do with this," he said quickly. "Leave them out of it."

"Okay by me," I said. "I'm not dragging them into it." I sat down at the table across from him, glanced down and was reassured to see it was bolted to the floor. "They came to the prison to see the warden. They wanted to know if you were okay. Seems they haven't been able to communicate with you directly."

"I don't want to talk to them," he said, looking away. "I've got nothing to say." He paused, then muttered, more to himself, it seemed, than to me. "They're not going to understand any of this."

"I'm sure they're not," I said. "But I'm just the messenger. I promised them I'd tell you that they love you and they'll keep loving you no matter what you've done. They want to hear from you when you're ready."

"Jesus Christ," he said, running his hand through what was left of his hair. "Why can't they leave me alone?" He sounded angry but there was something else going on in Clarence's face when he said it. Certainly, it wasn't blank the way it was when he first looked at me. Which meant that whatever else he was, he probably wasn't a psychopath. Psychopaths don't have any attachment to anybody.

"Well, that's not how that loving-people-thing works," I said. "And unfortunately for your plan, they do love you. Like it or not, they're probably gonna stick with you."

"What the hell do they want from me?" he said suddenly. "What am I supposed to say to them?"

"I don't know what you can say. You've got something inside they don't and they've got something inside you don't and there's not much of a match there. Most of us would throw up at the sight of a child being tortured. You get a high you can't even describe." He looked up quickly. "It's better than crack, better than cocaine, and you told yourself afterward you weren't ever going to do it again but of course you did because you couldn't get those fantasies out of your mind and every single time you thought about it you got a jolt of that drug again and after a while it was all you could think about. You began to live for the jolts and life without it became a kind of wasteland. And you got a lot bigger high from doing it than thinking about it. Actually, that's not true. The reality never quite lived up to the fantasies, but you needed the reality to feed the fantasies. Unless you kept doing it, the fantasies started to fade. They weren't as vivid anymore and the high wasn't as good."

Clarence was staring at me intently. "You seem to know a lot about this," he said quietly.

"That's because I've talked to people like you before," I said. "And, believe it or not, they all say the same thing. But don't be looking for a soul mate here, Mr. Clarence. I'm on the throw-up side of things. What I'm trying to say is you don't have to explain it to your parents because you can't. All they want is some contact with you. They've lost all their hopes and dreams for you. All they've got left to hope for is just some contact with you. They want to know you're safe, that you're okay."

Clarence sat for a minute silently and then he said, very quietly, "Get out of here. Leave me alone." It may have been quiet but I got a bad feeling from the way he said it and I got up promptly and headed for the door. Taking orders from an inmate is not something I'd do ordinarily but there are times to be macho and times not to be. I have never once disobeyed that feeling when I got it, even when somebody was small and shackled.

I had my hand on the doorknob when his voice stopped me. "What are you having?" he said suddenly. "A boy or a girl?" I froze for a moment at the question and then turned around slowly.

"A girl," I said. "Amnio says a girl. Definitely." Actually, I didn't have the foggiest idea, not to mention it was stupid to answer him anyway. But call me superstitious. I didn't want him sitting in his cell masturbating to thoughts of mutilating my little boy, that's for sure.

5

THERE WAS A NOTE FOR ME AT THE GUARD'S STATION WHEN
I walked out. I opened it absentmindedly, not sure
what to expect, but stopped dead in my tracks. I could
feel the smile start way down somewhere and just
explode on my face. "Stacy?" I said out loud. "Stacy's
here?

"Do you know Stacy James?" I said to the officer at
the desk.

"Sure," she said. "He's head of social work."

"Where's social work?"

She looked out the window and pointed to a building across the yard. "Right over there," she said. "Third
floor."

I practically raced over to the social work building—
or as close as I get to racing these days, which is sort of
a fast shuffle on flat surfaces and steady progress up
the stairs. It took a few light years but I finally made
it. The officer at the desk gave me the room number
and I was relieved to see that the door to room 305
was open—relieved because I couldn't really stop once
I got going, and I more or less skidded around the cor-

ner. Stacy was sitting behind his desk signing time
sheets. He looked up when he saw me and laughed.
"Michael," he said, standing up. "I was hoping you'd
make it by. Sweet Jesus, but you're a sight." He walked
around the desk and hugged me.

When he let me go I fell into a chair breathing heavily and took in the surroundings while I caught my
breath. Stacy's desk, the top of the bookshelves, every
empty space in sight was filled with tiny wind-up toys
that leaped and scuttled and whirled, and puzzles made
of metal rings that I couldn't imagine how to undo
short of a metal cutter. On the wall were what at first
looked like large framed pictures but a second glance
revealed as puzzles—the kind with so many pieces that
getting two or three pieces in one day was a triumph.

"My God," I said, when I had caught my breath.
"How many pieces?"

"Five thousand," he said, on that one. Seven thousand five hundred on the other one over there."

"I'm in awe," I said. "I can't even imagine that kind
of patience."

He shrugged. "Gotta have something to pass the
time. Jesus, you look good, even though you are truly
the size of a house. They told me you were pregnant
but I didn't expect this."

"I'm totally lost," I said honestly. "I can't move,
can't run, couldn't do a fade-away jumper to save my
life. Every morning I wake up and look down at my
ankles and wonder whose they are. I don't know what
I'm doing."

"You'll figure it out," he said with that confidence
people have when it's not them. I had caught my
breath enough to focus and I looked at him. He hadn't
changed at all. He was tall and thin with a large nose

that gave his whole face an eagle-like appearance. It had been years since I'd seen him but I thought exactly what I thought every time I saw him, that he had the kindest eyes I had ever seen.

He was more or less a "lifer," a staff member who was going to stay in corrections his whole career. He had worked every aspect of corrections from probation and parole agent to correctional officer to social worker. He had moved up the chain of command several times but always came back to working with the inmates. I didn't think his decision to stay in corrections had anything to do with security, like Eileen's did. Somewhere along the way, he had gotten hooked. He always joked he liked corrections because he was a voyeur at heart but I thought he was actually a closet do-gooder, although a savvy one. Most do-gooders were lunch in a prison.

"Go for coffee?" he said.

"Sure," I shrugged. "It's too early for a drink, as in about two months."

"You'll get there, Michael," he said grabbing his jacket and putting his arm around me as we walked out. He squeezed my shoulders and I got that strange feeling of natural affinity I had always felt for this man.

"Easy for a man who does five thousand-piece puzzles to say," I started in. "You're looking at a woman who can't stand in a five-minute line without fidgeting. I've been incubating for eight months. Eight months. Sweet Jesus! I'll be in a nursing home before this baby is born." I even felt comfortable whining around him.

"You need to take up meditation. All this rushing around can't be good for you."

"That's what my family says," I said, stopping in my

tracks. "What? You know my mother?" For a second I seriously considered it, which I'd like to put down to how crazy pregnancy had made me but really it wasn't true. Mama—even thinking about Mama—made me crazier than pregnancy ever could.

"Michael," he responded, gently moving me along. "It's just what anybody thinks who sees you rushing around like you do."

"You live by yourself?" I asked.

"I do now. Somebody's come and gone since last I saw you. But for the last few years, just me and the cat. Why?"

"You like it?"

"Love it."

"I gotta talk to you."

"This is your car?" We had negotiated our way through eight steel doors, two sally ports and a metal detector to finally hit the parking lot outside.

"It wasn't that expensive. It's ten years old."

"It's a Jaguar."

"It's an old Jaguar."

I walked around the sleek black exterior. "I don't even like cars and I can tell it's gorgeous."

"Gotta be back for anything?"

"Just the delivery."

"That should give us a little time. How about a drive out to Killington and dinner?"

I breathed a sigh of relief. It sounded fine to me. It sounded finer than fine. I wasn't worth a damn at intimacy. But friends? I could do friends just fine.

Dinner was in an old country inn high on Killington Mountain. We lucked out with a table by the window and the mountain fell away before us in layers like folds in a skirt. We could see small New England towns tucked in the folds and the failing sunlight gave everything an aura of grace. There was a kind of light that made even rusted cars look good. We seemed a million miles from steel doors and furniture bolted to the floors. I doubted there was anyone in the whole restaurant who thought a pencil was a nifty murder weapon.

"I didn't know you were at Nelson's Point," I said. "I'd have come by sooner." He just nodded, looking at me and smiling quietly. There was a sense of contentment in the air that wrapped around both of us and held us in the failing light. At one time or another each of us had run from something but we'd both made it through, and now it was a fine spring evening and we were two old friends having dinner at a country inn with a lazy blue haze drifting down the mountain.

Neither of us spoke for a few minutes when suddenly I put my fork down. "What happened to Eileen Steelwater?" I said. "I haven't seen her for fifteen years and I come back to find she is stone cold bonkers. She's screwing one inmate and defending another, a psychopathic lawyer, no less."

"Is there any other kind?" Stacy muttered. I shrugged and he went on, "I didn't know her as well as you did. But weird things have definitely been going on and it's not over yet. There's a guy whose chart I want you to read the next time you're over."

"Who?"

"The guy she was screwing."

"Okay, why?"

"You'll know when you read it. The thing I don't get—besides what you'll see in the chart—is he wasn't in her group. She never saw him for counseling. I don't even know how she met him."

"That is weird. What's she say?"

"Nothing. Eileen wouldn't discuss it. What do you mean it's not over yet?"

He shrugged. "A feeling, that's all. Something's in the air."

"Clarence?"

"It started before Clarence."

"Eileen?"

"I don't think so. It was still here after she left."

"So what?"

"I don't know. The whole place has that electric feel. I just know something's up. It's gotten worse since you've been here but it could be a coincidence."

"Maybe somebody's building a ladder," I said, but Stacy didn't laugh.

"You don't really have riots, do you?"

"Mostly not."

"Mostly?"

"Well, the last one we had they gathered to protest a change in the way good time was calculated. It was a sort of sit-down strike. Reminded me of the sixties. But . . . anything's possible. We may be small but we've got serious bad guys mixed in there with the small-time hoods."

"Bad guys like Clarence?"

"No, he's an exception. Torturing and mutilating children is out of almost everybody's league."

"Thank God for small favors. Have you talked to him?"

"Not yet."

"I did."

"What'd you think?"

"Small, nondescript guy. Moves very precisely. Probably a lot stronger than he looks, not that you'd have to be with four-year-olds. I was pretty careful with him. Always good to be careful around a lifer with a mean streak." It was true. In a state that didn't have capital punishment there wasn't much you could do about a guy who killed someone in prison if he already had eight life sentences.

We both fell silent. Finally, I spoke. "So what do you think about this electricity thing?"

"Nothing to do but wait," he said. "Feel out the snitches and hope someone gets greedy. But I don't like it. It just doesn't feel right."

"You talked to Gary about it?"

Stacy shook his head. "It's a little vague to go to the warden about." I wondered about that comment but didn't say it. The Gary I had known was somebody you could have gone to with a vague feeling. Maybe the times had changed. Or maybe Gary had.

On the way home we didn't talk much. For myself at least the sense of contentment that started at dinner had grown until it finally swallowed up the words whole. I did say one thing, though. I asked the question I had always wondered about and never asked, "Stacy, back when you and I were both single, how come we never got together?"

I saw the smile play at the corner of his mouth but he didn't look at me. "Ah, lassie," he said softly, "sometimes I have too much patience for my own good."

There was a message from Adam when I got home that he was working late on a burglary. I didn't mind. The sense of sweet contentment lingered on and an empty house seemed the perfect accompaniment. I sat on the deck letting the slow, easy sense of well-being run out the day. A small branch fluttered next to me slapping against the edge of the deck like water lapping against a boat and the brook below softened the coming night with its sounds. The day ran out like water pouring from a glass and it didn't take much to hear the noise of the brook as the sound of the day emptying and letting go.

There was people time and woods time. I didn't get tuned in very often to woods time where things weren't measured in minutes or meetings but in rhythms. When I was on woods time, I just could not bear to go back. I like hanging out where there is no time really, not as we know it, just the sounds of tapping and scraping and whooshing and chirping and Heraclitus's river rolling on. I don't think it's the demands of our day that make us crazy; it's that our rhythms are so wrong, so staccato, all the time staccato and abrupt and disconnected. We got time; the woods got rhythm. It was the same thing really for my money, only the woods got the better deal.

When the phone rang, I didn't even get up. To hell with it. I wasn't tempted even when I heard Brenda's voice on the line. She'd leave a message. Mama was at the Venetian, the voice said, which was a world away from woods time in Vermont.

I woke up early the next day with Mama on my mind. I went to Psychiatry and made myself wait until midmorning to call, which, okay, was still early in Vegas but respectable. Besides, I knew Mama wouldn't be in her room during the day and clearly she was going to be out at night so when else could I call? Not to mention, a senior citizen throwing away her retirement money was an emergency.

The hotel operator didn't blink at putting a call through at seven in the morning Vegas time—but then again she wouldn't have blinked if it had been four A.M., there being no such thing as time in Vegas.

"Yes," a sleepy voice said.

"Mama," I said. "It's Michael."

"Michael? What's wrong?"

"Nothing's wrong, except you're in Las Vegas, for Christ's sake. Mama, what are doing there?" I tried to say it gently but it didn't come out right.

There was silence while Mama got her wits about her. Then she went from zero to sixty with a speed a dragster would envy. "Let me get this straight. It's . . . ah, seven A.M., a little early to be calling your mother on the carpet, don't you think? You always had a nerve, girl, I'll say that for you, but this takes the cake. What makes you think I answer to you? It's none of your goddamn business what I'm doing in Vegas."

I took a deep breath. She wasn't entirely wrong about this. Actually, she wasn't at all wrong about this. "I'm sorry, Mama. I didn't say it right but I'm worried about you. I'm calling because I didn't know when I could reach you."

"So you're calling before dawn?"

"Mama, seven A.M. is not exactly before dawn. It's morning, okay, and maybe I should have waited until later but I didn't, so calm down. You've got everybody worried to death. You're in Vegas with a hundred and ten thousand of your retirement money. What, you think I wouldn't worry? What are you doing?"

There was a silence.

"Who told you that?"

"For Christ's sake. It's a small town. You know that. That's why I don't live there."

"You'd think a body could expect a little privacy."

"In Wilson's Pond? You know better. Mama, it's not the point. What are you doing?"

"What is the point, Michael? You calling your mother in the middle of the night over some rumor in Wilson's Pond?"

I took another deep breath. "Mama, I know you don't like to be fussed over—"

"Fussed over? Called on the carpet is more like it."

"All right, call it what you want, but what are you up to?" Now my limited patience was wearing thin. "Surely, you're not going to gamble away your retirement money. And who is this stranger you're hanging out with? Where'd you meet him? Who is he?"

There were days when I had been tactful in my life. I could remember maybe two. But I'd never had one with Mama. Not one. I didn't know why I don't have a graceful bone in my body when it comes to Mama. Listening to myself, I didn't like what I heard but I couldn't stop.

"Michael," the steely voice said. "I am seventy-six-years old and I don't believe I owe you or anybody an explanation for anything I do. If you don't like it, you can shove it where the sun don't shine. Now, don't call me again before dawn or I'll unplug the phone. You got that, girl?" and she hung up.

I stared at the phone. I could hardly blame Mama for her reaction. I likely would have reacted exactly the same way. But behind my rudeness, I truly was worried about her. Mama could handle anybody and anything in Wilson's Pond, but this was Vegas, for Christ's sake. Did she know the difference? It wasn't a small town; it was a Mecca for con men and the proverbial deal too-good-to-be-true. They had ways of getting money out of pros and my poor Mama, tough as she was, was not a pro. Somebody would see her coming, already had, from the sound of it.

Worse, I had a feeling no matter how I phrased it, Mama wouldn't have answered my questions. She didn't like people worrying about her. So what was the answer? What did you do with someone as prickly and strongheaded as Mama? I shrugged off the uncomfortable comparison and went out to the waiting room to pick up my next client.

6

I DIDN'T SEE MUCH OF ADAM FOR THE NEXT WEEK. TWICE
he came and went in the night leaving a note saying
he was tied up in a case, be back when he could. I
began to wonder what I was worried about. He was
never home anyway, so what was all the fuss?

I went to my group at the prison twice and came
back. It didn't seem to be going that well: in fact,
everybody was acting like they were just starting treatment for the first time. What had Eileen been doing
for six months if she hadn't been working on their
offenses, on their thinking patterns, on all the things
that are involved in their crimes? They were acting like
they were talking about these things for the first time.

On Friday, I woke with an aching back and sleet
pelting the windows. Winter was taking one last paw
swipe at the countryside but compared to the icy
slashes of January, it was halfhearted. The sleet stopped
abruptly a few minutes later and the sun struggled to
free itself from clouds clinging to it like lint. It looked
like someone with a hangover—or maybe just somebody pregnant—trying to get up for the day.

Despite the weather, my mood was anything but

somber; I woke with a kind of soaring joy. I got it at times—always had—and I knew right away when I woke up. It never seemed to come on in the middle of the day and it didn't have anything to do with anything that was going on in my life. It didn't matter that my back hurt or the baby was lying on a nerve. It was just this strange, fierce kind of joy I got for no reason at all.

I floated into Psychiatry and was cheerfully writing termination summaries—usually the most tedious of tasks—when my friend Marv sauntered in and sat down. I looked over at him but his ordinarily rotund and cheerful face looked somber. "What do you think about the news at Nelson's Point?" he asked quietly.

I stopped typing instantly and looked up. "What news?" I said carefully, the day's mood instantly on hold.

"I thought you knew," he said. "It was on television last night. I would have called you . . ."

"What news?" I said again evenly. But I had started to breathe again. It had dawned on me that Gary or his secretary would have called if it was anybody I knew well.

"There was a murder at Nelson's Point," Marv said. My heart jumped again and he must have seen it because he said quickly, "No one on the staff. Clarence."

"Clarence?" I said stupidly. "Clarence? But he just got there. He arrived a couple of weeks ago—max." As if that had anything to do with anything. "Jeez, he couldn't even have been out of seg that long . . . ."

Marv shrugged. "It's a mess, Michael. His attorney is accusing the prison of letting the inmates kill him. He's saying he should have been in protective segregation."

"Son of a bitch," I said. "He was on Gary's case to let him out."

"Not to hear him tell it," Marv said.

"Jeez," I said again, trying to let it sink in. I had to admit I couldn't make myself care about Clarence but there were a lot of other people involved, some of whom I did care about. "He had parents," I said to Marv. "They loved him. And I wonder how Gary's dealing with this." I was just thinking aloud.

Marv just shook his head. "The reaction of the public seems to have been 'good riddance,'" he said. "But it doesn't appear corrections is taking it that way. Not to mention they can't even find the murder weapon, much less the murderer."

"What do you mean they can't find the murder weapon?"

"Well, he was beaten to death with something. Something heavy and likely metal but they have apparently shaken down the entire prison and can't find anything that matches. They don't seem happy."

"No, they wouldn't be," I said. "It was their job to keep him safe and they blew it. They'll take it as a major embarrassment. Jesus, they can't even find the murder weapon? I don't get it. Max is not exactly an easy place to hide a big piece of metal. Damn near everything's nailed down and if it's not, it's checked in and checked out." Gary would be fit to be tied. And so would Headquarters. Security was king in corrections. If you couldn't keep the inmates from escaping or from killing themselves and each other, you had just completely failed in the only way that mattered in that world.

When Marv left I picked up the phone and tried to dial Nelson's Point. The switchboard was busy—and there were a whole lot of phone lines going in there. I got up and paced around the room trying to think if there was anything I could do for Gary if I drove out there. Well, what could I do? He probably wouldn't even have time to see me. I wrote an e-mail to him and sent it off. E-mail was hardly confidential, but I didn't have anything to say that couldn't be put in the papers. That I was sorry. Could I do anything to help?

On impulse I opened my desk drawer and started looking for an old address book. Gary's home phone was unlisted. Wardens didn't put their numbers in the phone book because they got too many threatening calls. Enough to scare the bejesus out of their children, not to mention unnerve the grown-ups a little, too. But I'd had Gary's number once upon a time, if I could just find the damn book. A ratty address book finally emerged from the caverns of my desk and I thumbed through it. I found the number and dialed. No one answered and I was leaving a message when Gary's wife, Susan, picked up the phone.

"Sorry, Michael," she said. "The phone's been ringing off the hook." So much for unlisted numbers.

"How are you?" I said. "It's been forever."

"Better than Gary," she said. "He was at the prison until two A.M. and he went back at five. I can't believe this, not on top of everything else."

There was a pause while I considered this and whether to ask. "On top of what, Susan?" I said, finally. "I don't know what you're talking about."

"Didn't Gary tell you? He told me you were back and he talked to you."

"Not about that, whatever it is."

I heard her sigh. "I don't want to get into it," she said. "Not on the phone, anyway, but I can tell you this, it's more than I can cope with."

I didn't know where to go with the conversation so I dropped it. "I've been wondering if I should drive out to Nelson's Point," I said. "I'm not sure I could do anything to help."

"You want my advice?" she said. "Go."

"You think I should?" I said, surprised at the firmness in her voice.

"Yes, I do," she said. "Not that he would admit he needs any support, but he does. He surely does."

Going was easier said than done. I had clients coming in all day so it was late afternoon before I headed off for Nelson's Point. It was okay with me to get there after hours. It would likely be saner than the day had been, but given they were in the middle of a murder investigation, I was certain that Gary would still be there.

The guard at the desk called Gary's office and he answered himself. His secretary was, not surprisingly, keeping saner hours than he was and had long since gone home. Gary told them to send me back and an officer in the central station behind bulletproof glass buzzed me through a series of steel doors. A warden's office was a fortress within a fortress. Wardens were a symbol for inmates of everything they hated about the system: courts, prosecutors, guards, witnesses, you name it. All those people had it in for them. The warden was "the man," and he represented all of them in their minds. Good idea to have security around.

I found Gary sitting all by himself watching a video. The room was dark except for the flickering light from the TV. For a second he didn't see me standing there but I could see him. He looked exhausted and so much older than he had just a few days ago. And something else. I couldn't quite put my finger on it but there was something in his face that didn't look right. I wondered if it had been there before but I hadn't noticed.

Maybe. The stress of this murder had laid his face bare like a bad wind stripping the covering leaves off trees. He looked up and saw me and his face brightened for a minute, enough to make me glad I'd come.

"Come on in," he said, waving me in and gesturing to a chair next to him.

"Lot of good I'll be," I said. "But I decided to come anyway."

I pulled up a chair and sat down, glancing at the screen. It looked like a security video of the yard taken from one of the towers. "He was killed in the yard?"

"No," Gary said. "He was a swamper. He was working inside the industries building, cleaning the floor in the hall." He kept staring at the screen.

"Uh, so why are you watching a video of the yard?"

"Do you believe in coincidence?"

"Not in a prison."

"Me either. There was a disturbance in the yard and the officer inside responded, just like he was supposed to. Drew the officer outside and that's when Clarence was killed."

"Ah," I said. "Doesn't sound good. Is it true you haven't found the murder weapon?"

"No, if you can believe it. It had to be big enough to cave in a man's head with one blow. Now, I don't care who he was or how big, we are not talking about a pencil or a pack of cigarettes here. There was absolutely nothing in that fucking hall and nothing in any of the classrooms and everything in the shops was locked up tight."

"What about their cells? People hide all kinds of things inside their cells. You've found weird stuff there before."

"Right. We find weird stuff there all the time. But

it's because they have time to hollow out the top of a table, that kind of thing. But they absolutely do not have that kind of time or opportunity in the classrooms or shop and the cells are on the other side of the complex. That disturbance took maybe ten minutes max. The area was secured immediately. No way did anyone have time to get back to their cells. And the moment he was found we locked down everything instantly and we searched everybody who was not in their cells. Nobody had anything on them. Nothing. What's more, we only found blood on the wall. It is fucking messy to beat someone to death and there wasn't a spot of blood on any inmate. We checked everybody who wasn't locked up when it happened."

"Jesus, Gary, you're talking me into thinking somebody on the staff did it."

"Not any blood on them either," Gary muttered, as if what I'd said had been a serious possibility. Which, who knows, maybe it was. Another serial killer had died a decade before, and rumor was the killer's family had been driving fancy cars ever since. Some of the families of victims tended to be a little vindictive about having their loved ones slaughtered for absolutely no reason except to give some somebody a thrill. Rumor was a relative of a victim had paid a lot of money for their version of justice. If an inmate could get rich off something like that, why not somebody else?

"He picked up a desk from the classroom," I said. "Carried it out to the hall and bonked Clarence on the head with it."

"The desks are bolted down," Gary said. I wondered if I could think of anything outlandish enough that he wouldn't consider it a possibility. "None of the bolts were disturbed and there was no blood, not even microscopic, on any of the desks. We ran a light over them. Besides, even the most dim-witted inmate might figure something was up if he saw someone coming at him with a desk in his hands. It looks like Clarence wasn't expecting it," he added. "He didn't yell and there were no signs of a struggle. Somebody had to have something small enough to conceal."

"Well, it's gotta be something from one of the shops," I said. "Woodworking? Welding? I mean, you have hammers and wrenches and saws in there. Where else could it be?"

"Easy to say," Gary said, rubbing his eyes. "The shop door was less than fifty feet away. We did think of that, Michael," he added dryly. "We did a complete inventory of every tool in the place and not one is missing. They were all in a locked cabinet."

"He had a key?"

"Possible, but again there was no blood, not even a microscopic trace on any of them."

"So the man knows how to clean up," I said lamely.

"It doesn't match."

"What doesn't?"

"The pathologist says it was a weird shape. Definitely not a hammer or a smooth bar or anything like that. It had something like teeth, or a series of short ragged edges on it. We can't even find a tool that *could* have done it."

"Oh dear," I said. "That *is* a problem." Like Gary, I fell silent and just watched the film. I had run out of ideas, even crazy ones.

Gary reached forward and ran the film backward a little.

"What do you see?" he said.

I watched silently. The camera was set to cover the

whole yard so the detail was poor. Raised in an era of TV camera work so good you could see the sweat on the quarterback's brow, I thought the film looked amateurish, which of course it was.

"Where is NBC when you need them?" I muttered, but Gary didn't smile.

There were clumps of inmates standing around the yard. Suddenly there was a scuffle in one of them. "Run that back," I asked.

Gary obligingly ran it back. I leaned forward and stared at the screen. It looked like one inmate just pushed another. Then all hell broke out. In a few seconds, guards came running and broke up the fight. But they had to push their way through the crowd that had gathered and it took a few minutes. Really the whole thing was over in ten minutes, as Gary had said. It was realistic enough from my point of view. You say the wrong thing. Somebody takes offense. A scuffle starts.

"Looks like the real thing," I said. "No way I would have known it was a decoy."

Gary snorted. "It's a phony," he said.

"Well, yeah, we know that now, but how could you tell if somebody hadn't gotten killed?"

In response, Gary leaned forward and ran it back again. "What do you watch when you're looking at a basketball game?" he asked. "The man with the ball?"

Now I snorted. "Never," I said. "You watch the pattern, what's going on under the boards. Who's setting a pick, who's moving into position. Who's cutting for the basket. The ball is the last thing you watch." I stopped short.

"Now," Gary said. "Don't look at the scuffle. Look at the groups." He pointed.

I stared while the tape ran but didn't see anything. I shook my head.

Gary ran it back again. "Where are they looking, Michael?" he asked.

Then I saw it. A couple of inmates turning their heads toward the group where the scuffle was going to break out. Before it started. Quick, furtive head movements. Nobody openly staring. Just looking and then looking away. That and one more thing. The same heads were turning to look at the towers. Glances at the groups, then the towers. Where the guns were.

"Somebody knew it was going to happen," I said. "And the towers—people don't keep looking at the towers like that, do they?" I asked. "Not on an ordinary day. Not before a fight."

"Bingo," Gary said.

"Whew," I said. "Somebody knew it was going to happen, at least the fight. Which means they likely know who killed Clarence."

"For sure, they know who set up the scuffle," Gary said. "And whoever set up the scuffle is involved in the killing."

"So?" I asked. "Where are the snitches?"

Gary leaned back. "I wish I knew. Usually this place is snitch city. People line up to rat on each other. Not this time. Nobody knows nothing about nothing. Worse, this place is still tense."

For the first time, I remembered what Stacy had said. Surely this had to be what he was sensing. "Stacy James said the same thing," I offered. "You think it's the investigation?"

Gary reached over and turned off the TV. "Must be," he said, but halfheartedly. Without the TV we were sitting in near darkness but Gary didn't switch on a light.

"This is not a good deal," I said softly. "I'm sorry."

"I told his parents we would take care of him," Gary said. "Jesus Christ, I practically promised he'd be safe."

"You didn't really. You said the staff would handle him professionally."

"You think letting him get killed is professional?"

"Gary, come on. You know nobody can guarantee anybody's safety—in or out of prison."

Gary completely ignored my feeble comments. "I'd say letting him out of solitary looks like a reasonably dumb thing to do right now. And we have gotten nowhere in figuring this out. Which means somebody has a level of control over the inmates I don't even want to think about, because ordinarily this would be an awful juicy bit of info to sell. But you want to know something funny? The one good thing is it distracts me from all the other shit going on in my life."

I thought about asking. I don't know why I didn't. I guess I thought if he wanted to talk about it he would. Somehow it didn't seem fair to ask him about something he hadn't chosen to tell me about at a time when he was so vulnerable I knew he would. Sometimes I think too much. The truth was I wanted to ask him and I should have. But I didn't know that until later.

I didn't realize I wasn't going home until I didn't turn off at the road heading out to my house. Sometimes I felt my car had a mind of its own and I just kept my hand on the wheel for appearances' sake. It wasn't a real surprise to me where I was heading. People find solace in different places when they're rattled. Mine wasn't a cathedral and it wasn't a casino but it was a place of solace to me.

Clarence was dead—no great loss to the world—but

he'd manage to wreak a certain amount of havoc on his way out. His murder would likely devastate his parents and cause all kinds of problems for Gary. There was a killer at the prison who'd gotten away with it and likely still had a murder weapon somewhere around where he could get his hands on it. That was a cheerful thought.

It didn't help that my group was completely off track and had learned nothing that would reduce their risk to reoffend in all the time they had been in treatment. And then there was my old colleague Eileen, who had gone off the deep end and didn't seem to have a clue she had lost it. Now my mother was busy trying to turn herself into a bag lady, seduced by hand-blown glass ceilings, hotels without clocks and the inevitable smooth-talking stranger.

I pulled up in front of the gym. There were university gyms I could have gone to but they were never, ever empty and an empty gym was my favorite place in the whole world. This gym was in an old recreational center that had been replaced a few years ago by a shiny, new one a few blocks away. Almost nobody ever used the old building anymore and certainly not the gym. In an age where kids were killed for the latest Nikes, old, decrepit gyms with nary a glass backboard in sight were not popular.

Except with me. I still liked Converse high-topped canvas basketball shoes and gyms where the floor was so uneven that home court advantage was a serious issue. This old gym was one of my favorites. I had played pick-up ball in it for years and still did sometimes when we couldn't get space in the new gym.

The question was whether it would be open, but I thought it might. A local church ran a bingo operation in the basement several nights a week and I thought this was one of them.

I headed for the back door to avoid running into anybody. I didn't want questions about why I was there and I didn't feel like chatting. It was open and I walked up a half flight of dusty stairs. Far away I could hear noise that sounded like people but there was nobody at all on the first floor that I could see. I turned right and headed for the steel door to the gym. I let it swing shut behind me and stood for a moment just looking at the silent baskets and the moonlight flooding in through the high windows, laying stripes on the old wooden floor.

Empty buildings are never empty. They simply have a different kind of spirit about them, one alien to people. Every building's feel is different but usually, the spirits of big buildings have a kind of grandeur about them you never find in small ones. This old gym's aura was both grand and kind at the same time, or so it seemed to me. It was old, that's all, and had seen a lot of shots, both good and bad. It seemed tolerant of both, kind even to the ball hogs and the occasional cheat who deliberately fouled and lied about it. I didn't ever have the feeling here that winning was everything. Some new gyms gave you that sense: win or die. But here, playing was the thing.

I crossed the floor, conscious my work shoes didn't sound right on the wooden floors—the clump of leather soles where there should have been the squeak of rubber. I was heading straight for the ball room, which stood with the door open on the far side of the court. The balls were neatly stacked in metal racks and I tried a couple, looking for one that was inflated just right, not dead, not so tight it bounced up to your chin. I found one and took it back to the center of the court to dribble and listen to the sound echo in the empty gym.

I shed the day like an old skin, just shrugged it off. I was one of Pavlov's dogs, for sure. Playing ball had always wiped the neurons clean and now, even listening to the sound of a ball bouncing in an empty gym did the same thing for me.

I always lost all sense of the day when playing ball. Somehow trying to figure out whether my opponent was overplaying me to the right or the left just scrubbed the neurons clean. No, that wasn't right. It wasn't what I was thinking that wiped the neurons. It was that a different part of my brain was running the show, one that wasn't consciously thinking at all. Something in the back of the brain took over far from my overactive frontal lobes.

Larry Bird once said he didn't know he was going to shoot until he saw the ball leave his fingertips. That explained how the slow awkward guy with white man's disease—he couldn't jump worth a damn—beat the gifted athletes he played. He had the advantage because he didn't have to think about what he did. His cerebellum never checked the decision out with the conscious part of his brain and it was just that split-second advantage he needed to get the shot off. I could never get my frontal lobes to pipe down quite that much but, on the other hand, I didn't exactly plan things on the court. However it happened, I got out of my thinking head somehow and it made me a new person when I walked off the court.

Tentatively, I tried to run a few steps but the awkwardness of it made me stop almost instantly. My God, where was my center of gravity? Who knew?

Somewhere about a foot and a half in front of my backbone, it seemed, where usually there wasn't any of me at all. If I couldn't deal with this new body very well standing still, it was a whole lot worse moving.

I tried a couple of shots, starting at the foul line. The effort it took nearly wiped me out. Out of curiosity I dribbled to the right and tried a jump shot. What a joke. My feet maybe cleared the floor by a quarter inch and physicists don't have machines that measured how short my hang time was. Not to mention I was now totally exhausted. Well, it wasn't exactly a surprise. Pregnancy was never designed to improve anybody's jump shot. I gave up and sat down cross-legged in the center of the court, wrapping my arms around the ball, just looking and listening.

Once again the sense of peace flooded over me. Silence was cumulative and seemed so much bigger in a big space than a little one. What was it like, I wondered, for the guys who cleaned the huge sports stadiums late at night? Did any of them, like me, hang around after everybody left just so they could get a sense of all that quiet filling them up?

I was home. Gyms had been more of a home for me in my adolescence than my own home. I played every day in the summer, eight hours a day, breaking in through a back window when they locked it. Who knows what I was hiding from? Everything, I guess: boys, a social world I didn't understand and wasn't any good at, a mother who didn't do "warm," a South I loved and hated. The only place I felt like me was on a basketball court.

Sure, the boys started out treating me like I was "different," showing off and making jokes—how many times had someone suggested that my team be "skins," meaning no shirts—but one blocked shot and all that disappeared. Suddenly you weren't a girl anymore; you were a ballplayer. Different altogether. And better— well to me, anyway.

In all those years I only had one bad memory in a gym—and it happened when I was grown. A killer had once stalked me in a gym and tried to kill me. It wasn't just that he wanted to *kill* me that upset me so much, but that he tried to do it in a gym! What an outrage. I felt like saying, "Sir, have you no sense of decency?"

I don't know how long I stayed. I always have trouble leaving a gym. But although I wasn't thinking anything in particular, when I walked out I knew I'd figured out a couple of things. Clarence's murder wasn't my problem. I couldn't do anything about it. And Gary, well, he'd probably survived worse. The group surely wasn't the issue. They were just being sex offenders. Some of them, at least, would con and manipulate and intimidate people any chance they got and that was just who they were. I was used to dealing with that and even had a track record of dealing pretty well with it. Eileen, well, as much I'd like to save the world I couldn't do much about the choices Eileen had made. People made their own calls.

My problem was sitting in my belly. And another one was leaving his shirt in my living room. My life was changing. All that space I had gathered around me to keep me safe was gone. There was a sweet face in my belly that was dependent on me to "do warm." And the truth was, I didn't know how.

7

"YOU DIDN'T LISTEN LAST TIME. WANNA GO FOR TWO?"

He knew how to get my attention. The note was sitting on my desk when I came up for group. Who knew how it got there? It wasn't signed but I knew who wrote it.

I put down my bag and headed straight for Gary's office. The one thing I knew, the one thing I did remember from working in a prison, was that until I handed that note in, Jim owned me. If I didn't hand that note in, I was in violation of a very serious rule about not giving and receiving things from inmates and the whole point of the note could well be that—just to get something to hang over my head. Then the second note would reference the first, so if you didn't hand in the first, you couldn't hand in the second and it would go on until you were in the middle of a full-scale secret correspondence with an inmate. Even if you wrote him back to tell him to stop, that would be kept as part of the arsenal. Staff have been blackmailed with far less.

"He's blowing smoke," Gary said, looking at the note.

I shrugged. "Maybe," I said.

Gary looked at my uncertain face. "Michael, we don't have people killed here every day. It may look like it right now but it just isn't so. We haven't had anyone killed here for over a decade before Clarence."

"Okay," I said again, but I was uneasy. Jim might be bluffing but I didn't have a sense of him and I wasn't as sure as Gary sounded.

"I want to talk to him," I said.

"Go ahead," Gary replied. The phone rang and he stared at it like it was a snake on his desk. He shook his head. "You wouldn't believe the shit that's coming down the pike over Clarence," he said, finally reaching for it.

"Probably not," I muttered on my way out.

"So what's up," I said. A Xeroxed copy of the note was sitting on the table. Jim had just been escorted to my office and was sitting across from me.

"You got Eileen's office," he said.

"I got Dr. Steelwater's," I replied.

"Look," he said, leaning forward confidentially. "You don't have to be like that. I'm just trying to help out here. I don't even know if I should be here. I could get killed just for talking to you about this."

"Get real, Mr. Walker," I replied. "If you even had a *chance* of losing your life for this, you wouldn't be here." Which sounded good but wasn't entirely true. Psychopaths loved to take chances. They got a thrill out of being on the edge of anything, including extinction. "You've got this visit covered some way, somehow, maybe with a bet you can con me up the same way you conned Dr. Steelwater." I leaned back and crossed my arms. "Question is, do you have something to talk about or are you just blowing smoke. Warden thinks you're blowing smoke."

Jim's eyes narrowed at my mention of the warden but he already knew I had handed the note in. The Xeroxed copy told him that. "He won't think that for long."

"Really?"

"Could be he'd better watch his back," he said grimly, watching my face.

My heart stopped for a moment. "Oh, come on," I said a split second too late. "The warden? I don't think so."

"Hey, I'm just passing along the rumor," he said. "All I know is somebody has gone to the gangs and asked for permission to make a hit on the warden."

"Get real," I said again but more weakly. How did I know what was possible and what wasn't? He saw my uncertainty.

"You can hurt anybody," he said. "You know that. Anybody—in or out of prison. You just have to want to bad enough." For some reason, the look Avery gave Gary flashed through my mind. If Avery hated Gary that much, who else did? And while Avery alone was capable of killing somebody—probably already had somewhere along the line—the truth was there were folks in this prison a whole lot worse than Avery. Who was I to scoff when an inmate told me a hit on the warden was in the works?

Jim went on. "The truth is, the staff only go home at night because we let them. Because we choose to let them go home. Any time somebody wants to hurt one of them real bad, they can. Not that the staff want to admit that. They didn't find the murder weapon, did they?" There was no point in denying it.

He probably knew more about the investigation than I did.

"So?"

"Weapon like that, it's like having a gun in your cell."

"What do you know about it?"

"Nothing much," he said casually. "Grapevine says Clarence was killed with one blow. I am a lawyer," he said, "and I'm not totally stupid. It's got to be small enough to hide on your person and heavy enough to kill someone with a single blow. Plus it's hidden somewhere in this godforsaken place. Not bad—from a certain point of view, of course."

"And what point of view would that be?"

"Somebody who wants to have a weapon handy."

"Are you telling me the same guy is going to make a hit on the warden?"

"Whoa, I didn't say that. How would I know? Could be it's somebody completely different and he's got a gun for all I know. For one thing, the rumor about the warden was around before somebody took a dislike to Clarence." Jim was sitting back with his hands behind his head and he was grinning. It seemed like he was in the mood to play games and he'd dribble out bits here and there, just enough to keep me interested. The problem was, how to get the right bits out of him.

"Tell me about that."

"About what?"

"About someone taking a dislike to Clarence."

He shrugged again. "I don't know anything about it."

"I'm not asking you to tell me *who* killed Clarence, because, of course, you wouldn't know anything about that—otherwise, I'm sure you'd do your civic duty. I'm asking you *why* somebody killed him. Because I am imagining, just imagining that someone like you might have a few ideas about that. Like you say, you're not exactly stupid and you are on the inside, which puts you in a good position to pick up things. So never mind what you know, what do you think?"

Jim leaned back. It's always difficult for a psychopath to resist a chance to show off.

"I'm not hearing much," he said shortly. "Someone's being very quiet about this—which is interesting because most inmates don't give a shit about Clarence getting killed. It's a little surprising really, that more shit isn't flying around. They may not know diddlysquat but everybody's usually got a theory."

"And yours is?"

"Hard to say. Could be Clarence was a throwaway. Maybe somebody was just trying to get on the playing board. I'm thinking whoever killed him may not have anything for or against him. For one thing, he wasn't here long enough to make enemies."

"On the playing board?"

"You know, establish themselves."

"By killing someone?"

"You know a better way in a place like this?"

I shrugged. Actually, I didn't. "Establishing themselves as what? For what?"

"Now that's the question, isn't it? How would I know? All I know is it's not as easy as you think to get taken seriously around here. Outside, you got enough money, you can join the country club. Here . . ." He raised both hands palms up. "Here, it's not money."

"So if nobody knows who did it, how does that get him on the playing board?"

Jim laughed. "Oh, somebody knows. Whoever he wants to know, knows."

"And the warden?"

"Well, that's different. Lots of inmates hate the warden."

"And you've just decided to tell us—about the rumor that someone's going after the warden."

"Didn't take it seriously until the hit on Clarence. People talk big but nothing had ever happened before this. Now . . . who knows?"

What could be the point of his telling me this? If it was a lie, if it didn't happen, Jim wouldn't get anything out of it except look like a fool, which psychopaths just hated. If it was true, somebody would kill him if they knew he passed it along. I needed to think about this.

"Anything else you want to tell me?"

"Nope." He just looked at me and grinned. "Now don't be having security come interview me about this. You know as well as I do that if you do that, somebody will figure out I told you and they *will* kill me. Which—although it may not bother you any—will certainly make the place look bad. For one thing, I doubt any warden in the system could survive two killings in a week. Not to mention it will prove I'm telling you the truth. But I don't think if they kill me for snitching you're going to get a lot of other volunteers."

"I don't make the decisions," I said, "but I doubt anybody would do anything they knew would put you at risk."

He seemed strangely satisfied at that and I wondered for the thousandth time what made people like Jim tick. In his situation, having ratted on a possible hit on the warden, I wouldn't close my eyes at night or walk into a shower alone. And having to be that paranoid wouldn't make me look satisfied.

"How's Eileen, excuse me, Dr. Steelwater?" he asked.

"Why do you want to know?"

"Jeez, why are you so suspicious all the time?" he asked. "I liked her. That's all. It may sound funny to you, but I thought what happened to her was sad. She was a genuinely nice person."

"You wouldn't know anything about what happened to her?" I asked. "Or how it happened? You wouldn't be involved in any way."

There was a pause. "I don't know what you're talking about. All I know is what the prison grapevine says. That she was bonking some guy over on unit five and got fired. What do you have against me, anyway?" he asked suddenly. "I've never done anything to you."

"What about Dr. Steelwater? You sold her a bill of goods about how innocent you were."

"Oh, are you a friend of hers?" he said casually. I didn't answer. "In any case, I didn't sell her anything," he replied firmly.

"That you were innocent?" I said. "Pleeeese."

"How do you know I'm not?" he said. "Stranger things have happened."

"Not recently," I said dryly. "It looks to me like you were working on her and somebody else got there first," I said. "You lost out."

He smiled and his look alone told me I was wrong. "I don't think so," he said quietly and then he said it again, even more quietly. It was the first, the very first time I knew he was telling me the truth. I filed it away. It was like tuning in on a radio station. Once you find the station, you can usually tell when you've got it again or you don't.

"Want to tell me about it?" I asked.

"Maybe sometime," he said smiling. "If you're nice."

"Don't hold your breath, Mr. Walker. Meeting's over."

I sent him back to his cell. Spending time with folks like him was like tracing a phone call. Give them enough time and sooner or later they'd figure you out enough to manipulate you. Already he'd figured out I cared about Eileen. No doubt his knowing that would come back to haunt me.

But it wasn't Jim who took me to Eileen's door that evening. It was Calvin, the inmate Eileen had screwed. After talking to Jim, I went back and read his records. The picture showed a sorry-looking specimen of humanity with a dull look in his eyes and bad teeth. His eyes were closely set together and from the side his face looked almost flat. Looking at him you couldn't help wondering about some kind of genetic syndrome, like whether he had an extra chromosome or two.

He was seriously violent, having attacked seven police officers in an elevator once as just one of the little incidents in his file and he seemed to have a thing about beating up women. He robbed convenience stores for cash and was suspected of having burglarized a series of businesses in his area. His last offense had been to walk into a motel, find a maid cleaning a room, rape her and cut her throat. The sheer senselessness of it made it stand out but not the violence. The violence had been escalating since he was fourteen.

No wonder Stacy didn't understand why Eileen had had sex with Calvin. It was pretty clear from the records Calvin hadn't charmed or conned Eileen: he wasn't the type. If he had threatened or forced her, why hadn't she asked for help when security walked in? And what about the question Stacy had asked: how had Eileen met Calvin? Nothing about this made any sense at all.

Eileen lived in an old farmhouse next to a dairy farm. The house was small and the outside needed painting but it had that patina that old things have and it looked comfortable. Nearly every inch of the lawn was taken up with perennials and it was easy to see that gardening was her passion. It would take a day or two a week just to maintain a garden like that. I stopped short at the garden and just stared at it for a moment. How many years had it taken to build this up? This was the house Eileen had sold to pay for a detective to investigate Jim's case? There was love in the placement of every rock. What on earth had compelled her to give this up?

I knocked and Eileen opened the door, understandably surprised to see me. I hadn't called. I didn't really want to give her time to prepare for the conversation. That was unfair, probably, but it seemed to me the stakes were pretty high right now and getting higher all the time. I hadn't done very well the last time when Eileen had been prepared to talk to me. I was hoping maybe I'd have better luck if she wasn't.

It was late afternoon but Eileen was still dressed in a bathrobe, which told me as much as the circles under her eyes. "Michael?" she said. "What's wrong? Has anything happened at the prison?"

"Well, yeah," I said. "But nothing you haven't heard about. Clarence was killed."

"Oh," she said. "Nothing else?"

"Like what?"

"Nothing. I just thought . . . Come on in."

"I'm sorry for barging in on you, Eileen, but I need to talk."

"It's okay. I just wasn't expecting visitors." That was pretty clear. The living room was a mess with what looked like legal papers, clothes, and dirty dishes strewn around everywhere.

She glanced around and shrugged, wisely deciding not to scurry about trying to straighten things. I followed her in and sat down on an easy chair, pulling the papers off first. Eileen sat down on the couch across from me. "How's the baby?" she said.

"She kicked a water glass over the other day," I replied. "I'm not kidding. She kicked so hard she knocked a water glass over on the table. Is she my child or what?"

Eileen laughed and it was a relief to hear it. She had a low, musical laugh and I remembered wondering if she could sing every time I heard it.

"Do you sing?" I asked impulsively.

"I used to," she said. "My mother was convinced I could have a career. She sang a little jazz, did I ever tell you, before she got married?" Her voice drifted off and she stared off for a moment.

"What happened?" I said.

"Nothing," she replied. "She died when I was twelve. Breast cancer. I gave up singing after that."

"Why?" I asked.

"Why what?"

"Why did you give it up?"

She looked squarely at me. "Because it reminded me of her, every time I sang. I sounded like her. Not that any of that matters anymore. I don't know why we're talking about this."

I shrugged. "Just curious, Eileen. Your laugh sounds

like you could sing, that's all. I wondered if you had."

"You were always curious."

It had an edge to it and without thinking I blurted out, "Eileen, what is it between us? It's always been there, something."

"Other than your judging me?" she said coolly. "Other than your thinking I'm a fool for staying in corrections while you went off to conquer the world. Other than the fact you think I'm stupid and naive and rule-bound. Other than that?"

"What?" I sat back and just stared at her. "I didn't . . . what are you saying?"

"What, you think I don't know how you see me?" She leaned forward and her lips thinned as people's lips do when they are well and truly angry. "I'm everything you think I am except stupid," she said, jabbing her finger at me at the word "stupid."

It was like a summer storm that comes out of nowhere. It could be that Eileen was tense and labile enough these days so that storms were pretty common. In any case, I didn't want to get into a fight with her. But there was some truth to what she'd said, although not to all of it.

"I never thought you were," I said. "All right, I don't think I felt it as harshly as you say it, but yes, there were these gaps between us. I couldn't stand all those rules and you seemed to care about them so much. I didn't know what you thought would happen if you broke one. What could the almighty authorities do—execute you? I didn't understand you, Eileen. You did all these things the same way all the time. You *liked* routine. I'd get bored if I had to eat the same thing for breakfast twice in a row."

"What I want to know," Eileen said, "is how you got

away with everything—with breaking every goddamn rule you ever ran into like a runner clearing hurdles. The first time I do something in my whole entire life, my whole world falls down around me like a house of cards."

"Eileen," I said, stunned, "there are rules and there are rules. Bringing car keys in your purse into the prison instead of leaving them in the locker is one thing; fucking an inmate is another. You didn't exactly break a minor rule. You make it sound like I ran around bringing contraband in and giving it to inmates. I never did anything like that."

"You ever do anything for love?"

"Sure, but that's what I don't get. You didn't. I've read the file on Calvin. He is a seriously unappealing person and you were not in love with him. You've never even mentioned him; all you talk about is Jim. What's Jim got to do with it?"

"You don't know shit about it."

"No question. I absolutely don't know shit about it."

"What are you here for, Michael? That insatiable curiosity of yours got the best of you?"

"Partly," I admitted. "Partly because I need to make sense of things. But there's also a rumor about another hit at the prison, and the rumor is coming out of your group. And somehow I suspect it's all involved with you and what happened, and I don't understand it."

"Another hit? I don't believe you. People don't kill each other in New England prisons. This isn't Miami. I was at Nelson's Point for fifteen years. Nothing like that ever happened." She dismissed it with a wave of her hand, but her anger seemed to deflate like a balloon. Silence fell. Eileen stared out the window at her garden and she didn't even really seem to be listening anymore. I didn't think she was in the present at all; she was in the past, fighting old battles with me and maybe with the singer she might have been.

I sat there feeling like I was caught in a time warp. This was probably the conversation we should have had fifteen years ago. I didn't know where to go with it. I started to open my mouth but Eileen spoke. "I was just always so afraid," she said, still not looking at me. "I never understood you. You never seemed to care. I worried all the time. For the first five years I held my breath, scared I'd be fired. I didn't even buy a house for almost ten years because if I lost my job I knew I wouldn't be able to pay for it.

"Then somewhere as the years kept going by, I went from feeling scared to feeling bored and there was nothing in between. I wanted . . . something . . . something that felt safe. I wanted to feel like I was . . . I don't know. There just should have been something between scared and bored and there wasn't.

"Suddenly I was forty and overweight and I had asthma and gout and men didn't even look at me anymore. I was like some kind of fixture. Inmates, guards, nobody, they didn't even notice me. You don't have a clue, Michael, what that's like. It's like you're not female anymore." There was a pause. "It was more than that. I didn't matter. I just didn't matter to anybody."

I didn't say anything. I was aging, too, but with a healthy baby in my belly and a good man in my bed, my aging wouldn't have impressed Eileen. And for better or worse—and often it was for worse—I was rarely ignored. People either liked me or hated me but I usually had an impact.

There was something else I didn't say. I was starting to get it. If you took risks a lot you knew which ones to take. If you walked on ice regularly, thin ice was pretty easy to recognize: you'd fallen through a few times and you knew how to spot the risky stuff. It was your business to know about ice.

But what if you'd stood in one place your whole life and you'd never stepped out on the ice. Probably you couldn't tell the difference between thin ice and ice six feet thick. Eileen had stood still until she felt herself petrifying and then she had panicked. She'd stepped out wildly and she had walked out on ice that wouldn't support a mouse.

It didn't make any sense to her. All those other people seemed to walk on ice all the time—people like me—bringing in car keys and forgetting to sign out and all those terrible things. The first time she did one thing against the rules, the sky had fallen in, just like she always thought it would.

She was like those parents I ran across who think their teenagers taking cocaine and wearing an earring are absolutely the same thing. You cannot convince them to let up on the earring because the drugs matter a whole lot more and that it is not possible to fight every single battle on every front with a kid, or else you lose the kid. The parents just looked at you like you were advocating cocaine for breakfast. They said things like, "You're saying we should just let him run wild."

There was a strange kind of rigidity that left people without depth perception. Things were right or they were wrong. Getting a parking ticket and killing strangers weren't as far apart for some folks as they were for the rest of us.

Realizing that, I knew how much Eileen must hate me. To her there was no difference between what she had done and things I had done, but I had always skated free and she had lost everything.

"Eileen," I said. "I don't know what to tell you about the differences between us. They've always been there. And it may not seem like it now, but I've taken my share of lumps for being the way I am. But this is not about you and me. There really is a serious risk of another hit at the prison and I need to understand some things. I know you're in love with Jim. That's so obvious you might as well be wearing a sign. Just tell me about him. I need to understand him better."

"He doesn't have anything to do with Clarence dying," she said defensively. "Don't tell me you're going to try to pin that on him."

"I'm not trying to pin anything on anybody," I said. "Besides, I don't have any evidence at all that Jim's involved in Clarence's death or anybody else's." I sort of crossed my fingers when I said that. I didn't really think Jim had offed Clarence or that even he was bold enough to advertise a hit on Gary and then try it, but "no involvement"—that might be stretching it. He surely knew something about it.

"I just want to understand his relationship with you." I held up both palms. "Honest to God, it isn't just curiosity. He's in my group, remember, and I need to know who I'm dealing with."

That seemed to satisfy her. "He's not who you think he is," she said.

"Okay, so who is he?"

She opened her mouth to speak and then shut it. I could see her struggling with the words. How do you paint a picture of someone so that someone else will see them as you do?

"He's kind," she said. She looked hard at me but I kept my face still and Eileen went on. "I know this is hard for you to believe, but he is. And he's perceptive. You know what he said to me? That first day we talked? He looked right at me and said, 'The people who work here, they're in prison just like we are. You see the same things we do. You eat the same food. You're in prison, too.'

"'But I can leave,' I said, 'and you can't.' But that thing he said, it was already thudding in my chest.

"'Yeah, but what are you doing at night?' he answered. 'I'm sitting in a room alone. You doing anything different?'"

Jesus, I thought, disgusted. He was good.

Eileen went on, "One day he told me—I still remember it—'There's something inside of you that's never had a chance to breathe. Don't you think just once in your life, just one time in your whole life you could let it breathe?'"

This time it was harder to keep my mouth shut, but I did.

"He was right," she added. "I couldn't even sleep for thinking about it. He saw things in me that nobody else saw. It was like I was in black-and-white to everybody else but to him I was in color.

"There's one thing I want you to know, Michael. I don't know why but it's important to me. That thing with Calvin. So help me God I'll deny this if you ever repeat it because it would get Jim in trouble. But I did it for Jim. He owed Calvin money, a lot of it, from gambling, and Calvin was going to kill him if he didn't pay up, and he couldn't. He saw Jim leaving my office one night, when he was working in the hall and he figured out that we were involved. He said he'd take sex as payment for the debt. I couldn't let him kill Jim and he would have. Don't look at me like that. Jim didn't want me to do it. He tried to talk me out of it. He felt really horrible. But after what he'd given me, I couldn't let anything happen to him."

This time my jaw ached from the effort of keeping my mouth shut.

8

I WAS TIRED OF PRISONS. TIRED OF LINOLEUM AND STEEL, OF cinderblock walls and exposed toilets. Tired of smooth surfaces without carpet or upholstery, of furniture designed to be washed down with disinfectant.

I didn't argue with the décor. On any given day, somebody was smearing feces on the wall. There were a fair number of psychotic folks in prison, the ones who were too violent to stay outside and eat out of garbage dumps the way society expected the rest of their brethren to do. But the truly crazy probably spread less feces than the malingerers and the plain old, in-your-face angry types.

The tangled knot of folks inhabiting those disinfectant-reeking cells were mostly young and poor and ill-educated. No small number had been raised to think drug dealing was a smart career choice. Some were seriously angry, with the kind of chronic, grinding anger that drew alcohol and drugs like water to a siphon. Occasionally they took it out on the people who caused the anger, but mostly not. Mostly it was you or I or an eight-year-old child in the wrong place at the wrong time.

But the violence would burn out of most of them by the time they hit their forties and they'd become more or less law-abiding, which was why almost everybody in a prison was young. Endless waves of the young washed up on the linoleum and steel shores every year, thrown up by the storms of their childhoods and controlled by whichever political currents were washing through the legislature.

Hundreds of miles away, carefully groomed middle-aged white men in pressed suits made speeches with an eye to the cameras and those speeches—quicker than Harry Potter's wand—made parole disappear or reappear, doubled sentences or cut them in half, transferred prisoners out of state or brought them back. Back at the prison, worried men who had never seen the legislature and some who didn't know where it was, read the newspapers anxiously—or had them read to them.

But mixed among "the scarred and the marred and the faulty," as Richard Selzer would say, were the truly cruel and vicious: sharp-eyed, watchful, ready to prey on anybody—in or out of prison. Prison was just a different playing field for these folks; the object of the game was the same and the rules, well, the rules were for everybody else.

I had been to the prison twice this week and wasn't due back until the following week. I was glad to have a few days at the hospital. True, the rooms there also smelled of disinfectant and the floors were covered with linoleum, but you could open any door yourself and there wasn't a single bar in sight. Also, everybody showed up at a hospital sooner or later. It was a thoroughly democratic place where the business executive in for back surgery wore the same backless gown as the welfare mom and sat in the same X-ray waiting room.

However, a whole lot of people who came through hospitals did just fine. They got better and went back to a real life on the outside. It was almost unheard of for people to make hospitals a permanent place to live: hardly any of them panicked when they were released to go home and checked themselves back in.

But how many inmates had I seen make an escape attempt two weeks before their release date? Prison had become the devil they knew. The outside world, with its requirements for earning a living and finding a place to live, with the necessity of shopping for groceries and doing laundry, had become just too scary.

I was meeting with the psych residents who did consults to pediatrics, going over the new referrals when a name caught my attention. "What was that name again?" I asked.

A dark-haired, first-year resident looked at his notes doubtfully. "Aphasia? Aspasia, maybe?" he replied.

I frowned. I had only run into that name once—outside of history books. Could there be two girls in the area with that unlikely name? "Last name?" I asked. He glanced through the referral.

"Raines," he said.

"Aspasia Raines?" I said. "What's wrong with her?"

"Diabetic coma," he said. "You might as well call it a suicide attempt. This kid *never*, and I mean *never*, tests her sugars or she takes her insulin only upon rare and unpredictable occasions. She eats what she damn well pleases and does what she pleases. The diabetes is controllable; she isn't. The staff are getting homicidal. They're going to kill her if she doesn't manage it herself. It's the third time she's been in the hospital in two months. She's had more education on diabetes than most of the staff. It doesn't do any good."

"Where is she?"

"Intensive care. Why, you know her?"

"I know her parents." Why hadn't Gary told me? "Anybody with her now?"

"Her mother, probably. She was here all day yesterday."

"Do you mind if I take it, for now? If her parents don't want me on it, I'll give her back, okay?"

He shrugged, looking relieved. "No problem," he said. "Just don't be too quick to give her back," he added.

Susan was curled up on the couch in the intensive care waiting room. There was very little visitation allowed in intensive care: a few minutes at a time for family members and none at all for friends. In between, the families hung out in the waiting room, which was often filled with more misery than should be legal in one room. It was a wonder the paint didn't cry.

"Susan," I said softly. Her eyes were shut and I wasn't sure whether or not she was awake.

"Michael," she said, opening her eyes and sitting up. "Thanks for coming."

"It was an accident," I said. "I didn't know Aspasia was here until I stumbled across it." I sat down beside her. "I'm so sorry, so very sorry. How are you doing with it?"

"The truth? Not so good."

"How long has it been going on?"

"A year," she said, stretching her arms over her head and blinking. "The year from hell." She put her head on the back of the couch, closing her eyes again. "She was diagnosed with diabetes a year ago and she will not do anything she's supposed to do. She just won't. I

have yelled until I'm hoarse. And Gary. He's worse."
She wasn't crying but I noticed dry tear tracks in the
light. It was always a bad sign when someone had run
out of tears.

"Where's Gary?" I asked.

"He was here all last night," she said. "He just left a
few minutes ago to go to work."

Whoa, at the hospital all night, working all day.
That would get to you after a while. "Susan," I said,
"I'm on call for psych consults. I can pick her up and
go talk to her—not that I'm promising any miracles.
I'm not. But I can work with you on this, if you want
me to. I can't see her for therapy because I'm a friend
but I can do a consult and try to help get her going in
the right direction. I can find someone to see her for
therapy, when she's ready. But Gary didn't tell me
about this, and I don't know if you want me
involved."

"Pick her up, Michael," she said firmly. "See if you
can do anything. I don't care what Gary wants."

"He doesn't want me involved?"

"No, he doesn't. That's another thing we've fought
about."

"But why?"

"He says you treat adults, that your specialty is
trauma. Yadda, yadda, yadda. It's all bullshit."

"So what's the real reason?"

"He's ashamed."

"Of Aspasia?"

"Of her, of us because we can't control her. I don't
even know what his problem is anymore. And I don't
care. I'm her mother and I'm telling you that if there's
any chance at all you can help her, then you need to
get involved. Because something horrible is going to

happen if she keeps this up." She rubbed her forehead absentmindedly, which I suspected meant her head was pounding. "I should have called you before now," she muttered. "It was just cowardice on my part, not wanting to set Gary off."

An elderly woman walked in with a nurse and sat down. The waiting room was far more often inhabited by the elderly than by parents of school-age children, which was as it should be. The nurse was talking softly but the old woman looked bewildered, as though she couldn't take it in. Susan glanced over and then shut her eyes again. "You wouldn't believe the terrible stories that come through here," she said.

"Oh, yes, I would," I replied. "Come on. Let's go get you some coffee and something to eat and then you can wait in my office for a while if you like. I've got meetings and I won't be there. Do you know where the cafeteria is?"

Susan nodded.

"Why don't you head on down and I'll meet you. I just want to take a look at her chart first—see what's up."

"You can see her," Susan said, rising. Evidently she wasn't going to fight me on food and a change of scene. "I saw her this morning. She's out of the coma and they're moving her to the ward today. She comes out of these things like a phoenix. I don't know how. I'd be dead by now."

"It's her age," I replied. "How old is she now?"

"Ten short years and one long one," Susan replied.

The chart was a nightmare of noncompliance. Aspasia was the kind of kid medicine hates most. She could live and should live and actually, the diabetes should be no more than a nuisance—given all the much worse things that kids can have. But Aspasia was having none of it. She was steadfastly refusing to do anything differently from the other kids. Just like the resident said, she would not test her sugars and she ate anything she wanted. Beginning and end of story. Before the willfulness of an eleven-year-old the vast arsenal of medical remedies lay useless.

Between the lines you could read the patience of the staff dwindling. After all, Aspasia was coming in next to kids with cystic fibrosis, who didn't have the choice she had. They were slowly suffocating from an incurable disease that would finally strangle them sometime in adolescence, and here was this kid with a normal life at her fingertips who was throwing it all away.

They'd have had a lot more sympathy if Dad had been a drunk and Mom a hooker. At least then they could have felt sorry for her. But faced with a normal and worried-out-of-their-minds family, they had no one to blame but Aspasia. And blame her they had. But by now they had mostly just given up.

She didn't look eleven under the covers. A small, white face and two thin arms were all I could see. Both arms were hooked up to IVs. She looked very small and very young but I'd yet to see a kid who looked their age in intensive care. They always looked small and pale and deathly ill—which they were.

Aspasia looked like she was dozing, but when she heard me come in she opened her eyes and I got a jolt. Maybe everybody else around her was defeated, but this kid wasn't. Her eyes were bright blue and her stare was singular and intense. The eyes belonged to a fighter, although one wholeheartedly on the wrong side. I sighed. I had had experience with that. I had relatives who'd fought for the South, which my whole family ought to be ashamed of but wasn't in the slightest. There was something about this child's face that reminded me of Roman despots and misguided Southern pride.

"You're well named," I said.

She didn't speak. "I'm Michael. I met you when you were little. I work with your dad. You have a great name."

This time she couldn't resist.

"My name is shit," she said. "It sounds like asparagus."

"Ah, well, I have a boy's name. How'd you like to live with that? Worse, Michael is just an ordinary name. But Aspasia isn't. She was one of my favorites."

"I don't care."

"That's probably what she would have said," I replied. "You going upstairs today."

"I guess."

"Good, at least you get TV."

"The channels here suck."

"What's your favorite show?"

"None of your business."

"Probably what she'd have said, too. You have a lot in common, really, although I truly don't think your parents would have approved of her. Actually," I said dryly, "I'm sure of it."

"What are you talking about? I don't know what you're talking about."

"A woman with your name. A long time ago. Your parents wouldn't have approved of her."

"Why? Was she a fuck-up too?" She said "fuck-up" with studied casualness, the way she had said "sucks," looking for a reaction.

"Well, depends on your point of view," I said. "I'm sure your dad would think so. He can be a little rigid. I don't know about your mom. I don't think so. Everybody sees someone like Aspasia differently."

She was too proud to ask. "It's still a dumb name."

"Then why don't you change it? Marie or Joan or Dweedle-Dee. People can just change their names, you know. What's anybody going to do about it if you don't answer to Aspasia anymore? Although, boy, that would be a hard one to let go. I bet there isn't another Aspasia at your school."

She snorted. "*Nobody* else has a name that stupid."

"I wonder if they teased her, too. Although it could be the name was more common back then."

"You're making that up. I've never heard of any Aspasia."

"Nobody ever told you the story of your name? Well, it's probably because she was such a black sheep. Or at least some people thought so. Do you have a computer? I'm sure you could find out about her on the Internet." Nobody went to the library anymore. The Internet was to kids what books were to the parents. "Or maybe not. There wasn't that much written about her."

"I don't care who she was."

"It's probably just as well. Really, I should get your parents' permission to tell you about her."

"Why? What'd she do?"

"Well, if it was a movie, it'd be X-rated, that's for sure. Anyway, what are you going to do today? Don't you get bored here? I think hospitals are seriously boring."

She shrugged. "It's all right."

"Yeah, well better you than me. I hate hospitals.

Having to stay in bed all day. I'm too antsy. You got anything to do?"

"TV."

"Oh, that's good. Grown-up talk shows and those seriously stupid game shows. Sounds like a fun time. I'll talk to your parents and see what we can do about a VCR. You get to know any of the staff on your visits?"

"Some."

"Anybody you like?"

She snorted. "They're all stupid."

"Well, they can be, that's for sure. And very dorky."

She smiled slightly. "Dorky," she said. "Dorky?" What's that?"

"Oops, you know grown-ups can't talk. Come on. You can translate."

She just looked at me.

"You okay for now?"

She shrugged.

"I'll be back," I said and left.

Why didn't hospitals ever have quiet little places where troubled families could gather over coffee or tea? Instead they have cafeterias the size of warehouses with all the charm of operating rooms. They're always clean, efficient and soulless. I always wondered if there were architectural firms specializing in "soulless." It just couldn't be an accident. You'd have to work to create some of the buildings around because some did not have a single smidgen of grace about them. There must be a "soulless" patrol somewhere, people especially trained to go over blueprints and say, "Hold it. There's a small alcove there where someone might have a quiet moment. Quick, get it out."

"Tell me about her," I said sitting down across from Susan. Her plate would have made an anorexic proud: there was a piece of toast on it and a teaspoon of fruit. It didn't matter; she wasn't eating it, anyway. She was probably living on coffee. "What does she like to do? Who are her friends? How's she doing at school, in activities, in other stuff outside of this? Who is she when she's not being a diabetic?"

"There is no outside of this," Susan said. "One by one we've cut out everything. Gary says taking care of her health is number one and if she can't do that, she can't do anything: play sports, anything. She has to go to school and come right home. It isn't working but he won't budge."

"Yes, he will," I said, emphatically. "He most certainly will. Because if he doesn't, she may die. She may die anyway, but if she does you won't want to think there was anything you could have done and didn't. Gary is stubborn, but he's not crazy. He will move on this."

"Well, good luck," she said. "I haven't had any."

"When's he coming back?"

"Right after work."

"All right, I'll be there. So tell me. Who is she?"

"I don't know who she is, but I can tell you who she was. Until a year ago. She was the apple of her daddy's eye. She was smart and funny and Gary thought the sun rose and set on her. I used to be jealous they were so close. She's a terrific athlete. Good at just about anything she tries. She was playing on a mixed soccer team for the first couple of years and I can tell you the boys were relieved when the teams divided by sexes. She just creamed them. She's never been afraid of anybody or anything on a field or court and she never met a ball she didn't like. I don't know what happened to her, Michael. She got diabetes and it all went to hell in a hand basket. She just never accepted it.

"It made Gary crazy. It still does. He's worried out of his mind but his way of handling it is to get angry. He just doesn't understand why she won't take care of herself."

"That's because he's using logic and it isn't logical."

"Well, what the hell is it? I don't understand it either."

"I don't know, Susan. I just met her. But it's something to do with who she thinks she is and what diabetes means to her. That's all I know."

"We have gotten books on diabetes. We have had her in educational classes. . . . We have—"

"Throw them away. She knows all that. It isn't knowledge that's the problem. Tell me something. Where'd she get her name?"

"Her name?"

"Yes, it's unusual."

"I named her for my aunt. She died when I was a child and she was my favorite."

"Do you know anything about where the name came from?"

"Michael, why are you talking about her name? What has this got to do with anything? Are you telling me this wouldn't have happened if we'd named her 'Joan'?"

"No, no, no. I'm looking for an 'in' with her. I'm wondering about her name."

"It's just my aunt."

I dropped it.

"So tell me what you've tried."

"I told you. We've tried making activities contingent on her taking care of herself. We tried a point system with stars and stuff. We've tried talking. We've tried yelling. Gary is taking it personally, like her non-compliance is something she's doing to hurt him. Which it isn't. Or at least I don't think it is. I'm not sure of anything anymore." She paused and stared off for a moment. "I have never felt so lost in my whole, entire life."

"Well, it sounds well and truly horrible. She's slipping through your fingers and you're frantic. I would be, too."

Tears came out of nowhere but Susan didn't seem to notice. At least for a moment. She just sat quietly, then suddenly she put her head down and sobbed. Nobody in the cafeteria even looked at her. It was a tertiary care hospital, after all. Most of the light stuff went elsewhere, to small local hospitals. Tears were not uncommon here.

"It's horrible, Susan," I said quietly, "and I'd be crying too, but it ain't over till the fat lady sings. She's still okay and she is a major fighter if she can turn this thing around. And don't think those ten good years are wasted. She's been well-loved and well-cared-for and she has a history of success. If anything makes the difference, that will—that and that fighting thing in her."

"Michael, if diabetes doesn't kill her, I will."

"I don't blame you," I said.

Gary was there at 5:40 sharp. Which means he had to have walked out the door of the prison at 5:01. Not easy if you're in the middle of a murder investigation and being seriously hounded by the media. I was sitting in the waiting room of intensive care with Susan when he arrived.

He stopped short when he saw me and then looked over at Susan. She shook her head. A mixture of emotions seemed to cross his face but I was glad to see that one of them looked like relief. It didn't appear he was going to throw me out instantly.

I got up and walked over to him and put my arms around him. He held on for a long time. Finally he said, "Michael, I didn't—"

"Look," I interrupted, "I stumbled across this and came over on my own. You can send me away if you want to, but what's the point? Let me see if I can help."

He let go and looked around for a Kleenex. He took a long time blowing his nose and finding a trash can for the Kleenex and then he said, "I don't see how anybody can help."

It was a kind of tacit acceptance. Susan looked surprised but didn't say anything. I wasn't. Gary had painted himself into a corner but he wasn't crazy enough not to take an out when he was offered one.

"Let's go to my office and talk," I said.

"I want to see Aspasia first," Gary said.

I took him by the shoulders and got my face very close to his. "Gary," I said, "Not unless you can promise not to say one negative thing to her. Not one."

He looked surprised and then sheepish. "What am I supposed to say? She damn near killed herself."

"Gary, you're on my turf now, so listen up. Tell her you love her and you're glad she's feeling better and that you'll be back, you have to see someone. And please don't tell her it's me. I am not going to be seen with you around Aspasia. And for God's sake, if she ever mentions me, do not say a single good thing about me. Promise? Just be neutral about me or hostile if you have to be something, but not positive."

Gary and Susan looked at each other. "Promise?" I said.

Gary looked uncertain. "Gary," I said, "has anything you've done worked?"

He snorted.

"Then why don't you try something different? Even if it doesn't work, at least you will have tried something different. If this were a car you wouldn't just sit in the ditch and spin your wheels. What's the point? The only thing you know for sure is that what you've tried thus far isn't working. So why keep doing it?"

"All right," he said, resigned—but not hopeful.

"Remember," I said. "Not one negative thing."

Gary just nodded.

I saw Susan slip her hand in his when they walked through the door.

Pediatrics was running their weekly diabetic clinic and after talking with Susan and Gary, I dropped by. I hadn't learned much more from the conversation than Susan had already told me. Gary was sick with worry but it came out as mad. If anybody else had hurt Aspasia he would have wanted to kill them. It didn't change anything that it was Aspasia hurting Aspasia.

I went into the back room where doctors write their notes looking for a pediatrician named Gene Brooks. He was Aspasia's primary doc when she was an outpatient but it didn't look like he had seen her much. She tended to come in only on emergency and that meant she got whoever was on the emergency room and then whoever was running the ward that month. But Gene would know something about her. Besides, I was really looking for something different from him.

I caught him between patients reading a chart.

"Gene," I said with genuine pleasure. He had always been one of my favorites. A mild-mannered guy, seldom ruffled by anything, he was endlessly patient with kids. Few people knew he took out his aggressions on the weekends by going over four-foot jumps on the back of an out-of-control thoroughbred.

The horse was called "Patience," but he didn't have any—not any at all. Patience had a lousy temperament. He bit anybody who came within four feet of him, and worse, he was erratic over jumps. Sometimes Patience jumped; sometimes he would screech to a halt right in front of one, half the time catapulting his rider to kingdom come. To complicate matters, he didn't seem to have a "tell," that characteristic something—a shiver, a slight slowing down, a movement of the head—that warns the rider the horse isn't going to jump. I would have been tempted to shoot that horse by now. Still I had to admit Patience could jump brilliantly when he wanted to. Gene loved that horse passionately—despite his emergency room bills.

As a rider Gene had more nerve than skill, and given that he wasn't getting that much better and the horse wasn't changing at all, I could see more bruises in his future than in his past. But you gotta like a guy who was as dopey over a horse as Gene was over Patience.

"Michael," he said, looking up and smiling. I sat down.

"How's Patience?" I said.

"Looking good," he said, rubbing his shoulder absentmindedly.

"You hurt?" I asked.

"Oh that?" he said, following my glance to his shoulder. He put his hand down. "It's nothing much. Just having a little trouble raising my arm. It's better than it was. I can get it up to my shoulder now."

I shook my head. "Gene, that horse is a menace."

He laughed. "Not really," he said. "My fault if I can't learn to stay on him."

I shook my head again. "I'm not getting into it," I said. "You're going to kill yourself on that horse if one of your friends doesn't shoot him first, but it's like telling someone to divorce a spouse. Better left alone. Aspasia Raines."

"Ah," he replied. "Kid's out of control. I can't get through to her at all. Parents are nice enough. Are you involved?"

"Psych consult from the ward," I said. "Anything about her I should know?"

"Sweet kid," he said, "but headed for a train wreck."

"Okay," I said. "Who do you have coming in today who's about her age and reasonable? No, don't make that reasonable, make that cool. I need a really cool kid, popular with her peers, maybe eleven to thirteen and handles her diabetes well."

He thought for a minute. "I've got a fourteen-year-old coming in. Named Kimberley Dent. Had it for four years. No big deal."

"Athlete?" I asked.

"I'm not sure," he said. He got up and walked over to a stack of charts and hunted through them. He picked up one and started thumbing through it. "Softball," he said finally. "Plays catcher."

"Sounds good," I said. "What time is she coming in?"

"Three P.M."

"Parents come with her?"

"Nope, she comes straight from school."

"Give me her phone number. I gotta call her mom."

9

THE PRISON WAS BEGINNING TO FEEL LIKE A FULL-TIME GIG. With two groups a week, there were only a couple of days between them, not to mention the time it took to read all the inmates' files and records, make notes on the current sessions and, of course, drive back and forth. In between I found a little time to hang out with Stacy.

I was sitting in his office after group, playing idly with a series of interconnected metal rings that slid up and down a U-shaped metal bar. They were supposed to come apart if you looped them the right way. I figured the thing had to be a joke. Just like Stacy to do something like that. There was absolutely no way those rings could come apart short of a metal cutter. "Your group's suddenly developed a work ethic," he commented, sorting through his mail.

"My group? Wrong guys," I said flatly. "Is this a joke?" I added, holding up the metal rings.

Stacy frowned without looking up. "Joke?" he said. "No, it's for real. They've all gotten jobs in the print shop, well, three of them, anyway, and a fourth one is trying. I sit on the committee that reviews job applications."

"I don't mean that," I said. "I mean this."

Stacy glanced up. "You're kidding," he replied.

I looked at it again, like Stacy's appraisal would somehow make the solution obvious.

When I didn't speak, he said again, "You're kidding, right?"

I shrugged. "So I only have neurons on one side of my brain. What? Is that a crime? My poor brain has never heard of spatial relations. You know who I really hate, the people who give directions by talking about the 'north' side of the building. Sadists for sure. I'd say do that twice and it's life without parole.

"So what does it mean?" I added, "The job thing?"

"Well, for sure, it means somebody's got the supervisor's ear and is getting his buddies in," he said. "The civilian supervisor is making the recommendations and he couldn't be recommending all those folks by chance."

"Let me guess," I said. "Jim Walker is working in the shop."

"You got it," Stacy replied.

"So what else does it mean?" I asked.

"Maybe nothing," he replied. "It may be that it's just an easy job and that they get to sit around all day and shoot the breeze and that's why everybody wants to work there."

"Or?"

"Or they're up to something," he said.

"Like what?"

"Who knows?" Stacy replied. "You heard about the ladder?"

"Yep."

"People get real ingenious in a prison."

"Well, it's a print shop so it's probably not a ladder this time . . ."

"Maybe they're printing their own prison newsletter," he said, putting the papers down and leaning back. "I can see it now: 'Razor Wire: Bad News Any Way You Slice It,' or 'Filing to Eternity: A Primer on Bars with Rotating Cores.' Maybe something less technical: 'Bundy: A Unanimous All-Star.'"

"Now you definitely have the wrong group," I said. "I run a sex offender group, remember. How 'bout 'How to Get a Job in a Shoe Store: A Primer for Foot Fetishes,' or 'Selecting a Safe Vacuum Cleaner.'"

"Vacuum cleaner?" Stacy said.

"You don't want to know," I replied. I thought for a moment. "If this were on the outside, I'd be going to visit their employer."

"What for?"

"Because sex offenders are always up to something. I'd be making sure they've disclosed they were sex offenders and that they didn't have access to pornography or potential victims. To be sure they weren't conning and manipulating."

"Oh no," Stacy replied. "This isn't the outside. None of those reasons apply here and if there is something going on, security will not like anybody mucking about. Leave it to them." He looked at me searchingly but I pulled an angelic expression from out of the blue and pasted it firmly on my face. Court had taught me a thing or two: how to lie without opening my mouth was one of them.

"I'm not kidding, Michael," he said. "There's that 'we' and 'they' thing with security. You know that. You are I are 'civilians' here. I've been here for twenty years and I'm still a civilian. And you? You're a part-time, contract employee. You're not even on the playing field."

"I didn't say I was going to do anything," I said innocently.

"And you didn't say you weren't," Stacy replied.

"Do I look stupid?" I asked. Stacy rolled his eyes but went back to the stack of papers on his desk. There was silence for a few minutes while Stacy thought about it. No doubt he was going to get into it again when something else caught his eye. "Uh oh," he said. "Gary's not going to like this." His voice had something almost like dread in it. "The guard's union thinks he's disciplined an officer too harshly. They're talking about a demonstration."

"How's he doing with all the pressure over Clarence?" I asked casually. I knew Gary was under pressure at home that Stacy didn't know about, but he had enough going at the prison alone to make the question reasonable.

"You want to know the truth?" Stacy said. "I think he's burning out. This murder is the first thing he's taken seriously in eons. He lets things slide he shouldn't and then when he does intervene, he comes in like Attila the Hun. Frankly, the union has probably got a point. They had in the other cases. Besides, half the time he's about as much fun to work with as a pit bull. Sorry, I know you like him but hardly anybody else around here does anymore."

I opened my mouth and shut it again. The look on Avery's face when he saw Gary in the hall flashed in my mind. "What's Avery got against him?" I asked.

"Nothing much," Stacy replied. "Just that Gary wouldn't let him go to his brother's funeral, the brother who raised him when his father died, Avery's mother having hit the road a long time ago."

"Do they let inmates out for things like that?"

"All the time," Stacy replied.

"So, why didn't Gary? Did he know the brother raised him and all that?"

"Sure he knew it," Stacy said. "But he also knew the killing was done by a rival gang and he wasn't at all sure Avery wouldn't use the occasion to even the score. Which he might have."

I realized I had been holding my breath. "So it was fair," I said.

"It was a reasonable call—in fact, it's the one most wardens would have made—but it would have made a whole lot more sense if he'd had one of us go tell Avery he couldn't go instead of just sending him a letter. The man's brother had died. He could have handled it better. But that's life in a prison. We're not a baby-sitting service, as the higher-ups like to say."

There was nothing I could say to that. Half the time it wasn't what you did, it was how you did it that pissed people off. I remembered a finding that the surgeons who got sued were the ones with poor communication skills, not the ones with poor surgical skills. Probably the same thing was true of wardens. But Stacy was right. Gary wasn't on the far side here. It would have been a little more graceful to have sent a staff member, but it wasn't exactly required.

Except in this case it wasn't really poor communication skills: it was a little girl named Aspasia making Gary crazy. He'd tried logic and he'd tried education and when neither had worked he'd put her in solitary. After that he didn't have a lot left in his repertoire. So he just got mad and—from the sound of it—had taken it out on everybody around him. Angry men weren't tactful or fair or fun to deal with. And they made mistakes.

"So what do you want to do about this print shop thing?" I asked.

"Not what you're thinking," Stacy said. "I'm going to take a little walk down the hall and mention it to my buddy, the captain. See what he thinks about it."

Stacy had me nailed—not that I'd admit it. I waited until he headed off to see the captain and then went on an errand of my own.

"Been here twenty-three years," the portly man in front of me said. "Been a printer all my life. Had my own business for fifteen years before I came here." Rudolph was in his sixties and his nose had the bloated look that went with the beer belly he was carrying. He liked his work and if my guess was right, he liked his beer, too. We were walking through the gymnasium-size room, empty now, and weaving through the huge machines that sprouted like giant metal cabbages on the floor.

"We do a lot of outside work here," he said. "Not just for corrections. And what we produce is as good as anything you'll find anywhere. Not that we always have the best equipment, mind you. Some of these machines are as old as I am." He laughed and patted his belly. I always wondered about that, men patting and rubbing their bellies like they were pets. It was peculiarly a male thing. Women never did it, no matter how big they were.

"We keep them together with string and Scotch tape. But we make do. We surely do," he said patting his belly again.

Reluctantly, I tore my attention away from his relationship with his belly. "What brought you here?" I asked. "I'm just curious. If you had a business on the outside."

"Oh, I know printing," he said. "But there's more to running a business these days than just printing. The bookkeeping alone damn near killed me. Got my wife involved and we sure as hell almost split up over it. Wouldn't be so bad if it weren't for the government. Government runs everything these days.

"I was at my wit's end, waking up nights worrying about everything and I saw an ad in the paper. They needed someone out here to run the print shop. I figured I was working for the government anyway, might as well work for the government, if you know what I mean. Let them have the headaches. It's worked out. If the work gets done, it gets done. If it doesn't, I'm still home in time for supper. I still get a paycheck. But it gets done," he added. "Especially now."

"Why now?" I said casually. I had been up front with Rudolph to a point. I had told him I was working part time at the prison and I was trying to learn more about the job placements the inmates had.

"Got a good crew," he said. "Best I've had in years. Maybe the best I've ever had. Got a guy who can keep the machines running, for one thing. That's no small problem with equipment as old as this. I swear if I gave that man some duct tape and a screwdriver, he could fix a space shuttle."

"And who would he be?" I said, but somehow I knew.

"Fellow named Jim Walker," he replied, smiling. "His dad was a machinist. He was practically raised in a machine shop. Said he had always loved machines,

would have followed in his father's footsteps but his
dad wanted him to go to law school. Said he was never
happy working as a lawyer. Feels more at home here
than anything he's done in fifteen years. I tell you
what. He's saved the state a ton of money. Not that
anybody gives a damn, but if they gave him a percentage of everything he's saved the state, he'd leave here
with a tidy sum."

I swallowed hard but didn't comment directly. "You
might want to take a look at his records sometime," I
said dryly. "It might make you appreciate what he's
been through."

"He's told me a lot," he said, dropping his voice,
although I couldn't imagine why. We were in something the size of a football stadium and there didn't
appear to be anyone within shouting distance. "About
his dad dying when he was twelve. Hard break for a
kid having to support all those siblings."

I made a mental note to check Jim's background
and see if anything he had told Rudolph was true.
Anything at all. Well, maybe some of it. Probably he
was once twelve years old.

I glanced at my watch and stopped short. I had told
Stacy I was heading for group early to catch up on
records, which wasn't a total lie, just a sort-of-maybe-
little-bit lie. I *was* planning to do records. I just took a
little detour first. The print shop was in the same
building as group anyway, so what was a little detour
among friends? But now I was running late enough
that I had to quickly excuse myself and head off.

I had a feeling there was more I should have
asked—something was rattling around in my overactive unconscious and trying hard to surface—but being
late for group would cause more trouble than it was

worth. The guys would be standing around on their
units, ready to go, pacing around and getting agitated.
The officers couldn't release them to go to group until
the announcement was made, so they'd be standing
around waiting, too. In a place where half the people
were pissed half the time, this would just increase it to
three-quarters.

I shuffled past the welding and the woodworking
shops, made it to the classrooms and then on to the
small conference room we used for group. The group
room was only at the other end of the corridor so it
shouldn't have taken eons to get there but it seemed
to, given how I was moving.

I called for the announcement to be made and only
a few minutes later, inmates started filtering in—everybody that is, except Jim. We waited for a few more
minutes then started group anyway, the rule being
that people were expected to come right away and if
they didn't, we weren't going to hang around waiting
for them. For God's sake, they were in prison, they
didn't exactly have to worry about traffic.

We were barely into layouts, however, when we
heard footsteps coming down the hall. Terrance, the
youngest offender in the group, broke off his layout
nervously and stared at the door. I made a mental
note to talk to Stacy about Terrance. He had grown
more nervous week by week in group, which was very
odd. Folks new to treatment tended to start off anxious
and then settle in as time went on. Terrance was doing
the opposite. His face looked tight and he was playing
nervously with an earring. He seemed to be a whole
different person from the kid who strolled in a few
weeks ago.

The door opened and Jim came in. Instead of going

to his seat, however, he headed straight for me, without even glancing at the other inmates. He bent down and said quietly in my ear, "Michael, could I see you for a moment? It's important."

I looked at Jim and then at the other group members. First Avery calling Eileen a "ho" and now this. Same thing for my money. Just different ways of making a run at the group leader.

"No," I said in a normal voice, not that the group wouldn't have heard a whisper they were listening so hard. "Mr. Walker, we're in the middle of group. If this is a life-threatening emergency, I will interrupt group briefly. But it needs to be something that absolutely cannot wait until after group. And it had better be something that only I can deal with. Otherwise, security is right down the hall and they can call a doctor or whatever. If it isn't that urgent, then have a seat."

Jim hesitated, then just shrugged. "It's just—" He saw the look on my face and broke off. "Never mind," he said and headed for his seat. I looked around the group and to my surprise saw alarm on nearly every face. In contrast, Terrance looked almost, well, relieved. Avery didn't look anything. He was staring straight ahead with nothing on his face at all.

The alarm took me aback. Why were people upset about my not talking to Jim? Did he really know something and, if so, how would they know and why would they care? This group was getting weirder by the minute.

It was too late to change my mind and too damn risky anyway to be having a private tête-à-tête with a sex offender while group was going on. I settled in, aware I was in the middle of something I didn't understand. This group just didn't feel like other groups I had run. On the surface, it was running smoothly—if you call people going through the motions smooth. But I'd never had a sense anyone in this group was taking treatment seriously except poor Terrance. He'd started out looking interested and was now acting like a one-legged rabbit in a room full of alligators.

We had barely finished layout and were just moving into the agenda for the day when Jim jumped up, suddenly. "This is bullshit," he said.

"Sit down," Mr. Walker," I said quietly.

"You know it's bullshit," he said to me. "Come on. You guys aren't serious about this." For a second he surprised me and I didn't answer. It was exactly what I was thinking. "I don't even know why I'm here. Okay, say I did what they said. At least it was adult women, not little kids." Jim had started pacing as he spoke. "I'm not some kind of pervert, like some of you creeps. And it's not like I hit anyone over the head or pulled a knife on them. I mean, how bad can it be to trade a little sex for working on a case? What would have happened if I hadn't taken the cases?" Everybody was staring at him and nobody answered.

"They didn't have enough money to pay full fare. You think other attorneys would have handled these stupid, messy custody cases for free? You're dreaming." He was pacing behind the line of chairs as he spoke, moving toward the end of the seats where Avery sat. The other offenders all turned to look at him except Avery, who never turned his head. Maybe it was the insult of that but when Jim passed Avery he said, "What kind of real man has to use a knife to get a woman anyway? A real man has women asking for it."

"Mr. Walker," I said firmly but Avery's voice drowned out mine. "You talkin' to me, Jim boy?" My heart jumped. It could happen that people tried to stomp on each other in group. Rare, but possible. "You better do something about this," Avery said to me, "or I will."

I started to speak to Jim, thinking for once, Avery was right. Jim was still walking and almost behind my chair when Avery spoke. I was turning around to follow him when something caught my eye. Jim's lips hadn't thinned. Sure, his face looked angry. Yes, he was waving his arms and stomping around the room. Nonetheless his lips hadn't thinned. When people get angry their lips thin—who knows why? Something about muscle contraction and capillary action. All the rest of it is fakable. The angry expression, the pacing, the arm waving, the angry words. Everything is fakable, except the lips.

For a split second I had a choice: let Jim get behind me or turn my back on the group. I couldn't do both. I decided whatever Jim wanted me to do was the wrong thing and Jim wanted me to turn my back on the group. I swung back around to the group and said firmly. "Mr. Walker, sit down. Right now or you are out of here."

Jim stood directly behind me, making the hair stand up on the back of my neck. The impulse to turn around was almost overwhelming. "You sit here week after week," he said, "like you think something is going on here. Well, nothing is going on here that has anything to do with treatment." His voice had that tone again, the one I'd heard once before, the one time I'd known he was telling me the truth.

"Something is going on here," I said quietly. "And

I'm pretty sure it doesn't have anything to do with treatment."

At that there was silence for a moment, then Jim resumed walking, heading back toward his seat. I breathed an internal sigh of relief when he entered my field of vision. The hand-waving and bitching continued but the oomph seemed to have gone out of the act. He sat down with a plop, crossing his arms on his chest. "Bullshit," was his final comment.

"Anybody else got anything they want to pull?" I said. There was silence.

"Uh," Leroy Warner said, "You think there's any chance we could get Eileen back?" Everybody laughed, even Jim and Avery. Everybody except me. And Terrance.

10

GROUP WAS ON MY MIND THE REST OF THE DAY. BY THE NEXT day it was still running in the background and I couldn't shake it or figure it out. I made my way to Aspasia's room vaguely distracted, and saw that fourteen-year-old Kimberley Dent was visiting. I had billed the contact between them as a new program called "Kids to Kids," a program where kids with chronic diseases make contact with each other. I never mentioned to either of them that it had exactly one pair of kids in it.

I also never mentioned that Aspasia was not taking care of her diabetes. I didn't want Kimberley lecturing her, which even a cool fourteen-year-old might be inclined to do if given the chance. After all, kids knew everything about everything at that age and they weren't inclined to be tolerant. What I had in mind was a little modeling, not a replay of finger-pointing adult lectures. So while I told the whole story to Kimberley's mother, I only said to Kimberley and Aspasia that they both played sports and might have some stuff in common. I told Kimberley truthfully that

Aspasia was new to diabetes and I thought having some contact with someone who'd had it for a while and dealt with it well might be a good thing.

From the looks of things, they were at least getting along. "Here's my e-mail," Kimberley said, handing a slip to Aspasia. "Let me know when you get home." Ah, the first generation that did not know life prior to e-mail. It was a scary thought.

When she had gone I dropped the book at the foot of Aspasia's bed. "A present," I said.

She picked it up. "What is it?" Aspasia had her normal color back. In fact, she was up and about and almost ready to go home. An adult might be sitting up by now.

"Greece," I replied. "At the time Aspasia lived." She looked at the picture of the Parthenon on the cover. "Her lover built that. Well, he had it built. That and about everything else that's considered great about ancient Greece."

"So," she said.

"So nothing," I said. "It's just interesting."

"What's interesting about it?"

"Aspasia," I said. "She was interesting. You don't get it," I said, sitting down on the edge of the bed. "At the time she lived, women stayed indoors, at least wives. They didn't compete in the Olympics. They weren't allowed to *go* to the Olympics on pain of death. They didn't vote. They didn't go out for dinner at a friend's house. They didn't go outside. They didn't read or write. If there had been movies they wouldn't have been allowed to go to one. If there were computers they wouldn't have been allowed to use one. They stayed home. Period.

"That is, all the respectable women did. The only

ones who had any freedom were the courtesans. The scandalous women who didn't get married and who lived with men. Some of them were paid for sleeping with men. Some were a whole lot higher level than that."

"Prostitutes," Aspasia said, disbelieving. "She was a prostitute?"

"Not exactly," I said dryly. "She was a freeborn woman from Miletus and she was the mistress of Pericles, who basically ran Athens for forty years. She was funny and smart and Socrates, one of the greatest philosophers in the history of the world, used to come and listen to her talk about politics and the art of public speaking. Men who thought women were as stupid as mules used to come and learn from Aspasia. It wasn't exactly a small thing to get anybody to take a woman seriously in those days."

Aspasia had opened the book and was looking through it idly. "That's dumb," she said. I wasn't sure which part she thought was dumb. "I wasn't named for her. I've never heard of her."

"You were named for your aunt," I said. "But somebody back there—your aunt or whoever she was named for or back further—somebody was named for this woman, because that name didn't exactly fall out of a hat. So you carry her name, and there is magic in a name, you know."

"That's really stupid," she said. "A name doesn't mean anything."

"Oh, yes, it does," I said. "A name draws the spirit of the person who had it. And you couldn't have anybody better hanging around you." Aspasia didn't look up. I took a deep breath. "What was special about her," I said softly, "was that she played the hand that was dealt her, and she made something of it. She made a whole lot out of it. And she drew a pretty lousy hand. She didn't whine about it or waste time bitching to the gods. She took the cards they gave her and she played them."

Angrily she snapped the book shut, "You don't understand," she said.

"So tell me," I said. "What's the deal?"

"You don't understand anything." She paused. "Diabetes isn't going to beat me," she said. "I'm too strong for it. It isn't going to win." There was silence.

"Okay," I said. "Wanna go out?"

"What?"

"I have permission from your parents and the docs to take you out. Wanna get out of here and go walk around the pond?"

She looked at me uncertainly. "Do I have to talk about this?"

"What's to talk about?" I said. "It's your call what you do. I'm just offering you a chance to get out of the hospital."

"Okay," she said, getting up. "I gotta get dressed."

"I'll sign us out," I said, and left.

The pond was a few miles away so we headed to the parking lot for the car. Aspasia wasn't talking on the way out and I kept up idle chatter to keep things from getting too awkward. When we both got into the car I fastened my seat belt, crossed my arms and said, "Start, car."

Aspasia looked over at me uncertainly and then at the dashboard as though she wasn't sure whether it would start or not. I repeated, "Start, car, I told you to start."

"What are you doing?" she said.

"This car is going to start," I said. "I told it to."

"You have to turn the key," she said. "What's wrong with you?"

"I'm too strong for that," I replied. "This car won't beat me." I got out of the car and started kicking the tires. "Start, goddamn it," I yelled. Someone walking to their car a few rows over stopped and stared.

Aspasia got out of the car and saw the person looking and said quietly, "Michael, stop it."

I just kicked the tires even harder and said, "It's going to do what I want it to do." I started hitting the car with my hand and then holding my hand and shaking it. "Ow," I said, "goddamn car."

"Michael," she said, "if you don't stop this I'm going back to the hospital."

"Get in," I said and quietly got into the car and turned it on. I didn't say a word, just drove out of the lot toward the road.

Aspasia turned around and looked back. The person had walked into our row and was staring as we left. She turned back around. "Michael," she said, "you're weird."

"Yeah, somebody would have to be weird to do that," I replied.

Aspasia was quiet after that and I started up the dumb chatter again just to give her a chance to think. I babbled on, pretending not to notice her silence, all the way to the lake.

We had walked halfway around when it started turning into an ordeal. The baby chose this moment to try to lie down on her favorite nerve again and every time she did, the pain was sharp enough that I broke out in a sweat. All I could do was wait until the pain passed. I was getting increasingly frustrated with all the starting and stopping.

"Why don't we just sit down?" Aspasia said. "Do you have to get back right away?"

I laughed. She was sounding like a sensible grown-up whereas I was acting like an impatient kid. We sat down and I breathed a sigh of relief.

"So," I said, "how're you doing with your dad?"

"All right," Aspasia said carefully, picking up a twig and drawing in the dirt with it.

"Yeah, right," I said. "So tell me how you really feel."

"I hate him," she said solemnly. She paused for a moment. "Are you going to tell him?"

"Nope," I said. "I wouldn't tell him what you say unless it was life-threatening. Besides, he already knows it. I think the way your father's acting, it's inevitable you're going to hate him," I remarked.

"I know he thinks he's helping," Aspasia said. If I wasn't going to defend him, she would have to. "I know he loves me."

"That too," I agreed. "But it probably doesn't help that much when he's yelling in your face."

"He's under a lot of pressure at work," she said.

"True," I said. "He doesn't know what to do at home and he doesn't know what to do at work right now, either. And he ought to throw up his hands, at least at home, and admit he doesn't know. But that's a little tough for your father to admit. He has some kind of stubborn thing—not that anyone else in your family has it, mind you," I said dryly.

Aspasia was silent. In front of us the light on the lake dazzled with a steady radiance that was mesmerizing. "I wonder what Aspasia would say about that," I said, gesturing to the lake. "How can anything that beautiful be so totally uncaring? It doesn't matter to that lake whether you or I live or die."

Aspasia glanced up and then back at me. She looked puzzled but didn't say anything. Not many eleven-year-olds worry about lakes.

"Do you ever talk to her?" I asked. The pain and the white light on the lake were getting to me and I had to admit I was getting a little spacy.

"Talk to who?"

"Aspasia," I said. "I'd be curious what she thinks about all this."

"Michael, you are too totally weird. You can't talk to ghosts. Besides, there isn't any such thing."

"Really?" I said. "Jung talked to ghosts and he was one of the greatest psychologists of all time. They used to come visit him in his house."

I turned to look at her to see how she was taking this and for a second I had a flash of an older woman, the eyes the same, the face thinner and her body without the easy fluidity that signals youth. Right after that I saw her much younger, a preschooler with her face shining as only kids' faces do.

That happened to me sometimes. The person was all those time periods, not one. Aspasia wasn't any more the eleven-year-old I saw in front of me than she was the forty-five-year-old she would be. She was all of it and sometimes I just lost track of what somebody looked like at the time. I had never told anybody that. It was just too weird even for a kid to appreciate and kids had a wider range than most adults.

"Besides," I said, "you gotta have somebody inside your head you run all this stuff by. How else are you gonna figure anything out?"

There was silence for a moment. Aspasia had just

been doing and not thinking. Pretty clearly she had not been running anything by anybody or figuring anything out.

"Michael," Aspasia said quietly, "I hate diabetes."

"Understandably," I said. "It's a hassle."

"It sucks," she added.

"Agreed," I said. "Which is why you confuse people so. Nobody gets it why you give it so much power." I shuddered. "I can't stand anything having power over me. You talk about me being weird? Give me a break. It's more than a little weird that you decide to turn an ant into King Kong."

"What do you mean?" she said. "I don't give it any power."

"You give it the power to put you in a hospital," I said. "That is not exactly something diabetes can do on its own. It has to have a lot of help from you to do something that big."

There was silence again. "I don't do anything," Aspasia said stubbornly. And then more quietly, "I'm not going to do anything."

"And nobody can make you," I said. "So don't worry about that. If you think they're going to make you, forget it. Nobody can make anybody do anything, really. You're on your own, kid." I got up. "Time for this two-ton truck to get moving. Let's head back."

Aspasia frowned and got up, looking uncertain. She looked like something didn't seem settled or finished about the conversation. Which was exactly where I wanted to leave it.

I slowly made my way back from dropping off Aspasia to my office in Psychiatry, speed of any sort being nothing but a sweet memory. Why wasn't there a blues song about this: "You got a belly like a wash-board, honey. I got one like a wash tub." I passed a corner I usually slid around and walked carefully down the stairs I always took two at a time. "You some kind of jack rabbit baby; I just like an ol' broken down truck."

The song only helped a little. Unexpectedly, tears came to my eyes. Which was dumb, dumb, dumb. This whole thing was temporary. Was I having some kind of hormonal tidal wave that I was acting like a nit? One thing was for sure. My reaction to pregnancy did not bode well for aging. No doubt about it. I was not going to do aging well.

The door of my office was open and to my surprise Carlotta was sitting cross-legged on the couch, reading. She was wearing pedal-pushers and a silk sleeveless striped shirt. I thought pedal-pushers went out twenty years ago but if Carlotta was wearing them they must be back. I smiled and lumbered in. Kibitzing with a friend was a whole lot better than pissing and moaning about a few extra pounds.

"Adam said you were still here," she said, looking up. "There are some weird women in the world," she added, holding up *Violent Attachments,* a book about women who fall in love with psychopaths. Her voice was cheerful but her eyes weren't. They had some funny thing in them that wasn't cheerful at all.

"Sick puppies everywhere," I replied. "Not just women. The men they're involved with are no slouches in the weird department.

"That's hardly your usual reading material," I added, plopping down in my desk chair and putting my feet up on the couch. As a lawyer in the attorney general's office, Carlotta sometimes dealt with child abuse and rape cases but they always upset the hell out of her. You wouldn't know from her calm and efficient demeanor in court, but they gave her nightmares. Ordinarily, she didn't read anything about deviancy she didn't have to.

"I'm just trying to feel better about Hank," she said, getting up and closing the door. "At least he's not a psychopath. It could be worse."

A wave of alarm shot through me followed by a jolt of rage. If that man had laid one finger on my oldest friend. . .

"It's not that," Carlotta said, seeing my face when she turned around. "Just listen. I need to talk."

She sat back down and crossed her legs. "He's cross-dressing," she said bluntly.

"Whoa," I replied. "You're kidding." I was silent for a moment, trying to take this in. Hank was a judge and had been Carlotta's steady boyfriend for about a year now. He was close to six-four and had a sort of Marlboro man look. It was hard to see him in a bra and panties. I wondered briefly if he wore black lace underneath his robes but decided not to make any jokes. Carlotta didn't look in the mood.

"How'd you find out?"

"Walked in on him." Carlotta took a sip of her coffee and stared into the cup like she was peering into tea leaves or maybe she was just watching the rerun. "He was wearing some pink frilly stuff of mine. I laughed without thinking. I thought for a second it was some kind of joke."

"Not likely," I said.

"No kidding. I feel like a shit."

"Why do you feel like a shit? What did you do?"

"What he wears shouldn't matter . . . but it does. She sighed and leaned back. I haven't had an orgasm with him since. I don't even want him to touch me. Every time he tries, I keep thinking about those pink panties. He looked ridiculous. I'm not supposed to say that. I'm not supposed to think that."

"Why not?"

"Well, it seems a little shallow."

"You're getting into that politically correct thing again, aren't you? I can't believe you are. Oh, come on, Carlotta. You know as well as I do: you can choose who you sleep with but you can't choose who you *want* to sleep with. Nobody gets to choose that." I could hear the vehemence in my voice. I was fiercely loyal to Carlotta and I couldn't stand it when she got down on herself.

"He says if I loved him it wouldn't matter. He's right. It shouldn't."

"Oh yeah, try gaining three hundred pounds and see how much he wants to hop into the sack with you."

Carlotta didn't answer but she didn't look reassured either. "Maybe I'm too uptight."

"Carlotta, for Christ's sake. These folks with special interests: golden showers, rubber corsets, men in garter belts—they're always quick to say there's no right or wrong involved, it's just what interests you. That's true, but the problem is they only apply it to them, never to you. So if they're turned on by wearing pink panties and that's legitimate, why isn't it legitimate for you *not* to be turned on by a man in pink panties? I don't get it. They never want you to be judgmental about them but they're wildly judgmental back."

"Have you dealt with this?"

"Not with Adam, thank God. Adam just likes sex, and he likes it plain and simple. That poet from New York. Remember him, a few years back? I don't know if

I ever told you. He wanted me to wear a rubber girdle—most damned uncomfortable thing I've ever had on. I thought I'd die of heat stroke. Somehow it killed the mood, wearing a rubber tube and developing a heat rash. He had a fit about my not liking it. Accused me of Puritanical ancestors. That really hurt," I muttered. "My ancestors were land pirates, used to make a living wrecking ships on the North Carolina coast and scavenging the wreckage. It's not much, but at least they weren't Puritans burning people at the stake."

"Michael, I'm talking about pink panties, not that North/South business which you Southerners keep fighting."

"Well," I said, "the South didn't win and you know how Southerners are when they don't win. They just keep trying. Never mind it was the most shameful cause that ever existed in—"

"Michael."

"What? Now we have to stay on one topic? When did this happen? A friend is someone you don't have to make sense with. It's right there in *Love Story.*"

Carlotta laughed. "It is not. Love is not having to say you're sorry."

"Since when? That's the stupidest thing I've ever heard. If you don't say you're sorry to somebody you love, who are you supposed to say you're sorry to? Someone you don't give a shit about? Why?"

Carlotta shook her head but her somber mood seemed to have lightened. "I don't know what to do," she said.

"Yes, you do," I said. And then, for once, I shut up. She did know. For my money there was a simple litmus test about relationships. Sooner or later it was the middle of the night and you were nude, toe to toe under the covers. And you either wanted to be there or you didn't. It was as simple as that.

Carlotta didn't. And try as she might, she wasn't going to be able to change that.

"So what happens now?" I asked.

"I'm having dinner with him. We're supposed to talk about it."

"Want me to come along?" I said. "I'll tell him you can like whatever you damn well please and he is not to guilt trip you and do that whining thing."

Carlotta laughed again. "Shit," she said. "I wish you could. I could just eat dinner and you could get on his case and then by contrast, I'd seem so reasonable."

"Usually works that way," I replied. "I've made all kinds of people seem reasonable in my time. I don't think people appreciate that aspect of my personality. Alas, I have to hang around to see the parents of a kid on the pediatric unit. Then I've got a doctor's appointment and therapy. Seems Marion thinks there's some work to be done."

"Imagine that," Carlotta said.

I was waiting after work to catch Susan and Gary when they came to take Aspasia home. The nurse called me from the nurse's station when they came and asked them to wait before they went in. I still didn't want Aspasia even to see me talking to them, so I met them in the hall and went into one of the small conference rooms on the pediatric ward.

After the greetings were over and we had settled in I turned to Gary. "You got any vices I don't know about?" I asked. "Ever smoke, anything like that?"

He and Susan looked at each other uncertainly. "What are you talking about?" he said.

"Leave your socks on the floor, anything?"

"Well, he's not the neatest," Susan said hesitantly. Gary just stared at her.

"Okay," I said, getting up. I leaned forward and got in Gary's face and said loudly, "You are not going to leave your socks on the floor. Do you hear me? You are not. So help me God, if you leave your socks on the floor one more time, you are going to be in more trouble than you've ever dreamed of. I can't believe I've raised someone stupid enough to leave their socks on the floor. What kind of stupid-ass person can't even pick up a pair of socks? Do you think I'm a personal servant or something, that I should spend my life following you around and picking up your socks? What are you trying to do? Make me crazy? Is this your idea of a fun time, making me miserable for no reason at all? Sometimes I think you don't have the sense God gave a gnat for some of the stupid-ass things you do. If you don't pick up your socks you are not going to leave this house. You are going to sit in this house and rot until you learn to pick up a pair of socks." I was going to go on for a while but something flared in Gary's eyes and I stopped.

I sat back down. "Okay," I said. "Feel like picking up your socks?"

"Fuck you," he said, with considerable force behind it.

"Exactly," I said.

"So what are you saying, Michael?" he exploded. "That we should just let her do whatever she goddamn well pleases? What she goddamn well pleases is to drink every soda and eat every candy bar she can beg, borrow or steal." The anger just poured out. I made a note not to get in his face again, even for a demonstration. He just wasn't that tightly wrapped right now.

"Whoa, Gary," I said softly. "I'm on your side. I'm not offering her candy bars."

"You might as well be," Gary snorted.

"Gary," I said, bluntly. "You want her alive or you want to be right? Because you may have to choose. All I'm saying is that when you order people around it gets their backs up. Even kids. Actually, especially kids. Certainly Aspasia. You don't have a gene in your body that *could* produce a kid passive enough to be that compliant. Besides, it's true for anybody. When you're ambivalent about something and somebody holds down one end of the ambivalence, the other just naturally pops up. So if you take responsibility for her diabetes, she doesn't have to."

"Michael," Susan said. "We can't just let go. She'll kill herself."

"Maybe," I said. "But she will surely kill herself if you don't." There was silence.

"I'm not saying abandon her," I replied. "I'm saying you've got to get *sneakier* about this thing. A kid named Kimberley Dent is going to invite her over to spend the night," I said, "and you need to let her go."

"You must be kidding," Gary said. "She'd end up in the hospital again."

"Kimberley has diabetes," I said. "And she takes care of it beautifully. She's also very cool and athletic and someone Aspasia could look up to. Her mother knows all about diabetes and I told her Aspasia was a hundred percent noncompliant. We'll work out a plan. But the plan will be that they have something very cool to do that Aspasia isn't going to want to miss for a trip to the hospital. Come on. They'll take their shots together."

Gary and Susan both looked stricken. They didn't

have any control over Aspasia anyway but they still had some fantasy they did, and having her go out of their sight overnight to anywhere *but* a hospital was almost too scary to contemplate. Clearly they thought they'd get a call in the morning that she was in intensive care or worse.

"And another thing. When she gets back, let's say she does okay—not a single 'I told you so.' You don't even ask how it went. You act like her taking care of herself is nothing unusual." I took a deep breath. The next part would be harder but I might as well go for broke as long as I was losing anyway.

"There's another thing. You have to lift this ban on activities," I said. "She has got to get back to sports and remember who she is."

"Why?" Gary said bluntly. "That's like rewarding her for this stupidity."

"Why is because you can't play well if you don't take care of your health," I said. "Why is because she'll miss some goals and she won't be able to keep up with the other kids and she won't be able to stand that. And then she'll see Kimberley playing well and she won't be able to tell herself that she can't do it anymore because of the diabetes because Kimberley can. Do you think for one second that Aspasia would rather lose than take her insulin? Get her in a close one, so to speak, and then offer her insulin. She won't turn it down unless she's caught in some major, stupid power struggle she feels she just has to win. She's already in a power struggle with diabetes, which she has got to get off if she wants to have a life. She can't be in one with you, too."

I looked back and forth from Gary to Susan, at the fear and uncertainty in both their faces. At the misplaced pride and stubbornness in Gary's. It was absolutely the moment of truth. The moment where a parent has to suck it up, back down, swallow their pride and lose a power struggle for the sake of the child. Even when they were right to begin with. Not every parent can do it, even with stakes this high. "Gary," I said softly. "That look on your face. You look just like Aspasia."

I was late getting to my therapy session but it didn't seem to phase Marion at all. Thank God she didn't make any kind of psychoanalytic interpretation of my tardiness. Sometimes being late just meant your last meeting ran over, but psychoanalytic theory never seemed to take the outside world into account. Except for Marion. She must be doing some kind of neo-Freudian adaptation, I decided, one that paid attention to the problem, left a lot of your childhood in the past and didn't pronounce you resistant if you got caught in traffic. Freud must be spinning.

She sat very still, very upright, with an air of complete serenity. Her long blue skirt draped naturally over her crossed knee with the kind of easy fluidity that meant it cost more than my car. Which, actually, wouldn't have been that much. I looked at her calm face and wondered vaguely what would happen if I confessed to being an ax murderer. Probably she'd ask me how I felt about it. Could serenity like that come from meditation, I wondered? Or maybe this was just better living through chemistry.

The night had turned warm and I pulled my hot, sticky shirt off my chest and took a moment to get my breathing back down to normal. The doctor had to have it wrong. I couldn't possibly have gained seventy-five pounds in this pregnancy and it was absolutely totally impossible that I was tipping the scales at 190 plus. I was going to break 200 pounds if this kept going and that was totally impossible. I spread my knees a little to keep my thighs from sticking together and looked at Marion. What? Was her side of the room air conditioned and mine wasn't?

"Marion," I said. "You know the best thing about basketball?"

She raised her eyebrows in a question mark but didn't speak.

"You always know if you're winning or losing. You do. It's right there on the scoreboard. You can look up any time and see. Football's even better. In football after every play you know if you gained five yards or lost five. There's nothing in real life like it. In life you never know what's going on and you sure as hell don't know if you're winning or losing.

"In sports, well, you can argue about *why* you're winning or losing but most of it is bullshit, anyway. You lose when they score more points than you do. That's it. But when is a coach ever going to say that when they shove a microphone in his face? 'Why'd you lose, coach?'

"'They scored more points than we did.' I'd vote for him for president if he said that. I love it when the commentators say, 'They've got to get some points on the board.' Uh, duh, what do you think? They don't know that? They haven't been trying? You know those bumper stickers that say, 'basketball is life.'"

"Yes."

"Well, it's not true. Basketball is better than life."

Marion had listened to me rant without saying much. Now she interjected, "With what, Michael." When I didn't answer, she said softly, "You don't know where you are with what? With the baby? With Adam?"

"I know some things," I said grumpily. "My friend Carlotta's boyfriend is cross-dressing and that ball game is over. She's going through the motions but it's one of those things that can turn a regular game into a sudden death overtime in a heartbeat." I glanced up. "Don't look at me like that. It's not a right or wrong thing. I'm sure there are millions of women out there dying for a man in pink panties but I can tell you Carlotta is not one of them. And there's another thing. It's not like telling somebody they're driving for the basket too much to the right and they need to go to the left some. It's like trying to coach reaction times. What you get is what you got. You're not gonna change what makes a person's toes curl up. Carlotta only likes one person in the family to be wearing panties, so to speak, and it ain't him."

Marion looked thoughtful but didn't speak. "Then I have this eleven-year-old kid. She's shooting at the wrong basket. It happens sometimes in the heat of a game. Somebody gets the ball on the rebound and puts it up again without thinking. But this kid is doing fast breaks to the other end of the court over and over again. Worse, she's playing in the majors. Carlotta isn't. Face it, Marion. Men come and go. Carlotta's just playing in a regular game. But this kid is betting the house."

"You can't persuade her of this?"

"Have you tried to persuade an eleven-year-old of anything? It would be easier to solve the Arab/Israeli conflict. And then there's my sex offender group. Ever seen someone playing badminton in the middle of a football game? Not a pretty sight. That was the last therapist who had this group I'm running. And they all knew she was playing badminton. I know what game I'm in but I can't figure out the plays."

"Is this really why you're feeling lost, Michael?" she said softly. "What about Adam and the baby?"

"It is not going to be a problem because this pregnancy is never going to end. I'm caught in the *Twilight Zone.* I'm just going to keep expanding until I am the size of a house and people come to stare at me in a circus. Nobody told me but there's an elephant somewhere in the family tree and my gestation period is two and a half years. No wonder my mother doesn't like me. She, by the way, is off to Vegas on a suicide mission."

"What did you used to do when you felt like this?"

"Shoot a few baskets. Try to kill someone in a pickup game. You know, normal stuff." I shook my head in frustration. "Now look at me."

"There's a package for you," Adam said when I climbed into bed. He reached over to the nightstand and handed me a small box.

I looked at it curiously. "It's from my mother. Think I should call the bomb squad?"

"Maybe she's trying to make amends," Adam replied.

I just looked at him. Clearly he didn't know my mother. I had never once heard Mama say the word "sorry" to anybody in her entire life. Make amends for what? You didn't need to make amends if you were never wrong.

I tore open the packaging and pulled a tiny jewelry box out. I opened the hinge and found myself staring at a large ruby ring with diamonds on either side. The note said, "If you don't want it, keep it for your daughter. Maybe she'll appreciate the finer things."

"Boy," Adam said. "Is that for real?"

"Oh, yes," I replied. "It's for real. Mama doesn't like fake anything."

"Does your mother have that kind of money?"

"She appears to be liquidating her retirement fund. Adam, I do not know what to do about this. Mama's in Vegas with a hundred and ten thou of her retirement money and I can't stop her. But it just doesn't seem right to stand by and let my mother turn herself into a bag lady. And there's some con man she's hooked up with."

"So why don't you go after him?"

"What?"

"You can't always get through to victims. You know that. The perp often has too much control over them. So, why don't you get a line on the guy? See if you can scare him a little. Maybe he doesn't know she's got you for a daughter. That would scare most people."

I thought about it. How would I find him? Brenda. I'd call Brenda. One way or another, I could probably get his name. And then?

"Not bad," I said. I put the ring down and turned on my side to face Adam. Gently, I put my hand on the soft hair curling through his open shirt. He put the book down he was reading and turned to me, a question in his eyes. I started to answer it in the way he liked best, when, for some reason, Carlotta came to mind.

"Adam," I said. "Have you ever even considered wearing pink panties?"

"Excuse me?" he said. "You want me to wear pink panties? Did I hear that right?"

"No, no, no. I don't want you to wear pink panties."

"I distinctly heard you raise the question." He looked amused. "Now don't be shy."

"Adam," I said firmly, "I'm not voting for pink panties. I swear. I'm just trying to figure out why a man would *want* to wear pink panties. I mean, what are they thinking about? Are they trying to imagine they're female and if so, then they're having sex with another female. Which makes it being gay by proxy, which seems like kind of a stretch. I mean they're doing a male/female thing really, so that's quite the imagination. Or maybe they're not pretending to be female, maybe they think the wrong sex got the pink panties. It *could* have evolved that men got the pink panties. When you think about it, in most species, men got the colors and the frills. Maybe they're just bitching about evolution. Do you think that's it?"

"Didn't they teach you about that kind of thing in graduate school?"

"As if anybody has a clue why a guy wants to wear pink panties."

"This is the kind of thing you think about?"

"Well, yeah, sometimes."

"You sticking with therapy?"

"Never mind," I said frostily. "That's the last time I'll be asking you about pink panties."

"Oh no," he said, grabbing me around my voluminous belly and snuggling his head in my neck. "Don't take away the pink panties. You're so sexy when you're talking pink."

"Adam, you never take me seriously. You think I'm funny when I'm dead serious."

"Especially then," he agreed.

11

"DR. STONE," HE SAID, GETTING UP AND LEANING OVER THE desk to shake hands. Behind him I saw a set of framed handcuffs on the wall. What on earth would induce someone to put a set of framed handcuffs on the wall? The first time he handcuffed someone? A famous person he handcuffed? A little S&M on the side? I shook it off.

"Michael," I said.

"Arnie Watkins," he said, sitting back down. The note from Captain Watkins had been at my desk when I got out of another unproductive group session. Dutifully, I'd gone straight to his office.

There was a pause while the captain sized me up. I didn't mind. I was doing the same. He was a big guy, close to six-five, and easy on the eyes, as Wyonna would say. He had a buzz cut and a nicely shaped head under it. He looked like a marine—a very young marine. You could say eighteen just because of his job but he could have passed for sixteen. I wondered idly why everybody was getting so young these days. Here was a captain in corrections who wouldn't be allowed to order a drink with a driver's license in his hand. You go in for surgery these days and you're lucky if your surgeon can grow a beard.

He crossed his arms when he sat back down and I noticed the bulging muscles in his shirt. It was always a mystery to me why cops and criminals had such a shared passion for weight-lifting, but you could build a lot of rapport discussing reps with either one of them.

"You wanted to see me?" I asked, when Arnie didn't speak. He seemed to be making up his mind about something and when he started in, he did so tentatively.

"Stacy says you're a good guy." He paused, blinking. "Now if that's not politically correct . . . I don't know what the heck you're supposed to say these days."

"Don't turn yourself into a pretzel," I replied. "It doesn't matter to me. I think you were going to warn me about something. Probably being nosy."

He laughed. "We've got an investigation going, Michael. You can't be futzing about."

"Investigation of what?"

"Stacy didn't tell you?" he asked. "Drugs." I guess he had made up his mind. "The drug rate here has doubled. We usually test four percent positives on our urine screens and we're edging up to ten."

"My guys?" I said, aghast.

"What would make you think that?" he said, looking at me curiously.

I shrugged. "I'd suspect my crew of anything."

Arnie laughed. "Not that we know. But that's the point. We don't know. We can't find a snitch to save our lives."

"Anything going on in the print shop?"

"Why?"

"Nothing really. Just Stacy mentioning there's a sudden rush to be a printer."

"I doubt it. We've gone over all the shops and the classrooms with dogs. Nothing doing. Could be the print shop is just an easy gig."

"But what if the drugs just weren't there that day?"

"Wouldn't matter," he said. "The dogs will pick up the residue of drugs, even if they're gone. Clean as a whistle."

"How long has this been going on?"

"Awhile," he said. "Several months. Although the drugs seem to come and go. I don't need to tell you, I hope, not to tell anyone about this."

I shook my head.

"We thought we had it solved," he said. "Thought it might be a staff member who got fired," he added.

"Eileen?" I asked, incredulous.

"You said it, I didn't," he responded.

"I don't think so," I said emphatically. Then I paused. "At least I wouldn't have thought so. But . . ." I threw up my hands, "What do I know? Who would have thunk she'd have done what she did?"

"The theory was when she went away the drugs might go away. But they didn't. So probably not Eileen."

"So why is it a problem for me to talk to the guy who runs the print shop?"

"It's not that big a deal if you do it once and leave it alone. But Stacy seems to think you're not likely to because your guys are congregating there. You've got to remember the whole place is hypersensitive right now and they'll be wondering if you're involved with the investigation—either of them. There's the murder investigation going on, too, you know."

"You talking about the inmates? They didn't know I talked to him. I went in when no one was there."

He looked at me like I'd grown two heads. "Don't kid yourself," he said. "They know everything and anything that happens in a prison. Like they say: the staff have a life. You are the inmates' life."

I didn't say anything. I knew he was right the moment he said it.

"Just be careful, Michael. Don't forget somebody's got a weapon in there somewhere and they've used it once already. You could end up getting close to something you don't even know you're close to and freaking somebody."

I digested that. Not a pretty thought. "Arnie," I said slowly. "Why would inmates want you to turn your back on them in a group?"

"Did they?" he said. "What group? Your sex offender group?"

"Yep."

"You're sure."

"Positive. Guy started arm-waving, stomping about, grandstanding, got behind me. I came within a hair's breadth of turning around to see him. Didn't feel right about it and didn't do it. Everybody looked upset that I didn't except a kid named Terrance. I thought he looked relieved, but I don't know. Afterward . . ." I broke off. I'd started to tell him they'd asked for Eileen back but didn't want to somehow.

"Terrance," Arnie said quickly and picked up a pen. "What's his full name?"

Afterward, I had second thoughts about the eager way he copied down Terrance's name and decided to check it out with Stacy. I walked slowly over to the social work building and, on the way, passed the print shop. I glanced inside through the open door and saw Jim and Rudolph standing next to a huge machine that was partially disassembled on the floor.

Jim wasn't lying about his mechanical ability. I would not have a clue how to fix that machine but if Jim didn't know how, Rudolph would have spotted it by now. But it wasn't the machine that drew me. It was the easy way Jim had his hand on Rudolph's shoulder. I cringed at the sight. It crossed all sorts of boundaries to be touching an inmate or letting an inmate touch you. I didn't casually put my hand on my dentist's shoulder or straighten my surgeon's tie. In a prison, being allowed to casually touch staff was the final stage of grooming. It meant Jim had Rudolph completely in his pocket.

"Sure is easy to find you these days," I said, finding Stacy sitting at his desk buried behind a mound of paper.

"Too easy," he said, irritably. "There's a reason they call it a desk job. By God, that's just what they mean. And people wonder why I give this kind of thing up every few years and go back to being on the front lines. Everyone treats me like I'm some kind of freak for doing that. They're all clawing to go up and I'm taking the escalator down but I ask you, Michael, how long could you sit in a chair and sign time sheets?"

"Two minutes," I said, "counting the getting up and the getting down. I'm never surprised when you throw this kind of thing over. I'm just surprised you keep coming back to it."

"The truth? I get tired of incompetence at the top," he said, pushing the paper away and sitting back. "Sooner or later I get enough seniority that I can move up and I start thinking about all the asinine decisions that have come down the pike. Then I start thinking my Jaguar needs a tune-up which—considering what the state pays line workers—almost guarantees I have to get an administrative job. Come on," he said. "Let's go to the cafeteria and get a cup of coffee. I'd like to take a walk somewhere away from the prison but it's too much trouble to get in and out of here and I have to work late tonight."

I followed him out of the room and down the corridor. "Well, if you're supporting a car like that, it's a wonder you're not selling drugs. Speaking of which," I said, "I am royally pissed at you. A captain I don't know trusts me enough to tell me there's an avalanche of drugs at the prison and my good old buddy Stacy doesn't?"

"His to tell," Stacy said. "Besides, I don't trust you. You'd go mucking around in it for sure and that's a scary thing here, Michael. The drug business is pretty lucrative in prison. There aren't a lot of other shows in town."

"Oh, give me a break. You told me yourself you've had one killing in a decade. Besides, you talk as though I act like a total and complete fool, and I insist it's a sometimes thing. Mostly, I act reasonably sane."

"Most times," he said.

"Beats most people," I said.

"That too," he added.

We walked in silence out of the building. When we were crossing the courtyard and away from any of the buildings I spoke again. "Stacy, I told Arnie about something that happened in group. Not a big thing, but somebody got behind me, ranting and raving. I'm pretty sure they wanted me to look at him, which would have meant turning my back on the group. I didn't do it."

"Good idea," Stacy said.

"Anyway, afterward everybody looked upset that I hadn't, except a new kid in the group, a guy named Terrance. He looked relieved—well, I thought so, anyway. So, anyway, I told the captain—what's his name—about it today and he got all excited. Wrote Terrance's name down. What's he going to do?"

We were approaching the cafeteria building and Stacy stopped. Both of us knew enough not to discuss anything around the inmate workers in the cafeteria, the prison grapevine being a fearsome thing. He shrugged. "He'll call him in," he said. "Talk to him."

"Yeah, but why would Terrance talk to *him?*" I asked. "Terrance doesn't strike me as a snitch. I don't think he's psychopathic and he grew up in the criminal subculture. Cops are the enemy; snitching is for shit. It's against his code to snitch. Doesn't Arnie know that?"

"Sure," Stacy said dryly. "Arnie knows that. But it won't matter. Terrance'll talk to him."

"Why?"

"He'll make him an offer he can't refuse," Jim said. "They do it all the time."

"Like what?"

"Standard procedure," Jim said. "Tell him he'll be out of there in ten minutes if he talks and the word would go out he "didn't tell those motherfuckers nothing." If he won't talk, they'll hold him for an hour and a half and spread the word he did. Hard for an inmate to turn down."

"You're kidding," I said, but Stacy looked so grim I knew he wasn't. "That stinks. Isn't that a little dangerous for the inmate?"

"Could be," Stacy said, "but it does work. And the stakes are pretty high here, in case you haven't noticed." He started walking again.

"Works unless he's young," I muttered more to myself than Stacy. "Young and not that savvy yet." I caught up to Stacy. "I don't know what Terrance would do with an offer like that."

"He'll take it," Stacy said confidently. "Be a fool not to. Trust me, whatever Terrance knows, Arnie will have within . . ." he glanced at his watch. . . "I'd say the next twenty minutes. Arnie's a good guy but a little gung ho. He's over there by now."

I didn't say anything but I didn't like it. I'd just set up the only member of my group who wasn't up to something. Didn't anybody except me think that was a problem?

I was on my way out of the prison when I saw Rudolph in the sally port ahead of me. I hurried through—as much as you can when you're waiting for giant slabs of steel to inch forward at the speed glaciers move—and caught up with him outside. It was my good luck to run into him outside the walls. I had remembered what I wanted to ask him and Arnie was right; anything inside a prison was seen by some inmate somewhere.

"Rudolph," I yelled. He had started off down the street but he turned and paused when I called out, frowning when he saw me.

"Wait up," I said, smiling and acting as though my welcome had been a warm one. He looked uncertain and shifted nervously from one foot to the other while he waited, but stood there while I hurried up. "Remember me?" I asked.

He nodded, but looked distracted and a whole lot less cheerful than when I saw him last. Why did I think Jim had warned him about me? Maybe it was because he looked like a cobra had just slithered across the sidewalk toward him.

"I'm the person who came to visit your shop. I run a sex offender group and I was checking on the men's placements." He had already acknowledged me so obviously he remembered me, but the key to coming across as an airhead-blonde—which is a very useful thing to be at times—is constant dithering without saying anything. Deep down most men think women are oblivious dingbats, anyway, so airhead-blonde will work almost anytime, anywhere, with almost any male, even in this so-called enlightened age. Rudolph looked nervously around while I was speaking as though he was worried somebody might see him talking to me but I, of course, didn't notice.

"Going this way? My car's down here; I'll walk with you." I started walking in the direction he'd been heading and Rudolph reluctantly fell in step. He had already committed himself to that direction so he could hardly say he was going some other way.

"I had a question I forgot to ask the other day," I said. "Have you ever done any follow-up to see how many men who are released get jobs in printing once they get out?"

He shook his head.

"Because I think that having a job is the whole key to keeping people out of prison. You look at these guys' histories. They have terrible employment records. They get unemployed, need some money, maybe they pick up a drug problem. You know, one thing leads to another and before you know it, they hold up a convenience store. But if someone had taken the time to give them a hand, give them a good work ethic, it might never have happened. You know so many of these guys just come from dreadful homes, just dreadful. The job wouldn't have to be in printing for you to have made a difference. Do you have any idea how many people just get jobs and hold onto them once they get out? I would think they could learn a lot about a work ethic just by being in your shop."

We were a half block from the prison by now and Rudolph's shoulders seemed to relax a trifle. He glanced over at me. "Well, I've never followed it up but I've always thought holding a job would make a difference. The problem is all these people on welfare just waiting for a handout. If people got up and went to work every day they wouldn't have time to get in all that trouble. They'd be too damned tired."

"I couldn't agree more," I said. "And if you keep one guy from going back to prison, well just think, it costs thirty thousand a year or something like that to incarcerate one prisoner. Every five years, that's a hundred and fifty thou per prisoner. That's a fair amount of money. But I never get it. The state never seems to want to spend a little bit to save a lot. They scrimp on the programs that would save them the most. Good programs end up trying to make do and get by. I bet you've had to fix those old machines of yours a time or two. Weren't you telling me that some inmate had found a way to save the state money? What's the guy's name? The one who's a lawyer? I'll bet they hassled you endlessly when you tried to get that through. Did it ever work out?"

"Finally," he snorted. "I had to make the calls myself to get the bids. He was right, too. The supplier he knew about was a whole lot cheaper than the one we had or any of the new bidders, for that matter."

"It just amazes you, doesn't it? How did he know that, given that he was in prison?"

"His father is a machinist, has all sorts of connections."

I chuckled. "Shame they don't give you a percentage of what you saved them."

"Damn straight it is," he said. "I had enough trouble just getting them to switch. Even when the guy was way less than the state was paying. The state likes to do things the way the state likes to do them. And don't look for rhyme or reason."

"Amen," I said. "Say, I have a friend that runs a little newsletter for a nonprofit over in Nashua. Was this a paper supplier by any chance? I know my friend was complaining about the high cost of paper, especially since some of the mills shut down."

"Paper, toner, cartridges. Any kind of disposable supplies. Anything but hardware."

"What's the name? Is it anywhere near Nashua?"

"Armand Brothers," he said. "They're up in Berlin, New Hampshire. It's probably not any further than where he's getting it now. It's a small firm, but they've been fine with us. Deliveries are on time and a whole lot less. Frankly, I hope they stay in business. I don't know how they would make a profit on what they're charging us."

I was pondering Rudolph's words uneasily in the car on the way home. No way was Jim Walker trying to save the state money. That was a given. So what was he up to? I was thinking maybe I should go see this supplier and find out when the car phone rang out Beethoven's Ninth. My car phone had somehow gotten stuck on musical rings. To save my soul I couldn't get it to make a normal, mechanical ringing sound. It was a sure sign machines were malevolent.

I stared at it for a moment like I always did. I didn't like the idea of someone being able to find me wherever I was. It was like someone always tapping you on the back when you were dancing. I was doing something, for Christ's sake; I was obsessing about why Jim was trying to save the state money. Besides, when was my car phone ever good news? I hardly gave the number to anyone and nobody called me unless it was really, really important. And really, really important was like having some disease that made you a great case in medicine—never good.

I gave up on the third ring. My relentless curiosity won out. "Michael," the voice said. "Run that thing by me you were saying again in the cafeteria."

Stacy's voice always had a slight burr in it. It was slow and a little bluesy with an easy, almost Southern rhythm. Usually just hearing it made me smile. But say one thing for the phone: you pay a whole lot more attention to sound when you can't see anybody's face. Today his voice sounded different, more staccato and slightly more high-pitched. Underneath there was an undercurrent of excitement or nervousness or something else with an afterburner.

"What thing?"

"That thing you were telling me about seeing Jim and Rudolph. What were they doing?"

"Working on a machine."

"Come on, Michael," he said, impatiently. "Tell me exactly what you saw."

"He had his hand on Rudolph's shoulder," I said slowly, wondering what Stacy was looking for. "They were staring at the machine and there were parts laid out everywhere. It was one of the really big machines, I don't know which one. It looked like they had taken the whole thing apart. Jim was standing really close to Rudolph and talking up a storm."

"Was Rudolph looking at the machine?"

"Sort of . . . I don't know. He was looking at the floor, I think. Like people do when someone's too close to look at directly. All I remember was he had that look on his face like a deer frozen in headlights, you know that look that people get when psychopaths are pouring on the charm and they've bought it big time."

"Jesus Christ," Stacy said. "Jesus H. Christ . . . Like pieces of a puzzle."

"What is?" I said. "What are you talking about?"

"Gotta go," he said suddenly, so abruptly I wasn't sure if he was talking about our conversation or something else. It was almost like someone had walked in. "Gotta go," he said again.

"Is someone there?" I asked. There was silence. "Stacy," I said. "What's going on?"

"I'll call you," he said and the phone went dead.

I felt left high and dry, unsettled and uneasy. I hadn't wanted to be on the phone. Now I didn't want to be off. Stacy had put something together but I didn't know what. What kind of news could it be that Jim had had his hand on Rudolph's shoulder and why did it matter where Rudolph was looking? The more I thought the more annoyed I got at Stacy for leaving me in the lurch like that—but getting ticked didn't make me feel any less uneasy. What if someone had walked in? From the sound of it, it couldn't have been good. I picked up the phone and dialed the prison. The officer on the desk put me through but I got nothing but Stacy's voice mail. Reluctantly I hung up. I'd call Stacy at home later and find out what was going on. That was the plan, anyway.

Eileen was waiting at the house. "How'd you know where I live?" I asked, the moment I was out of the car.

I'd kept the phone number of my little house in the country unlisted and never gave out the address. It didn't just have to do with my obsession for privacy; it was a safety thing. Eileen was a smart lady but hardly a detective. If she could find it, a whole lot of other people could, too. And besides, just looking at her, I realized I didn't trust her. She'd gotten suckered big time and I didn't have a doubt in the world Jim still ran her.

She raised her eyebrows like Groucho Marx and said lightly, "We have our ways."

I stared at her for a moment. Maybe it was the phone call from Stacy and my sense of unease but it didn't seem funny.

"Like what?" I said evenly.

There was silence and then she said, "Jim told me."

"Oh great," I said. "That's just great. Jesus Christ." I blew out a long breath. "Oh, shit, Eileen. That's just marvelous. . . . What the hell. Come on in."

I led her through the house out on the back deck. "Iced tea?" I asked. "Glass of wine?"

"You got anything harder?" Eileen said.

"Sure. You trying to drown your troubles these days?"

"Once in a while," she said, sitting down on the deck and putting her feet up on a chair. I noticed her ankles when she put them up. They looked as swollen as mine. Eileen wasn't living right. She said she had gout. From the looks of her ankles, it wasn't going well.

"Gin and tonic okay?" I asked.

"Sure," she said, taking the glass I brought out and downing a long thirsty drink. I put my iced tea down and walked back into the house. Absentmindedly, I dialed Stacy's number. No answer. I walked back outside with the phone. "Sorry," I said. "I'd gotta keep trying this number."

Eileen shrugged. "No problem," she said. I sat down and we both looked at each other.

"So," I said. "Something brings you here."

She took another drink. "I want to know some things, Michael, but if I ask, you're going to ask me some questions back and then I need to know you'll keep what I say confidential."

"Whoa," I said. "You're way ahead of me. Depends on what it is. Is it illegal?"

"Maybe," she said. "Well, sort of."

"Sort of," I echoed. "There's not much that's 'sort of' illegal."

"Some prison rules are just rules," she said. "You can be fired but you can't be tried so I don't know if that means it's illegal or not."

"So this involves at the least breaking some prison rules."

"Maybe," she said.

"But you don't know for sure if it's actually illegal."

"I'm not sure."

I drank some more iced tea. "I don't know," I said. "Depends."

"That's not good enough."

"Listen, I don't even know what we're talking about. I can't give you any blanket guarantees. For one thing, I don't know if you know what's really going on. Excuse me, Eileen, but I think you're up to your neck in something that maybe you don't even know about."

"Maybe," she said. "Maybe that's why I'm here."

"Let's do this a piece at a time," I said. "What do you want to ask me?"

"What's your relationship with Jim?"

I smiled incredulously. "I beg your pardon? I think that's my line."

She looked down at her drink. It was already three-quarters gone. I began to wonder if I'd have a guest tonight. If she kept this up, she wouldn't be in any shape to drive. "I'm serious, Michael."

"The truth?"

She nodded.

"You won't like it."

"Tell me the truth."

"I think he's a stone-cold psychopath and he's up to his ears in something illegal at the prison. I think he took you for a ride big time and cost you damn near everything. I don't know if he was involved in Clarence's murder or not but I'd bet anything he knows who was."

She was still staring at her drink. "I didn't ask you what you thought about him. I asked what your relationship was."

"He's in my group."

"You're not involved with him?"

"Involved? What are you talking about? Why would you ask?"

She sighed, relieved. "Because you're all he talks about. And he keeps trying to learn everything he can about you."

I digested this. It surprised me and it didn't.

"When do you talk to him?"

She stared into her drink. "There you go."

"That's what you were afraid I'd ask?"

She nodded.

"Because you're not on his visitor list," I said, thinking it through. "The prison wouldn't allow it because you're ex-staff. And standard policy is that ex-staff don't get to visit inmates because they know too much about security. He'll be on a mail monitor for the same reason. And all phone calls are recorded, which means he really wouldn't want to ask these questions on the phone. Right? So how are you in contact with him?"

She shrugged. "Does it matter?"

"It might," I said, after a moment. I picked up the cell phone and dialed again. "It might not. Hell, I don't know." The phone rang out. I glanced at my watch. Stacy surely should be home by now if he had come straight from the prison. I dialed the prison again and asked them to page Stacy. The officer put me on hold.

"So," I said, while I waited. "It couldn't be you're seeing him in person. So, it's either phone calls or letters, but Jim's too savvy to use the phone because he'd know they're recorded. So it's letters or notes. Right?"

"What if it were?"

"How's he getting them past the mail monitor? He's gotta be running another staff member, who's helping him. Why are you telling me this, Eileen? If I tell them and they find out how he's doing it they'll cut the lines of communication and fire the staff. And that'll nearly kill you, because you're so caught up in him."

My voice sounded more impatient than I meant it to. Mostly it was the frustration of trying to reach Stacy. I was still on hold because Stacy wasn't answering and the officer didn't come back on. Finally I gave up and hung up the phone. I needed to pay attention to what Eileen was trying to tell me.

"Why's he asking about you?" she said in reply.

I just looked at her. "Good point," I said, finally. She held out her glass. Silently, I got up and went back to the kitchen to refill it. I felt a little guilty doing it. I was stone sober and Eileen wasn't and it didn't seem a fair match. But Eileen was choosing to get drunk, and I had a feeling she couldn't say what she wanted to say without the alcohol. So who was I to cut her off? Especially with the stakes what they were.

I returned with the glass and sat down again, resisting the impulse to pick up the phone. Two minutes had lapsed, max. I needed to get a grip.

"Here," Eileen said, reaching in her purse. "I want to know the truth. What do you think?"

I took the envelope she handed me and opened it. It was mailed from Burlington, which was nowhere near the prison. Somebody had carried it out and mailed it, for sure. Slowly I read it and then reread it. It started with "My dearest," but the sweet tone was gone by the third sentence. She had apparently already told Jim a fair amount about me because he was asking for details of things she'd already said. Exactly when had she first met me? What did she mean I never cared about the rules? What was my life like outside of prison? Who was the baby's father? And so on. If a lover had asked me all that about another woman, I'd be freaked, too.

I closed the letter and put it back into the envelope. Then I looked at my fingers. There were faint smudges on them. I held the envelope up for a closer look. There was something dark and dusty clinging to it. I rubbed my fingers together and then tried to smell the faint dust. What on earth was it?

"Do they all have these smudges?" I asked.

"Yeah," Eileen said. "I don't know what it is."

"So what do you make of this?" I asked her.

"Well," she said. "I don't know. He's either inter-ested in you as a girlfriend or he's trying to set you up. Either way it doesn't look too good for who I thought he was." She paused. "Maybe I better tell you about group."

I nodded, but just then the phone rang.

I jumped and grabbed it. "Michael," Gary said. "I've got bad news. Really bad. Stacy James is hurt."

"Oh my God," I said, my stomach knotting so hard I put my hand over it. "How bad?"

"He's unconscious," Gary replied. "He was attacked and beaten."

"Alive?"

"Alive, but hurt bad. I don't know, Michael. It's pretty bad. He had bled a lot by the time we found him."

No matter how much you worry about bad news, you're never ready for it. You might see some dark clouds and *think* about rain, but that doesn't prepare you for the storm that rolls in faster than you can run and knocks a tree down on your house. I was stunned. There was the age-old temptation to think it was a dream, that reality would return any minute. "What happened?"

"No fucking idea," Gary said. "He'd been moved. He was in one of the classrooms but I think the attack happened in the hall. A guard found him. Michael, it doesn't look good."

"Which hospital?" was all I said.

Eileen sat silently beside me, which was just as well because I was talking nonstop. "Son of a bitch. Son of a bitch. He told me not to go mucking about. Now what does he do?"

"Michael," she said firmly. "I need to tell you about group."

"Well, you can't," I said. "You can't because I couldn't retain a word of it. I cannot believe somebody like Stacy walked into something like that. He knew his way around." I chattered on while Eileen sat slumped in the side of the car. "Was someone in the office? It sounded like someone came in." I glanced over.

"Later, Eileen," I said more softly. "I just can't concentrate right now."

She closed her eyes as the back end of the car skidded a little on a curve. "Michael, I don't think it's going to help if we get in an accident on the way there."

"That? That's nothing," I said. "Don't worry. I drove like a maniac as a kid."

"You could easily have nine lives," she said solemnly. "But I'm pretty sure I don't.

"I know," she said straightening up. "What was that thing you said to me once—'If you lose the ball, don't make a foul trying to get it back?'"

I looked over at her curiously. "I'm surprised you remember something like that," I said. It seemed strange. Why would Eileen remember something I said in passing fifteen years ago?

"I remember," she said quietly. "You said it the day I brought in the knife."

I glanced over at her. What was she talking about? "What knife?"

"Isn't that funny," she said. "You don't even remember. It was back when we were interns. We had just finished the security training for nonsecurity staff, the one where they talk about all the dos and don'ts. They had made a really big deal, really big, out of contraband and a knife was just about the worst sort, short of a gun. And I opened up my lunch box one day and I had left a paring knife in it." She fell silent.

"So?" I said. "It was just a paring knife, right?"

"Michael," she said. "It was a knife."

"Okay," I said slowly. "So what happened."

"I started to hand it in, of course, turn myself in, but I was really upset. I wasn't sure what would happen. I got up and that's when you said it. You said, 'If you lose the ball, don't make a foul trying to get it back.' I didn't have a clue what you were talking about. I guess you figured that out because you just shook your head and took the knife out of my hand and put it into your purse."

I didn't remember any of this. "Eileen, help me out here," I said. "I don't know why this was important to you."

"Because," she said, "I knew they could have fired you and you wouldn't have told them whose knife it was. Michael, please slow down. It's not going to help Stacy if you get us killed."

I slowed down a little and fell silent as I swung onto the interstate. It just seem so sad to me that something I didn't even remember seemed so important to her. How scared had she been all those years when something as simple as putting her knife into my purse still stood for safety in her mind? But then again there was the cup of tea on the mountain that still stood for solace in mine.

I glanced out at the blackness flying by. Granite

cliffs rose on both sides and I remembered a quarry nearby where I used to rock climb. New England was full of granite, hard and unyielding, strong enough that a quarter-inch ledge would hold your weight without question. The granite was reassuring, in a way. I'd climbed mountains in Colorado that crumbled beneath every step, threatening to take you down with every miniature avalanche. At least whatever you could find to hold you in those old New England cliffs wouldn't let go from under you. Which maybe was Eileen's whole point.

But there was something else here too, a strange harshness in the land I never felt anywhere else in the country. Mount Washington next door was only 5,000 feet but had killed more climbers than the 14,000-foot mountains in Colorado. The weather could shift on a dime in New England and 200-mile-an-hour winds weren't uncommon at the top. Whiteouts—where the fog was so thick you had to hold your hand close to your face to see it—happened all the time and unlucky hikers were found dead at the top in shorts and tee shirts. They had climbed one mountain—a sunny, spring mountain with crocuses budding—and died on another, a mountain locked in an icy storm with high winds and no visibility.

It was more than that, I had to admit, looking at the moonlight slide over the rocks. The harshness was spiritual as well. I had only felt such harshness in one other place in my whole life: Alsace-Lorraine, the drive from Brussels into France, where the land was soaked in blood for hundreds of years and nobody—no matter how little they believed in spiritual things—was untouched by the sense of oppression.

It's those damned Puritans, I thought, as we moved

from the rocks to dairy farms. Even the silos looked forbidding against the sky. Puritan land. What would you expect? And for all I knew that was Eileen's point, too. That she felt the harshness here, enough to expect someone to fire her for a paring knife inside a lunch box.

We turned into the emergency room lot of Conway Regional Hospital, a small hospital halfway between Jefferson and the border. The lot had several ambulances parked here and there and the same kind of loading dock that factories did, only this time the cargo was mostly the human refuge from highways, the true killing fields in this country. "How did this happen?" Eileen said softly. She sounded like a bewildered child.

"I don't know," I said as I pulled into a parking space. "But Eileen, so help me God, when we have time, when Stacy's okay, you are going to tell me everything you know, everything that was happening in group, everything Jim ever said to you. You are going to tell me because I am pretty sure that Gary could be next." Eileen just looked at me, her face sickly in the yellow light from the sodium lamp high above.

I started to get out of the car but she caught my arm.

"Do you think Jim could do something like this?" she said urgently. "He couldn't, Michael. Maybe some other things, but not this. Maybe he would con. Maybe he lied to me. But not this. Not anything like this."

"In a heartbeat," I said and shook her off.

12

GARY WAS STANDING IN THE WAITING ROOM WHEN I ARRIVED, looking haggard and beaten and a little wild all at once. He stopped short when he saw Eileen trailing in behind me. "What's she doing here?" he said as I walked up. Staff who fraternized with inmates were seen as traitors by other staff, turncoats who compromised everybody's safety.

"We were in a meeting," I said. "She was telling me about the group." He didn't look placated. "Jesus Christ, Gary, we don't shun people who screw up. We just fire them. She's still a person. You knew her for fifteen years, for Christ's sake. Who cares now, anyway? How's Stacy?"

"He's in surgery," he said, tearing his eyes reluctantly from Eileen, who stood a few feet back. "They're drilling a hole in his head to relieve the pressure on his brain." He paused. "He's a mess. His head was all caved in when we found him. There was so much blood one of the officers slipped in it."

His tough guy manner had an undertone of fear in it, like things were slipping out of control, which truly they were. I put my arms around him and hugged him and neither of us spoke for a moment. Wisely, Eileen didn't move. We were just standing there frozen when Aspasia walked through the door from the parking lot.

"I told you to wait in the car," Gary barked.

"I have to go to the bathroom," she threw back. He pointed and she headed for it, sullenly.

"What's she doing here?" I asked.

"Susan had gone to a meeting and we were home alone. I couldn't leave her there by herself." Prison wardens did not leave their children alone at home. They had heard too many stories.

"She can't just sit in the car," I offered tentatively. "Maybe there's a—"

"I don't want her involved in this," Gary said. "It won't kill her to wait in the car. It's the least of the problem right now."

Aspasia came back and Gary said, "Get back to the car."

"I'm bored out there," Aspasia said. "I want to look at magazines if I have to hang around."

"She's okay, Gary," I said gently. "Here you can keep an eye on her."

His face clouded over for a moment but he shrugged and Aspasia went over to a seat.

"What happened?" I said.

"An officer was just making his rounds when he found him hidden behind a desk in a classroom. He saw some blood and followed it. Someone had tried to clean up but it wasn't a good job. We found some blood in the hall and some on the floor in the class-room. That's all I know, Michael. No inmate activity in that area at all. It was after hours and the classrooms, the shops, everything was shut down. I don't even know why he was there."

"I do," I said, "At least I know why he was in that building." I told him about the phone call and what Stacy had said. "That's all I know. I sort of thought someone might have come in but I don't even know that for sure. I'm thinking now maybe he was just excited to go check out whatever he was thinking about. I tried to call him later but never got through."

Just then the door to the waiting room swung open and a woman walked in wearing surgical scrubs. She was tall, over six feet, lean and strong, and she had spiked green hair. Gary visibly gasped when he saw it. She looked at him. "Not a word. Not a single one about my hair. I told myself if I ever finished that god-damn residency I'd do whatever I damn well pleased. So it's none of anybody's business."

Gary looked rooted to the spot, like he'd been struck dumb. No way was he going to think anybody could be competent to do surgery with green hair. Out of the corner of my eye, I saw Aspasia look up, inter-ested. "Forget the hair," I said. "How's Stacy?"

She glanced over at Gary with a, "yeah, right" look but answered my question. "He's stable. He'll live, but functioning? Can't say anything now. We'll know more in forty-eight hours."

I started to speak but she held up her hands. "I'd tell you more if I knew anything. That's all I know."

"Speculation? Off the record? Not to be held to it?"

She eyed me carefully. "Well, I think he's got a shot at being okay, if he's not blind, that is. He got beat up in the occipital lobe. But he was still conscious enough after the first blow to cover his head with his hands. Both forearms are broken," she said casually, "multiple fractures. But they broke the force of the blows. Somebody really beat the shit out of him."

Gary finally found his voice. "What was it?" he asked.

"Not sure," she replied.

"Could it have been an odd-shaped metal instrument with ragged teeth on it?" I knew why Gary was thinking that. If it killed Clarence and they never found it, and Stacy was also beat half to death, odds were it was the same one.

"No," she said slowly. "What would make you think that?" She looked at Gary strangely. "Where did you come up with that?" she said again.

"Just a wild guess," he said. "So what was it?"

"Did this guy know it was coming?"

Gary and I looked at each other. "No," Gary said. "There were no signs of a struggle and he didn't call out. He was hit in the back of the head so we don't think he was expecting it. Why do you ask?"

"Because he drew the murder weapon," she said. "That and that other thing you were just describing." She reached into her pocket and came up with a folded piece of paper. It had a drawing on it of three rods, one with jagged teeth, one with something that looked like a ball near the end with some raised indentations on them, and a third that was a straight rod with something like a hook on it.

"This one," she said, pointing at the middle one with raised indentations on it. "This one matches the wounds." Gary and I stared at it dumbstruck.

"He drew this after he was hit?" Gary asked, confused.

"Oh no," she said. "He didn't do this after he was hit. He didn't do anything after he was hit except curl up in a ball and try to survive. I'm sure his lights went out pretty quick. Anyway, there was no blood on this and there was blood all over him. This was in his pants pocket. He must have drawn it before the attack."

Aspasia had tiptoed up to see the picture and now she spoke. "It looks like parts of a car," she said.

"There are no cars inside a prison," Gary said impatiently.

"Well, it's a machine," she said, stubbornly. "It's stuff from a machine even if it isn't a car."

In the movies when all the pieces fall into place, there's a soundtrack that thunders in. In real life you just stand there drooling and feeling like a fool. I don't remember breathing for several minutes and then I just slowly turned to Aspasia in amazement.

"Well, it is." Aspasia said. "What else could it be? I took shop, you know." I sat down cross-legged on the floor, feeling a little dizzy. Like pieces of a puzzle, he had said. "What a dumb-ass I've been," I said. "I walked right by it."

"Are you okay?" Gary asked, looking down at me.

"Oh yeah," I said. "I'm just feeling like an idiot. I'm okay."

"No wonder we couldn't find it," Gary said.

There were a few moments of silence and then he looked down at me again.

"Don't even think about it," he said.

"Think about what?"

"Going over there tonight to look at the machines."

"Don't be ridiculous."

Without a word, he pulled out a cell phone and

dialed the prison. He gave instructions to cordon off the shop as a crime scene.

"This is about preserving evidence, right? You're not seriously thinking I'd go over there and do what Stacy did," I said.

"I'm not thinking anything," Gary replied. "The classroom's already cordoned off as a crime scene. I'm just extending it."

He shook his head and dialed back. Someone needed to go into the personnel files and find out where Stacy's family was. It was time for the lousy middle-of-the-night-emergency phone call that is painful to make and heartbreaking to get.

I didn't stay to hear it. I got Eileen to help me up and went looking for the surgeon. She had disappeared somewhere in the middle of the phone calls and I found her in the doctors' room dictating the surgery. "Sorry to interrupt," I said. "but is he going to wake up before morning?"

"Probably not," she said. "But even if he does, he isn't going to be seeing any visitors."

"You on all night?" I asked.

"Nope, I just came in for the surgery."

"Who do I see about calling me if anything changes?"

"You family?"

"Sister-in-law."

"Yeah, right."

"Closest thing he's got here. Since when is family someone you're related to?"

"All too true," she said. "See the head nurse. Tell her I cleared it."

"What's your name?"

"Dr. Docteur. Don't start in. Just tell her."

* * *

When I got back Gary was sitting in a chair looking thoughtful. "Will you take Aspasia home?" he asked. "Susan'll be back by now."

"Why, where are you going?"

"Nowhere," he said. "I think I'll stay for a while."

"Why? He isn't going to wake up. The doctor just said so and they won't let him have visitors, anyway."

"Just take her home, Michael."

I sat down beside him. "You're not feeling too good about this."

"I should be?"

"You couldn't do anything about it. Shit happens. You couldn't predict Stacy would figure things out and go down there after hours without a backup."

"What'd you mean without a backup? It should have been safe down there. What the hell was an inmate doing out?"

I didn't have an answer for that but started to say some other chirpy, reassuring thing when he held up his hand wearily. "Just take her home," he said. "Okay?"

I looked at him: at the skin which was the sickly color of worried; at the white shirt with a prominent coffee stain on the front. Gary was former military. Maybe he had a bit of a pot belly now and wasn't in the shape he used to be, but nonetheless he usually dressed like his old sergeant might show up at any minute. I had never seen him with a dirty shirt or a rumpled anything. Now he looked halfway to home-less. "Okay," I said, resigned.

I couldn't fix it. Not everything could be redeemed. Gary was ultimately responsible for everybody at the prison and he took that very seriously. An inmate was dead and a staff member nearly so. He'd failed no matter what I said.

At the door Aspasia stopped and turned. She looked at her father uncertainly and then back at me. I just shrugged. She walked back slowly and gently kissed his check, "Good night, Daddy," she said and turned to go.

He looked up and I caught a bit of light in his eyes that hadn't been there before. I take it back. I couldn't fix it, but she'd come close.

The three of us headed for the car. Even Aspasia seemed somber and, as far as I knew, she had never even met Stacy. It had started raining while we were inside but none of us made a dash for the car. Nothing like an assault to make a little rain seem inconsequential. I was tired and wired all at the same time and sleep, that fair-weather friend, wouldn't show up anytime soon. I had a thing about friends who took off just when you needed them but sleep got a bye. It could do whatever it damn well pleased and when it finally dragged its sorry ass back home, you were so glad to see it you didn't say a word.

I started up the car and drove back slowly. The night had turned pitch black. There was a half moon but clouds had rolled in to cover it and the rain just made it worse. It hit me that this was the perfect night to run into a deer. Deer were worth worrying about on a good day in Vermont and at night they were almost impossible to see. Dodging deer on the highway was such an essential skill in Vermont they really ought to put it on the driving test. It wasn't like hitting a rabbit, either. Hitting a deer meant you clipped their tall, spindly legs and threw their big, solid bodies right through the windshield, half the time wiping out everybody in the front seat. Try as I might, I couldn't think of anything more cheerful.

I wondered idly if Gary had been right. If Aspasia and Eileen weren't in the car, would I have made a detour to the prison to check out the machine room? No. Definitely not. Okay, maybe not.

Just then, Aspasia leaned forward and said, "My daddy's really upset, isn't he?"

"Yeah, he is," I replied.

"Why? It wasn't his fault."

"True. Very true. But he feels responsible for everything that happens at the prison, everything bad. It's his job to keep bad things from happening."

"But he can't control everything."

"He knows it in his head but he still feels that way."

"He does the same thing at home."

"Does what?"

"Thinks he can control everything."

"True."

"He must really hate me."

"He doesn't hate you, Aspasia. He thinks he's failed you."

"Why does he think *he's* failed? I'm the one who screws up all the time."

"Because you got diabetes in the first place."

"That wasn't his fault."

"He knows it in his head but he still feels that way."

"Jeez," she said, and leaned back.

Eileen hadn't spoken. Her face looked like a beach after a storm: stripped of old things and laid bare. Thoughts seemed to flicker across her eyes like driftwood floating by. I didn't speak. There was a conversation coming up after Aspasia left and we both knew it.

Adam was asleep when Eileen and I got home and I found his presence strangely reassuring. It crossed my mind that being home alone was usually my idea of peace but somehow Adam's solid, sleeping form seemed . . . well, okay. It meant when this miserable night was over I could fling one arm over his side and feel his breath rise and fall. Not too shabby really, to feel a live creature lying next to you. Probably I'd touch the back of his head and it wouldn't even be caved in or anything. And I didn't see a single drop of blood anywhere. Heck of a thing.

It also dawned on me it helped that he was asleep. Great. A sleeping person was halfway between having nobody there and having a real live human being to contend with. Well, one step at a time. Maybe that was the real reason for pregnancy. It gave you a chance to get used to having somebody around before they actually showed up.

I rubbed my belly absentmindedly and headed down the stairs from the loft to the deck where I'd left Eileen. My belly hurt or ached or felt like lead most of the time now. It felt less and less like a part of me and more and more like a bowling ball somebody duct-taped to my abdomen.

The rain had cleared but the deck was soaked and I put towels on the chairs to sit on. The night had turned luminous and warm with a glistening sheen individually tailored for each leaf and blade of grass. A spider web on the corner of the deck held huge drops of water and I spied a small dot in the corner. The spider was at home, sitting next to raindrops as big as she was. Must be interesting, I thought idly, to be sitting on a shining steel cable with a drop of water as big as you are hanging next to you.

And what did we look like to her? Big galumphing creatures, heedless of all the misery we caused. We probably killed something every time we took a step. She would see it, sitting in the corner. The ants I stepped on. The small spider I brushed away and sent flying into space. I never looked to see if its back was broken by the fall but she might. Point of view was pretty much all there was, when you got right down to it.

"Wow," Eileen said dreamily, watching the moonlight weave together the stream and the woods beyond. "This place is magic."

"No more so than your garden," I replied.

She frowned and I remembered, too late, she had sold it. Probably it was not the best thing to remind her of. "I've been working on that garden for ten years," she said, with no particular regret in her voice.

"It shows."

"Do you think it's ever time to let go of things?"

"Sure."

"I've never been good at letting go."

"We ought to split the difference. I've never been good at holding on."

"So how come you have the baby and I don't."

I digested that. I didn't have an answer. "Did you want one?"

"I don't know. Maybe. But I couldn't imagine doing it on my own."

"I'm not sure it's harder."

She looked at me.

"I've never been much good at that couple thing." Eileen laughed and the sound brought up that other woman, the one whose voice Eileen heard every time she sang. Probably I wouldn't hear Eileen laugh now without thinking about her now, too.

What did all this talk sound like, I wondered, if you were the size of a spider. Rumbling, like thunder? Or maybe spiders had broken the code for human speech hundreds of years ago and she was sitting over there with an opinion.

"Eileen," I said. "Did you ever consider that the roots of trees are suspiciously like synapses?" I was tired and my head was jumping around like it always did when I was tired.

"Synapses?"

"Synapses. You know, how nerve impulses flow from one synapse to another. They jump across a small distance at the end of nerve endings and those endings look exactly like the roots of trees. And absolutely the roots of those trees are all tangled up with each other, just like synapses."

Eileen stared at the trees. "That oak there," I went on, "the big guy. You could be standing half a mile away and you might still be standing on its toes. The roots go that far, easy."

She blinked several times. "Your point?"

"There is absolutely no way those guys can't be passing information from one to the other."

"Michael?"

"Yeah."

"This is the kind of thing you think about?"

"Sometimes."

"You in therapy?"

Why was everybody always asking me if I was in therapy?

I ignored it. "So what was going on in group?"

"I don't know," she said. "I play the videotape in my head, you know, and it begins to look different. I thought I knew what was going on. Now I'm not so sure."

"What did you think was going on?"

"I thought Jim was needy, that he was innocent and didn't belong there in the first place."

I looked at her.

"It's not the same stuff I was telling you about before. I'm not trying to tell you about Jim. I'm trying to tell you about group. I'm trying to tell you what I did. Maybe what I didn't do."

"Which was?"

"I didn't run much of a group."

I had gotten that far on my own. "Meaning what exactly?" I was too tired to just let her tell it in her own way, even though I knew I should.

"Michael," she said dryly. "Do you know how impatient you sound all the time? I always feel like you're in such a hurry and I'm holding you up. It's crazy-making if somebody is trying to talk to you."

I sighed. How many times had I heard "slow down" in my life? I should have been a bank robber. Now that's a profession that values speed.

"I promise to zip my lip if you will just tell me what was going on," I said firmly and shut up.

"I'm trying to tell you that I spent most of the time talking to Jim in group."

I considered what to say. I didn't know what she meant. Finally, I came up with the most neutral thing I could think of.

"Tell me about it."

"He would come in and he would ask if he could talk to me, privately. Sometimes he did that. A lot of times, really," she added thoughtfully as though watching the video-memory play. "He was depressed a lot and needed to talk. Sometimes I'd take him outside in the hall. It was so personal that it didn't seem right to have the rest of the group listening in. Sometimes, we'd go off to a corner of the room and talk."

"In group?" I said incredulously. "What was the rest of the group doing while you talked with Jim?"

She flushed but didn't deny it. "I'd give them an assignment if it looked like it would be a while. Sometimes, I just let them talk. . . . I don't want to admit it. I don't think I faced it, but it became kind of a regular thing. Now I wonder—"

"What?"

"If it was planned or something. I swear to you, I never even thought about it at the time. I began to look forward to it. That's hard to admit but it's true. I began to feel disappointed if he didn't need to talk. I guess I think now I needed it more than he did."

"He didn't always want to?"

"No, not always."

I asked the question I had to ask even though I knew the answer. "Eileen, think about this very carefully. Could you always see what was going on in the group when you were talking to Jim? Did you always, and I mean always, keep your eye on them?"

She paused so long I thought she wasn't going to answer but I wired my jaw together and kept my mouth shut. Finally she said, "No, I didn't."

"What were you thinking about just now?"

"Not that. I knew the answer to that right away. I never even thought about keeping my eye on the group. It's just that . . . what I was thinking about was how Jim always seemed to."

I raised my eyebrows quizzically.

"Have his eye on the group. He kept an eye on them. I'm not sure, but I think he did. The picture I have is Jim with his back to the wall and me with my back to the group. If it didn't start out that way he moved around until it was. Then, in the hall, he'd stand in the doorway or close to it. I guess I'm wondering if all that was deliberate. I don't get this. What were they doing?"

"Passing drugs," I said.

13

I OPENED MY EYES THE NEXT MORNING AND PICKED UP THE phone. Adam was gone and for the first time I wondered if this was a plan. Maybe Adam really didn't stay home that much or maybe he was lying low until the baby came. Whatever. But he wasn't giving me much of an excuse for throwing him out, that's for sure. Not, of course, that I was looking for one.

A new nurse was on the ward where Stacy was staying but word had been passed and she was willing to talk to me. Stacy's vital signs were stable and he was no longer on the critical list. But he wasn't awake and the anesthesia had long ago worn off. She refused to speculate. He was unconscious, that's all she could say. They'd know more in forty-eight hours.

"Meaning what?" I said, trying to keep the serrated edge out of my voice when I couldn't get anybody to say what I wanted to hear. "If he doesn't wake up in forty-eight hours he's not going to?"

"Meaning we'll know more in forty-eight hours," she replied firmly. Hospital personnel were used to people trying to get them to say things that they couldn't say. I took a deep breath and tried to smooth out my rough edges a little. Alienating this woman wouldn't help.

"If I came up, could I sit with him for a while?" I asked, impulsively.

"He's in intensive care," she replied crisply. "Are you family? No visitors but family."

"Absolutely," I said. "Sister-in-law and his brother is out of the country. He'd never forgive me if I didn't take care of Stacy." How did I get so good at lying? *I* might have believed me.

"Well, even family aren't allowed in for very long," she said reluctantly, "but you could sit with him for a short while . . . if you were quiet and didn't disturb him." Her tone was disapproving and not at all welcoming. Moreover, she'd said absolutely nothing to give me any comfort or reassurance. I suppressed my annoyance at the chilly reception I was getting. I was usually on the other side of this medical situation and knew staff didn't always rank high on "callous" and "unemotional." Then again, it wasn't all that unusual.

"On my way," I replied simply.

I looked at Stacy and felt relieved. There were tubes everywhere, of course. Tubes were the hallmark of the ICU. But Stacy had only seven or eight lines hooked up to the two IVs in his arms and that was encouraging. I'd seen a small child with as many as sixteen lines piggy-backed on each other so if you went by the line count, Stacy wasn't doing that badly.

I didn't know exactly what was flowing into him but I knew the territory: somewhere in those rubber ribbons would be a mixture of dextrose and potassium and saline, just to sustain and hydrate. There would be a catheter, of course, and if I stayed long enough I'd hear the sound of the automatic blood pressure cuff. These were just support and monitoring troops. Then there were the big guys: drugs to maintain his blood pressure and drugs to keep swelling down. The line going into his head told me they were monitoring his intracranial pressure, which meant they were worried about it.

I tried to ignore the *whoosh* of the respirator. People in comas almost always had them, I reminded myself. Even when they could breathe on their own, it was usually shallow and erratic. Besides which, the docs would use the respirator to hyperventilate him. They'd want to lower his CO_2 to keep the swelling down. Still, it made me uneasy; nobody likes to see a respirator.

Mostly, medicine these days comes down to two things: cutting people up and pouring drugs in. Even if you cut them up, you still have to pour drugs in before, during and after. Drugs aren't a part of medicine: they are medicine. Mostly what doctors do these days is fine-tune the array of chemical troops at their fingertips.

Oh, sure, there are PET scanners and MRIs and CAT scanners and machines of all sorts: huge, fancy expensive toys that probe and scan and analyze, and make the doctors' eyes light up like kids playing with erector sets. But it is all in the service of figuring out where to cut and why—or more typically, which drugs to give. Drugs are still king and IVs are the highways that deliver them.

I sat down by the bedside. The sheet was pulled up to Stacy's chest and tucked in tight, military style. His hands were lying down limply at his sides with IVs on the backs of them. It all looked strangely formal and

made me uneasy underscoring, as it did, that Stacy
wasn't moving. Anybody moving would disturb that
crisp, smooth expanse and the careful placement of his
limbs in two minutes flat but Stacy looked like he had
lain that way all night.

The tableau made him seem more dead than alive
and I focused on his breathing to remind myself that
he was *not* dead or dying. I had to work to remember
that, here in this sparse, utilitarian room where the
dead might look more at home than the living. I lifted
my hand to put it on his still one and realized mine
wasn't steady.

The nurse walked in, the same one I'd spoken to on
the phone and who had curtly admitted me a few
minutes earlier. She was in her fifties and stocky, with
short brown hair cut just below her ears. She wore no
makeup or jewelry and her haircut was graceless, as
though she'd gone to the cheapest beautician she
could find and not paid much attention to the results.
I remembered what Eileen said, that the point had
come where no man had looked at her as more than a
fixture. No one would pay much attention to this lady,
I suspected, and it wasn't just the lack of attention to
her appearance. It was the lack of vitality in the face,
the hard set of the jaw as though something had settled and closed off in her life. A private grief, I
thought, or maybe just a series of bad years that had
worn her down.

I stiffened when she turned toward me, sure she
was already throwing me out even though I'd just
gotten there: "a short while" could mean anything,
really. But she just nodded and went over to check
the IV bottles. She picked up one and inspected the
line going down to Stacy's hand. She picked his hand

up and looked closely at the needle taped on the skin.

"Mr. James," she said softly, "I'm sorry, but this vein has shut down and we need to open up another one. I'll call the IV team and they'll be up in a minute." I was startled to hear her speak to him at all given he looked totally, completely, flat-out unconscious. I was even more surprised at the exquisite gentleness of her tone. Her whole manner had changed when she'd turned to Stacy and I realized in an instant how much I had misjudged her. She might be one way with the world, but she was another way altogether here, in this room, with her patient.

I looked at Stacy's face but it hadn't seemed to register anything. "Can he hear you?" I said.

"We don't know," she said, some of the softness still lingering in her voice like perfume trailing. Her abrasiveness toward me had ebbed anyway, as though somehow just by being in the room, I fell under some of the same protectiveness her patient did. "There have been some studies of unconscious people, mostly anecdotal reports of people reporting conversations while they were under that turned out to be true. Now we act as though they can hear. I think they can," she said, and with a small backward glance at Stacy, she left to call the IV team.

When she was gone, I turned back to Stacy. Who knew if Stacy could hear, but why not try? "Stacy," I said, "it's me, Michael. You're in a hospital. You got beat half to death at the prison. I am so sorry, so very sorry it happened but I think you're going to be okay." I don't know why I said that last part. I wasn't really sure he'd be okay, but it seemed to me telling him he might be blind when he woke up wasn't very encouraging.

"I think we've figured out what's going on, part of it anyway, so don't worry about that. What we think happened is . . ." but the rest of it died in my throat. Stacy was beyond all that, beyond caring about what had happened in the prison, beyond *any* kind of meaning or narrative or even threat. He was at the end of a long tunnel, listening to the sound of his heart beating and his breath rising and falling. These would be the rhythms his life returned to, the same ones it began with. And what else would be at the end of that tunnel, I wondered, when all else was taken away? What would be there for me?

An image rose suddenly, so forcefully it hit me like sea spray. I was floating in water, my legs dangling under me, one foot behind the other tucked into the hard rubber of a slalom ski. In the distance I could hear the droning of the speedboat growing fainter, a strangely natural sound, as it headed off to drop a passenger ashore.

I put my head back into the water and let my hair fan out on all sides, closing my eyes, the better to feel the water lapping against my shoulders and neck. When I opened them it was to an infinite expanse of powder blue above me. "If God isn't a tarheel," the bumper stickers read, "why is the sky Carolina blue?" And anyone who thinks that is a joke has never looked up at the sky from the center of a Carolina cove.

The water on my lips had a faint salt taste, halfway between the sharper tang of the sea and the sterility of lake water, salty enough for dolphins to use the inland waterway as a nursery, fresh enough for the water snakes who lived in the marshes nearby, underneath willows garnished with Spanish moss.

When the boat came back I would rise from the

lapping bay with a great *whoosh,* throwing water left and right. I'd lean hard to one side, straighten both my legs and feel the shock of the turn rivet through my shoulders and down my spine. I'd almost touch my shoulder to the surface as I cut. I'd hold that sharp edge on the water until I was almost even with the boat on one side and then straighten to start my lean the other way. But for a moment when I straightened, I'd pause to raise my face to the sun and feel the wind whip through my hair. I'd laugh from sheer exuberance, joy fed by the power in that toned, youthful body and laugh, too, at the glory of the shiny water I slid over—Jesus Lord! the shiny water—millions of bright sequins dancing like alien life forms on the surface of the sea. No doubt it is we who are cousin to the porpoise, after all, and not the other way around. I never saw a porpoise with any particular joy at being on land.

This image would be there, I knew, at the end of any tunnel I ever peered through. Not people, surely not accomplishments or achievements or jobs. At the end of the tunnel for me, there would be the water lapping on my shoulders and the taste of salt on my lips and the wide expanse of Carolina blue.

But I lied. There would be one person at the end of that tunnel and she had not lived long enough to see a water ski: my sweet baby Jordan, who got blind-sided by SIDS before her first birthday. Abruptly, I looked around the room, trying to distract myself from the feelings that had caught me like a tidal wave, but the stark hospital room offered nothing. I stood up quickly, knowing movement was the only thing now that would keep her at bay.

Some people think I am a brave woman. They point

out I have never hesitated to confront rapists and mur-
derers, sadists and psychopaths. They note that I go
under the boards with people who have six inches and
a hundred pounds on me and don't give an inch. I
can't deny I have swum and skied in snake-infested
water most of my life and never stopped when the sun
went down. And too, I wouldn't give up jumping
horses over rigid, cross-country jumps for all the jumps
I've hit, hurt so bad sometimes that I couldn't brush
my teeth afterward because it shook my head too
much. Maybe all that was true, but it was also true
that I knew my limits. I'd run from the memory of my
sweet baby girl dying, every single day for the rest of
my life. It would take a tunnel the size of Stacy's to
stop me.

And for Stacy? What was in his tunnel? I could only
guess.

I kissed Stacy and squeezed his hand as I headed
out. I was on the move now, trying to outrun a memory. I should have gone to work, work being an effective analgesic and where I was supposed to be, anyway.
But something about a friend lying unconscious makes
the normal day seem irrelevant. I wanted to do something useful but there was no sense in going to the
prison. Security would be taking the place apart and
putting the pieces under a microscope. There was no
way I could help. I doubted they'd even let me get
close enough to get in the way.

I drove aimlessly for a while just thinking about the
attack on Stacy and what we knew and what we didn't.
My sweet baby girl started to recede and I felt the
tightness in my chest ease as I puzzled over what all
this meant. Finally, I pulled out a map. There was one
piece of the puzzle security didn't have. I found the

route I was looking for and headed up to Berlin, New Hampshire, where the printing supplier was located, the one that Jim had recommended to Rudolph.

So why did Jim do that? He could have done it just to get in Rudolph's good graces, but it could also be he got in Rudolph's good graces to bring the supplier in. So which was it? It couldn't be as simple as the supplier smuggling drugs in, or the dogs would have found them. But it was part of the puzzle. It had to be.

Berlin was a paper town and the smell of the paper mill hit me full force when I got out of the car to ask for directions. If noses could stagger, mine would have reeled like a drunk. As it was, my eyes watered in a gesture of neighborly sympathy.

You gotta wonder how people could live there but I suspected the residents didn't notice the smell. Anything that happened all the time—odors, traffic noise, violence—ceased to register after a while. It just became part of the way things were. Still, who knew what all those chemicals in the air did to people's lungs? But the smell of the paper mill was the least of a logging town's worries. Bad smells didn't kill you, at least not right away.

There was a time when the logs were floated down the river to the mill, a giant log drive once a year, with millions of tons of logs alternating between wild, uncontrolled tumbling and locked up jams that stretched as far as the eye could see. It was hard to know which was more dangerous. Men rode the logs while they flew down the river, rode them through rapids and even sluicing over dams, all the time perched precariously on top of rolling cylinders, sometimes scarcely wider than their shoulders. They were gymnasts of the first order. There were tales of men riding the logs doing handstands, just to show off. "River gods," they were called by the local people, known for their skill, their red shirts, their fearlessness and swagger, not to mention their ability to drink themselves blind three weeks out of the year.

But logs were indifferent to the confidence and bravado of the river men and were endlessly inventive in their turning and twisting. Even the most experienced river man could be thrown when they slammed into each other. If it was hard for a normal mortal to stand on one in calm water; imagine standing on one that's being rammed by other logs in the middle of the rapids.

The river men fared little better at the jams because it was their job to free them. Whether that occurred by pushing with peavies—long wooden sticks with hooks on the end—or by blowing them up with dynamite, they never knew when a jam would break free, carrying the men working on it with the sudden force of a wooden tidal wave.

Slips were common and often fatal. Between the icy water and the tons of logs running together there was frequently no second chance. The boots of dead river men were hung on trees in tribute and there were a lot of trees with boots hanging on them. Probably half the residents of the town had lost someone to a logging accident way back when.

I stopped at the 7-11 and asked for Armand Brothers Suppliers, but the kid behind the counter was clueless. His hair was pulled back in an unkempt ponytail and he wore three earrings in his poor tortured earlobe. No doubt he could have rattled off the names of rock bands I had never heard of, complete with which members were currently in rehab, but knowing where a local business was located was another story. He counted out my change in a slow, rhythmic manner—seeming to find every coin fascinating—so much so that I finally looked closely at his eyes. Could be he could use a little rehab himself.

Was one of his ancestors a river man, I wondered? Quite possibly, and they would have understood the stoned look in his eyes. Most of the river men went through a natural rehab every winter when they headed back to the woods. For the time they were off work, they drank as hard as they rode the logs. But what was this generation of kids medicating? Not the cold and wet and danger that the river men faced. Maybe a lack of rivers to ride. Somehow, starting a dot.com just wasn't the same thing.

I stopped at a hairdresser's shop for directions—it's true hairdressers know everything about a town—and soon found myself standing in front of a building up a side street off the main drag. I stared dubiously at a tiny building that looked like a Quonset hut without the curved roof. It was made of prefab metal and was not much broader than a double-wide. It was hard to imagine that a business of any size could be run out of a place that small. Adding to my skepticism was the children's play equipment on one side of the entrance. If someone lived as well as worked there, it was a very small business indeed.

I opened the front door and walked in to find a long counter in front of me and a small waiting area with vinyl covered metal chairs sitting randomly against the wall—the kind of chairs you associate with kitchens. The place surely wasn't geared for walk-in business. No one was behind the counter and the building was silent. There was a corridor stretching toward the back of the building on one side behind the counter and I leaned across to yell, "Hello, anybody here?"

There was a noise in the back and then silence. I started to yell again but a woman nearly as pregnant as I walked slowly from the back room. When she got closer I realized she didn't look well at all: she had dark circles under her eyes and her face was pale and sweating. Her black hair, short on the sides and long in back, was matted against the sides of her cheeks.

I stepped back a little so she could see I was pregnant too and then said, "Are you all right? You look like you don't feel so good."

"Just a little nausea," she said, leaning on the counter. "I'll be okay."

"When are you due?"

"Not until July," she replied.

"Whoa," I said looking at the size of her.

"Twins," she said. "Twice as much nausea. Twice as big. Let me tell you, it's something."

I didn't think she sounded all that pleased about it. "First child?" I asked.

There was a pause and then she said, "What can I do for you?" and her voice was distinctly chillier than it had been before. Everybody's got a story.

"I'm Michael Stone," I said. "I work at the prison."

"Which prison?" she said, and it seemed to me she had grown very still.

"Nelson's Point. I'm here about Jim Walker."

She didn't say anything for a moment but her face got instantly tense. Funny, I hadn't noticed all the lines in it before but suddenly they were everywhere: steep lines running from her nose to her mouth, worry lines between her eyebrows, aging lines at the corners of her eyes. No wonder Lincoln said every man over forty was responsible for his face. Feelings changed faces as if they were putty.

"We have nothing to do with him," she said tensely after a moment. "He's gotten Jeffrey in enough trouble. He's caused enough misery in our lives. Jeffrey promised me that was the end of it, last time. He has nothing to do with his cousin anymore. What do you want from us? Jim isn't staying here when he gets out, if that's what you're thinking."

I filed away that Jim and the printer were cousins and that they had a history of getting into trouble together. Corrections would have a fit at that, I knew. "Well, you do have a contract with the prison," I said. Her eyes widened. "Jim set that up, you know," I added, surprised at her response.

"What?" she said straightening up from leaning on the counter. The circles under her eyes looked darker, if anything, but she didn't look sick now; she looked mad.

"What? What are you saying? We don't have a contract with any prison."

"But you do. You have a contract to provide printing supplies to Nelson's Point. Didn't you know?"

"That's not true," she said. "He wouldn't dare. Jeffrey," she yelled. "Come out here." When he didn't answer she went back down the corridor, stuck her head out a side door and yelled again, "Jeffrey, come in here!"

He yelled something back I couldn't hear but it must have been in the affirmative because she stood by the door and waited, staring at me the whole time. I tried to think of something that would get her talking.

"It sounds like you've had a hard time with Jim Walker," I offered. It sounded lame.

She snorted but didn't speak.

I opened my mouth to try again when the side door opened and a small man walked in, drying his hands on a rag. He looked wiry and fit as though he did hard physical work of some sort. His face looked puzzled but wary, and he glanced first at her, and then at me. "What's up?" he asked quietly.

"This woman says we have a contract with a prison for printing supplies. Do we?" she said bluntly.

"Who wants to know?" he asked, looking at me, but it seemed to me his face had grown wary. The hand-drying had abruptly stopped.

"Jesus Christ," she said. "You mean it's true. It's fucking true that we're involved with Jim Walker again. I can't believe this. You promised me, you son of a bitch."

She was less than a foot away from him and her voice had risen but he didn't look at her and he didn't respond.

"Who wants to know?" he said, again, still looking at me.

"I'm Michael Stone," I said. "I'm a psychologist at the prison and Jim Walker is in my group." I started to say more but stopped. How was I supposed to justify my meddling? I shut my mouth abruptly.

"It isn't illegal to have a contract with the prison," he said slowly. "What do you want? Why are you here?"

"Hello," the woman said. "Are you listening to me? We are not getting involved with Jim again. You know what happened last time, goddammit. You promised me."

"Shut up, Joanna," he said, finally turning to her. "Just shut the fuck up, for once in your miserable fucking life." His voice had enough venom in it to poison, say, the entire city of Los Angeles, and his right hand had balled into a fist. Although he didn't raise it, Joanna saw it and involuntarily took a step back.

A jolt of adrenaline went through me like a bolt. I just hated big people picking on little people—always had, always will. And between a woman pregnant with twins and an adult male with his hand in a fist, that counted as big versus little in my book. The adrenaline sent heat to my face and made me dizzy for a moment. That much adrenaline could not be good for the baby, I knew, and I put both hands on the counter to steady myself and try to calm down. I took a deep breath, and when I spoke I was pleased to hear my voice sounded reasonably under control.

"Actually, it probably is illegal," I said. "Because I'm pretty sure corrections inquired as to whether you had any connections with any inmates and if you didn't disclose any, then it's considered fraud. But that's the least of your problems, because an inmate is dead—as I'm sure you know from the papers—and a staff member has been beaten half to death. If he dies, then somebody is looking at two murder raps. And I'd bet dollars to doughnuts that Jim Walker and this contract are involved. Does the term 'accessory to murder' mean anything to you? Because that's what you could be looking at if you're involved with this."

Neither spoke. They looked completely frozen. Nobody seemed even to be breathing. Finally Jeffrey said, "Get off my property. I've got nothing to say to you."

I walked to the door but stopped there. I turned and

they were standing exactly where they had been; nobody had moved an inch. "Murder's a whole lot worse than whatever you've been up to," I said. "Here's what you can do. Get an attorney. You're going to need one. Then have them call the prison and offer to cooperate. Cut a deal with the DA. Tell him what you've been up to and offer to testify against Jim. They're going to be a lot more interested in the beating and the killing than in you and you likely weren't involved in either because you weren't there. Maybe you could get probation, stay out of prison, I don't know. It's better than getting tagged for the whole thing."

"Get out," he said, and this time the clenched fist was for me. With one last look at Joanna, I did.

I stood outside for a minute trying to get myself under control. The shakes had started, which they always did after a major adrenaline rush. Inside I could hear Joanna screaming at Jeffrey that he was an asshole, which I had to agree with. He was yelling back, even louder, with more of the "shut the fuck up" type of helpful response. After a few minutes the voices started to fade. Evidently, one of them, likely Jeffrey, had gone back down the corridor, no doubt with the other following. They were still yelling but the voices had grown fainter.

Quietly, I opened the door and went back in. I heard a door slam in the back and then crying, Joanna, for sure. I took a business card out of my purse and wrote something on the back. I put it on the counter and left.

I remembered a Jerry Springer show on the way home, one that made me wonder why pouring garbage into people's homes day after day wasn't a felony. The show started with a video of two women fighting in the mud of a farmyard—a wife and her husband's mistress. The two women were both slipping and sliding in the mud, both wearing tee shirts, of course. The wife won that fight but not the war. Her husband came on with a second video, this one of him in the hot tub with his new mistress. At the end of the video he invited the mistress to try a swing he showed the camera, one with a seat and two foot straps to hold the woman's legs in the air, all suspended on chains. The swing was homemade but the film footage seemed suspiciously professional.

Of course, the mistress and husband trooped onto the show and the audience booed both of them. They yelled back, sitting close together and united. The public fight and the widening gulf with her husband seemed to frighten the wife. In the middle of it she got on her knees in front of the husband, ignored the boos of the audience, and begged him to stay with her. There was a complete look of childlike dependence on her face, shot through with the fear of abandonment. She didn't care about the mistresses, although she said she did. She cared about being abandoned.

Why did Joanna stay? I had witnessed only fireworks but these were rarely moments of truth. Truth came at quieter times, odd moments when the fighting ebbed like a tide going out. If I could hang around enough—after the arguing and the hitting and the sobbing were over—sooner or later something deep and fundamental would slide across her face.

It was almost always fear: fear of poverty or loss or abandonment, maybe of Jeffrey exacting revenge. "You don't understand, Michael," one woman had once said to me. "The moment I leave him he's a shadow outside my door." I shook my head wanting it to be different. People made their own choices but I spent half my time wishing some of them would make different ones.

On the way back I called in for messages. Melissa went through the day's crop and I listened listlessly—somehow it was hard to concentrate on normal stuff with Stacy in the hospital and this poor woman pregnant with twins somewhere in the back of my mind—until Melissa got to the call from Mrs. Clarence. When Melissa hung up I stared at the phone for a moment. Nothing against the Clarences, but exactly what could I do? Some part of me was secretly relieved that their son had exited this world. At least it meant there was no chance he'd someday be on the loose again. But that was hardly an excuse for not calling back a woman whose son had just been murdered. Reluctantly, I picked up the phone.

"Hello," I said, "Mrs. Clarence? This is Michael Stone returning your call."

"Thank you for calling back, Dr. Stone. We've been meaning to call you for a while now but time just seemed to get away from us. We've been doing a lot of thinking and a lot of praying since Ed's death."

"I'm sorry you lost your son," I said. "No matter what he did, I know you loved him." I gritted my teeth when I said it. If anybody in the world deserved to die it was Edward Clarence, and I felt like a hypocrite for saying anything else.

"We did. We do," she said simply. "I know most people are happy he's dead, but they didn't know him when he was little. He wasn't always that way. I don't know what happened," she said, still in that vague, wondering voice. "I just wish I knew what happened."

I didn't say anything. I didn't know either and there wasn't any kind of easy reassurance I could give. They'd raised a monster. Who knew how that happened?

"Anyway," she went on. "We didn't call to talk about that. We wanted to thank you."

"Thank me?" I said.

"Yes, thanks to you, we got to see him before he died. I'm sure that wouldn't have happened if you hadn't talked to him."

"You did?" I said, surprised.

"Yes, I believe it was shortly after you talked to him. He said he talked to you anyway. He called and said we could come visit. We came right up the next day. Now I'm so glad we did. There wouldn't have been a second chance."

I didn't know any of this. "How did the visit go?" I asked, cautiously.

"Good, it was good," she said. "We talked to our pastor first. We went right over to see him that night after Ed called. We said we didn't know what to say. We were afraid we'd blow it. He said to trust in the Lord, that we didn't have to say anything. Just to let him know we loved him and the Lord loved him, no matter what he did."

"Pretty good advice," I said.

"We took it," she said simply. "We told him we were just there to tell him we loved him, that we'd always love him."

"What'd he say?"

"He said he was sorry he hurt us," she said. "It meant the world to his father and me."

Now it was my turn to sigh. Maybe it meant the world to her and her husband, but Jesus Christ, try telling that to the mothers of the preschoolers he raped and killed. He didn't sound one bit sorry about those children and Mr. and Mrs. Clarence in their loving him were trying to ignore all that. I couldn't judge them for it—loving a child was the atomic bomb of the feelings world. Instead, I just felt weary and sad and wanted to get off the phone.

"Did you find his killer?" she said.

"No," I said. "I'm not in security so I'm not in on the investigation, but if they'd found him, they'd have charged him and it would be in the papers."

"We were completely shocked," she said, "after what he said. We just didn't expect it."

"I don't think Gary meant to promise that nothing would happen," I said quickly. Nobody can promise—" but she interrupted me.

"Oh, I don't mean what Warden Raines said. I meant after what *Edward* said."

"What'd he say?"

"That he'd made a friend. That it wasn't going to be so bad, after all. He said he didn't have a very good job but he'd have a better one soon."

"Really? Did he say anything else about it?"

"Not really."

"Not really?"

"Well, he just said one thing I didn't understand. But it wasn't important."

"What was it?"

"Nothing really. He just said he always had had a 'nose for trouble,' and he laughed when he said it like it was a joke or something. We didn't know what he meant really or why he was laughing. He didn't get in a lot of trouble as a kid. He was quiet, too quiet really, and withdrawn.

"I'm making him sound crazy and he didn't seem that way at all. It was just that nose comment that didn't make a lot of sense. He was fine, really he was. He was upbeat. I think he was relieved to be in prison, relieved that he couldn't hurt anyone anymore."

It had started. They were going to rework Clarence into someone who wanted to be caught, who was sorry for what he had done and who was relieved to be incarcerated. Easy to do now that he was dead and couldn't contradict them. God knows it would be a whole lot easier to live with. And who was I to judge them for it?

"Probably," was all I said.

14

IT WAS DARK BY THE TIME I MADE IT HOME. NOTHING WAS close to anything else in Vermont. All the towns were small and everything seemed an hour or two apart. The day had flitted by in pictures of dairy farms with hilly pastures set on small, tired mountains with a few defiant cliffs refusing to be worn down. Just like people, I thought. But which was I? A small, tired mountain or a defiant edge refusing to be worn down? A small, tired mountain, I decided.

I didn't regret the drive to see Stacy and the drive to Berlin and back. Driving was a kind of meditation for me. I didn't have to talk to anybody or see anybody. I didn't have to face the people who didn't know about Stacy and expected me to act normal or the people who did know about Stacy and wanted to talk. A car was like a little capsule that I could sit in all by myself and watch the farmhouses roll by.

Not that I had illusions that what was outside this car was as idyllic as it looked. "You look at those scattered houses, and you are impressed by their beauty," Sherlock Holmes had said to Watson. "I look at them and the only thought which comes to me is a feeling of their isolation and of the impunity with which crimes can be committed there." But Sherlock had more faith than I did that the proximity of the city offered any protection.

Adam's car wasn't in the driveway and for a second I kicked myself that I hadn't called him on the way. It sounded stupid given we were currently if temporarily—yes temporarily—living together, but it looked like I'd have to make an appointment to see the man. I thought for a moment about driving back into town to have dinner with him but realized how silly that was and got out of the car. I'd call him first. He might already be on his way home, for Pete's sake, and we'd be cars passing in the night. Besides, in all the craziness of Stacy getting hurt, I still hadn't dealt with Mama. I needed to track down that guy she was with and see what he was up to.

I headed for the house, thinking that there was one more phone call that needed to be made. I'd best check in with Gary about Jeffrey. Jeffrey and Jim Walker were up to something for sure and ten to one it had to do with drugs. What I didn't know was whether it had anything to do with Clarence or Stacy. But I hated to bother Gary at home. Tomorrow would be good enough.

I only heard one step behind me, the crunching sound of a single footstep on gravel. But before I could even startle there was an arm around my throat cutting off my wind. I grabbed the arm automatically to try to pull it away, a sharp fear going through me that he was going to break my Adam's apple, he had my neck so tight. But I barely got my hands up before he jerked me off my feet and dragged me backward. As I

was struggling to get my feet back under me, I felt a
steel blade on my belly. I stopped struggling instantly.

The voice in my ear was so close it was strangely
intimate. No one whispers in your ear but a lover or a
child. But this was neither. "Leave it alone," he said,
very quietly, the voice utterly calm. "Leave Jim and his
cousin alone or I'll cut that bastard out of your belly
right in front of you. Do you understand?" He was
whispering, which even in my fright I knew was a
good sign. People who killed you didn't bother to dis-
guise their voices.

I tried to say something but his grip was too tight
and I only made a hissing sound. I tried to nod but
couldn't do that either. He saw me try and loosened
his grip slightly. "Yes," I said, nothing but survival of
the baby on my mind. Terror held me tighter than his
arm did. It coursed through every neuron in my head,
every cell in my body. I don't want to think what I'd
have done to save that baby at that moment but for
starters, I'd have killed this man in a heartbeat if I
could have.

"You fucking bitch," he said. "Don't mess with me.
I'll kill you just to prove I can."

I said nothing, did nothing.

"You tell anybody about this and I'll find you, no
matter where you are. You have no idea how vulnerable you are, you fucking cunt. From the house to the
car, from the car to the house. I'm a patient man,
remember that."

I said nothing and then, because he seemed to be
waiting, I nodded again.

I thought he'd let me go then, but he didn't.
Increasing his grip, he started drawing the knife across
my belly. It could have been a scalpel it was so sharp

and it cut through my clothes like they were paper. At the moment it starting slicing skin, my fear level exploded and then suddenly I was floating up, away from it all. I looked down and watched the man hold me with his forearm around my throat, methodically cutting across my belly. I noticed with detachment how white my face was.

Completely detached and floating now, I watched the panicked woman below me pick up her leg and kick it backward. I think she was aiming for his balls but she caught his knee instead. It was a desperate kick and harder than she could normally have done. The man's leg slipped out from under him and he swore in surprise. The knife cut deeper as he fell but then she was free. She started running for the woods and I noticed with approval she was moving at a pretty good clip, even pregnant. He started to go after her, then he stopped.

The woods closed around her like Harry Potter's invisibility cloak and then she was running through small bush in the pitch black, what moon there was being completely obscured by the overhanging trees. She was running way too fast to be careful and she tripped on something in the dark, got off-balance and crashed into a tree. Her shoulder and belly hit first and she grabbed her belly, too late to protect it.

The blow shook me up and suddenly I wasn't hovering anymore. I was back inside the panicked figure. I stood up, still holding my belly with both hands as if somehow I could protect it that way and started running again, this time feeling blood drip through my fingers. "It isn't bad. It isn't bad," I kept telling myself over and over. I didn't know that was true but I had to believe it or the fear would swallow me like quicksand. All I could hear was my labored breathing.

I had no thought of trying to make it to a road. The only road would be deserted this late at night and whoever had threatened me had to have driven here. If I ran along the road, he'd just run me down.

Or maybe it was instinct that drew me to the woods. I had climbed out of my window at night many times as a teenager, not to go party with other kids but to walk in the woods and swim in the inland waterway. I had never run into any other people in the woods at night. People would walk down dark alleys and streets a lot more dangerous than these benign New England woods, but the city was the devil they knew.

Finally I stopped and collapsed behind a tree. I couldn't run anymore. My breathing was so loud, I couldn't even tell if anyone was still after me, but eventually it slowed a little and I still heard nothing. The myriad of small animals that made up the forest community had all frozen at my intrusion, so the residents weren't making any noise.

I took off the sweater I was wearing and used it to blot the blood on my belly. Everything hurt but I couldn't tell what was the cut, the running, or even whether I was in labor, my belly hurt so much. Why didn't I carry a cell phone? Why didn't I carry a gun? Pepper spray if nothing else? For Christ's sake, nerve gas, anything. How many times did I have to get blind-sided before I quit thinking it was a safe world and started trying to protect myself.

Something rustled in the bushes and my heart leaped up to warp speed again, but the rustling stopped and I remembered how loud small animals sounded in the woods at night. If the man hadn't caught me by now, I told myself, he wasn't going to. He'd never find me in the dark of the woods. The woods at night were more my territory than his—at least I hoped so. I leaned my back against a tree and felt the tears come, blood still running through the fingers holding my belly.

Eventually I made my way back to the house but I didn't go in. I couldn't be sure he was gone. He'd said he was a patient man and I'd take him at his word. I stayed hidden at the edge of the woods, pressed hard on the cut to stop the bleeding, then sat down to wait. I started shivering almost right away but what was shock and what was the cold of the New England spring I couldn't say. I don't know how much time passed before Adam's car pulled in. The wait seemed endless. When he did finally show up, relief surged through me like an electrical current and I got to my feet with my new-found energy and called to him. The lights of his car had temporarily blinded me so I couldn't see his expression but I saw the body language. He turned quickly at the sound of my voice, then took a step toward me before he stopped abruptly.

"Adam," I said wearily in the car on the way to the ER, "why do you always blame me when something happens? You're worse than my mother. If I got hit by a truck and broke my arm in three places, she'd just say, 'What'd you do that for?'"

"Like you don't have anything to do with it," Adam shot back. It wasn't hard to tell when he was angry. His lips turned into a thin line and there was a certain set to his jaw.

"Well, you think maybe whoever pulled a knife on me might have a little responsibility here?"

"I plan on taking that up with him," Adam said shortly and something about the tightness in his voice silenced me. "How's the bleeding?" he asked.

"It isn't that bad," I replied. "I really think it's just a surface wound. It has to be," I muttered, "or something would have happened by now."

"Michael—"

"Don't lecture me, I'm not in the mood."

Adam went on as though I hadn't even spoken. "You have to understand something," he said, speaking very slowly. "There are bad people in the world. There are some people who are trained to deal with them. We carry guns and nightsticks and handcuffs and radios. There are other people called civilians who aren't trained to deal with them. When civilians start poking around bad guys, they usually get hurt. Sometimes they get killed. Do you know which side of this you're on?" He spoke with exaggerated simplicity and I bristled.

"Adam, you sound like you're talking to a child. Cut it out."

"I'm just trying to be clear," he replied. "Because it seems like a really clear thing to me and a really true thing but no matter how I say it or how many times, I'm still not getting through. Let me count the ways someone has tried to kill you. Someone tried to strangle you—"

"That was in a gym," I said indignantly.

"Meaning?"

"Who would expect to be strangled in a gym? That's sacrilege."

"And then someone tried to kneecap you with, I

might add, plans on torturing you and murdering you afterward. I believe that was in a church, for what it's worth."

"I didn't have anything to do with that. Some stupid-ass judge let him out."

"And now someone has threatened, maybe tried, to kill," he paused, "our baby."

"You almost said—"

"My baby. You keep this up, I'm going to sue for custody before this baby's born."

"Oh, come on."

But if Adam was kidding he gave no sign of it. "I think I might win. In fact, I'm going to get Carlotta to represent me. She would too, you know."

I didn't comment. She probably would.

"Some people favor putting pregnant crack addicts in jail. There might be precedence . . ."

By the time we got to the emergency room I was royally pissed. I got out of the car and slammed the door. Adam started to follow me in but I turned around and stopped him. "I can walk in on my own steam," I said. "The baby's fine and frankly, I'm tired of being yelled at. Go find out who this Jeffrey character is because that's probably who it was. Isn't that what you people who have the guns and the nightsticks do?"

Adam ignored me and headed to the ER. "Where are you going?" I asked, exasperated.

"I'm leaving," Adam said, "but I want to talk to the nurse first."

I followed him up to the emergency room counter and before I could speak he pulled out his card and put it on the counter. "I'm Adam Bowers," he said. "I'm the baby's father. Michael will tell you what happened but if there are any problems with this baby, I want to know about it." He gave the receptionist a look that said that he would take out her throat with a spoon if she left him out of the loop.

I saw her blink at the intensity on his face and then she took one look at my bloody belly and picked up the phone.

I didn't know the emergency room doc. Which was happening more and more as Jefferson University Hospital got bigger. We might be in a rural area but given we were the main tertiary care center for much of New Hampshire and Vermont, we were still growing by leaps and bounds.

He was tall and thin and he had one of those heads that looked a little big for his skinny frame. Still, he was good-looking with black hair a little longer than most men his age and eyes with that kind of light in them that's better than an IQ test for telling you who's bright. He introduced himself briefly and walked over to the sink to wash his hands. The glance he'd given me had appeared casual but I didn't think so. It might have been brief but so are X rays. I had a feeling those bright eyes didn't miss much.

I was sitting in a chair still holding my sweater over my bloody belly. A more novice doc would have rushed over to check my belly but this one had taken in my color and the absence of fresh blood, and then gone quietly off to wash his hands. My level of trauma was not going to impress an emergency room doc. When he finished, he briefly checked the chart, which had just recorded my blood pressure and heart rate, then hopped up on the examining table himself and swung his legs over the edge. "You're on the staff?"

"Yep," I replied. "Are you new? I don't think we've met."

"Just here for the weekend." He didn't explain but I knew what he meant. There was such a shortage of emergency room docs in the country that emergency medicine specialists flew all over to do weekend coverage. Some docs were traveling full time. They'd fly in on Friday, work all weekend and fly out Monday morning, then have the rest of the week off. Mostly, I didn't like it. The flying docs didn't have a clue what the local resources were or who to refer to. But I had to admit it was better than being short-staffed and long-lined in the emergency room.

"Boy, I didn't know we were that low on docs."

"Everybody is."

"You like it?"

"Yep, gives me time for other things. I'm one of those perpetual student types."

"Other medical specialties?"

He shook his head. "No, one residency was enough for me. I go a little farther afield. What's your area?"

"Psychology."

"I took a Masters in psychology on one of my binges. Interesting stuff although some of it is a little weird. So," he said, "you're about to have a baby. Your first?"

I never knew how to answer that question. "More or less," I replied.

"Ah," he replied. "Sorry."

"You have kids?" I asked, impulsively. It was a totally inappropriate question and I don't know why I asked it. Maybe it had to do with how tired and punchy I was getting now that the adrenaline was draining away.

"Not me," he replied. "You know that cartoon where the man has his head on his desk and he says, 'I can't believe I forgot to have children.' That's me. I just forgot to put it on the list." He managed to draw a small laugh from me but before it had died, he'd picked up again.

"So," he said with studied casualness. "Receptionist says you've got a husband with a temper." He said it flatly as though it were an established fact but he managed to leave a question hanging in the air all the same. So that explained it. Docs were trained to worry a lot more about domestic violence these days than about relatively minor trauma. What I had this time wouldn't kill me. But any man who would cut my belly could do something a whole lot worse next time.

"One of those specialties wouldn't have been inter-rogation techniques, would it?"

It was his turn to laugh but he dropped his slouched, leg-swinging, good-buddy posture, sat up and crossed his arms. "All right, then," he said still smiling. "So what's the deal?"

"Well, for starters, he's my boyfriend, not my hus-band, but that's neither here nor there. It was a stranger," I said, "or maybe an acquaintance. He came up behind me and I didn't see him. Cross my heart and hope to die."

"Stranger?" he said, neutrally.

"Look, my boyfriend is pissed because it's his baby in my belly. He's pissed at whoever did this and he's also pissed at me because he thinks I put myself in sit-uations where getting hurt is practically inevitable. He's being an asshole, in my opinion, but one thing's for sure, he doesn't have a temper in the way you mean it and he sure as hell didn't carve up my belly.

"I don't want to get picky here but do you think you could check out my belly? What I need right now is to be sure everything's okay medically. I realize you can tell I'm not dying but I'm still nervous about this baby thing." Actually, what I needed was to finish this up and get out of there. I was feeling so tired it was an effort to sit up.

"Sure," he said, hopping up. "I'll check you out but I'd still like to hear what happened. Deal?"

So I told him. It just sort of all spilled out. I told him about an inmate getting killed at the prison and about the drugs and about Stacy getting bonked and about my visit to the printer and about the man with the knife. I didn't mean to tell him that much but once I got going I got a bad case of verbal diarrhea and it all came out. He checked me over thoroughly while he listened, brought a nurse in and did an internal. When the exam was over he sat down at the small writing desk while I sat on the examining table. He took a few minutes to write in the chart and then looked up.

"Medically, it's all minor. That cut is marginal for stitches but I'm not going to bother because I don't think they'll hold across that stretched belly and tape will do just about as good a job, maybe better. It's going to tear open when you deliver anyway. Okay?" I nodded.

"You're two centimeters dilated so I think you'd better stop running around and take it a little easier. You can save the world after the baby comes. You've still got about a month to go and it wouldn't be a disaster to deliver now, but the baby will benefit by having a little more meat on its bones. So, cool it.

"By the way, I take it back. Your boyfriend is a saint.

He can't have any temper at all or he'd have throttled you long before now. If you were running around chasing crooks with my baby in your belly, I'd be tempted to put you in a pumpkin shell and lock you up, too. And you're wrong," he added.

"About what?"

"Either the printer didn't do this or the printer isn't the poor-guy-who-gets-dragged-into-things-by-his-big-bad-cousin like his wife thinks. I mean, it sounds like she thinks this Jeffrey guy keeps getting dragged into things by his cousin, but she's wrong."

"Why is she wrong?"

"Because whoever attacked you wasn't a fear-biter."

"Excuse me?"

"Dogs. Do you know anything about dogs?"

"No." Although Mama did. If it was something about dogs I should run it past Mama.

"One of my hobbies. I breed Dobermans. A nice dog. Totally misunderstood. In any case, in the dog world, dogs will bite you for only two reasons. Either they're fear-biters—they bite you if they're cornered and only then—or they're just plain vicious. Canine psychopaths, if you will."

"How do you know this guy wasn't a fear-biter?"

"Because fear-biters don't say things like, 'I'll kill you just to prove I can.' That's more on the psychopathic end of things. They also don't talk about 'from the house to the car and the car to the house.' That's that fantasy thing psychopaths do. You probably know that better than I do when you think about it. Fear-biters see you as backing them into a corner and giving them no choice. Their fantasies all revolve around self-defense. They say things like, 'Don't make me. . . . You give me no choice,' that kind of thing. This guy wasn't thinking self-defense; he was thinking the 'Joy of Violence.'"

What was it Wallace Stevens had said about watching a snowstorm all night until the "bright obvious" stands clear in the sunlight the next day? I had been influenced by Joanna's view of Jeffrey, at least to some extent, and she, for sure, was too close to see the bright obvious. But I knew the gospel truth when I heard it. The doc was right: the man who had carved on my belly wasn't a regular person dragged into this by someone else. He wasn't even a normal thug. He talked like, well, a psychopath.

Jim and Jeffrey. It wouldn't be the first time two psychopaths teamed up together, but every time I had ever heard about it, it had produced results that were definitely not pleasant. It wasn't like you added the harm two psychopaths could do: it was more like you multiplied it.

Carlotta was waiting when I walked out to the lobby, which was a good thing because until then I hadn't even thought about how I was getting home. I'd guess Adam was at the police station, using the computer to find out what he could about Jeffrey, or maybe he was on his way to Berlin but, either way, I was without a car. I hadn't called Carlotta but obviously he had.

I was feeling self-conscious about my sliced-up clothes and had put the bloody sweater over my belly. Carlotta stood up when I walked into the lobby and I saw her eyes slide to the bloody sweater. Alarm instantly stripped away some of her usual composure and just as quickly she slid it back on. "It's all right," I said, when we'd closed the distance across the small room. "The baby's all right and I'm just a little tired." She took off her coat and wrapped it around me. Then she put her arm around me and we headed out. She hadn't spoken at all and I didn't feel the need to say anything, either. I was just glad not to be explaining anything to anybody or arguing with anybody and Carlotta, with that weird tact she had, seemed to know that.

I put my head against the car door and fell asleep on the way to her house. She hadn't asked but it was clear I wasn't going back to my house in the country tonight. Despite my usual preference for solitude, tonight the lighted windows in her neighborhood looked warm and reassuring.

I found my way to the guest bedroom while Carlotta futzed around in the kitchen. When I emerged from the shower I found a terry cloth robe waiting for me on the back of the bathroom door and a cup of tea on a stand beside the bed with a lit candle next to it. Some lute music was playing softly from a CD player she'd brought in. Carlotta still hadn't spoken and it appeared she wasn't going to as there was no light under her door. As I sat alone in the darkened bedroom sipping the tea I marveled at how useful it can be to keep words out of it when you're trying to say something.

15

I WOKE UP THINKING OF ACHILLES, A CLEAR PICTURE IN MY head of Achilles' chariot circling Troy and dragging the body of Hector in the dust. I had a decent relationship with my unconscious as far as I could tell, but clearly it didn't think I was very smart. My unconscious used very little veiling when it sent me messages; it more often hit me over the head with a two-by-four. I mean, duh. Why would I be thinking about Achilles after someone had held a knife to my unborn child? Maybe my unconscious was just opposed to paying therapy bills. You sure didn't need a therapist to interpret the kind of dreams I had.

No question, my own Achilles' heel was sitting in my lap. That's the way it often was with women. We got attached. Agamemnon, on the other hand, was perfectly willing to sacrifice his daughter to get fair winds for his ships to go off on a fool's errand to Troy. You just cannot imagine a woman doing that. It was just like the Alamo in my book. Not the kind of really stupid thing a woman would do.

I had nearly worked up a good case of early morn-

ing feminist indignation when I thought about
Adam. Guilt slipped into place like a familiar gear
engaging. Adam was after me for taking too many
chances with this baby and I sure as hell wouldn't
want to be Jeffrey when he caught up with him. That
was the problem with stereotyping: it was satisfying
as hell. It filled you up like a good meal. It just felt
good to do it—if you didn't mind being wrong half
the time. I dropped the internal rant and dragged
myself out of bed.

Every piece of me ached or hurt. I sat up and
looked at the phone on the nightstand. Beaten up
as I was, I knew there were some things I had
to deal with. I picked up the phone and dialed the
hospital to check on Stacy but the line to the ward
was busy. Frustrated, I hung up and called Mama.
With Stacy unconscious and somebody coming at
me with a knife, there had been no time for Mama.
But really, Mama losing her life savings was a bit of
an emergency, too. I picked up the phone and
dialed.

"Well, I'm sure I don't know," Brenda said. "I think
she called him 'Richard,' but she never mentioned a
last name. Land sakes, I was so curious, I'd have
remembered it if she had."

"Well, find out," I said bluntly.

"Michael, how am I supposed to find out? If I just
outright ask your mother, she'll want to know why I
want to know. And if I tell her you asked me, well,
that's the end of that. And I don't have any other reason to ask her. Besides, I can't imagine lying to your
mother. I don't think she'd like it."

"Brenda," I said bluntly. "Think devious for once. I
know you are the most straightforward soul in the uni-

verse, but I have got to locate this guy and we both know I don't have any other way of doing it. Call the travel agent. Maybe they flew together."

"I don't think so. Your mother mentioned he was coming from Raleigh. She said something about meeting him there—in Vegas. At least I think she did."

"Well, think of something," I said. "Draw her out in conversation. Ask her about him."

"Oh, no," Brenda said quickly. "I don't think I could do that. Your mother would figure out I was up to something."

"Brenda . . ."

"All right, I'll think about it. I will."

"You were a teenager once. Think of something a teenager would do."

"I'll think of something you would do, Michael," she said dryly. "That might help."

Slowly, wincing all the way, I stuffed my aching limbs into a huge pair of maternity pants big enough for a clown suit and a shirt bigger than a Burger King flag. I looked at the angry cut on my belly while I was doing it and more guilt rocked me. Adam was right, of course. Why was I hassling strange people when I was pregnant?

When I walked out to the kitchen, Carlotta was sitting at the table reading the newspaper. She raised her eyebrows when she saw me as though trying to gauge whether I wanted to talk or not. "I'm all right," I said, sitting down. Carlotta had made some decaf— pregnancy meant you couldn't eat or drink anything remotely interesting; really, it gave babies a totally false sense of life on this planet. She poured me a cup and sat back down.

"Adam feels like a shit," she said. "He knows his timing was lousy."

"Even though he was right," I said.

"Even though," she echoed. "You mad at him?"

"Only a little. Enough of my stuff." I knew it was stupid but I didn't want to talk about it. I was embarrassed about getting caught from behind and cut up. No matter whose fault it was, helplessness always produced shame. "What's happening with Hank?"

"He's gone," she said.

"You threw him out?"

She shook her head. "On his own steam."

"So what happened?"

"We were sitting at breakfast a few days ago. He had wanted to make love that night and I didn't. I was just sitting there trying to figure out how to avoid talking about it. It was very awkward and worse, it was Saturday, so I couldn't just get up and go to work—although I was thinking about it—when he put down his newspaper and just sort of looked at me.

"I didn't want to talk so I kept reading and then I couldn't stand it anymore so I gave up and said, 'What is it?' And, he just said, 'It's over, isn't it?'

"And I didn't want to say it quite that baldly but he called it so I wouldn't lie to him. I didn't know what to say. I didn't say anything."

"And then what?"

"Nothing. He didn't argue. He didn't ask me anything. He didn't accuse me of anything. He just got up, folded his newspaper, came over and kissed me on the forehead and then he walked out."

"Just like that?"

"Just like that."

"Wow," I said.

"Yeah," she said, a kind of longing woven through the word.

We both sat there. There were times you needed to play out a hand and times you needed to fold. But how many people did we know who could tell the difference and act on it? I walked away too soon, no matter what was on the table. Most people walked away too late. Maybe Hank was somebody who got it right. Which wouldn't make Carlotta miss him any less.

"It's strange," I said, "about this secret-keeping thing. It's not just the pink panties, is it? It's thinking he was one way and finding out he was another." I wasn't just thinking about what Hank had kept from Carlotta. Jim had a few secrets he was keeping from Eileen and how long had Jeffrey waited before he started beating his wife? In every single case, I'd bet the betrayal itself would be a big piece of the damage. What was behind the screen was almost secondary.

"The pink panties are there," she said. "Maybe they shouldn't be but they are. But it's the other thing, too. I mean, I've got all the sympathy in the world. I don't know what I'd do. He can hardly tell someone he likes to cross-dress on the first date, and by the time he feels safe enough to tell, he's got someone thinking he's a whole different way. I don't have an answer to it." Carlotta looked miserable. Truly, loss was what made this planet a tough place. Her world had just grown smaller. What's to like about that? As far as I could tell, the only people who didn't pay in blood for loving were psychopaths, who never had the problem because they weren't attached to anybody.

It wasn't supposed to be like this. I believed in a "Just World" as much as anybody. People who did bad things were supposed to suffer. People who were nice, kind, ate their Wheaties and loved other people were supposed to thrive. But psychopaths were driven more by joy than angst, I knew. They had more delight in conning and manipulating, in having power over others, than most of us got from anything. The rest of us were struggling along—loving and losing, telling our secrets or keeping them—while they circled the herd with about as much conscience as lions going after a zebra. And if you just voted according to who was having more fun, you'd have to think the psychopaths came out ahead. What kind of a joker was running this place, anyway?

We talked for a while longer but finally I got up, put my arms around Carlotta and kissed her on the top of the head. I'd be back, but right now there was something I needed to do. It was time to fess up. Put my cards on the table and leave at least one game. Not the way Hank had done. I wasn't folding really: I had some valuable cards. I just needed to hand them over to someone else to play. I walked into the living room, picked up the phone and called Gary.

I wasn't looking forward to the meeting and I drove listlessly, wishing I was going somewhere else. Gary wouldn't like it any more than Adam had that I had gone off looking for the printing supplier. And he'd be appalled that someone had come after me. I didn't know anybody who didn't think I was an idiot for what had seemed like a simple inquiry at the time. Somehow I felt surrounded by a male view of the world—"Just leave it to us, little lady. Now you run on home and have your baby. Don't bother your pretty little head with the big, bad world." Well, maybe there was one person. She was pregnant, too, and taking a hell of lot more risks than I was. On impulse I picked up the phone in the car and dialed.

"What'd you want?" she said.

"Jeffrey was gone last night, wasn't he? Don't answer. I'm not asking you anything. I just wanted to tell you where he was."

"I know what you're going to say," she said quickly. "The police have already been here. I told them already and I'll tell you. He was home last night, all night," but her voice was dull and unconvincing.

"Really?" I said, and some of the anger bubbled up that had been simmering all night. "Really. Let me tell you what happened, Joanna. Because I'll bet dollars to doughnuts the police didn't tell you much and I'll bet he didn't tell you shit.

"Did they tell you he came up behind me and cut off my wind so I couldn't breathe? Or that he jerked me off my feet and dragged me backward? Or that he said he'd kill me just to prove he could? Did they tell you he said he was a patient man and that if I didn't back off, he'd be there—from the house to the car, from the car to the house? Did he tell you that?

"Did they tell you he cut my belly where the baby is? I don't know what he had in mind because I panicked and kicked him and got away. Even if he didn't plan on cutting me open, a slight slip or a half inch too deep and that would have been it. Amniotic fluid gone. Do you think he would have helped with an unscheduled C-section, Joanna, or do you think the baby would be dead now and maybe me too?"

"He wouldn't do anything like that," she said, quickly. "He loses his temper sometimes, that's all, but he's got a good side to him. He does. He's not what you think. He's just had some bad luck."

"He wouldn't do it?" I yelled. "You're dreaming. But we can test it out. Has he ever threatened to cut you, Joanna? Threatened to cut 'that bastard you're carrying,' quote, unquote? Because I'm willing to bet a man who'd say that to a stranger has already said it to someone a whole lot closer to him. So, tell me, Joanna, has he said it or not?" Again there was silence.

"Because if he did, then you know every word I'm saying is the truth. Where'd he tell you he was last night? Because he told you he was somewhere else. Am I right?"

"You're wrong about him," she said, and her voice had dropped so much I had to strain to hear her. Who was she talking to—me or herself? "Men talk. They say things when they're mad. Everybody says things they don't mean when they're mad. It doesn't mean anything."

"Bullshit. His 'talk' landed me in the emergency room. I should send you a picture of the cut. If you won't help me for my sake, remember this. If he kills someone he is going to jail for the rest of his life. That police chief around here is not somebody who'll let this go. He has a problem with Jeffrey going after a pregnant woman, and if Jeffrey kills me or the baby he will make sure that Jeffrey never sees a window without a bar across it for the rest of his life. So, if you won't do me a favor, do Jeffrey one."

"I can't," she whispered. "He'd kill me." I closed my eyes and shook my head. She was sure he was such a nice guy that he couldn't possibly have cut me but nonetheless he'd kill her if she ratted on him. Sure, that made sense.

"Then do this," I said. "Take down this number. If he leaves the house without your knowing where he's going, drop a dime on him. You don't have to testify. You don't have to break his alibi. You'd don't have to say anything. Just give me a chance to get away from him. It's in his best interest not to kill me or the baby, not just mine. You know that."

She didn't speak. "Here's the number, Joanna. Write it down." I gave her the number but heard nothing. I had no way of knowing if she wrote it down or not.

I took a seat across from Gary. He looked tired and glum and he hadn't even heard from me yet. On the table between us lay three metal objects and a plastic bag sitting next to the drawing Stacy had made of the three pieces of metal. "Jeez," I said, looking back and forth between the drawing and the objects. "Stacy's pretty good. Where were they?"

"That machine in the print shop that kept breaking down," Gary said. "Small wonder it wouldn't work if half its parts were missing. You gotta admit it was clever. Take the murder weapon out of a machine and then just put it back and close the damn thing up afterward. No way anybody's going to find it."

"What's this?" I asked, pointing to the plastic bag.

"Ah, that," he said. "We found that in the oil tray. It had a jumpsuit in it with blood all over it. Somebody knew it was messy to beat someone to death. So they simply put a jumpsuit on, stripped it off afterward and hid it in the oil tray. We're analyzing the blood now, but you want to bet it's Clarence's or Stacy's or both?"

"What's Rudolph's role in this?" I asked.

"Ah," said Gary. "We're establishing that now. He's looking pretty sheepish and he's at least guilty of trusting some of the inmates enough to leave them alone unsupervised—which means he broke a lot of rules.

But I thought he'd have a heart attack when he realized what the parts had been used for. I don't think he knew what was going on.

"Just so you know," he added. "I've canceled all treatment groups—yours, alcohol and drug, domestic violence, everything—until we get to the bottom of this. I don't want a repeat of Stacy anywhere down the line."

I nodded. I expected it and I wasn't that upset. I'd been doing treatment for a number of years and this was the first group where I felt that not a single inmate was getting anything out of it. The group had had a bad feel from the beginning and after the talk with Eileen, I was pretty sure why. If my treatment group was an excuse for distributing drugs in the prison, it was hardly a surprise no one was taking treatment seriously.

"So," he said, running a hand through his hair and looking distracted. "What's up?"

Feeling a little sheepish myself, I started slowly, not looking at Gary. I told him about the trip to New Hampshire, about the connection between the printer and Jim Walker. "I was going to tell you about the supplier when I first heard about it," I added quickly, "but Rudolph told me the same day Stacy got hurt and the whole thing slipped my mind when I heard about Stacy." Gary didn't speak—although it was pretty clear he was not a happy camper—but I kept going. I walked lightly over the attack but his face darkened predictably anyway. "I'm all right," I finished lamely. "I think he was just trying to scare me." I told him briefly of my suspicions that the group was used to distribute the drugs. Gary looked puzzled and I had to tell him I thought Eileen had been distracted and not keeping a close eye, but didn't say too much more. Nonetheless, he rolled his eyes. I hated to be the one getting Eileen into any more trouble than she was already, but there it was. I couldn't leave her out entirely.

When I stopped we both sat there, neither of us speaking for a few minutes, then the phone rang. Relief surged through me and I realized I didn't care if it was nuclear war, I was so glad for an interruption. Gary snatched the phone and said "What is it?" in a voice so abrupt I winced. He listened for a moment and then handed it to me.

"Michael," Julie, Gary's secretary, said carefully—no doubt Gary's reaction had had an impact—"sorry to interrupt, but there's someone here who would like to see you."

"Who?" I said surprised.

"The office says it's a Mrs. Terrance. She says you're her son's counselor."

"Really?" I said. It had to be Joey Terrance's mom, the only guy in the whole group I had any hope for. The guy I had accidentally set up for Captain Watkins to harass. "Okay, I'll be right down." Probably Mrs. Terrance could have waited for a few minutes. Probably—I wouldn't tell Gary that.

"Gotta go," I said, getting up with more speed than I'd managed for months. "That's all I've got, anyway." I turned to go, then stopped and turned back around. "Take it easy, Gary," I said softly. "Hey, you're making progress on this thing. You've got most of it."

Gary snorted. "After one inmate is killed and a staff member maimed? Fine time to be making progress."

I shrugged. "It wasn't a murder weapon until somebody used it," I said. "It was just a part in a machine." I turned to go.

I got to the door before he spoke again. "Michael," he said, his voice gentler than I expected. I stopped but didn't turn around.

"Don't do that again."

"What?"

"Withhold information. Go off on your own investigating things. Trust us a little, okay? It may not seem like it, but we do know what we're doing—most of the time, anyway."

"Okay," I said simply, and opened the door.

"Michael," he said again.

I stopped, waiting, but he didn't speak, so I turned around.

"Is he coming back?"

I wouldn't have told him. I hadn't told Adam or Carlotta or anybody. But he asked. And the answer had been there since I'd talked to the doc in the emergency room. I wouldn't lie to him. What was the point?

"I think so," I said. "Adam's already harassed him and he knows I told. He'll take it personally. Sure, it's possible."

"And your plan?"

I shrugged. "Haven't got that far. Figured I had a couple of days, anyway."

"Get that far," Gary said.

I just nodded and left.

I walked down to the waiting room not looking forward to seeing Joey Terrance's mother. I had a daily relationship with guilt anyway, but I just hated the times it trailed out behind me like tin cans after a wedding car. No doubt Mrs. Terrance had heard about the guards threatening Terrance—I'd be ticked about that too, if I was his mother. But how had she known I had given them the info? It wasn't likely that Arnie had

told Joey anything about where he got the information. It would just make him seem more omniscient if
he didn't say. Hell of a thing. Gary was on my case for
withholding information. Mrs. Terrance would be on
my case for sharing it.

She was sitting bolt upright on one of the chairs in
the waiting room, clutching her pocketbook in front
of her. She was a large woman with very dark skin and
hair that had been severely straightened. She was
neatly dressed in clothes that reminded me of the
fifties. She seemed ill at ease, like a woman caught in a
place that felt completely alien to her.

"Hi," I said softly, not sure why she looked so dis-
tressed. I had thought she might be angry but this was
different. "I'm Michael Stone."

"You be Joey's counselor?" she said.

"I'm his group leader," I said. "I don't see him for
individual counseling." She looked blank and I realized that whether it was group or individual probably
didn't make much sense to a regular person. "Yes," I
said. "I'm his counselor."

"I gotta talk to you."

"Sure," I said without enthusiasm. "Why don't we
go next door to the canteen?"

She followed me, still holding her pocketbook in
front of her as we sat down at a table in a far corner.

"What can I do for you?" I said, apprehensively.

"My Joey," she said. "He's a good boy, not like his
brother."

"His brother?"

"Daryl was trouble from the day he was born, just
like his father. But Joey, he was different. He was a real
sweet little boy, couldn't stand to see an animal hurt,
used to steal food from the table to feed stray dogs.

He's gonna be somebody, you could tell that right away. If it weren't for his no-good brother, he wouldn't be in no prison. He'd be a preacher like his granddaddy. He still gonna be a preacher like his granddaddy. The Lord don't care you make mistakes, just so long you come to Jesus."

"Joey's here on a charge of molesting his brother and two friends," I said dryly. "Is that the same brother or a different one?" I wasn't going to touch the religious stuff but I was wondering whether she was blaming the victim for the molestation.

"That weren't nothing," she said. "He was just fooling around with his little brother, Rodney. That weren't nothing they shoulda put anybody in prison for. Lord, if every time two kids fooled around you put one of them in prison, you're not gonna have nobody left to go to school. Joey's older brother, Daryl, he's the one who taught Joey to do that, anyway. My baby woulda never done that on his own. Daryl got Joey into all kinds of trouble growing up. I used to pray to God why he gave me Daryl, but I know now it was just to test me. The Lord works in mysterious ways."

Oh boy. Why did families do this? Between the one who could do no right and the one who could do no wrong, it was hard to know who was harmed most.

"I didn't spare the rod, if that's what you're thinking," she said when I didn't speak. "I wailed on Joey regular like—just like the rest, just like the Bible says. 'Spare the rod and spoil the child.' Ain't nobody ever gonna say I didn't do right by those children." She nodded vigorously as though defending herself against imaginary charges. "I worked two jobs. Sixteen hours a day I worked to put food on the table. Worked in that

factory till my fingers got all big and stiff." She held
them out and they looked arthritic, all gnarled and
swollen.

"I done right by them. I gave them everything they
needed. Those kids didn't go without. Not like I did."

"Okay," I said slowly. "What did you want to see me
about?" I knew better than to comment on her choice
of discipline. She wasn't going to convince me that
beating kids was a good idea—and the fact that Joey
was in prison didn't help her case in my mind—but I
knew I wouldn't convince her, either. Not to mention
people who worked sixteen-hour days to support their
children were *trying* to do right by them, whether they
succeeded or not. All the same, life probably hadn't
been much fun for Joey—Mom gone all day every day
and when she was home, "wailing" on him as her
Christian duty.

"He's up to something," she said. "I asked him how
he's doing here and he stare me straight in the eye."

"Eye contact?" I said, confused. "He kept eye contact?" I had to remember it didn't mean the same
thing in her culture as mine.

"He stared at me and stuck his jaw out. I know he's
been talking to Daryl again. That's the only time my
boy goes wrong, when he's listening to his no-'count
brother. I told him he can't throw his life away like
that. We're all done with that kind of mess. Shames
me to think of my boy being here. What am I supposed to tell the Reverend? I just got to hang my head.
I've worked too hard for him to waste his life in a
prison. So he's gonna tell you."

"Excuse me?"

"I told him I didn't wanna hear it. I don't wanna
hear what kind of mess he's got himself in now. He's

gotta tell somebody what he's doing and he told me he'd tell his counselor. You be his counselor?"

"Well, I guess. I don't know of any other."

"Then you go talk to Joey. If he don't come clean, I wanna hear about it. I'll come down here with Reverend Carter and straighten that boy out."

"Joey wants to talk to me?"

She looked at me like I was dense. "Joey's gonna talk to you; it don't matter what he want."

I walked back up to my office and called for Joey Terrance to be brought up. My cut was hurting and I was tired already. But maybe he had something; then again, maybe not. Anyway, this was one I couldn't turn over. Mrs. Terrance had told Joey to talk to me and it was clear that was exactly what she meant. I closed my eyes and almost fell asleep while I waited. Really, running through the woods had exhausted my quota of energy for the next month at least.

"Joey," I said, literally rubbing my eyes when he was brought in. "Your mama said you wanted to talk to me." He started to speak but I held up my hands. "Wait," I said. "You need to know something. Outside, when you speak to a counselor, it's confidential. It is not confidential here. Read my lips about this, Joey. Nothing you say to a prison counselor is confidential—ever. So if you're up to something illegal, you can tell me if you want to but you need to know it will go to the prison authorities. You can also talk to your attorney first." Fair was fair. He had a right to know.

"I was gonna talk to you anyway," Joey muttered. "I'm not doin' nothin'. Well, not really. I just know some stuff, that's all."

"Okay," I said. "Like what?"

"Do they need to know I told you? Not that I'm scared of them or nothin' like that."

"Who's they? Other inmates?"

He nodded.

"I won't tell them, that's for sure. But prisons are funny places. Once this goes to security, I lose control of it and everybody knows the prison grapevine gets a lot of stuff it shouldn't. Or they could figure it out for themselves if they get some heat."

"I don't care," he said defiantly. "They mess with me they gonna have to deal with Daryl." He shook his head solemnly. "Not too many people wanna deal with Daryl. That's the thing, anyway. Jim, that white lawyer, he want me to hook him up with Daryl. And my mama gonna kill me I start runnin' with Daryl again."

"Why is Jim interested in Daryl?" I asked.

"Daryl got connections. Down in Hartford and New Haven. He in tight with some people down there."

"Gangs?"

He nodded. "So Jim wants to get hooked up with a gang? Why?"

"He say they can do some business. I don't know why he want Daryl. He already got Avery. Avery know people."

"In New Haven?"

"No, I think Avery from Boston. That's all he talk about anyway. Hear him tell it, he the man in Boston."

I thought about it. What kind of business? Only thing I knew about was drugs. Could it be Jim and Jeffrey were expanding their enterprise?

"I heard somethin'. Maybe it don't mean nothin'. But I keep thinkin' about it. Maybe it just be the way he said it. Said it like it mean somethin'." He paused.

"I was comin' out the shower and Avery and Jim were standin' there at the urinals. I didn't hear what Jim say but Avery, he say, 'I keep my end of the bargain when you keep yours.'

"Then Jim say he got no chance. Security be too tight. Not his fault. Everybody uptight since Clarence killed."

"What did Avery say?"

"Nothin'. He already said it. Man like Avery, he not gonna say it twice. Man said what he had to say. Jim whinin' about it don't mean nothin'."

"Did they see you?"

"Sure, but I acted like a dumb kid, like I don't hear nothin'."

"Jesus. You think they bought it?"

"Sure," Joey said, "They bought it 'cause they wanted to. Like I said, I got Daryl. They wanna believe I don't hear nothin'. They think different, they might end up dealin' with Daryl."

"Joey, just one thing. Your brother Daryl. Is he as bad as your mama thinks he is?"

"And then some." Joey nodded.

I didn't go to my office at the hospital. The knife cut, the adrenaline flood, the pregnancy, everything seemed to catch up to me. I drove straight home and by the time I got there I was so sleepy I could hardly drive. I took the cell phone and got out my .357 Magnum and put them both on the coffee table. Then I dived onto the couch and spent the day sleeping off and on. The phone rang several times but I just turned the answering machine down and ignored it.

I was finally up and sitting with my feet in the hot tub wishing the rest of me was there too when Adam came home. "You know, the baby's completely formed now," he said. "You could probably sit in it okay."

"Who knows?" I said. "Weren't you the one telling me not to take any chances?"

"Well, that's with men wielding knives," Adam said. "That's a little different." I didn't comment and Adam sat down on the edge of the tub, moving my .357 Magnum over first: I was lugging it with me when I went to the bathroom, just in case. Adam took off his shoes and socks, rolled his pants up and wiggled his toes in the crisp night air before he dropped them into the tub next to me. "You need to come down and make a statement," he said. "I tried to call."

"I was here," I said. "I just fell asleep. I'll do it tomorrow. Any luck with Jeffrey?"

"Girlfriend says he was there all night," Adam said, which I already knew.

"She's lying."

"Probably, but we have to prove it. He didn't leave much behind. Anyway, he knows he's on tap for it. He's a weasely little guy. Not exactly likable."

"Like you thought he would be?"

"That's not what I'm saying. There's something sneaky about him, beyond what you run into ordinarily." I knew what he was talking about. There were degrees of bad guys. The big-time thugs like Avery were actually the easiest to deal with. You knew who they were and what they did. Everybody understood the rules when dealing with Avery. But the Jeffreys of the world? There was something there you were never sure of. For one thing, you really didn't know what they were capable of.

"You mad at me?" he asked.

"No," I said honestly, "not really. It's just . . ."

"What?" he prompted when I didn't go on.

"I do things," I said, "that don't seem like any big deal at the time. Sometimes they aren't. But sometimes they *are* a big deal and some pretty weird stuff happens. The problem is I can't always tell the stuff that turns out to be a big deal from the stuff that isn't. I didn't know going up to look for the printing supplier was going to start anything. I'm not *trying* to act like an asshole. Maybe the world's just weird or maybe I have shit for a compass on this kind of stuff."

"Maybe both," Adam said dryly.

"So what's the answer?" I asked. "I just keep doing stuff and you keep yelling at me that I'm an idiot?"

"I never said you were an idiot," he replied. We both just sat there. I hadn't turned on any lights and I could barely see his face in the dark, which somehow made it easier. "How are you doing with me living here?" he asked suddenly, and although his face hadn't changed, something in the atmosphere between us picked up a charge.

"You're not really living here," I said quickly. "You're sort of hanging out for a while." Adam didn't say anything. "All right, maybe you're living here—for now, until the baby's born and everything settles down." I glanced over. Adam still didn't speak. "Shit, I don't know, Adam. Sometimes I can't believe it. I come home and you're here or you walk in and I'm like 'Whoa, how did this happen?' and I think I have to talk to you or entertain you or something. Everything gets small . . . I don't know how to say it . . . all around me, everything gets small and crowded and I think if I don't get out of here my chest will burst. And when that happens I really don't understand how I did this.

"And sometimes . . ." I sighed. Why was this harder

to admit? "Sometimes, it's not so bad. Not bad at all, really, sometimes." I glanced over at Adam's face but I couldn't read anything on it at all.

"Michael," he said slowly, "I'm not going to be a part-time father. I'm just not. So, I don't want to bring this up, but you didn't exactly mention it to me when you discontinued birth control."

"I was over forty," I said sullenly. "I didn't think I could get pregnant."

"Okay," he said slowly, but he didn't sound convinced. "What I'm trying to say is you've got some responsibility in this thing. To work this thing out. So you need to get used to me," he said bluntly. "Because I'm here and I'm staying."

"Jesus," I said. "Couldn't you just lie to me a little, give me time to get used to this thing?"

Adam laughed.

I left it alone. I didn't know where to go with it. Adam's voice had that "word with the bark on it" tone, as my grandmother used to say. Where did that leave me?

"Adam . . ." I said slowly. "I'm not me anymore."

"What do you mean?" he said softly.

"Sometimes I think I stopped growing at around thirteen, maybe twelve. When I close my eyes and pull up a picture of myself, it's always the same. I have on blue shorts and a white tee shirt, white socks and tennis shoes. I'm flat-chested and lean-hipped and my legs have those long, lean muscles in them that kids have. I have reflexes so fast I can catch a cup if it falls off a table. Hell, people have thrown eggs at me when I wasn't expecting it, just to test me, and I've caught them sometimes even with my left hand.

"Only . . . well, look at me now. Who is this person?

I don't even know her. My ankles look like something you'd see in a medical book under 'bad ideas.' I can't walk across a room without needing to take a break in the middle. And you, and everybody else I know, is patting me on the head and telling me to run on home and let them handle it, little lady. I don't feel like me anymore.

"And what does this baby mean, anyway? That I'm going to have to worry about how what I do impacts someone else every day for the rest of my life? Am I going to have to be afraid to stand up to anybody who's even vaguely, possibly, remotely dangerous because they could come after my kid? Get real. That's all I deal with. Face it. Criminals are dangerous. That's why they're in jail. I don't know who I am anymore."

Adam put his arms around me and said nothing at all. He just kissed the top of my head and then rested his cheek on it. Strangely, a vague sense of peace passed over me, paused hesitantly, then seemed to settle in. I don't know why. Adam hadn't said anything. Nothing chirpy or reassuring, none of that this-too-shall-pass crap, nothing drippy about "the bright side." He hadn't said I was wrong or I was still me or even did that light-at-the-end-of-the-tunnel thing. He just sat there, saying nothing at all, with his arms around me.

I laid my head on his chest and closed my eyes, drinking in the smell of his aftershave and feeling the heat from his body. A spring inside me, the one that stays tight all the time, began to ease off and let go.

"Beyond this point there be dragons" the old maps read and I had always believed it. Get into strange, uncharted territory, and no question, you'll run into a dragon or two. But what drew the explorers weren't the dragons, it was the Spice Islands they hoped to find. And it turned out, maybe it was true: maybe there weren't just dragons, maybe there was a Spice Island or two out there as well.

If so, they weren't on any map I had. I didn't have a name or a description and certainly not a latitude or longitude. I just had the smell of Adam's aftershave and the warmth spreading from his chest all the way down to my palms. There was some kind of shape looming out of the fog off the starboard bow. Something was out there and it wasn't all bad.

16

"MICHAEL," THE VOICE ON THE PHONE WAS TRIUMPHANT. "IT'S
Brenda."

"Brenda," I said, rubbing the sleep out of my eyes
and glancing at the clock. It was a respectable hour for
my cousin to call. I was just running late again. "Did
you find something?"

"Yes, I did. I did. The man's name is Richard
Thompson and I've got his phone number in Raleigh.
Here it is."

"Good job," I said as I wrote it down. "How'd you
get it?"

I heard Brenda clear her throat. "Well, your mama's
back so I had to wait till she went shopping. Then I
went to her house and I stole her phone bill. I did. She
locks the house but I have a key, don't you know, and I
walked right in the house and in the bedroom. I knew
she kept her bills in that little desk in the corner. I
can't believe I did it but I took her phone bill. I got his
name by calling the operator. They can give you the
name if you've got the number now. It's called 'reverse
directory' or something like that. Only . . ."

"What's the number?" I asked. Brenda gave it to me and then she said again, "Only . . ."

"Only what?" When she didn't speak I said, "Come on, Brenda. Whatever it is, tell me."

"Well, there's another thing I wanted to tell you about. I'd have called you anyway. I mean, it's none of my business and I hate to always be talking behind her back—"

"Brenda, I just can't cope with all this dilly-dallying. Just tell me."

"All right. All right. I'm just worried because your mother's spending so much time on the computer."

"A computer? My mother has a computer?"

"Yes, she does. I don't know when she got it. I tried calling her, Lord, I don't know how many days in a row last week and the line was always busy so I stopped by. She was on the Internet and she told me that's why the line is busy, but goodness, Michael, it can't be healthy to be sitting at a computer that long. She's given up the soaps."

"She's on the Internet? Doing what?"

"I don't know, Michael. How would I know? I don't know anything about computers. I'm just worried about her. These trips back and forth to Vegas. Now this computer thing."

"Did you ask her what she was doing?"

"I most certainly did not. You know your mother. What do you think she would have told me?"

Good point. But what was my mother doing on the Internet? Chat rooms? Gambling? Supposedly there was gambling on the Net. Had Mama discovered she didn't have to go to Vegas to gamble? If she wasn't gambling, what was she doing? Surfing for what? Talking to whom? Somehow I just knew she wasn't reading the news. Why was I in my forties having to worry about my seventy-six-year-old mama on the Internet?

"Brenda," I said. "Do you remember when that tour group called me from Greece because Mama was wandering off by herself?"

"Yes, I remember but—"

"But nothing, Brenda. Do you remember when she got arrested at the Acropolis for wandering behind the roped-off areas?"

"Yes, but—"

"Did I have any solutions then?"

"Well, I believe you talked her into coming home."

"I did not, Brenda. I absolutely did not. They *shipped* her home. I had nothing to do with it." I took a deep breath. "I'm trying to say I don't know what to do about Mama any more than you do. So if you have any ideas feel free to share them, because I don't know what she's up to or what to do about it."

"Michael, you told me to get that man's number. Do you want it or not?"

There was silence. "Oh, hell, Brenda, I'll give Richard Thompson a call. Not that it will help."

And I hung up.

It didn't help. I picked up the phone immediately and called the number Brenda had given me. I didn't even know if it was an office or a home number but wherever it was, Richard Thompson answered immediately.

"Mr. Thompson," I said. "I'm Michael Stone, Mrs. Stone's daughter."

"Ah," he said. "I am very pleased to meet you. Your mother is a remarkable woman, Ms. Stone. I don't think I've ever met anyone quite like her. What can I do for you?"

"Well, to tell you the truth, I'm concerned about my mother, Mr. Thompson," I said bluntly. "About her and your relationship with her and about what she's doing in Vegas."

"Well, now," he said. "She is an unusual woman and I'm not surprised at your calling. I haven't been involved with anyone her age before, it's true, but I think this will all work out. Really, with this kind of thing, age has nothing to do with it."

"And what is your age, Mr. Thompson?"

There was a pause. "I'm not sure why you ask," he said. "I'm not sure that's any of your business."

"It seems obvious to me why I'd ask," I replied.

"Then you need to enlighten me," he said.

"Mr. Thompson, exactly what are your plans for my mother?"

"I don't have any plans for your mother," he said stiffly. "You should know better than I do that your mother does what she wants to do. I have given her information, that's all. It's good information, I believe, but your mother doesn't always take my advice and she is definitely the one making the decisions. I might add that she came to me, Ms. Stone. I didn't go to her."

"Do the words 'undue influence' mean anything to you?"

"Excuse me?"

"If you talk my mother into losing her life savings in some Las Vegas scam, then I will make damn sure you spend every cent you get defending yourself in court. Not to mention people who do this once do it more than once. It might be very interesting to look into how many other elderly widows you've been 'involved with.'"

There was a long pause, then he said stiffly. "I think you have the wrong idea about this but I'll relay your concerns to your mother." And he hung up.

I got myself dressed, still thinking about Thompson and what he meant, and getting an uneasy feeling I was off-track somewhere. What I never understood and probably never would understand was why I could read criminals so well and didn't understand anything at all about Mama. I'd grown up in the same house with her. I hadn't grown up with a single psychopath or sadist or even pedophile anywhere in my family tree, thank God. So why was it I could read them on sight and couldn't make sense of anything about Mama?

I just always had a vague uneasy feeling about her and around her. Maybe the whole thing was predictability. Psychopaths and sadists and pedophiles were incredibly predictable. They ran true to form, no matter what it cost them. Once you saw where they were coming from you knew without a doubt where they were going. But Mama was a broken field runner who could turn on a dime. You just never knew what direction she was going in. But why was I trying to tackle her? Sometimes I thought I was supposed to learn something from my relationship with Mama. But what?

I drove to the police station and spent the morning making a long and embarrassing statement about being attacked to a tape recorder while Adam sat quietly nearby. It was embarrassing because getting caught unawares always makes you feel like a dork. Outsiders always thought the fact that you were the innocent party and were just minding your own business when someone jumped on you with both feet would make you feel okay about it. But right and wrong weren't the whole story. People were wired to care about efficacy. Having your head in the mud under someone's boot was never a good moment, never mind how "wrong" they were.

I went to my office afterward and spent the afternoon restlessly seeing clients. Nobody I saw had anything very wrong with them and after a while I got impatient, which wasn't fair in the slightest. Fair or not, I had moments when I wanted to stand up and yell, "You think you've got problems? You think your life isn't exciting enough? I've got a friend who's daughter is trying to kill herself with diabetes and another one trying to wake up from a coma. Now we're talking problems."

I didn't say it. I just nodded and asked what I hoped passed as thoughtful questions. It was a strange fact in life that everybody had some sort of worry sack inside their heads. It filled up with something, no matter how trivial. The people who had it good never seemed to know it until they got it not so good. Then they remembered but by then it was too late: once you get cancer, the annoyance of your daughter not doing her homework fades, but you can never go back. So the day made me more sad than anything. It seemed a waste to be talking to people who were crying over their horse trainers quitting or their husbands wanting to move to a different town or their mothers still calling them every day. Get an answering machine. Get a life. But I was just as bad as anybody else. Hadn't I just been pissing and moaning about being fat and slow like it was the end of the world?

I did get one piece of good news. Late in the day the phone rang and the nurse I had talked to in Stacy's room actually remembered me and called to say he'd come around. He was off the respirator, but unlike the movies he hadn't woken up bright and cheerful with tales of lights calling him to peace and serenity. He'd woken up groggy and confused and not sure where he was. He was in an "acute confusional state," to use the official language and, no, I couldn't see him yet. They didn't know anything yet about residual damage. You couldn't assess much when someone was this out of it. All they knew was that he could see and he could hear, which was certainly a start. And light years better than being the mummy he had been.

My delight at the news faded some on the way home as I thought about Jeffrey coming back. It was only 5:30 but already it was getting dark, and there was something about the dark that made you think twice about going home to face an unwelcome visitor. Just heading toward the house brought up the knife on my belly, the slippery voice in my ear. I shuddered. Maybe I should check in with Adam and see what his plans were. We hadn't talked that morning about our schedules but I knew he'd want to coordinate our going home. And maybe I did, too. But the day had likely gotten away from him—it had me—and neither of us had called.

His number was busy at work so idly I dialed my own office number to see if he had left a message after I left. The first message, however, stopped me in my tracks. The voice was slurred and very small but there was no mistaking it, even though I'd only heard it a couple of times before.

"He's gone," she said and it sounded like she was

crying. "He's got his guns with him and I . . . I don't know for sure but . . . Jesus, call me if you get this." I thought she'd hung up but suddenly she rattled off a number and then the phone went dead.

Frantically I tried to remember the number while I searched for a pen. I slowed down and pulled the car over at the first wide space in the road, dumped my purse upside down and finally pulled a pen out of the debris. I grabbed the first piece of paper I saw and wrote the number on the back. I grabbed the phone and dialed, noticing, as I did, the low battery light on the phone flash. I had been carrying the darn thing around with me without a thought of recharging it. Please, please, hang in there, I thought, and goddammit, Joanna, answer this phone.

The phone rang four times and just as I was giving up she answered. "Jeffrey?" she said and I closed my eyes for a second against the desperation that came across in the single word.

"Sorry," I said, "it's me, Michael Stone."

"Oh, shit," she said. "I shouldn't have called you."

"Why?" I said. "You want him to go to prison forever?"

"Some days," she said.

"Not enough days," I muttered. "What happened?"

"He got a letter this morning."

The phone beeped three times, which I hadn't heard before but didn't think was a good sign.

"And?" When she didn't speak, I added, "What was in it?"

"I don't know. He didn't show it to me. It's gone now. He burned it."

"Joanna, help me here. What are you talking about?"

"He wrote down an address. All I saw was 'River Road.' Then he loaded his guns in the car. We had . . . I tried to stop him."

"What's he got for firepower?"

"You're not going to kill him, are you?"

"I think the problem is the other way around. Tell me what I'm facing."

"A rifle and a .45. I wouldn't try to get into it with him. He'd . . . it wouldn't work. He was a ranger. He's got a shooting thing out back. He shoots . . . well, a lot, anytime he's mad." Which I already knew was a lot. "I think you'd better make yourself scarce." There was a pause. "If you tell him . . ."

"I won't tell him. Are you all right?"

"I think so. It's not bad. My ribs just hurt a little."

"He hit you in the ribs?" I was outraged and then regretted showing it.

The phone beeped three times again.

"He . . . he doesn't know what he's doing when he gets like that. I shouldn't have got in his face. I know it sets him off. I'm all right, really. You live on River Road?"

"No."

"You don't?"

"No, I don't," I said. "But I know who does."

"Don't let them hurt him," she said. "He's not a bad person. I don't know what I'd do without him."

Maybe get a life, I almost said, but didn't.

"Joanna, when did he—" but the phone beeped three last times and went completely stone dead.

The problem with a rural state was it was rural. That was fine when you were leaf-peeping or cow-gazing or whatever but not so fine when you were try-ing to find a telephone. There were no gas stations or shopping malls along this road, just an occasional farmhouse set back from the road. I passed a couple and slowed down each time but neither had any lights on or cars out front and finally I gave up. I could search all night for a goddamn house with somebody home. Or I could drive out and warn him myself. There was only one thing wrong with that idea, but I put it aside.

Could I find Gary's house after all these years? Maybe. I was only fifteen or twenty minutes away if I cut over by the old highway that ran from Clarion to Newport. If I did that though, there wasn't a chance in hell I'd find a place to call from along the way. Still, if I kept driving toward home, it would take longer to get there than going to Gary's house. Turning around and going back to Jefferson would take even more time. Goddamn cell phone, I swore. This could have been so simple if the damn thing was just working.

I put the pedal to the metal and headed for the old highway that would take me to River Road. Maybe for once there would be a highway patrolman lurking somewhere in the shadows and he'd pull me over and have a nice fat car phone just sitting on his dashboard. Fat chance, I thought.

The road was mostly dry for which I was grateful beyond belief. I had driven like a maniac as a kid and had a reasonable sense of how fast you could go and still hold a curve, but it was all on Southern roads. I didn't know ice. Didn't understand it. Couldn't compensate for it. The damn stuff just seemed to come out of nowhere and who could tell when it was thin enough that it wasn't a problem or thick enough that you lost traction completely. And there was still plenty of it on the back roads in Vermont, even though officially we were into spring, whatever that meant in New England.

I held my breath as I skidded a little on a curve, grateful I had only run into a small patch of ice. There was a covered bridge ahead and I slowed down. One thing I did understand: bridges were colder than roads because they had nothing under them but air. If there was ice anywhere it would be on a bridge.

The bridge was slippery and I felt the traction go. Suddenly the car had that steering-a-ship feeling it gets when there's only a vague relationship between the steering wheel and where you end up. I slid across the bridge, hands frozen on the wheel, just hoping I wouldn't start drifting sideways. Thank God the bridge was straight; nobody had been dumb enough to put a curve in the middle of any Vermont bridge I had ever run into and the straightforward momentum took me safely onto the dry pavement beyond.

I hit the accelerator and my old "basic car" shot forward with a gratifying leap. How much of a lead over Jeffrey did I have? That was really the question. It would take him at least two hours to drive from Berlin to Gary's house, but how long had Joanna waited before she called? How long had he been gone?

I hadn't been to Gary's house in so long I missed the turn-off and had to back up. Goddammit, his house was more isolated than mine. What was it with people who saw the worst of humanity that we liked to hide out in the woods? Good idea when it meant someone couldn't find you. Not such a good idea when they did.

Gary's house was maybe a quarter mile away when I hit the brakes and slowed down. Didn't I need a plan or something? What if Jeffrey's car was in the yard? I

hadn't seen one parked on the side of the road so pre-
sumably if his car wasn't in the yard, he wasn't there
yet. On the other hand Jeffrey was coming from
Berlin, a whole different direction from me. Without
looking at a map I didn't know if he'd end up coming
from my direction on River Road, or coming from the
other end. I could go past Gary's house and scout the
road on the other side to see if there was a car there. If
there was I could give it up and go for help—wherever
that was. Or I could just hightail it to Gary's, warn the
family and call the state police. I didn't know which
way to call it.

Gary's driveway rose up suddenly in front of me
and I had to decide. It dawned on me that if I did
scout farther down River Road and find Jeffrey's car,
Jeffrey might still be in it, which wouldn't help at all. I
turned into Gary's driveway and grabbed my Magnum
out of the debris from my dumped purse. Vaguely, it
crossed my mind that what I was doing was likely the
sort of thing Adam was bitching about. But this was
going to be simple, I hoped. Jeffrey was probably still
an hour away. I'd warn the family. We'd call the police.
They'd be waiting for him if he showed up. What
could go wrong? If I was too late, that's what could go
wrong.

There was only one car in the driveway and it had a
Vermont license plate; likely it was Gary's or Susan's
since Jeffrey lived in New Hampshire. There were
lights on in the house and, from the outside at least,
nothing looked wrong. Relieved, I pulled my car in
behind the other one and was out of it as soon as it
stopped, gun in hand. I crouched and ran awkwardly,
slowed down by my belly, which just seemed even bigger when I tried to bend over. I didn't think he was

there but I wasn't taking chances. I stayed close to the cars, which was smart if Jeffrey was out there on the *other* side of the cars, pointless if he was on my side, but who knew? I got to the end of the second car and made a break for the door.

The door was locked as I knew it would be. I crouched down, hidden in shadow and started banging on the door and yelling for Susan.

Eternity passed and then Susan opened the door. She looked at eye level and then down, startled as I scurried past her and into the house. I slammed the door, reached up and locked it. "Where's Gary?" I said.

"On his way home," she said, looking frightened. "What's wrong?"

"Where's the phone?" I asked.

"It's not working," she said.

"Since when?"

"Maybe twenty minutes ago. What's going on? What's wrong?"

"Shit, shit, shit," I said. "Pull the blinds. I got a call. Someone's on his way here. Already here, I'd guess. He's after Gary. Or maybe you and Aspasia, I don't know."

Susan paled and took a step backward. She glanced toward the kitchen and I saw Aspasia sitting at the kitchen table with a spoon frozen halfway to her mouth. "Get down," I yelled to Aspasia. She didn't do anything, just sat there for a minute and then Susan hurriedly crossed the room and pulled her off her seat, the spoon still in her hand.

I headed for the blinds and heard Susan coming up behind me. I grabbed her arm when she passed and said, "Get down." Her face looked so blank I didn't think she heard me but she nodded and dropped down beside me. Together we crawled around the house dropping blinds and turning off lights.

"Any chance he's already in the house?" I whispered.

"I don't think so," Susan said. "We've been here all afternoon and we haven't heard anything. You're sure about this?"

"No, but the fact your phone is out isn't reassuring me. You have a cell phone?"

She shook her head. "Gary does. Big help that is," she muttered.

"Do you have a security system?"

"Sure," she said.

"Is it wired independent of the phone?"

"I think so."

"It's supposed to go to the police?" She nodded. "On a separate phone line?"

"I think so. A monitoring center, anyway, and they call the police. It's been so long I don't remember all the details."

"Set it off."

Susan thought for a minute, then crawled to the front hall. She stood up long enough to set the system and then crawled to a window. She opened it slowly but nothing happened. She turned to me, confusion on her face. "It isn't working. It's supposed to make a siren noise and then dial the police."

"On a separate line?" I asked again.

"I'm pretty sure."

"Then he's here. They wouldn't both be out by accident."

Susan sat down heavily on the floor. "Jesus Christ, Jesus Christ," she muttered. "I've worried about something like this for years. I've dreamed about it. I can't believe it's happening."

"How long before Gary's due home?"

"He called," she said, looking at her watch. "About half an hour ago. He was just leaving. It was right after that the phone went out."

"So how long?"

She shrugged. "Maybe another half an hour. Maybe less. Why is he after Gary? Never mind," she said. "It doesn't matter. But if he's here, why did he let you through?"

"I'm not the one he's after. Not this time, anyway. Also, maybe he wasn't in position. Or maybe," I added, "he thought a dead body on the lawn might be a clue. I don't know." I turned back to stare out of the window while Aspasia crawled up. She looked really frightened and curled up next to her mother. Susan put her arms around her. "Is this for real?" Aspasia said in a small voice.

"Maybe," I said. "I don't know. It could be. We have to assume it is. I don't know how seriously I'd take it except we've got one dead body at the prison and a staff member maimed. I don't think we'd better ignore it. He's not after you two," I added, thinking it through. "He's after Gary or he would have come in by now" . . . unless, I thought but didn't say it, he was planning on killing them in front of Gary, which would be a pretty horrible kind of thing. But this wasn't Jeffrey's personal vendetta, it was somebody else's, so probably not. Although Avery could have some weird idea about sending Gary to a family funeral too, like the one Gary hadn't let him go to. I decided not to mention that possibility.

"What's he going to do?" Susan asked.

"I think he told me," I said. "I had a run-in with him once. He jumped me getting out of the car and then he started rattling on about 'from the house to the car, from the car to the house' and how vulnerable people were. My guess is he'll try to shoot Gary when he gets out of the car. Nobody sees him. He picks up the shell and he's gone. If he's really smart, he'll be wearing boots one size too big, that sort of thing." I heard a sharp intake of breath from Aspasia and turned to look at her. Her pupils had dilated widely and then they got very small. I cursed myself for being so blunt. "We'll figure something out," I said, although truly it didn't seem very likely. "Come on," I said. "Let's go upstairs and see if we can spot him from there."

We crawled to the stairs single file and then got up and ran up to the second floor. We gathered in Aspasia's bedroom, which overlooked the front yard. Darkness had completely fallen but bright moonlight lit up the scene below. I could see pretty clearly but everything looked perfectly normal. Nothing to alarm Gary at all that something was amiss, except maybe the lights in the house being off.

"Great," I said, disgusted. There was no way we could pick out a sniper in those woods. No way at all. The distance from the driveway to the woods was forty feet or less. It was hardly possible to miss with a rifle at that distance, even at night. Certainly not with a moon like that. I doubted Jeffrey would even bother with a scope.

"Anything else?" I asked. "Gary got any tricks up his sleeve for protection here?"

"Like what?"

"Weapons? Anything."

"Sure, there's a handgun next to the bed and a shotgun in the attic."

"Anything to keep people out?"

She thought for a moment. "Deadbolts."

"Where? On the outside doors?"

"That too. No, on all the doors. You can barricade yourself in any room. There's a deadbolt on every door."

"Hollow doors?"

"No, solid. Is this going to help?"

"I hope not." I didn't say any more but Susan knew what I meant. If we needed to barricade ourselves in a room, it meant Jeffrey was inside the house and that wasn't a happy scenario any way you looked at it.

Aspasia crawled over to a window and looked out of it. "You have to do something," she said and her voice sounded shaky. "You can't let him shoot my daddy."

"Okay," I said. "Let's think about this. No cell phone, no regular phone. I don't see any way we can get to the outside world—"

"You can't just—" Aspasia sounded shrill.

"Hold on, Aspasia. What we need is for Gary to back right out of there without ever getting out of the car. Better yet, not drive in at all. But not driving in at all . . . that would mean one of us has to get through the woods to the road. Too risky. I don't know how good this guy is, but I'm told he was a ranger, which means he's probably pretty good in the woods. Not to mention we don't know where he is. And I can't go. I'm practically disabled. Aspasia can't go. She's a kid."

"I'll go," said Susan.

"Why can't I go?" Aspasia asked. "I'm smaller and I can hide better than you and I know these woods better, anyway. I played in them all the time, Mom, remember? I can find my way around in the dark."

"I'm sure you could," I said, "but it would be crazy for either of you. Likely, this guy's got night glasses. He could have them anyway. And, I repeat: we don't know where he is. If he gets hold of either of you, Gary will just give himself up."

"So that leaves warning Gary, from the house, when he gets here, before he gets out of the car."

"We could yell," Aspasia said.

"Too late," I said. "He wouldn't hear us until he got out of the car and then he'd stop to listen."

"We could set the house on fire," Aspasia said.

Her mother rolled her eyes but I said, "Well, it would get his attention, but it would also burn us up or force us out of the house, neither of which is too good."

"Turn on music really loud," Aspasia offered.

"Shoot the gun?" Susan suggested.

"Gary'd probably head for the house," I said to Susan, "thinking you were in danger. Same problem with the music. He wouldn't know to go away. Or if he thought the shots were coming from the house he wouldn't be watching the woods and then Jeffrey could ambush him."

"We could shoot at the woods now," Aspasia said. "Maybe this guy would shoot back and then we'd know where he is and I could go out the other door."

"The problem is the shooting back," I said. "He probably wouldn't and we'd be wasting ammo for nothing since we don't know where he is. But if he did . . . it's kind of risky to start shooting at people, especially people who are good with guns. Bullets go through windows, you know, and some bullets even go through walls. You don't want to do something like that until you have to."

We all fell silent. "Can you get on the roof from inside the house?" I asked.

"No," Susan said.

"That's not true, Mom," Aspasia said. "I've gotten on the roof before from inside the house."

"What?"

"From the attic. From the window in the attic."

"You're joking," Susan said. "How could you do that? You could have been killed. I can't believe you did that. The window up there is on the side of the house. There's nothing under it but the driveway."

Aspasia nodded. "Julian and I. We decided to climb up and see the stars from the roof. That's all. It wasn't that hard. The window doesn't have a screen. I just opened up the window and stood on the sill and got my leg over the roof. It bent the gutter some. I was afraid you'd notice. Julian held on to me in case I fell. It wasn't that hard."

"Aspasia, do you know how stupid that is? You could have been—"

"Later," I said. "Can you do it?" I asked Susan.

"Maybe," she said.

"She can't do it," Aspasia said. "She gets vertigo. She can't do anything that's up high."

Susan shrugged. "I can try."

"Okay," I said. "We're running out of time. Let's get a sheet. We're going to make a sign."

"Will he see it?" Susan said doubtfully.

"You got an extension cord and some kind of portable light?"

"Maybe, if I can find it. It might be in the garage. There's a portable clip-on light that we use to spotlight some outdoor decorations at Christmas."

"Perfect," I said. Maybe this crazy thing had a shot.

"Wait a minute," Susan said. "It's a full moon, for Christ's sake. Even without the light why won't this guy, whoever he is, see it?"

"Jeffrey," I said. "His name is Jeffrey and he's too close. I think he is, anyway. You can't see the top of the roof from the front lawn. That's basically where he is, on the edge of the woods. He can't be that far back in the woods. If he was, he couldn't see the roof through the trees, anyway. But he isn't because he wouldn't have a clear shot at Gary if there were trees in the way."

"Mom can't do this," Aspasia said again. "She'll fall. She can't even climb a stepladder. Why won't you let me?"

I looked at Susan.

"Out of the question," she said. "If he sees her, he could shoot her."

"Right," I said. "I forgot about that. She is seriously right, Aspasia. It's not the climbing thing. It's the getting shot thing that's the problem."

"And it's not a problem if he shoots my mother?" Aspasia asked. "That's not a problem?"

"I don't have time to argue," Susan said. "Aspasia, you're not going and that's final."

"It's the diabetes, isn't it?"

"What?"

"If I didn't have diabetes, you'd let me go. You used to believe in me."

"Aspasia, there's a madman outside with a gun. It's got nothing to do with diabetes."

"Yes, it does," Aspasia said. "You used to think I could do anything. Now you treat me like a freak. I can't do this; I can't do that. You don't let me play sports. You don't let me go anywhere."

"Aspasia, can it," Susan said, irritated. "You don't know what you're talking about."

"Uh, guys," I said. "We need to get this banner going or this conversation isn't going to matter because Gary's going to be here before we have any way to warn him. We're going to be sitting here arguing and listening to gunshots. So, where're the sheets? And paint? Do you have any paint and a brush?"

Susan went to the basement and came back with a can of blue paint. We pulled off the lid but when I saw it, my heart fell. It was light blue. "Nothing darker?" I asked.

Susan shook her head. After all, who had black paint lying around? We all looked at it, discouraged. "What about the red?" Aspasia said. "For my windows, remember?"

"There isn't enough," Susan said. "There wasn't that much."

"We could mix it in," I replied. "Let's get it."

I was feeling the time pressure. It had taken us forever to get this far. No question, Gary would be pulling in soon.

"Before we do this thing," I said, "I just want to be sure we haven't missed anything. Two-way radio?"

"No."

"E-mail?"

"Dial-up connection," Susan said. "Needs a phone line."

Try as I might, I couldn't think of anything else. Admittedly, the whole thing was a hare-brained idea, but it was something. Sometimes you had to go with "something" when your alternative was "nothing."

Thank God kids liked bright colors. The red was a fire engine red and turned the light blue into a kind of medium purple that had a shot, anyway, of being dark enough to be seen.

We spread out a king size white sheet on the living room floor and hurriedly painted giant letters the length of the sheet. "TRAP. RUN" it said. It was the shortest thing we could think of.

"Here's what's important," I said to Susan. "You gotta do this just right. You'll be on the roof so you'll be the first one to see him drive in. You have to yell at just the right time for Aspasia to plug the light in. If we plug it in too soon before Gary's anywhere that he can see it, Jeffrey will see the light and get someplace where he can shoot the light out or rip the whole thing to shreds with bullets. Too late and Gary's out of the car. Besides, if Gary gets all the way in, he won't be able to see the roof, either. You have to do this the first moment Gary can see it. And there's the light, too. If the light doesn't shine on it just right, he won't see it. Where can you hook up the light?"

"Maybe the chimney," Susan said, doubtful. "If it isn't too tall."

"It isn't," Aspasia said. "I can reach the top of it from the roof."

We both looked at her but neither of us spoke. It just wasn't the time to get into it. If the truth be known, almost every kid had done a whole lot more stuff than their parents knew about. At one point I'd done an informal survey in pediatrics. Every single adolescent I talked to had had some kind of close call their parents knew absolutely nothing about.

Aspasia got a hair dryer and tried to dry the paint but it was too slow and we ended up shaking the sheet, knowing the letters would smear some but hoping it would still be readable. We stuffed the sheet and the clip-on light into a day pack. Susan and I headed up to the attic while Aspasia went off to get a hammer and nails to hold the banner down and some duct tape for the light.

Susan had grown quieter as we'd gotten closer to finishing. On the stairs I said, "Susan, are you all right?"

"No," she said.

"Can you do this?"

"I don't know," she said.

She didn't seem inclined to discuss it so I shut up. What was there to say, anyway? She was in a box and it was going to be between her and the vertigo. Lot of help any of us would be.

We got to the attic and walked over to the small side window set into the attic wall. I looked down. Truly, the concrete driveway looked a long way away and the roof looked a long way up. There was really no easy way to swing from that window to the roof. "Holy shit," I said. "Aspasia did this? This is not going to be easy." I was just thinking aloud. I glanced at Susan's face and wished I'd kept my mouth shut. She looked even paler than before and she said suddenly, "Be right back," and headed for the stairs.

I followed her down and waited while she threw up in the bathroom. "Susan," I said, "don't you have any meds for this? For when you have to fly or something?"

"Oh, yeah," Susan said. "I do have some for flying. I never thought about it. I don't think it will work, though. I'm supposed to take them half an hour before I go."

"Let's try it anyway. It can't hurt. They might kick in." I was also thinking that even a placebo effect might do something.

Susan found the meds and swallowed them. Her hands were shaking and I realized with a sinking heart that this absolutely could not work. She would either fail to do it or fall or get up on the roof and panic. I had mountain climbed once with someone who had panicked on a cliff and it had been hell getting him down. I had had to give up belaying him and climb up beside him to talk him down. We could have both been killed very easily. Very, very easily. If Susan got on that roof and froze, she'd be a sitting duck, especially if she was making any noise—and she might be.

Great. We had a crazy solution that was worse than the problem we had in the first place. "Susan," I said. "This isn't going to work. It just isn't. You can't do what you can't do. You can't do this any more than I can, just for different reasons."

"I'm going to try," Susan said and headed for the stairs.

But we were too late. When we got to the attic, the window was open and the pack and Aspasia were gone.

"Oh Jesus, oh Jesus," Susan said, running to the window and putting her head out. She started to yell for Aspasia but I grabbed her and pulled her back in.

"Don't yell," I said. "He'll know she's there. You'll get her killed."

"Oh Jesus," she said again, still holding onto the windowsill and sinking to her knees on the floor. If anything happens to her . . ." Just then one end of an extension cord flew through the window, hitting me in the face. I grabbed it and then we heard movement on the roof.

"Good girl," I said.

"What?"

"She's setting up the light first." I looked at Susan, who just looked scared out of her mind. "It's a good idea," I said lamely. I didn't want to say why. My guess was Aspasia was setting up the light first because she wasn't sure she could get back up once she went down the roof to nail the bottom of the banner. And that's because the roof was likely as icy as that bridge. Up above we heard more movement and then quiet tapping.

"She's all right," I said. "She's laying out the banner." Susan put her hands to her mouth. "If he hears her . . ."

"Uh oh," I said, "Music." I started to go down the stairs and turned back. "I don't know where the stereo is," I said. Susan got up and made a beeline for the stairs. The quiet tapping had stopped and up above I could hear Aspasia moving across the roof. It sounded hugely noisy from inside the house but there was no way to know how far it carried outside.

The noise was only half the problem. Trying to move down an icy roof and not slip was going to be a doozy. Up high Aspasia could straddle the roofline. But down lower there wouldn't be anything to hold on to. And if she couldn't get back up she'd just be sitting there when the lights went on and the shooting started.

Britney Spears started up suddenly. Susan had stopped in Aspasia's room to turn on her boom box rather than going all the way to the first floor. It was an inspired choice, I thought. If this lasted long enough we could play "Oops, I Did It Again," over and over and drive Jeffrey insane within minutes. He'd go home just to get away from it. I shook my head to clear it. I had to get a grip. I heard the telltale sounds of someone slipping down the roof and my stomach lurched.

Susan was back and I turned to her. "How solid are the gutters in front?" I asked. She didn't answer. What a stupid question. How does anyone know how solid their gutters are? It's not like people jump on them to find out. The sliding stopped and we both held our breath for the thud that meant Aspasia had gone over the edge but there was no sound. Neither of us dared to move for few moments.

"What are we doing?" I said, startling. "We're not set up. Go get ready to plug in the light. I'm going to get all the guns and set up at the window in Aspasia's room to cover Gary. When he comes, I'll yell. You plug in the light and wait to help Aspasia in case she tries to get back in the window. I don't think she'll come back until it starts. It would make too much noise."

"Michael," Susan said. "You've got a baby. Do you want me to take the guns and you do the light?"

"Can you shoot?" I asked.

"No," she said. "I hate guns."

"Forget it," I said. "It wouldn't help. Go get the light."

I got the guns and all the ammo I could find and sat by the window straining to see into the woods. The shotgun and a .45 were sitting next to me and my .357 Magnum was in my hands. Beside me lay two speed loaders for the Magnum, a box of cartridges for the .45 and a box of shells for the shotgun. I had quietly pulled up the screen so there was nothing between me and the woods except darkness and distance. I eyed the shotgun longingly but it wouldn't reach that far so there was no point. Still, it was a hell of a weapon when you didn't know exactly where someone was.

The noises on the roof stopped and I cut off the stereo. The silence was a relief.

I wondered if Jeffrey had enough firepower with him to penetrate the walls of the house. No question he'd try if we screwed up his chance to get Gary. The big deal was I had to see that first flash of light. I couldn't shoot until Jeffrey opened fire: Gary might really think someone was shooting at him from the house if I shot first. It meant I couldn't stop Jeffrey from taking one shot at Gary but I needed to make it hard for him to take any more until Gary got out of range. Then I'd hightail it for the back of the house, away from the windows and the deafening noise and the lethal bits of steel that would be zigzagging around.

We were minutes away, had to be. Unless Gary had taken some bizarre detour he'd be home any second. I hadn't heard anything from Susan and there were no more sounds from the roof, so I was pretty sure Aspasia hadn't come back. I didn't want to think about it, but there was a good chance she wouldn't survive a volley at a lit roof, which would surely happen when the light went on—not unless she got back before Jeffrey turned his attention to her. But knowing kids, she'd stay to see what happened to her daddy first. And there wasn't anything I could do about it.

I put the gun down, took a deep breath and rubbed both my eyes. Time to gather myself and focus on this thing. I looked out the window again. The night hung still and easy and a faint hooting drifted up lazily from the woods below. Darkness was nestling in and through the trees like some kind of packing material, cushioning them from the relentless moonlight.

Nonetheless, out there in those quiet woods, somebody was killing somebody. The killing never stopped out there. For all my bitching about people, we were the only species that even questioned whether might made right. Out there, if you could catch it, you could eat it and the catching and the eating never stopped.

My mind settled down clear and completely present. I'd obsess about all this later, I knew, and wonder how I got there. I'd think Adam was right and I'd feel guilt right down to the marrow of my bones for involving an unborn child in anything to do with guns. But for now, nothing existed except the woods out front and the shiny piece of metal resting easy in my hands.

I had always liked guns, though I wished I didn't. I didn't approve of them and thought the Europeans had it right: ban the goddamn things. But there was no accounting for liking. I liked handling them, liked shooting them. I felt comfortable around guns. I had to admit I felt a whole lot safer when I had one in my hands. Go figure.

Strange how at ease I felt—if you call being in an altered state at ease. I could see the leaves shining on the trees, hear faint scratchings and scramblings in the forest. I had been afraid driving over, anxious when we couldn't figure out a plan, scared we wouldn't get the banner done in time and terrified when we had found Aspasia gone. Even now if I looked at it rationally, I'd say we didn't have a snowball's chance in hell of pulling this off. But there was a time when all the planning and the anticipation were over and there you were, face-to-face with the moment.

I knew where I was. It was the second when you're standing on the edge of the airplane right before you jump. It was those few minutes on the foul line with no time left, one point behind and a one-in-one in your hands. It was the last three strides before the jump. I always entered a different zone, one where the past stops as though a steel door has slammed and there is no future at all. You can't see past the ball in your sweaty hands.

Jeffrey didn't trigger it when he jumped me from behind. Helplessness never does, only the one-in-one foul shot where you make it or you don't and everything is different depending on whether the ball circling the rim drops in or out.

Lord, I'm ashamed to say what a glorious moment it is. Time stretches out and the present becomes as big and wide as a Montana sky. Everything slows down. But whereas every saint and seer who ever lived can find that moment patting a puppy, the door to the present only opens for me here, at times like this, when there's a fork in the road and one way leads to a cliff. It's just one of those places that you either like being or you don't. It's the stuff of some people's nightmares, the stuff of Michael Jordan's dreams.

And here I was again. In a few seconds it was going to matter a whole lot whether I heard the car in time, whether I saw the first flash of the gun, and most certainly whether my reaction time was a tenth of a second too slow or a tenth of a second too fast.

And that's why I was sitting here smiling in the dark with no reason at all to smile. Because I was here and it was too late to be anywhere else. And nothing but this moment existed with the moonlight warring with the clouds that had suddenly come from nowhere. For reasons I never could fathom, this moment was someplace I lived.

I scanned the forest again. "Make a mistake, Jeffrey," I thought. "Just one cigarette. It's been a long wait. Surely, no one would see. Don't even think about anyone seeing you. Just light up." I could end this with a single lucky shot, and moral or not, I knew I'd try if I had the chance. But the woods remained dark.

Where would I be? I thought suddenly. If it was me. Close enough to the house, I knew, to keep people from leaving. On my right, I realized suddenly. Duh. That's the only place you'd get a clean shot when Gary got out of the left side of the car. And at the closest point to the car where there was good cover. I narrowed it down to two or three vantage points. Why hadn't I thought of this before? Of course, he wouldn't be on the other side. The car would be between him and Gary. Especially with people yelling at Gary, he couldn't count on him walking all the way to the door. And he would have figured out the people in the house had been warned when he saw me go inside and the lights went out. The most he could count on was Gary getting out of the car.

In the distance I heard a car motor, low at first and then steadily growing louder. I waited, each moment more liquid and more luminous than the last.

17

I STRAINED FORWARD IN THE DARK TRYING TO GAUGE THE FIRST moment that Gary could see the banner. The house was set back from the road and the driveway was long enough that it officially qualified as a private road. It started off to the side and then curved around so that it ended up in front of the house. If there were fewer evergreens, Gary might have seen the roof before the curve or at least once he was into it, but I thought the evergreens by the driveway were thick enough that you couldn't see through them. Hell, I was guessing. It was night and the moonlight was coming and going now, depending on the cloud cover drifting by. I realized belatedly I should have talked more to Susan about what you could see coming down the driveway. I just hadn't thought to.

It was too late now. My best guess was that Gary could see the roof for the first time when he came out of the curve in the driveway. But that wasn't all that far from the front door and well within Jeffrey's rifle range. Even if he saw the banner, Jeffrey would be close enough that Gary'd need to be lucky. I steadied the pistol on the windowsill and sighted along the barrel. There was no time now, just stillness and the sound of my breathing.

In a few moments I saw the moonlight reflect off a strip of chrome coming around the curve and I yelled "lights" at the top of my lungs. Light flooded on instantly from above and suddenly I was blind. I hadn't realized that light on the roof would spill over and work like a flashlight in the dark, making everything invisible to me that wasn't directly lit up. And nothing beyond a few feet from the house was lit by that light.

I stopped, helpless. I had nothing to fire at. Jeffrey could have been standing up in the yard for all I knew and I couldn't see him. For a moment the motor kept growling forward and then I heard the brakes catch, heard the car slam into reverse and the squeal of tires on gravel. Relief poured through my system as though my heart were pumping it instead of blood. If nothing else, at least Gary was warned.

I squinted and could vaguely see the car. It was then I heard the first shots. They sounded soft, like hail hitting the car. Jeffrey had thought about the problem of potential neighbors and brought a silencer, Goddamn his soul. I yelled "Cut the lights; I can't see!" and the light went dead almost instantly.

I didn't wait for my eyes to clear. I started firing at the woods on my right where the shots were coming from, just hoping that nothing bizarre enough had happened to somehow land Gary over there. By all rights he should still be in the car. I went deaf from my Magnum and as my eyes started clearing from the light, I saw the car was stalled. Gary hadn't made it out. The tire was down on the driver's side; maybe the engine was gone as well, who knew? But the car wasn't moving and I could see Jeffrey's bullets ricocheting off it.

My revolver ran out of bullets and I didn't take time to load it. I picked up Gary's .45 and opened fire on the woods again. His was a semiautomatic and as I got a burst off, I saw Gary open up the door on the passenger side and throw himself to the ground. He half-crawled, half-ran to the woods on that side and I lost him in the dark. Hopefully, Jeffrey had, too. The glass on my window exploded as Jeffrey turned his attention to me. I ducked and then crawled away from the window to the corner, curling up into a fetal position and hiding from the glass that was exploding all around me. I expected this to happen but it didn't help. The room seemed suddenly alive with bullets and sounds of shattering glass. I lay in the corner stunned, cursing to myself and just sort of praying at the same time.

The shooting stopped and after a moment, I dragged myself to a different window and peeked out. All seemed still in the woods and I didn't see anything move or fire. Minutes went by and nothing happened. Then distantly, through my ringing ears, I heard Aspasia scream, "Daddy, he's behind you!" She sounded very far away to my poor traumatized ears and I could only barely hear her. Gary must have heard her though, because the moon came out long enough for me to see a dark form leap, followed by a burst of gunfire. Suddenly, the gunfire came back on the house, but this time higher up, toward the roof.

I opened fire again and my ears started hurting from the incessant sound. I could see Gary firing from beyond where he had landed. At least I hoped it was Gary. I had a moment of doubt thinking it was easy to get people mixed up in the woods at night. But you had to place your bets and I had made mine. Mine said Jeffrey was caught in a cross fire and that Gary and I had him pinned. The gun ran out and I picked up my Magnum, threw in a speed loader and started up again. My ears got steadily worse and soon even the sound of the firing couldn't get through. I heard nothing at all, just felt the shock of the gun kicking back.

I saw it, though. I'd be lying if I said I didn't. I saw someone break for the road holding a rifle and I stopped firing and yelled, "He's on the driveway!" My voice sounded strange to me, far away, as though it were someone else's. I saw Gary step out on the road, shooter's stance, pistol straight out in front in both hands. He must have yelled something to Jeffrey but I couldn't hear it: Gary was turned away and my hearing was almost completely gone. But I know he said it because Jeffrey stopped and turned around and dropped his rifle. And then Gary shot him twice.

I put the pistol down, not believing what I'd seen. Maybe I was wrong. Joanna had said Jeffrey had a .45. Maybe he had pulled it. Jesus, I hope he had pulled it. And then I got my wits about me and ran for the stairs. The attic was empty and for a second I couldn't think where Susan was until I realized she had to be on the roof with Aspasia. I stuck my head out. "Are you okay up there?" I yelled. "It's over."

"No," Susan yelled back. "She's hit."

I don't remember the rest of it very well. Which is funny because I remember everything that happened before then exactly. I can still remember the way the moonlight brushed the tops of the trees while I sat and waited for Gary's car, the way the darkness clung to the trunks and pressed itself against the forest floor. I still see in my dreams Gary's dark form hurtling from the car and always, I hear the sound of the gun assaulting my ears and the high ringing that followed afterward. But more than anything, I see Jeffrey standing there with his hands up and I see Gary, shooter's stance, facing him.

Afterward, I have a flashbulb memory of seeing a ladder on the side of the house. I guess Gary must have gotten it. I don't know how he got Susan down or whether she came under her own steam. But I do remember seeing Aspasia being carried over his shoulder. And I remember the relief that hit a second time when he said she only had a shoulder wound.

I know I sat down on the front steps. I don't think I felt much like standing up. I remember seeing Gary dial his cell phone and I know he must have spoken to me because I remember his face up close to mine for a moment. I gave him my car keys, I guess. I must have because he and Susan put Aspasia in my car and backed out of the driveway, around his shot-to-hell wreck. For a second I thought he was going to run over Jeffrey—really, there was almost no way to avoid it—but at the last second he swerved and went around. I was left, sitting in the moonlight, waiting for the police I knew would come while Gary went off to meet the ambulance.

Then it was just me and Jeffrey waiting in the moonlight. I got up slowly and walked around the car to where he lay. I wanted to be sure that he was dead, given there were just the two of us—life could get awkward if he wasn't. And there was something else I wanted to check.

He lay on his back with both arms out, all life

unmistakably drained. The moonlight made his face look waxen, as though he were a life-size mannequin that had never been alive. "Sorry specimen of humanity," I said aloud. I couldn't make myself care about this man. He had beaten his woman, cut my belly and tried to kill all of us, including an eleven-year-old child. And that was just the stuff I knew about. Yes, Virginia, there are bad guys in the world.

I didn't feel particularly afraid standing there in the moonlight with a dead man at my feet—I've always been a lot more wary of the living than of those who aren't. Gently, I knelt down beside him. The shots were centered on his heart and so close together you couldn't tell through his clothes he'd been shot more than once: Gary was a very good shot and he hadn't aimed to wound. Near his outstretched arm lay a .45. But whose fingerprints were on it, I wondered? His or Gary's?

If they were Gary's, he was smart. He had waited until Jeffrey turned around to shoot him. A bullet wound in the back is always hard to sell as self-defense. But what, I wondered, had Aspasia seen?

The young police officer was incredulous. There really wasn't much crime in the back country to speak of. An occasional B&E. A few people who drank and drove. But a cold-blooded, premeditated murder attempt on a prison warden? That happened in Boston or Milwaukee or L.A. But here we were, standing in somebody's front yard in the middle of the night with a dead body in the driveway and a car and a house looking like a war zone. He hardly seemed to believe his eyes and kept staring at Jeffrey as though if he looked away he'd disappear.

There were two of them and they had introduced themselves as Officers Rogers and Kline. Officer Kline didn't seem to share his younger partner's astonishment. He was in his late forties or early fifties and was clearly ex-military. They can take off the uniform and grow out their hair but they can't change the way they stand or move—or the way they react to dead bodies on the lawn.

He quietly checked Jeffrey to make sure of the obvious, that he was dead, then he told the younger Rogers to stay put while he checked the perimeter with a flashlight, examining footprints and looking for Jeffrey's car. Although he didn't say so, I had the feeling he was making sure Jeffrey was alone.

He came back and quietly pulled out a stick of gum, offered me one and asked me what had happened. I was pretty tired and still sitting on the steps. I sighed and gave them the Readers' Digest version—no point in the unabridged. I'd have to say it all again into a tape recorder, anyway.

Both officers remained standing. Rogers kept glancing at the woods, apparently not reassured by his partner's survey, all the time keeping his hand on his holster. I had a feeling if a squirrel moved he was a goner. I had a feeling if I moved too fast—which wasn't likely—there might be a problem. Kline never once glanced at the woods or at Rogers. He knew there was no one else in the woods and he knew Rogers was too young and too green to believe him.

"I couldn't see that much," I was saying. "The light from the roof blinded me at first and by the time I could see they were both in the woods. The cloud cover was coming and going and when it was there, you couldn't see dip. I fired when I could see him but never hit anything. I saw him make a break for it, though, after he got caught in a cross fire between me and Gary. I yelled to Gary and saw him go after him. He'll have to tell you the rest."

Kline grunted and glanced up at the roof. "A sheet?" was all he said.

"Yeah, it seemed ridiculous but we couldn't think of anything else."

"Worked."

"If you can believe it."

"Hell of a kid," he added.

"That too," I replied. But already I was moving away from Jeffrey and the sheet. I didn't even want to talk about it anymore. I was coming out of crisis mode, out of the stillness and the singularity and the moments where life got down to a very few, simple things. The present moment was fading and I was back in the real world. I was wondering already what the deafening sound and the adrenaline had done to this sweet child inside my belly and thinking about facing Adam.

18

"SHIT, SHIT, SHIT," I SAID. "YOU ARE KIDDING ME."

"Don't blame me," she said. "I'm just the messenger." Which was being a little modest. Lucy was actually the lawyer sent by the Office of the Attorney General to assess the attack on Gary and see if there was a case against any of the other folks we all knew were involved. And it looked like there wasn't.

We were sitting in Gary's office, gathered around the conference table. Gary and I looked at each other, disgusted. "You know as well as we do," Gary said, "that Jim Walker and John Avery were involved in this thing."

"Prove it," she said. Lucy was a petite woman wearing a lime green suit with a short skirt. Her silky hair was tied up into a bun on top of her head and strands too silky to stay up had escaped on all sides. She didn't seem to notice or care. I wondered if she looked like that in court, hair more or less flying out everywhere. If she did, it probably helped. It made her look human to a jury and careless to an opponent. Not that the latter impression would last very long.

"What do you think," Lucy went on, "we can go in and say, 'John Avery had a grudge against the warden'? Right, him and half the inmates here. 'He and Jim Walker had a deal so Walker signed up his cousin to kill Gary'?"

"Yeah," I said, "but you've got Terrance over-hearing that conversation."

"You think that'll stand up? First of all, Mr. Terrance is a known felon with three counts of child molesta-tion against him. Juries don't like taking a child moles-ter's word for dip shit. Here, let's try it. You be Terrance. 'Mr. Terrance, did you know what Mr. Walker and Mr. Avery were talking about when you overheard that conversation by the urinal? Just so there's no mis-take, Mr. Terrance, I am referring to the conversation in which Mr. Avery *allegedly* stated that he would keep his end of the bargain when Mr. Walker kept his. The conversation in which Mr. Walker *allegedly* replied that he could not do so, that security was too tight since Clarence's death. Even assuming this conversation occurred, do you have any way of knowing what they were talking about?' Go ahead," she said, still looking at me.

"No," I said. There wasn't anything else I could say.

"'So, Mr. Terrance, you had no idea this had any-thing to do with Warden Raines?'"

"No," I said, again.

"'And did Mr. Avery or Mr. Walker ever say or do anything after that to give you the idea that conversa-tion related to Warden Raines?'"

"No," I said.

"'Do you know for a fact, as you sit here today, that that conversation had anything to do with Warden Raines?'"

"No," I said.

"'So that conversation could have been about anything, anything at all. It could have been about paying back a poker debt. It could have been about doing a favor that involved some very minor infraction, if any, of the rules and regulations of the prison.'"

"Yes," I said reluctantly.

"I could go on," she said. "In fact, if I were the defense, I'd give Terrance a list of possible scenarios and ask him if he knew for a fact that it was not about any one of them. The list could take a while.

"And there's the other stuff we don't know dip shit about. Who killed Clarence?"

We were both silent.

"Who tried to turn Stacy into a vegetable?"

"One of them," I said. "Had to be."

"Give me a break," Lucy said. "Had to be? We don't have squat."

"Well," Gary said grimly. "At least we got Jeffrey."

"And that's all you're going to get," she said.

I didn't comment. Yeah, we got Jeffrey—or rather, Gary did—and listening to Lucy reminded me exactly why he had shot him. But on the other hand, we also might have had Jeffrey and Jim lining up to sell each other out if Jeffrey were still alive. The truth was, without Jeffrey as a potential witness against Jim, Jim was going to skate. So was Avery.

"Let me remind you," Lucy went on, "of what you don't have. What you don't have is any idea how the drugs got into the prison."

"It's the print shop—somehow," I said weakly. Lucy didn't even bother to ask me to prove that.

"You don't have Avery or Walker tied into either the murder of Clarence or the attack on Stacy James. You don't have any proof that Walker arranged the hit on Gary."

"Oh, come on," I said. "Jeffrey didn't even know Gary. He had nothing against him. Why else would he go out there and try to kill him unless it was some deal whereby he'd pay Avery's grudge debt for him and Avery would hand over some drug contacts. Or something like that."

"'Why else' doesn't cut it in court," she said. "And I'm pretty sure 'something like that' isn't even admissible. They'd probably declare a mistrial if you said 'something like that' in court."

We were all silent. "Look, guys," Lucy said finally. "I hate to be the hardass here. If somebody tried to kill me, shot my daughter, destroyed my car and damn near wrecked my house, I'd be pissed, too. Royally pissed. But being royally pissed ain't the same thing as having a winnable case. We don't even have a triable case here, screw winnable." She closed up her briefcase. "Let me know if anything develops. I'll revisit it. I swear to you, bring me anything at all on any of this, however flimsy, and I'll go to war. But right now you got a whole lot of nothing. You guys want to go out for a beer?"

"Look at me," I said. "I can't even drink caffeine."

"Sorry," she said. "Sprite?"

"I'm too depressed," I said.

"I'll pass," said Gary.

"All right," she said. "Be that way. You guys take it easy," and she walked out.

"We have to think of something," I said after the door closed. "I just cannot bear the thought of these guys getting away with this."

It was the first time Gary and I had been alone since

the shooting, which only happened three days ago but felt like three months. We both seemed to realize it at the same time. There was a silence, then Gary spoke. "Michael," he said awkwardly, "I haven't even thanked you. For coming that night. If you hadn't, I wouldn't have walked away from it." He looked extremely uncomfortable. I had been in his position before and there was something strange about it. Sure, you're glad someone saved your life but you still feel weird, all helpless and indebted.

"Tell Adam that," I said. "He's ready to divorce me and we aren't even married."

"He'll get over it," he said. "Wait till he sees the baby. I went from not-sure-I-wanted-one to ready-to-kill-for-Aspasia in the time it took to pick her up. There's no trip like it."

There was another silence and I realized with a sinking feeling Gary was going to get into the thing I didn't want to talk about. "Michael, I don't know what you saw that night at the house . . . or thought you saw."

"I didn't see anything," I said firmly. "And I don't think I saw anything. I told the police I was sorry I couldn't be more helpful about what happened but the cloud cover came in at the end and I couldn't see a thing. I sent them to you to tell them what happened because I didn't see it."

"Okay," he said slowly.

"And I don't need to talk about what I didn't see," I added. "The bigger question," I said, "is what Aspasia saw. She might have been in a better position to see than I was."

He just looked at me and I realized he hadn't even thought about it. It was just the way grown-ups were.

They always oriented to other grown-ups. Really, what I thought and saw was of no consequence. If I had said I thought Gary shot him in cold blood, Gary would just have denied it and I doubted any prosecutor would even have asked for an indictment. It would be easy to prove I was pretty far away and that it was dark and that I couldn't be sure. And right or wrong, juries were reluctant to second-guess someone who's defending himself from an assassin. But what Aspasia saw—that was going to matter.

"You think she saw it?" Gary said.

"Maybe," I replied. "She hasn't talked about it?"

"She hasn't talked about anything that happened that night," he said thoughtfully. "We haven't pushed her."

"She'll need to—sometime," I replied. "Hey, good news," I said, as much to change the subject as anything. "Stacy's talking and he's even making sense."

"I know," Gary said. "He said a few words on the phone this morning."

"You called today?" I asked.

"Today," he replied. "And every day."

I wouldn't say Adam had exactly forgiven me. But he seemed to have given up and stopped talking about it. Actually, he hadn't said that much about it, period. Maybe, I thought, even he understood I'd been in a box. Or maybe he'd decided I was hopeless. In either case, the pressure was off with Jeffrey dead. Nobody was coming after me as far as either of us knew and consequently I hadn't seen that much of him. If I didn't know better, I'd have thought he was avoiding me.

"I checked out Richard Thompson," Adam said over

dinner. We had arranged dinner in town to try to catch up but it wasn't working that well. Conversation still wasn't right between us. It was stilted and awkward and we seemed to be looking for things to talk about. Richard Thompson, Mama's new friend, would do nicely. "He doesn't have any criminal record at all. He had one traffic ticket four years ago for speeding and that's the extent of his police contacts for the last fifteen years."

"So he's clever," I said.

"I think that's a little beyond clever," Adam said. "Are you sure about this? That he's up to something with your mother?"

"Sort of," I said. "I mean, he admitted it. But I'm no longer sure it's what I thought it was." I had replayed the conversation with Thompson in my mind a hundred times and it just did not sound right. I had the feeling you get when you're just plain wrong about something but try as I might I could not think of an innocent interpretation of Mama taking one hundred and ten thousand dollars to Vegas with Richard Thompson.

"What's he do for a living?" I asked. "If anything."

"He's retired."

"From what?"

"He was CEO of a small company." Which didn't fit at all. "Here's the thing, Michael. He's a member of SCORE."

"SCORE?"

"It's a volunteer organization of retired business executives who help new businesses to get started."

"Mama is starting a new business in Vegas?" I said incredulously. "Like what? Like what, exactly?"

"Why don't you ask her," he said, picking up the bill the waiter had just left. What happened to the days when we used to irritate the management because we stayed and talked so long? "You going home?" he asked.

"Later," I said. "I have a session with Marion. Don't say it." Wisely, he didn't.

I had some time to kill before the session so I went back to my office to work on records. But I had barely pulled the charts when the phone rang.

"You weren't at home," Mama said. "So I figured you'd be at the office."

"That's good, Mama," I replied. "I was going to call you anyway."

"I heard about you on the news," she went on. "Land sakes, Michael. What are you doing running around getting in gunfights pregnant? I don't think God gave you the sense he gave a potted plant, to be doing something like that."

"Yes, I'm well," I said. "And the baby's doing fine. Thank you for asking."

"Well, you're never on the news for anything good," she said. "It's always shooting somebody or getting shot at or something like that."

"I have never shot anybody," I replied. "I have tried to but I missed. And I don't get shot at that often."

"Michael, most people never get shot at."

"Thank you for your support," I said. "Mama, I give up. You're not gambling away your retirement fund, I've gotten that far. You're starting some kind of business in Vegas. So what is it?"

"In Vegas? Why would I start a business in Vegas? I don't live in Vegas."

"Mama."

"Michael, you get yourself in such an uproar over

nothing. Why don't you ever trust your old mama. Just look up my website."

"Excuse me?"

"You do have a computer, don't you?"

"Yes," I said slowly.

"Well then," she said. "Look it up. You got a pencil?" and she gave me a web address. I was already turning on my computer by the time she hung up.

My problem was I thought of everybody as a victim or an offender. Okay, so I allowed for bystanders. But Mama wasn't a bystander anywhere in life; she was always something, and I tend to get a little narrow in my categories.

"Mama's Jewelry Emporium," I said to Marion later that evening. "My mother is buying jewelry from pawn shops in Vegas. She's got a jeweler to go around with her to pick out the real stuff and she's selling it over the web."

"Your mother is how old?" Marion asked.

"Trust me, it's not relevant," I said. "That's not the point."

"It's a clever idea," she said.

"That's not the point, either."

"What is?"

"The land pirates are back." Marion didn't reply. "It's this thing in my family tree. I'm serious. My mother is a land pirate. She's a scavenger. She is going on the beach after the storm, picking up the debris from the shipwrecks. Okay, my family tree has moved up a step. She isn't standing at the tables encouraging people to gamble. The last time my family went through this they were standing on the shore putting a lantern around the necks of horses to mislead ships and wreck them. That's a little worse."

At least I hoped she wasn't doing anything like that. For a second, an image surfaced of Mama standing next to some little old lady with a diamond ring she liked, telling her to "go for it, girl." "No, I don't think she'd do that," I said to the image. "Hell," I said to Marion, "I don't know if she'd wreck the ships or not but she isn't doing that because she doesn't need to. There are plenty of desperate people down there betting their engagement rings and their mother's pearls. And they'll always 'be right back' but they don't come back. Not ever. So here comes my mother."

"It is not a crime," she said slowly.

"No," I said. "There's that."

"You don't approve."

"I don't know," I said. "The thing is, I couldn't do it. Every ring I picked up I'd be wondering about the story behind it. I'd be thinking about all the sadness and lost dreams of every one of those people. I can't be feeding off misfortune like that. It just would make me sad. But my mother would just think they are dorks for being that stupid and if they're going to be that stupid, what's it to her? Somebody's going to buy that ring, she'd say, so why not her?"

"She does not have that need you have, to redeem or restore."

"I didn't say that."

"Think about it," she said. "That's all I'm asking." And then she just flat changed the topic—or I thought she did. "What is going to happen to your friend Eileen?"

"Eileen? What made you think of her?"

"It's just that you and her seem so much alike—in some ways."

"What? We have nothing in common, absolutely nothing."

"Really?"

"Marion, what are you talking about?"

"Michael, field mice flee when they're attacked and forest mice freeze. Are they so different?"

"I don't know. That's just environment. Field mice are trapped in the open. They might as well run. They'll get picked off if they stand still. Forest mice have cover. Of course, they'll freeze. Then no one could see them. That's just practical. It's got nothing to do with anything."

"Oh, did I say it that way? My mistake. The truth is that field mice freeze and forest mice run."

There was silence.

"You're saying . . ."

"That people can make up reasons for anything, to explain anything. But at some point the explanations don't matter. Look in your past for reasons if you want, and in Eileen's. But it won't change your basic natures. For whatever reasons, Eileen has always felt safety lay in standing still—and you—you have always, always felt safety lay in moving on. You are very much alike, really. You're driven by the same thing. Except that need you have to reach out and redeem things for others. She does not have that."

She laughed at my stricken face. "Don't look so upset, Michael. Safety drives everybody, everybody that is, except maybe your mother. The only difference is, what is safety to one may seem like foolish risk-taking to another."

I didn't say anything. I'd like to think my love of staying on the move had something to do with a sense of adventure, but no doubt there was some fear mixed in there, too. Okay, a lot of fear. Intimacy had always seemed scarier to me than belaying down a 200-foot cliff at night in the rain. Actually, that hadn't been so bad.

"Only . . ." she added.

"Only what?" I asked.

She shrugged. "Only Eileen must now redeem her life by moving on, while you," she glanced at my belly, "you must now learn how to stand still. It will be a stretch, I think, for both of you."

I woke up the next morning with a plan. And despite Marion's fantasy that I was some goody-two-shoes running around trying to save the world, it didn't have anything at all to do with saving anybody. It had to do with holding Jim Walker accountable and Avery, too. All right, so it might help Eileen redeem her lost pride a little. So what if it might let her back into the pawn shop with enough money and the ticket in her hand. That was okay, but it was a side effect. That wasn't why I was doing it. Screw Marion.

I thought about it all during breakfast and then sat on the deck afterward in the cool morning air drinking coffee, still thinking about it. After a while, I decided the idea wasn't going away. Not to mention it felt better to try *something* rather than sitting around saying what a shame it was we couldn't do anything. So I picked up the phone and called Gary.

The drive out to Nelson's Point seemed to whiz by. It always does when you are somewhere else in your head and paying no attention. I ran through a dozen scenarios where the plan might fail, but couldn't find any reason not to try. So what if it failed. Sometimes you had to see a possible line through things and follow it. It was like a kayak run. You knew there were rocks and you knew where you might crash. But if you were going on the river those were the chances you took. This line through the rapids was perilous, but then again it had a shot.

When I finally got to the prison and negotiated all the barriers, I sat down across from Gary, barely able to contain my excitement. "I've been thinking about this," I said. "We have no evidence linking Jim or Avery to anything, right?"

"Thus far," he said, doggedly.

"Give it up," I said. "We're not going to find any. We need them turning on each other."

"I can't see it," he replied.

"Well, hold on a minute. We need some leverage, which means we need somebody who knows something to start the dominos tumbling. So who knows something?"

"Besides them?"

I nodded.

"The inmates whose heads were turning right before the scuffle," Gary replied instantly. "Assuming that's connected." We both knew it was.

"Sure, but we don't have any leverage on them. They have no reason whatsoever to risk Jim or Avery killing them or having them killed. And don't say it can't happen in a Vermont prison. Nobody's going to believe that now. In fact, that might well have been part of the reason for killing Clarence, just to make that point. I'm thinking outside the prison."

He looked blank.

"Two people," I said. "Joanna, Jeffrey's wife. She's a possibility but she doesn't know much—although Jim may not know that. And she might help. She hates Jim and I bet she blames him for Jeffrey's death. The other person is Eileen."

He sat up straight and his face got grim. "Eileen's involved in this?"

"No," I said, "not in the murders, not in the attack on you. She still doesn't believe Jim would do anything like that. But she's wavering about Jim. And I know what would push her over the edge."

"Okay, but even if you could, she doesn't have anything."

"Yes, she does, but she doesn't know it. She's got something that will tell us how drugs got into the prison. If we can figure that out, it's a start." I didn't tell him the rest of it. Might as well break it to him slowly.

"All right," he said. "Are you going to talk to Eileen?"

"Not yet," I said. "First I need to talk to Calvin, that guy she was screwing. And I need permission to cut him a deal."

"Why you?" Gary said. "Let security handle it. Tell us what you want and we'll deal with it."

"I can't," I said. "Because I'm the one who has to talk to Eileen. I need to convince Eileen that Calvin's telling the truth and not making up stuff because you're pressuring him. Because he's gonna say something she absolutely won't want to believe and she'll take any out she can find. How am I supposed to do that if I have it thirdhand? She'll be sure you pressured Calvin and it's all a big lie. You know she will. She doesn't trust you on this."

"Why would she trust you?" he replied. "She's hardly seen you in the last fifteen years."

"She does trust me," I said. "It has to do with a paring knife in a lunch pail."

Gary just looked at me.

"It doesn't matter," I said. "She does, I'm telling you."

Calvin was leering from the moment he walked into the room. Maybe nailing Eileen had gone to his head. He looked me up and down like boys do in high school when they want to be obnoxious. He was a singularly unattractive man with a flat face, bad skin, bad teeth, and a burn on the side of his face and neck. His eyes were small and hard and dull. He was also huge; each leg being roughly the size of my waist. I thought briefly about his long and varied history of violence, dating all the way back to adolescence. I thought too about the maid whose throat he had cut after raping her. This was one scary guy. I felt bad for Eileen. It must have taken a lot to get Eileen to drop her pants for this guy.

"Mr. Calvin," I said. "I am Dr. Stone. I am here to talk to you about Dr. Steelwater."

He snorted and just sort of smiled. "I got nothing to say," he said.

"Mr. Calvin. I'm going to lay it on the line. You drew three hundred and sixty in seg for that infraction. Seg is not a fun place. How'd you like to drop it to one-eighty?"

His eyes narrowed and he stopped leering and looked at me closely. "Now that I have your attention, what we want is very simple. You have never been willing to discuss the incident. I'd like to know what happened."

"I told them what happened. Me and the doctor were getting it on. What do you want me to say?"

"I don't want you to lie to me. If you make up anything—and I mean anything at all because you think I want to hear it—I will do anything I can to make sure you serve the entire time in seg and I will personally ask every officer there to check you constantly for the smallest infraction in hopes of extending it. I repeat, don't lie to me, Mr. Calvin. It's not what I'm here for."

He shrugged.

"Here's the deal. We have evidence that another inmate was involved in this. The story he's telling is that you threatened his life if he didn't persuade Dr. Steelwater to have sex with you."

His eyes widened slightly and he frowned. "I didn't threaten nobody. Who said that?"

"Actually, I suspect you didn't threaten anybody. But the inmate certainly made a case that you did. Which is why I'm here. I don't think he should walk and you should take the whole fall if he was involved. I know Dr. Steelwater did not have sex with you because you and she had a thing going. He says you threatened him. It's a plausible story. So you get one chance to tell your side of this, Mr. Calvin.

"Here are your choices. You can tell me what happened between you and the other inmate and you can tell me the truth. If you do, you get your seg time reduced by fifty percent if what you say checks out. Or you can face charges of criminal threatening. If you don't tell us what happened, we have no choice but to go with what the other guy said. So we'll charge you with threatening in addition to the current charges and you'll probably get another three-sixty on top of what you've got. Your choice, Mr. Calvin. It makes no difference to me."

Calvin pondered it for a minute. "Could be dangerous. Talking about people around here."

"We'll send you to another prison," I said, "if you're worried. They do that all the time if they're concerned about someone's safety. Besides, you're in seg. You can't get much safer than that. And anyway, you don't strike me as the kind of guy who's afraid of very many people. With your track record, *he'd* better be worried." He chuckled and his eyes lit up with pride. Boy, the things people were proud of. It was all bullshit, anyway. He was buying time while he thought about it.

"He's sticking to his story, Mr. Calvin. We have to go with what we've got if we don't have your side. I don't see how you've got anything to lose. If you're protecting him, he sure as hell ain't returning the favor. So you're going to take the fall for somebody who's selling you down the river? God didn't make anybody that dumb." Actually, God did, but I didn't want to get into it.

"Jim Walker is full of shit," he said, finally. "That's not what happened." And then he told me.

I sat in my car in Eileen's yard with the tape in my hands. But I didn't get out. I was wondering if anything we'd get out of the conversation I was about to have was worth what it would do to this woman. It's one thing to bet on somebody and lose. It's another thing to find out you were betting at a rigged table. Eileen had her doubts about Jim, but she had no clue, no real clue who he was. "Hello, Eileen," I said in my head. "I'm here to introduce total and complete shame into your life. Just make room for it on the couch. It'll follow me in very shortly."

I started as the door to the house opened and Eileen walked out. "Michael," she said, walking up to the car.

"What are you doing sitting out here? Are you all right?" She looked worried, which made me feel even worse.

"I'm fine." I sighed. "I'm just thinking."

"Are you having pains?"

"No, no really. I'm okay." I opened the door and got out of the car. My stomach felt worse than it had on the way to Gary's house the night Jeffrey went after him. "Can I come in? I need to talk to you."

She led the way, still looking worried, but now there was a kind of fear mixed in with the worry. Clearly, she'd figured out my hesitation at getting out of the car had something to do with her.

I sat down on the couch and Eileen sat down across from me. She looked thoroughly frightened by this point. She didn't offer coffee or tea and she seemed to be just holding her breath. "You know about the attack on Gary?" I began.

She nodded. "I tried to call him but I couldn't get through. I left a message."

"Did you know the guy was Jim Walker's cousin?"

Eileen just seemed to sink into the couch.

"The news didn't carry it because DOC didn't tell the media. The police are still investigating and they didn't want to screw it up. So," I said, taking a deep breath, "we're looking at Jim, again."

"Michael, he—"

I cut it short. "And this is what we came up with," I said, holding out the tape in my hand.

She didn't take it. She just looked at it like it was a snake. I had a strange feeling I was the serpent holding out the apple to Eve. Things would not be the same. "It's bad, isn't it?" she said finally.

"Yes," I said gently. "It most certainly is."

"Why should I listen?" she said desperately. "Maybe I don't want to know."

"Because we need your help," I said. "Or he's going to walk for what he did to Gary. And don't forget his cousin didn't just try to kill Gary. He shot Gary's daughter, too. She's eleven years old, Eileen, and he tried to kill her. Besides, you can come out of this better than you know now. But you have to go through this first."

She still didn't move. "I can't make you listen," I said. "But I'm telling you that you need to. I don't know much, Eileen. But I know a dead-end illusion when I see one. It's going to take too much energy to hold on to your belief in Jim. He's not who you think he is and the more you try to deny who he really is, the more of you you'll have to spend to do it. The only good thing about reality, that I can find, is that it holds itself up. Things that aren't true are just expensive, that's all. You end up spending so much time and energy and psychic something or other holding these illusions up, that there isn't enough of you left to live. Do you know what I mean?"

She didn't say anything for a moment. Then she nodded slightly. She hadn't looked at me at all. She was still looking at the tape and I was still holding it out.

"Besides, at least some of this can be redeemed." She glanced at me quickly. "Yes," I said. "It can."

Slowly, Eileen took the tape and without a word she walked over to a stereo on a shelf next to the sofa. She put the tape in and hit Play, then she sat back down. My voice came on first and I watched her as she listened to how I had set it up with Calvin. I wanted her to hear it because I wanted her to make her own deci-

sion as to whether we had pressured him into lying.
Then came the part I was dreading.

"I saw him come out of her office, when I was emp-
tyin' the trash cans in the hall. He was buttonin' up
his shirt and he was just kind of smilin', you know
what I mean? He winked at me when he walked by
and I stopped him.

"I say 'Jim, boy, what are you up to? You gettin'
some a that?' He didn't say he wasn't. He just sorta
smiled and said, 'Now what would make you think
that?' He started to go on but I say, 'Jim, you gotta
learn to share with your friends. I sure would like to
get me some of that white bread.'

"'Why should I do that?' he said.

"'Because a man never knows when he's goin' to
need a friend,' I say. 'You runnin' with a wild bunch.
You get on Avery's wrong side, he turn on you and you
gonna find a knife between your ribs one fine mornin'.
And there's nothin' your skinny white ass can do
about it. You need some backup, boy. Get me some of
that white bread and you got yourself some real help.
Avery think twice before he take me on.'

"He just stop for a minute and then he say, 'You got
a point there, buddy. Maybe we can work something
out. I'll think about it.'

"One night after that he pull me over when I was
leavin' the rec room and he say, 'You still interested?'

"I tell him, 'Sure I'm interested. What else is goin'
on around here? I'll take anything I can get.'

"He say he can get me one shot. He don't think he
could get me any more. 'Is that enough?'

"So I tell him, 'It's more than I got now.'

"But nothin' happened and I was thinkin' he forgot
about it. A couple of weeks went by and I don't hear

nothin'. Then I'm in the hall cleanin' up one night and Jim sticks his head out the door and he say, 'You ready?' That's all he say.

"I say, 'Hell yes.' Jim come out the door and he wink at me. He whispers, 'Screw her brains out, buddy. It's the only chance you're gonna get.' I come in and she waitin' for me. She got no underwear on under her dress. I don't say nothin'. I just unzip my pants, lift her dress and put it to her. She keep her face turned away but I don't care. I fuck her standin' up, leanin' against the desk and I fucked her good. Real good."

There was a pause on the tape and I remembered it well. Calvin had looked off into the distance with a smile on his lips that had made my stomach churn. Then he said softly, "She wet when I put it to her. I think Jim fucked her before I got there. But I don't mind sloppy seconds. Make no difference to me. Kind of liked havin' a bitch wet for a change." Calvin paused again thinking about it. Then he glanced over at me, still smiling, looking for what? Revulsion? Fear? I wouldn't give him the satisfaction and kept my face blank. In a few seconds he went on.

"Afterwards, Jim want me to tell him all about it. There weren't that much to tell. I just fucked her, that's all. I don't know what he want me to say. But he ask me to tell him over and over all about it. He like to talk about it. Ask me if I liked them hairy. He kept saying she one hairy broad.

"Man, I start dreamin' about it. I decide Jim gettin' it all the time, why not me? So I go back to Jim, I say, 'Jim, I want more a that stuff.' He act all pissed. 'We had a deal,' he tell me.

"'We still got a deal,' I say. 'But what's it to you if I get a little more. You like hearing about it anyway.' He ask me if I told anybody and I said 'Hell, no.' He don't agree at first but I keep after him. I keep thinkin' I let her get off too easy.

"So, same thing happen. Same way. Jim don't give me no warning. I be working one night in the hall. He stick out his head and say, 'You ready?' I'm there in a flash. This time I take my time. Made her get on her knees and suck me off. Turn her over the desk and fuck her in the ass. I don't have nothing with me and she whimpering when I fuck her in the ass. Sure felt good to be the one in charge for a change. They all so high and mighty. I do all the stuff I been thinkin' about, all the stuff I didn't do last time I was in such a hurry.

"But then security walk in and spoil the party. That's it. He lyin' through his teeth if he say I threatened him. I might a threatened him. Tell you the truth, I was thinkin' about it. But I didn't have to."

Eileen got up woodenly and walked over to the stereo. Her hand was shaking as she turned it off. She put her hand on the shelf and stood for a moment just holding on and I wondered if she was holding herself up. Then she turned without a word and went into the bathroom. I just sat there feeling helpless and listening to her throw up. After a while, the sounds stopped, the door opened and Eileen went into her bedroom and shut the door. There was silence and then I heard her sobbing.

I got up and went into the kitchen and put on some hot water. The house was easily as messy as it had been the first time I was there. Idly I started straightening up while I waited for Eileen. I figured I needed to leave her alone for a while and I just wanted something to do. I filled the dishwasher and turned it on and started wiping down the counters. I finished the entire first floor, and had two cups of tea before the door opened.

Eileen came out and didn't even notice the changes in the house. She sat down in a chair in the living room facing the empty fireplace and her face was very pale. She had a shawl around her shoulders but she was shivering even so. She looked almost disoriented, like she wasn't sure where she was. I started to speak but she got up abruptly and started walking around aimlessly. She'd go over to a shelf, pick something up, finger it slowly, then put it back down. It took her a few minutes but then she focused on me. "You?" she said. "Why are you still here?"

"How are you doing?" I asked.

She laughed and the sound scared me more than what she was doing. I got up, went back to the kitchen and fixed some tea. I came in and put a cup on the end table next to her chair. "Drink some," I said.

"I am such a fool," she said, not touching the tea. "I am such a fool."

"It's gotta feel that way," I said. "But you're not the first person to be taken in. And you won't be the last. People give them their life savings. They let them baby-sit their kids. They're good. That's all. They're just really good at what they do."

"I am such a fool," she said again. She was looping on the words and she wasn't listening to anything I said. I didn't think she even heard me. Scenes were running through her head, I was almost sure of it. Scenes and conversations and letters and sex. Every single interaction she had ever had with Jim Walker was blowing like a hard wind through her head and every single one of them was being reinterpreted in the light of that tape. Eileen wouldn't come back to the world for a while. She was rearranging the furniture inside her head and everybody knows that moving furniture is a big job. I just sat there waiting. I didn't know what else to do. I knew I wasn't going anywhere anytime soon.

It was the next morning before I got to talk to Eileen. I wasn't invited to stay over, I just did. For one thing, I was worried about Eileen's being suicidal. She had thrown away everything for nothing. The noble sacrifice she'd made had been nothing but a cheap trick. She had been a complete fool, no way to sugar-coat it. She had lost her job, her house, her license, her profession, almost twenty years of work, not to mention the respect and friendship of her colleagues. And now she knew she wasn't going to ride into the sunset with her "innocent" lover. There was no way back and no way forward. She had been used and abused and discarded and she had colluded in her own destruction. She'd just been too needy to figure it out. People had definitely killed themselves over less.

"How are you?" I asked. She had emerged from the bedroom and this time she took the cup of coffee I offered.

"Shitty," she said. "How should I be?"

"Shitty," I responded.

"You're still here." She sounded flat but she was present, oriented and in the house, which was definitely an improvement.

"I was worried about you."

"Has Gary heard the tape?"

"Yes."

"Who else?"

"Nobody."

"Who's going to hear it?"

"I can't promise because it may be out of our hands but we're going to try for 'nobody.'"

"I was such a fool," she said.

"It happens," I replied. "I'm sorry, really sorry."

"How come you know these people?" she said suddenly. "I don't get it. You always had some kind of radar for psychopaths."

I shrugged. "I've never figured it out. I make a lot of mistakes in the rest of my life. But for whatever reasons, I've always gotten it with these guys. I know how they think and I can usually spot them. Don't ask me."

"What happens now? That's part of why you're here, isn't it."

"That's part of why I came. It's not why I stayed. Now? Now we go talk to Gary. You admit to having sex with Jim. Yes, I know it opens you up to more charges legally but I have a feeling we'll be able to cut a deal on that. It also gives us something to squeeze Jim with. Plus you bring Gary the letter. I keep thinking about the letter with the smudges. You still have it?" I realized I was holding my breath.

She nodded. "You give him the letter and the other ones Jim sent and we let the crime lab go over them. Those smudges might even tell us how the drugs got into the prison. I think he'd use the same mechanism to smuggle the drugs in as the letters out. And then," I said quietly, "you set Jim up."

She just looked at me. "I set Jim up?"

"Yes," I said. "You got a problem with it?"

"Just tell me how."

"How is doable," I said. "'How' we figure out. The hard part is behind you."

"Which is?"

"Wanting to."

19

IT WAS THE FIRST TIME I HAD SEEN GARY LOOK SORRY FOR Eileen since this whole thing started. But hearing what Jim had told Eileen and then hearing the tape had its effect. He got up when we walked in, came around his desk and hugged her. She burst into tears and kept saying, "I am so sorry, Gary. I am so sorry."

Gary didn't say anything. He just hugged her for a few minutes. When he let go he picked up a box of Kleenex and handed them to her. "Sit down," he said. "We've got work to do. It's time to end this fucker's reign."

It sounded good to me and we all sat down. I started to say something, then shut up. Eileen needed to do this herself.

"There's one more thing you don't know," Eileen said. She took the letters out and handed them to Gary.

He looked at them, puzzled. "They're from Jim," she said. "After I was kicked out. I don't know how he got them out."

"Smell them," I said to Gary. "Before Clarence died

he told his mother he was going to have a new job and that he had a 'nose for trouble.' He laughed and his mother thought it was odd enough to tell me about it. I'm thinking those smudges have something to do with what he was talking about. I'm also thinking that the smell might throw a dog off. I thought we could send them to the crime lab and see what they are."

Gary smelled them and then he snorted. "I don't think we'll need to send them anywhere," he said. "It smells like toner, like you find in copiers." He picked up the phone and dialed.

"Can I speak to Henry," he said. "This is Warden Raines."

"Henry?" I mouthed silently.

Gary covered the phone. "Rudolph's suspended until we finish the investigation," he said. "We got a new guy there for the interim."

He took his hand off and turned his attention back to the telephone. "Henry," he said. "What kind of toner do you use in the printing machines?" We couldn't hear Henry's response but I'm willing to bet he thought it was a weird question.

"Is it dry?" he asked. "Powdery?" This time the answer was instant. "Can you bring one down?" he said finally, and his voice had taken on a disgusted tone. "To my office. Right away. Thanks."

"Sealed cartridges," he said. "I don't know how we'd ever prove it. I feel like a goddamn fool," he added. "Jim's cousin simply doctors the cartridges and the inmates take the cartridges out when they 'fix' the machines."

"While, no doubt," I added, "Jim is off talking to Rudolph about his lousy childhood."

"Gary," Eileen added. "I think they used my group

to distribute them to inmates in different cell blocks."
He looked at her. "While my back was turned. I didn't
know about it." She took a deep breath and looked
Gary in the eye. "I was talking to Jim. I thought he was
depressed and needed help."

Gary started to say something and I shook my
head very slightly. He didn't usually listen to me, but
for once he did. "It's water over the dam," he said
shortly. "I should have looked more closely at the
machines before now, anyway. We pulled the contract right away when we learned the printer was
related to Walker. The drug rates have started dropping. The good news—and the bad news—is the
drugs have stopped coming in so we don't have any
way to prove any of this."

"Jesus," I said. "We're always a day late and a dollar
short. We keep figuring things out after somebody's
dead, somebody's maimed, after the smuggling's over.
We have got to get ahead of this game. And that," I
looked at Gary, "is where Eileen comes in. She can set
Jim up."

"I'm listening," Gary said.

We rehearsed it and rehearsed it and rehearsed it
until everybody was grouchy and frustrated. Two different officers had role-played Jim, both of whom
knew him and both of whom knew psychopaths well.
Sometimes Eileen had done okay and sometimes she
hadn't. "What I don't get," she said finally. "What's
stopping me is I just can't see him going for this. What
makes you think he would believe me? That I would
do something like this?"

"Eileen," I said. "You're just too goddamn good-
hearted and moral. What you're not getting is every-

body thinks everybody else is the same way they are.
You believed Jim because you thought he was like you.
He's going to believe you for the same reason.

"Every psychopath, every single one I have ever
met, without exception, thinks everybody is running a
scam all the time. If they run a better scam than you,
they just think that's part of the game. Every human
interaction to a psychopath is like a play in football. If
you beat somebody, if you gain five yards, you win the
down. It's as simple as that. And they think you're
playing the same game they are. Either they win or
you do. You have to believe Jim won't have a problem
thinking you could betray people or you won't be able
to pull it off. Can you do it?"

"If I think he'll buy it, I can do it. Michael," she
added, "you're scary."

"Yeah, it's going to be hard to explain at the Pearly
Gates," I replied. "'But St. Peter, I can think like a psy-
chopath. I'm telling you it's useful—even up here.
Maybe especially up here.' You think it'll work?"
Nobody laughed but at least they smiled.

She walked into the visiting room and Jim stood up
in surprise. There were only a few other visitors in the
room, all of whom had been placed at a discreet distance. "Eileen," he said warmly. "They told me I had a
visitor but they wouldn't tell me who. My God, they
let you in?"

She crossed the short distance and sat down carefully across from him with her back to the uniformed
officer standing by the door. "You can thank my
attorney," she said. "He went to court over it. They
can stop me from seeing Calvin but they've got no
reason to keep me from seeing you. I was never

accused of any impropriety in regard to my relationship with you."

Jim glanced at the officer and back at Eileen. He smiled again but his eyes were wary. The surprise had worn off and clearly he was questioning this. Eileen half-turned and glanced at the officer too. He was watching another couple farther over. The man at the table reached out to take the woman's hand and the officer walked over to tell him no contact was allowed. While he was walking away, Eileen turned back to Jim and quietly pulled the collar of her shirt back to reveal a small microphone taped to the inside of her blouse. She straightened up and Jim stared at her. He leaned back and waited. Eileen turned around and looked again but the officer was still standing by the couple and still had his back to them.

Quickly, she reached inside her shirt and pulled the cord from the mike. Then she leaned forward. "They want me to set you up," she said very softly. "But I couldn't do it. I only agreed so I could talk to you." The officer strolled back to his post, which was too close for Eileen to talk privately so she sat up and said in a normal tone, "I think you should talk to your attorney about why the appeal is taking so long. There may be something he could do."

The officer stretched and then started walking around the perimeter of the room. As he passed Eileen, she continued to talk about legal issues. The moment he was out of earshot she leaned forward and whispered, "We don't have much time. They'll come get me to fix the mike. Someone named Joanna called me. Listen, all she wants is for you to tell Avery to put her on his visiting list."

Jim didn't said anything for a moment. Then he

said softly, "Why? Why does she want to see Avery? What's she doing?"

"What she thinks," Eileen said, looking around for the officer, who was over getting a drink of water, "what Jeffrey told her, was that he was going after Gary in exchange for Avery coming up with some contacts he could sell drugs to."

"I don't know what you're talking about," Jim said.

"You don't have to know what I'm talking about," Eileen responded. "Just ask Avery to put her on his list. She'll make it worth his while."

"Why would Joanna come to you?" Jim said.

"Who else did she have?" Eileen replied. "There wasn't anybody else she could call. Jeffrey told her about you and me and she thought I might be able to get through to you. And I wouldn't help her unless I knew what was going on.

"Anyway, a large shipment has come in and Jeffrey's dead and she doesn't know what to do with it. So she wants to talk to Avery. That's all. Just tell him."

Eileen turned around again to look for the officer. He had completed his circuit but had stopped over by the second door. He was too far to hear.

"I don't believe you," Jim whispered. "Joanna didn't know anything about this. Jeffrey wouldn't have told her. Besides, she wouldn't get involved in anything like that."

"Oh really? If she doesn't know about it, then how did she tell me?" Eileen countered. "What do you think, she's working from a Ouija board? Jeffrey told her about more than you know. As for not getting involved, the woman is pregnant with twins and Jeffrey's dead. How do you think she's going to support herself? Not with that printing business, especially now that the prison contract is kaput."

"You're different," he said. "This doesn't sound like you."

"Well, there's nothing like losing your job, your livelihood and facing jail to change a girl. I'm different because I have to be. Nobody's going to look after number one but me."

"So what are you getting out of this?"

"One third of the profits. Get real, Jim. I owe fifteen thousand in legal fees and that's just the beginning. I've lost everything. I've been thinking a lot about this. I know things weren't like I thought between us. But I don't care. I need to make some money. I have to make some money because the only thing that stands between me and going to jail is a good attorney. Right now, I don't have a job and I can't get one. Working with Joanna is the only way I know.

"Listen," she added, glancing back at the officer discreetly, who was still on the other side of the room, "I don't care what you think. You don't have to believe me about any of this. Joanna doesn't want anything from you. Just tell Avery to put her on the list." She started to rise.

"I deal with Avery," Jim said. "Sit down. Tell her to come see me. I'll put her on my list."

"I don't think so," she said, but she sat back down. "Because you, Jim boy, and that incompetent husband of hers fucked up. You did not produce the desired result and Joanna doesn't think you have any clout left with Avery. She wants to talk to him herself. She figures she can make a money deal, one that doesn't involve anything as stupid as going after a warden."

Just then a secretary stuck her head in the door and said, "Dr. Steelwater, you have a phone call."

"I'll be right there," Eileen said and turned back around. But she didn't get up.

"She can't make a deal with Avery," Jim said. "Avery isn't going to move on this. He's got one thing on his mind, that's all. Unless she's got some way to finish what Jeffrey started, there isn't going to be a deal."

"Well, she wants to try and she doesn't want to go through you," Eileen said. "She blames you for Jeffrey's death. She says you should have known better than to send Jeffrey after someone who was, for Christ's sake, a former military pistol champion. Did you know that? If you wanted to get Gary, you should have tried something better than shooting him. You don't try to shoot someone who outshoots the entire U.S. military."

Just then the secretary put her head in the door again. "They say it's urgent, Dr. Steelwater. You're needed right away."

"Nothing is ever as urgent as they think it is," Eileen replied coolly. "Tell them to give me five minutes."

Jim looked surprised. "How was I supposed to know that?" he answered. "Besides, Jeffrey was a good shot. It should have worked. He had surprise on his side. Tell Joanna it was just a fluke. Tell her to come talk to me. She has to talk to me if she wants to get to Avery."

Eileen sat back and smiled. Even on closed circuit TV you could see the look in her eyes. She pulled open the collar of her blouse, carefully unpinned the mike and spoke into it. "That should about do it," she said. "Come on in." Then she turned to Jim. "Welcome to wireless, asshole. Ain't technology grand."

* * *

They rolled on each other, as I knew they would. Avery was less of a sure bet than Jim. The problem with having no attachment was you had no attachment. You took the best deal you could at any given minute and turning state's witness and blaming it all on Avery looked like a better deal than going into court with that tape—even if the defense did cry entrapment.

Of course, once Jim rolled on Avery, Avery was through with him and had no compunction about returning the favor. Which meant they couldn't wait to tell on each other. In the end, we never got all of it straight. Both Avery and Jim blamed the other for assaulting Stacy. They were both there, supposedly working on the machines while Rudolph went off for a smoke break. Probably nobody would ever know for sure which one actually hit Stacy but it hardly mattered. They both carried him to the classroom. The law would see them as co-conspirators.

The attack on Clarence was something else again. It was just what Jim told me, if I'd had the wit to listen, when I first talked to him about it. I should have remembered how much psychopaths like to brag and at least considered he might be talking about himself when he said Clarence was killed just to get someone on the playing board. Jim just wanted to show Avery he was one of the big boys and was capable of killing somebody. That's how he played it to Avery, anyway. But I suspected Jim also wanted the "thrill" of killing someone. It's not something the rest of us are likely to understand, but he just wanted to try it out.

So he befriended Clarence and introduced him to the print shop. Clarence got close enough to figure out the drugs, which meant he definitely had to go. No problem—it was already in the works. But Jim hadn't counted on how tight security would get after a murder and he never got a chance to do the same thing to the warden—so he brought in Jeffrey.

In the end, there were a lot of conversations with investigators and a lot of talk about deals but none ever materialized. Lucy was hell to deal with when she had two confessions in her little briefcase.

It all depended on which judge they drew, of course, but the easiest judge they could possibly draw was not going to do anything they'd like. The problem with trying to shoot a warden is that a warden was too close to a judge in most judges' minds. Not that we weren't all equal, but we weren't. When it came to killing people, trying to kill a major authority figure in the criminal justice system was frowned on by the judiciary.

Lucy decided not to use the tape. We turned it over, as we had to, but Lucy told me to tell Eileen she hadn't listened to it. I had filled her in over a beer—hers, of course—so she knew the gist of it. It nearly killed her not to use it. Lucy's idea of heaven was to play that tape before a woman judge at sentencing. But I pointed out she was in overkill already. The other guys in the group had been all too happy to talk about the drugs in exchange for being kept out of the murder raps, which I truly don't think they were involved in, anyway.

Just to make sure, Gary transferred Terrance. He was the only one who didn't draw any extra time and we knew that would look suspicious, despite the fact that those on the inside knew he had stayed away from moving the drugs.

All in all, given we were down forty points at the

half, it seemed like a reasonable end score. Everybody was alive except Jeffrey and Clarence—and I hate to sound callous, but the world hadn't lost a lot. Stacy was on the mend. Joanna was free to make another choice, though who knew whether it would be any better. Eileen wasn't going to jail for having sex with an inmate, although she could have. It was a felony but the state deferred prosecution if she stayed clean for two years. She'd eventually get her license back, although it would take a few years and she'd never practice in a prison again. Gary had written her a letter that helped the licensing board to start thinking about temporary suspension rather than banishment. There was just one thing left.

20

"How's Wonder Woman?" I said. "Jesus, you look great. Are you sure you got shot?"

"I got shot," she said. "And it hurts. They don't make it seem like it hurts in the movies."

"No, they don't emphasize that part too much. People might not like watching it if they did."

"I'm glad you came to see me," she said. "It's boring here and it seems so weird to be here for something different."

"Well, there are probably better things to do with your time," I said. "Just a thought."

"I've been thinking about that. That man made the thing with diabetes seem . . . seem something, not so big or something."

"One reason I work with them," I said. "They make losing your car keys look pretty good too. I have this thing, Aspasia. Now don't laugh, because it's going to sound dorky and don't tell me you don't know what dorky means. I'm going to get on my soapbox one time and then I swear to you I'll shut up forever. But now that you mention it, there is one thing I want to say. I have this thing that at times in your life, somebody or something is going to try to beat you. And they might be pretty good. In fact, sometimes they are going to be really good, as good as Jeffrey was when he was shooting real bullets while you stood on that roof."

She didn't laugh. She looked down at the sheets and then straight up in my face. "So," she said.

"So don't beat yourself. Make them do it—if they can. Make it hard for them. That's all. Just never ever beat yourself—that's like giving them forty points. Even if they beat you once in a while, make them miserable doing it. End of sermon."

Aspasia didn't say anything and neither did I. Then she said, "You're saying Jeffrey isn't the last thing like that."

"I'm saying he's not even the first. Somebody or something is always out there. Whether it's Jeffrey or diabetes, as Gilda Radner said, 'It's always something.' Don't throw away any cards you might need; that's all I'm saying. So. Are your parents coming by?"

"Soon," she said. "I thought you were them. I'm glad you're here first, though. I wanted to tell you something. No, ask you . . . that night. No, not that night. What if . . . what if somebody, say, just say . . ."

"Hypothetically speaking," I said.

"Yeah, that," she said. "What if somebody had their hands up and somebody else had a gun . . . aren't they supposed to stop . . . just hypothetically, that is."

I sat down on the bed. "Yes," I said. "They are. I won't sugarcoat it. They're supposed to stop."

"And what if they don't? What if they shoot the person—the one with their hands up?"

"Well," I said, "if you're far and they're close, you

can't be sure what they saw, or thought they saw. They might have thought the person was going for their gun." She didn't look convinced. "Or they might not," I admitted.

"Suppose they didn't think that," she said.

"In that case it might help to understand it a little before you start judging them. The thing is, when you come to somebody's house and try to kill them and especially their child, you are truly taking your life in your hands. And the child's the thing. Any parent in that situation will kill you if they can. It's this primordial thing between parents and kids. You gotta remember. At that point in time, a parent in that situation might not even have known if their child *had* been killed."

"Pri . . . what?"

"It's a thing. They will kill you, I guarantee it. And if you suddenly stop and go, 'okay I give up,' some people—actually, those with the most experience in the criminal justice system, to tell you the truth—are likely to start thinking about all those guys who got off, who did something like that and somehow beat the rap. I'm not saying it's right, Aspasia. I'm not saying it's a good thing. I'm just saying I can see how it could happen."

"But if you saw something like that and somebody found out about it, what would happen to the person who did the shooting?" She got very still.

"What I'm going to say to you isn't anything you're going to get in a sixth-grade civics book. But actually, I don't think much would happen. The person would say you were mistaken and since there wouldn't be any way to prove it one way or the other and the other guy started it and *was* trying to kill people, I don't think most judges would second guess the guy who was defending himself and his family. They'd probably take his word for it. So anybody who saw something like that wouldn't need to feel guilty about not telling, if that's what they decided, because I don't think there's much they could do about it, anyway."

I laughed. "It's this protective thing parents have about kids. You should see what your father would do to diabetes if he could. If it was a person, it would be in big trouble. That's his problem with you. You're hurting you and there's no way he can stop it. It makes him crazy."

Aspasia didn't say anything, not anything at all. She just sat there. Strange, we seemed like old friends. You always know who your friends are because they're the ones you don't have to talk around.

Just then Gary and Susan walked in. I was sorry because I thought there might be more to talk about. "We can talk about this later," I said, "If you want."

"That's all right," she said. "I don't think I need to."

Gary and Susan both kissed her and Gary sat down on the chair while Susan sat on the bed. I got up to go but Aspasia stopped me. "No," she said. "I want you to stay because there's something I have to say to Daddy and I want you here."

"Okay," I said, slowly, but I wasn't happy about it. I thought for sure she was going to bring up the shooting.

"Daddy, I don't want you messing with the diabetes anymore. I don't want you telling me to take my shots or asking me anything about what I've been eating. I just don't. I'm big enough and it's my business anyway and I'll handle it."

Gary and Susan looked at each other. I kept my mouth shut. I was just the bench team.

"Okay," Gary said. "As long as you can handle it."

"No as long as anything," Aspasia said firmly. "It's none of your business, whether I handle it or not."

Gary started to speak but Susan interrupted. "We can try, honey," she said. "That's not easy for us but at least we can try."

"Baby," Gary said, "I just want—"

"You want me to be like I used to," Aspasia said bitterly, "when I didn't have diabetes. When I was your little princess."

"What do you mean?" he said. "That's not true. I don't care about the diabetes."

"Yes you do," she said. "It's true, Daddy. You should have seen your face when they told you I had diabetes. It was like I wasn't perfect anymore. I'm not lying. You haven't treated me the same way since. I know I've screwed up but you have, too. And I know you don't believe me but I think you've been a little bit mad at me for having it." Gary and Susan both looked at me.

"First I've heard of it," I said, holding up my hands.

"Why do you look at her like I can't think for myself? That's what I mean. You act like I'm stupid or something and you didn't used to."

"You're not stupid," Gary said. "You're the bravest girl I've ever met in my whole life, bar none. And you saved my life by disobeying your mother and climbing up on that roof. So I guess we'll have to trust you because you make pretty good choices when people get off your back. I'll have to think about what you said because I didn't think I was doing it and it's hard for me to believe it. But one thing I do know: you are so my little princess."

"Here's to you, kid," I said out loud on the way home and mentally raised a toast to the girl with the old name. "Your namesake would be proud." In my own mind, I knew Aspasia was up there somewhere in a toga yelling, "Yes!" I rubbed my swollen belly absent-mindedly as I drove. "You could do worse than hang around that kid," I added, "that is, if you ever show up."

I pulled up to my A-frame and was glad to see lights on. "I'm getting used to him," I thought. "It's just like some corny song. I'm getting . . ." I shuddered, "comfortable." It was a truly scary thought.

But all that changed when I saw the suitcase on the bed. "You're packing?" I said, and something that wasn't the baby turned over in my stomach.

"Yep," he said.

"Adam," I said. "Why are you packing? What happened to that stick-it-out-thing? What happened to that not-a-part-time father thing? This is all it takes to send you packing? I haven't even been that obnoxious. One gunfight? That's all it takes?"

"Now you believe in that stick-it-out thing?" he said, but he didn't stop putting his things into the suitcase. "You serious about that?"

"Well, sort of. At least I thought you were. I was trying to make my peace with it—for your sake. For the baby's sake. I don't know, for somebody's sake."

"How about your sake?"

"Well, sort of. It wasn't that bad." Adam kept packing. "Sometimes it wasn't bad at all," I added.

"So you want me to stay?"

"Well, yeah," I said sitting down on the bed. "I think I do . . . if you can believe it."

"Good," he said. "Because your bag is already packed."

"What? I can't fly. Where are we going?"

"We're not flying. We're driving. To Maine."

"For what? We can't go to Maine. Why are we going to Maine?"

"Because," he said, "you have two weeks to go. And I cannot think of any other possible way to keep you out of trouble other than to rent a cabin in Booth Bay, Maine, which is not a bad place, if you remember. I don't think even you can find a way to get in trouble if you're not working. And I just cannot put up with your screwing around with my kid anymore. Not until she or he is out and has a fighting chance, anyway. And Booth Bay is near a very fine medical center that already has your records. Melissa has canceled your schedule and I have packed your bag. So bring the baby and let's go." He looked at me and held out his arm.

Outmaneuvered, outgunned, and outmanned—and not all that upset about it—I took his arm.

Visit
❖ **Pocket Books** ❖
online at

....

www.SimonSays.com

....

Keep up on the latest new
releases from your favorite
authors, as well as author
appearances, news, chats,
special offers and more.

SIMON & SCHUSTER
A VIACOM COMPANY
www.SimonSays.com

Pocket
Books

2381-01

ANNA SALTER

"Dr. Michael Stone is sure to take her place
beside the major characters in crime fiction."
—Andrew Vachss

WHITE LIES

FAULT LINES

SHINY WATER

POCKET BOOKS